WICKED DESIRE

"Tell me what you fear now," he whispered, leaning close enough that his nose touched her cheek.

The scent of his skin, his touch, his nearness, they made her limbs feel sensitized, and her lips, and her breasts. Every part of her lit with heat, a liquid glow deep in her belly. She was left quivering with something far more complicated than fear.

A realization, an awakening of sorts.

It was not him she feared most, but *herself*. Her reaction to him. Her unbridled climax. Even in the wretchedness of her distress, she found him beautiful. Alluring. Fascinating.

She thought that if he touched her, drew her close, wrapped her in the shelter of his embrace, she would not be afraid.

He was warm and hard and solid.

Dear heaven, what madness was this?

He moved his head so he drew his nose down, along her cheek, her jaw, the side of her neck. "Tell me," he whispered again, drawing back so his gaze snared hers. There was hunger there, such hunger, feral and stark. The strength of it touched her, lured her.

"You. I fear you." A half-truth. She feared the frightening urge to turn her face to his, to breathe the scent of his body as he breathed hers, to touch her tongue to his skin and know the taste of him . . .

Books by Eve Silver

DARK DESIRES

HIS DARK KISS

DARK PRINCE

HIS WICKED SINS

Published by Zebra Books

His Wicked Sins

Eve Silver

ZEBRA BOOKS
Kensington Publishing Corp.
www.kensingtonbooks.com

ZEBRA BOOKS are published by

Kensington Publishing Corp.
850 Third Avenue
New York, NY 10022

All Kensington titles, imprints, and distributed lines are available at special quantity discounts for bulk purchases for sales promotion, premiums, fund-raising, educational, or institutional use.

Special book excerpts or customized printings can also be created to fit specific needs. For details, write or phone the office of the Kensington Special Sales Manager: Attn. Special Sales Department. Kensington Publishing Corp., 850 Third Avenue, New York, NY 10022. Phone: 1-800-221-2647.

Zebra and the Z logo Reg. U.S. Pat. & TM Off.

ISBN-13: 978-0-8217-8129-6
ISBN-10: 0-8217-8129-4

First Printing: August 2008
10 9 8 7 6 5 4 3 2 1

Printed in the United States of America

Acknowledgments

I thank my editor, John Scognamiglio, for believing in me enough to push me harder. I thank my agent, Sha-Shana Crichton, for always saying what needs to be said and doing what needs to be done.

To my critique partners, Nancy and Brenda, I offer my thanks for their willingness to read any amount of pages, any time, anywhere, and for the immeasurable gift of their input. A special shout-out to Caroline Linden for purple bacteria and for telling me to figure out who my hero is.

To my family, my mom and dad, my brothers and sisters-in-law, nieces and nephews, I offer my love and thanks.

Dylan, my light; Sheridan, my joy; and Henning, my forever love—I thank you for so much more than I can express.

Finally, I dedicated this story to the memory of Brix, my companion, my friend. Six years wasn't long enough. I miss you.

Chapter One

Crimson splatter painted a gruesome landscape on the pale walls of the Black Swan Tavern.

Parish constable Henry Pugh picked his way around the stiffening corpse, taking note of the arc of blood that splashed far and wide and the congealing pool at his feet. Dark and glossy, it reflected the flickering candlelight and colored the air with a cloying, heavy scent, both sweet and sour.

He had never seen so much blood.

But then, today was Henry's first day with the Shadwell Police Office, and he had never before seen foul murder.

Outside, on the cobbled street, the night watchman called out the time. Half past midnight.

Raising his candle, Henry squinted at the floor, noting the bloody footprints that moved along the hallway. Then his gaze slid back to the dead man, William Trotter, the landlord of the Black Swan. He lay on his back, sprawled over the steps that led to the taproom, eyes wide and staring, face twisted in a look of surprise. From all appearances, he had been attacked from behind, likely never knowing the identity of his assailant.

Bits of brain and bone speckled the landlord's clothes, the wood of the step, the wall at his side. His head was bashed in, and his throat slit for good measure. Rivulets of blood wended down the stairs and across the floor, merging and puddling a small distance away.

Henry squatted low. The stink of human refuse slapped him, and he reared back, appalled to witness such ultimate humiliation. Death was neither kind nor dignified.

An ugly thing, this. An ugly thing.

The coal-heaver, Jack Browne, a lodger here at 34 New Gravel Lane, had run to summon Henry when his banging and ringing failed to rouse Mr. Trotter to come open the door. On hearing the tale, Henry had expected that Jack was locked out for the night, and the Trotters gone to bed of an early hour as was their custom. Mrs. Trotter was insistent upon that, and lodgers, most of them sailors taking a room for a short while, knew that should they come late, the door would be barred against them. Odd, for a tavern to keep such hours, but that was the way at the Black Swan.

Henry's benign suppositions had proven bitterly untrue. Before him lay Mr. Trotter's savaged remains. He'd not be answering the door this night, or any other. This man who had laughed and joked and drawn ale just hours past was cold and dead now, his life snuffed in a manner that was purely evil. Henry's shock at discovering the body had been so great that he had barely managed to hold his composure and instruct Jack Browne to fetch more men.

With a sigh, Henry reached out now and closed the landlord's eyes.

As he drew his hand away, Mr. Trotter's lids flipped open once more, pinning him with a blank and eerie stare, the eyes filmy, the whites gone gray.

Startled, Henry cried out and scuttled back, slapping one palm against the floor to steady himself. The stare seemed to judge him and find him guilty. He should have listened earlier that day when Mr. Trotter complained of a stranger lurking in the shadows outside the parlor window. He should have listened.

But in the end the landlord had clapped him on the back and made light of his own concerns, and so Henry had laughed along with him.

Swallowing against the sting of bile that clawed up his throat, Henry shifted his gaze from the dead man's eyes to the gaping slash across his throat, to the blood and brains and shards of bone. He lacked the experience to know how to set his feelings and abhorrence aside, to see only the crime that need be solved. Still, he was determined that he would not disgrace himself. He would not, though the provocation and justification were strong.

Fingers trembling, he closed the landlord's eyes once more, willing them to stay shut. Then he rose and went to find the others.

He felt chillingly certain there were others.

Chapter Two

The Great North Road, Yorkshire, England,
September 1, 1828

A lone tree endured atop a distant, windswept hill, its dead branches stretched skyward. Charred, begrimed stones sat in the tree's twisted shadow, burned and blackened remains of old cottage walls. They prevailed against time and weather, with the desolate landscape stretched behind like a joyless painting colored in flat hues.

Elizabeth Canham found she could not look away, for the scene touched a place inside her, one that nagged and ached like a sore tooth.

That cottage must once have been a home, a haven.

Surrounded by harsh moorlands, it was now a friendless place, steeped in loneliness, calling to her as the stagecoach rumbled on its way. There was a haunting beauty to the sight, and an odd, disturbing afterthought, a warning . . . but perhaps that was only the tuneless echo of her own melancholy.

Beth turned in her seat and leaned close to the window, watching the ruin until it disappeared from view.

What had happened to them, the family who had

once lived there? Her imagination conjured all manner of terrible visions, but in the end, she decided to lean toward the hope that they had escaped the fire and gone on to live healthful and content lives. To think otherwise was horrific, for she had intimate knowledge of the damage that fire could do.

After a time, she glanced down and unclenched her fingers where they curled and crushed the material of her black bombazine skirt. She was not in mourning, but the dress had been both available and inexpensive, two factors in favor of its purchase.

The drone of a woman's voice buzzed through the confined space of the coach. Today, Beth was not alone in the conveyance, but tomorrow she would be. *That* was an eventuality she could not despise.

Her carriage-mate, Mrs. Beacon, had nattered on the entire trip from the coach yard at the Saracen's Head in London. A well-meaning and fine woman of incomparable verbosity, she was free with both her words and her advice.

"You are pale as a shroud," Mrs. Beacon offered now, shifting on the seat beside Beth and leaning close to peer at her from beneath her bonnet. She evinced no hesitation to offer such personal observation to a near stranger.

"That dull black makes you look whiter than a cod's belly. With your blond hair and fair skin, you need a bit of color." Mrs. Beacon softened her words by producing a tin of peppermints and offering one to Beth, then to each of the two gentlemen occupying the opposite seat.

One was plump and pasty, and rather green about the gills. Coach travel appeared to disagree with him.

The other was bland as oat pudding, with thin sandy hair worn in a disheveled style, and small, pale eyes that darted nervously about.

Glancing down, Beth smoothed her palm over her skirt. Mrs. Beacon's observations aside, Beth was well pleased with her drab and sad wardrobe, purchased at a significant discount when the young widow who had ordered it never arrived to claim the dresses from the seamstress. Mindful of her limited funds, Beth had bought only the bare minimum that she needed, serviceable garments of black and gray, clothing suitable for her new position.

"Blond hair and blue eyes . . . my youngest daughter has the same coloring as you, though she is by no means as skinny. There, there"—Mrs. Beacon patted Beth's knee consolingly—"you'll put on a bit of meat when you reach my age."

Her monologue continued throughout the ride, and then, close to Grantham, the sandy-haired gentleman took advantage of Mrs. Beacon's need to draw breath and spoke in the rare instant of silence.

"We are near to Gonerby Hill. 'Tis just to the north of Grantham," he said, leaning forward in his seat. The movement pushed his high collar and stock even higher, and his chin was nearly swallowed by the cloth. "Steep it is. The steepest on the Great North Road. Why, I heard that last winter, there was so much ice and snow that the wheels could not hold to the road and the stagecoach slipped and careened down to the bottom, flipping end over end and crushing the driver and guard."

No one said a word.

"*Everyone* died," he continued, his tone tinged with morbid glee. "And the horses, as well."

A cheering thought.

"Oh." Beth could summon no more appropriate rejoinder.

Mrs. Beacon made a sound low in her throat and, after a moment, leaned close to Beth and spoke for her ears alone.

"Remember, love, you must pay the coachman an extra shilling per stage, and the guard, lest you find he loses your luggage. At the inn where you stay the night

you must give sixpence to the chambermaid and tuppence to the boots. My son and his wife are in
Grantham, and their twelve little ones. I'll not be going
on with you to Northallerton . . ."

There, Mrs. Beacon made a lengthy pause, cleared
her throat, blinked again and again, her rheumy gaze
locked on Beth's, until at last Beth understood the hint.
In truth, her thoughts were consumed by Mrs. Beacon's
talk of shillings and sixpence and tuppence, inordinate
sums when compared with Beth's rapidly dwindling re-
sources. Nonetheless, she summoned a rejoinder to satisfy the other woman.

"I am bereft to lose your fortifying companionship,
Mrs. Beacon," she murmured, attempting to instill the
observation with the appropriate tone of regret.

Closing her eyes, Beth battled a sharp pang of loss,
not for the thought of leaving Mrs. Beacon, but for her
home, her parents, her brother, for everything known
and customary.

She opened her eyes to find the gentleman who had
spoken of the carriage accident studying her with interest.

"I believe you mentioned Northallerton. Do you stay
on there?" he asked.

"No. I go to the village of Burndale, to Burndale Academy. I am to be a teacher."

To Burndale Academy. Her mother had not wanted
her to go, but there had been little choice that Beth
could see. Unless starvation was an option. Food was not
free, nor lodging, nor coal.

The gentleman made a rude sound that snuffled out his
nose. "I know of such places, such *academies*." He sneered
and nudged the man next to him. "William Shaw, the
headmaster at Bowes Academy, was prosecuted . . . oh . . .
some years past, on account of two boys went blind from
his beatings. And he starved them, too."

Beth felt a wary tension creep through the muscles of
her limbs, her shoulders, her back. His assertion shocked

and horrified her. Pressing her lips together, she suppressed a shudder.

Her horror would only burgeon and grow to unmanageable proportions if she let it.

Beatings and starvation.

"Burndale Academy has no such reputation," she said firmly.

"So you say." The man shrugged. "But such schools always harbor death, from maltreatment, neglect, disease."

"If that is the case, who would send their children to such a place?" Beth demanded.

"Well, I suppose some do not know, and others do not care. Some of the children are born on the wrong side of the blank—"

Mrs. Beacon cleared her throat loudly, and the gentleman broke off and gave a nervous little laugh.

"I would not lodge a dog at Bowes Academy," he said, vehemently.

"You ain't got a dog!" the second gentleman pointed out, and gave a loud guffaw, the noise drowning out Beth's rejoinder as she said, "Then it is a fine gift of fortune that I do not travel to Bowes."

For some inexplicable reason, Mrs. Beacon chose this moment to cocoon herself in silence. Beth gritted her teeth and turned her gaze back to the window, her heart heavy.

What viciousness had precipitated such discourse?

She recalled the gleam in the gentleman's icy pale eyes as he spoke of the carriage accident. Some people were malicious creatures who thrived on tales of horror and pain. Perhaps he was such a one and had set out with the purpose of creating unease.

She should not allow it.

Still, a troubling wariness gnawed at her. Was there a possibility that the man's horrific assertions sprouted from a seed of truth? She truly knew almost nothing of Burndale Academy . . .

No, she would not cast her mind to needless worry. Her correspondence with the headmistress of Burndale had been most pleasant, and she would carry that positive expectation until such time as it might be proved faulty.

Not so very far now, she thought, though she felt as though she had been traveling for an eternity. The jolt of the wheels as they dipped into grooves and ruts in the road shook her bones, leaving her feeling bruised and broken.

But the worst of it for her was the confining nature of the carriage, the walls close, the space small and tight. She felt the tug of panic, and she tamped it down lest it surge free and drown her in an icy deluge that would rob her of breath, of rational thought, leave her in a despised state of mindless terror.

An *attack of dismay*, her mother called it. Beth thought that a polite and benign term for the ugly reality of her secret infirmity.

Forcing her shoulders to relax, she turned her gaze to the carriage window and the vast space beyond. She could only be grateful that her destination was not so far as Edinburgh, which would take a full fourteen days of travel.

A fortnight in a small, restricting coach. Dear heaven, what a thought.

Mrs. Beacon shifted closer, pressing her tight to the corner. Beth fixed her gaze on the patch of sky she could see through the window and deliberately ignored the walls that surrounded her.

Despite her current discomfort, she knew herself to be fortunate. Many women in her position would be driven to truly desperate ventures. Surely traveling to Yorkshire, alone, with only a letter to guide her and without friend or even acquaintance, was not desperate.

After all, she had secured honest employment as a teacher at Burndale Academy, and so must count herself as privileged.

Her strengths lay in French, English language, music, and drawing, and she was quite competent in geography and history. She was glad of her mother's tutelage these many years, else they would all be in a terrible fix.

Yes, well, a *worse* fix than they were in.

You must not be afraid.

The thought brought a sad smile to her lips, for she could hear her mother's voice, kind but firm, recalling that exact sentiment so many times over the years.

She must not be afraid.

Yet, in a secret corner of her heart, a place she shared with no one, Beth admitted only to herself that she was *always* afraid of so many things . . . the memories . . . the dreams.

The truth.

Northallerton, Yorkshire, September 3, 1828

Sarah Ashton lugged her third load of coal up the stairs to the fireplaces of Briar House. So many fireplaces in this cursed place. Midmorning sun streamed through the window, showing the dust on the table and the mantel. Sarah sighed. She would need to take care of that before her workday ended, else Mrs. Sykes, the housekeeper, would make her stay back on her afternoon off.

When the last of the coal was done with, she scrubbed her hands over her apron, careful not to soil her dress. It was a pale blue cotton print, unlovely and faded from many washings, but the color was fine on her. She hoped to keep herself clean until the afternoon.

Fetching a wooden bucket, she started on her next

task. Down on her knees, she dragged forth the chamber pot from beneath the bed. She emptied the contents into her slops bucket, then wiped out the pot with a wet cloth that hung from the waist of her apron. Her nose wrinkled at the smell and she thought herself better than this, better than chamber pots and slops and fetid rags.

He thought so, too, her gentleman. He thought her worth pretty ribbons, a silver thimble, a lace handkerchief, a silver watch. Imagine! She kept the delicate little watch pinned to her dress, hidden beneath her apron so none would see. No sense inviting questions. Likely, the housekeeper would think she'd pinched it.

In turn, she had gifted him with a lock of her hair. It was all he had asked of her, and she had been happy enough to give it.

Sarah moved to the next room, the next chamber pot, and the next. Seven bedrooms. Almost done now.

She paused and smiled as she thought of *him*. She'd not let him do more than hold her hand and kiss her cheek. Only once, she'd been brave and bussed him on the lips. They had been smooth and warm, and she thought perhaps today was the day she would let him do more. He had been true, meeting her every week on her free afternoon. Today marked the sixth week.

Sarah was no fool. He was taken with her, but no man of his ilk would stoop to marry such as she. The best she hoped was that he might set her up, nice and quiet, and barring that, well, a few trinkets and gifts. She was sentimental, but only to her limit. In the end, she would sell what he gave her in order to buy herself a better life.

There was a sound in the hallway, barely a whisper. Sarah quickly fell to her knees and dragged out the chamber pot. It would not do to be caught woolgathering. She emptied the pot and wiped it as she had done with the others already that morning, then she rose and turned toward the door. As she had expected, Mrs. Sykes stood in the doorway.

Sarah bobbed a quick curtsey.

Mrs. Sykes frowned, her brows drawing together to gouge deep furrows, her fingers worrying the ring of keys at her waist. She looked as though she meant to say something, and Sarah wished she would not.

Perhaps the housekeeper knew what Sarah did with her free afternoon. Perhaps she meant to warn her away. If that was the case, Sarah wanted no part of it. 'Twas her own affair, and she meant to keep it that way.

Pressing her lips together, Mrs. Sykes shook her head, and after a moment, she turned and left Sarah alone.

Sarah's breath left her in a harsh whoosh as, hefting the half-full bucket, she moved to the next room. There, she repeated her motions, emptying the slops, the stink from the bucket heavy in her nostrils. Hot, revolting work, it was, and she dragged the back of her wrist across her forehead, anxious to be done.

In the final chamber was a pitcher and bowl, and when she had emptied the last pot, she poured fresh water, and was thrilled to see a sliver of soap—too dry to work a good lather—laid by the side. The servants here at Briar House were allowed to take the remnants of the soap and the worn-down stubs of candles for their own use. That was not considered thieving, though she would catch a tongue-lashing at the very least if Mrs. Sykes caught her washing up here.

With a glance at the open door, she used the water and soap to wash her hands and scrub her face. She'd not go to him smelling like a hog rooting in the mud, and if she emptied the basin and wiped it clean, none would be the wiser.

Above the hearth was a looking glass, and Sarah checked her appearance. Her hair, a bright guinea-gold, was naturally straight as a pin, and fine. Her man liked curls. Thick, bouncing curls. He had said as much, more than once,

So early this morning, long before the sun came up, she had wet her hair, doused it in a mixture made from water and sugar. She had turned the strands with a hot iron—she had a horrible blister at the top of her right ear where she'd not been careful enough—until she had a head full of curls. They weren't soft and fine, for the sugar water made them hard. Instead, they were solid, fat ringlets.

When Mrs. Sykes had seen them, she had frowned something fierce and made tsking sounds and clicked her tongue. In the end, she had said nothing, just shook her graying head with its white cap and let Sarah go see to her chores.

Sarah turned from the mirror and did a cursory dusting of the room. Finally, finally, her work was done, and she walked as quickly as she could along the dark hallway, down the servants' stairs, and out the back door. She was careful to avoid the other servants, having no wish to be enveloped by a group of chattering girls off to buy ribbons in town on their half day.

Stepping out, she found that the afternoon was warm enough, if a little gray. Anxious now, she lifted her skirt and flew along the muddy lane, past the icehouse and into the woods. Their special place was a clearing deep in the trees. As she came upon it, she saw he was waiting, tapping his crop lightly against his thigh, impatient.

A fine figure he was, in his cord breeches and square-cut coat.

Turning at her approach, he stilled and stared hard for a moment, saying nothing. At length, he stepped forward to take her arm and hold her in place, his fingers biting deep until she gasped.

"You've done your hair in curls," he said in a strange, dead voice. His grip tightened, making her flinch and jerk in response, but he held fast, raising his free hand to touch her hair.

His gaze slid to hers, cold and dark and pitiless, and

his lips curved in a terrible smile. It was only then that Sarah thought to be afraid.

Burndale, Yorkshire, September 3, 1828

Resolutely shoving aside the incertitude that spiraled through her, Beth drew forth the letter from the head-mistress of Burndale Academy. She showed it to the stagecoach guard when he appeared loath to leave her alone on the road.

"This is the place I was instructed to wait. The letter states that someone shall come for me by six o'clock on the third of September," Beth said, attempting to infuse her words with confidence. She was uncertain if the guard could read, but he stared at the page for a time, then nodded.

As the guard strode toward the stage once more, Beth called, "Wait. I have one question. Is there another route between Grantham and Northallerton? Another stage that would have reached here more quickly?"

The guard frowned and shook his head. "No, miss. Why do you ask?"

"The two gentlemen who traveled with us from London to Grantham . . . I thought I saw one of them on the road in Northallerton this morning . . ." She had glimpsed his face through the open coach window and, surprised to see him, had half raised her hand in greet-ing. In truth, his were not memorable features, but for an instant, she had been so certain it was he—thin, sandy hair, pale eyes, pale skin, his stock so high and tight he looked as though he had neither neck nor chin—and then she had thought perhaps not.

"Not likely, miss. There's no other stage that goes this way."

No, of course not. She wondered why she thought of

him at all. Likely, because his presence in Northallerton was a puzzle that tickled her thoughts, and she had ever been fond of puzzles. Or rather, of *solutions*.

She liked everything neat and tidy, everything in its place.

The guard tapped his foot, impatient now. Raising his head, he met Beth's gaze, his brow furrowed, and she realized that it was not impatience that made him edgy, but something else. Worry.

"You have a care, miss. Burndale's a small place, but there are goings-on—"

"Oy, Bill, come on, then!" the driver called, shifting on his seat as he glanced at them over his shoulder.

Beth knew he must stay on schedule as measured by a chronometer held under lock and key. He had already done her a great kindness, leaving her at the crossroads by the church as defined in her letter rather than at a pre-scribed stage on his route. Had he declined her request, she would have been forced to hire a cart in Northaller-ton, an expense she could ill afford. She was very grate-ful that he had chosen to acquiesce, and she knew it was churlish to hold him up any longer.

Stepping back, she watched in silence as the guard climbed up and the coach rocked into motion, creaking and jingling as it picked up speed, the wheels crunching on the road. A place right below her ribs, deep inside, tightened and did an odd little dip as the carriage grew smaller and smaller, and finally disappeared from view.

She was left utterly alone as the dust slowly settled and her thoughts churned.

What had the guard meant about goings-on in Burn-dale? From his tone and his frown, she could surmise it was nothing good.

Reaching up to settle her bonnet more securely on her head, Beth tamped down her apprehension. She turned to the north, and then to the south. There was no sign of an approaching vehicle. Not the sound of a bridle. Not a cloud of dust on the road. Her trepidation surged as she wondered if she and the guard had both erred, trusting that someone from Burndale Academy would soon come to fetch her. Perhaps she would be left here as the sun sank low and the shadows grew and blended with the night.

She made a huffing little laugh, laced more with anxiety than humor. To be left alone in the dark in a strange and foreign place was a less than appealing outcome.

Resolutely, she concentrated her thoughts on the facts at hand, shutting away her incertitude. Here was the stonebuilt church, with its peaked roof and squared tower, and the crossroads just as the letter described. She most definitely had come to the location outlined in the letter, and she must trust that someone would arrive forthwith to fetch her.

Only . . . she had presupposed the crossroads to be at the hub of the village. She had not expected this place to be so very solitary, with not a single living soul in sight.

Wrapping her arms about her waist, she glanced about at the unfamiliar surroundings, then up at the bruised sky. Heavy clouds of pewter and dark purple hung brooding on the horizon, but at least it was not fearfully cold. Her cloak was in her canvas-covered trunk, and with the breeze temperate and light, she felt no need of it.

Beth pressed her lips together and gave a last look along the empty road as she assessed her options. There was still time until six o'clock, over an hour, but she would feel more secure if she formulated a plan for the eventuality that no one arrived to greet her. She could not possibly drag her trunk all the way to Northallerton, some five miles to the south, and she disliked the idea of leaving her every possession untended here in the roadway while she trudged the distance unencumbered.

The village of Burndale was closer, but in which direction? Not south, for they had not passed it on their way from Northallerton, but that left three possibilities and she was more likely to choose wrong than right.

Unfortunately, the landscape provided no clue. From where she stood, she had a clear view of rolling hills on all sides, and in the immediate vicinity, the church, the graveyard, and the drystone wall that surrounded it.

She ran her fingers over the small cloth bag she carried at her wrist wherein were colored threads and needles and linen squares she meant to embroider with her mother's initials and send home as a birthday gift. But she could not imagine sitting on the low wall and sewing neat, tidy stitches while her skin fairly tingled with both excitement and anxiety.

How could she feel aught but anticipatory as to the end of her journey? She was filled with curiosity and interest, even as each passing moment stoked her genuine concern that no one would come for her and she would greet the night here on the road.

That thought was not one she wished to dwell upon.

With a last look about, she determined to walk through the graveyard, to read the stones and know a little of the inhabitants of Burndale, or at least a little of those who had passed some time in this place. Anything to carry her thoughts from the uneasy contemplation of the dire possibility that she would be left here, forgotten, and the full dark of night would come upon her like a pall.

From the graveyard, her trunk would still be in view should she turn to glance back at it, and she would be able to see the cart from Burndale Academy should it arrive—No!—*when* it arrived.

She reached the low wall around the yard and saw that a broad, pebbled path cut a swath to the wooden front doors of the church. She supposed that if it rained, she could drag her trunk along the path and under the overhang so that both she and her belongings might remain dry. The plan offered her some small comfort.

Meandering through the rows of headstones, she

paused now and again to read one or another, refusing to allow her thoughts to wander to supposition and desperation.

She had made her decision, and it was a sound one. Her employment at Burndale Academy offered her family a small spot of hope in an otherwise desperate situation. Worry and exhaustion could not change that.

She was inordinately fortunate to have secured this teaching placement. One advertisement she had read in the London paper had asked that a governess come for no pay at all, merely room and board. Another position as companion to an elderly widow would have paid a pittance in comparison to the thirty-five pounds per annum offered her as a teacher at Burndale Academy. Once she had earned her pay and could send monies home to help her family, she would feel far better, far more secure, than she did now.

The thought cheered her and she turned her attention once more to reading the words etched in the stones.

Here was a cherished wife and mother, and here a loving husband. A son. A daughter. She stopped, head cocked to one side as she studied the epitaph before her. With a vague sense of unease, she read the words a second time to be certain she had not misunderstood.

Helen Bodie-Stuart. Born July 5, 1798. Died January 10, 1828, at Burndale Academy of this place.

A chill of foreboding touched her skin, or perhaps it was only the gathering wind that made her shiver so.

Distressing recollections of the guard's warning that she have a care, and of the conversation with the rather nasty gentleman in the carriage—his assertions of beatings and starvation and death at schools such as Burndale—burgeoned, giving rise to all manner of horrific suppositions.

This woman, Helen Bodie-Stuart, had died at Burndale Academy, the exact destination Beth sought. A portent? She did not like to think so.

The cry of a raven made her stiffen, and she glanced at the leaden sky, and then the still-empty road. Swallowing, she shook off her disquietude and continued on to the next grave marker, and the next.

Some moments later, she read another epitaph that made a second, stronger surge of unease snake through her veins like a poison, leaving her heart thudding in her chest.

Katherine Anne Stillwell of Burndale Academy of this Parish who departed this life 13ᵗʰ day of September in the year of our Lord 1825 aged 24 years.

Two women had died at Burndale Academy.

Died there.

Had Beth been a crying sort, she might have shed tears then, from fatigue and distress and dismay.

Pressing her palms flat against her skirt, she steadied her thoughts, willing the darkest part of her, the desperate, ever-fearful part, back to its dusty corner. She silently remonstrated herself for allowing her imagination such free rein.

She ought to know better; open the gate just a little and the tugging, black mire would suck her deep, shrouding her in memories and waking dreams more terrifying than any nightmare.

She breathed deeply, then exhaled, resting her fingers on the cold gravestone. Yes, 'twas a sad thing when one died so very young, but perhaps there had been cholera here, or typhoid fever. Surely there was no sinister implication in the death of the two women some two years apart.

Despite her silent reasoning, Beth could not help the wariness that scratched at her, could not dampen the need to glance around the graveyard, suddenly painfully aware of its isolation . . . her own isolation . . .

With a shudder, she turned away.

Her gaze lit on the road, and she saw a carriage in the distance coming from the same direction that she herself had traveled earlier, the road from Northallerton.

With her heart tripping, Beth hurried back to her trunk and stood waiting as the conveyance drew near. She had the impression of fine horses with glossy black coats and flashing hooves, all moving at a frantic pace. For a fraught moment, she thought the carriage would not stop, so great was its speed and so disinterested its driver, but at the last, he drew rein and halted a dozen feet beyond her place.

She glanced down at her travel-rumpled clothes—far dustier now than they had been a moment past—and then up again at the vehicle. She had expected a dray or a wagon to fetch her, a simple cart, and so she was startled by the quality of the curricle, sitting high on two wheels, drawn by two magnificent, perfectly matched horses. All so very sporty.

Her attention shifted from the beasts to the driver. She could see only his broad back clothed in a dark brown riding coat, a glimpse of one leg in buff-colored cord breeches, and a booted foot, splattered with dried mud.

"Bloody hell. They'll likely have forgotten you."

The words, spoken in a gruff male tone—the words coarse, the clipped vowels cultured—gave Beth pause. She froze, one foot before the other, halfway to moving in the direction of the curricle. With a quick, shuffling step, she retreated. He swung down then, lithe agility and leashed impatience.

A gentleman, she thought, and then her gaze met his for the briefest instant, shadowy and cold as the Thames in winter, and she wondered. *Perhaps not.*

He was taller than she by a head, his shoulders broad, his frame lean and hard. His gaze flicked over her, from her face to her dusty hem and back again. She clenched her fist at her side, refusing to succumb to the silly urge to reach up and smooth her hair.

A half dozen steps brought him closer, and the sinuous grace of his movements made her think that he would dance well, this curricle driver. He exhibited innate balance and masculine elegance. Something about the way he moved made her think of her mother's stories, of foils and fencing masters, and men who feinted and parried and moved as if in a deadly dance.

That was the world her mother had been born to.

"Do you fence?" she blurted, thinking surely he must. Then she thought she ought to have tempered her tongue. She was accustomed to asking question upon question, had been encouraged by her father to do exactly that. But this was not home, and she would be wise to guard her words.

He blinked, drew up short at her odd address, and his brows rose as he said, "I do."

His clothes—fine cut, fine cloth—defined his station, but even without them, she would have known. There was a way he held himself, a steady confidence to his gaze. He looked . . . unconquerable . . . a walled fortress. But there was something else . . . an impression that his wall not only held others out, but held himself in.

She shook her head. What an odd notion.

One thing was certain. This man was not a driver sent here to fetch her, and his words when first he had stopped suggested that no other was coming.

Her father would be proud to know she noted all these bits of the puzzle. The thought was misty sad.

"You are *not* sent from Burndale Academy to fetch me," Beth observed.

"No, not sent from Burndale, but willing to fetch you nonetheless."

He walked closer still, studying her with a curious air, frank perusal, the light in his liquid dark eyes mesmerizing. Her heart did an odd little dance, tripping faster than it ought.

"I am on my way there now and would be pleased to

offer you a ride," he continued. "May I presume that you are the new teacher?" He raised a brow in question.

So he knew there was a teacher expected. She supposed that was a recommendation of sorts.

Studying him, she assessed both his appearance and her options. His hair was dark, wind rumpled and over-long, with a thick hank falling across his brow at the front, and the ends curling slightly where they brushed the back of his collar. He was close enough now that she could see that his dark eyes were lit by a shimmer of gold and, when he turned his head just so, a whisper of green.

Unfamiliar stimulation shimmered in her veins. He was studying her as she studied him, and something she saw there made her pulse trip over itself with eager glee.

She was startled by such unprecedented and strange excitement.

Well. He was . . . beautiful. Like the exotic panther she had seen when her father took her once to Peddleton's Menagerie. She had felt sick for the panther, locked away in his cage, had wished for a way to break the bars even as she had recognized that if she did somehow release him, she would likely be his next meal. And a bloody and screaming one at that.

This man had that same look, that dangerous, feral look. Only there was no safe cage around him, save the one he built for himself.

"I am Miss Elizabeth Canham, come to Burndale Academy to teach history and geography and literature." She waited a moment and, hoping she did not sound forlorn, asked, "Why will they have forgotten me?"

That hard mouth curved a little. She thought his smile held more darkness than mirth or amiability. A cynical sensuality that even she, an untutored girl, recognized.

He glanced at the laden sky and said, "The head-mistress has a weighty matter to occupy her afternoon, and Mr. Waters is not known for his remarkable memory. Unless it is remarkable for its unreliability."

Something in his tone made Beth uncertain if she should step back in unease or smile in collusion.

"Your name, sir?" she asked boldly, not pausing to wonder how she dared.

He sent her a look she could not read.

"My apologies, Miss Canham. My manners are rusty, indeed. Griffin Fairfax." He bowed, most gentlemanly, but she had the impression he was somehow mocking her. Or perhaps himself. He had placed a strange inflection on the word "manners."

"Yours?" he asked, with a gesture toward her luggage. At her nod of assent, he hefted her trunk as though it weighed nothing and made quick work of tying it to the back of the curricle.

Turning to her once more, he held out his hand in open invitation. His features were purely sculpted and artful, fine enough to be cast in bright polished bronze, carved by a skilled hand, kissed by the sun.

She studied his hand, hesitating, wondering if accepting a ride with this stranger was indeed her best course. He was dressed well enough, like a gentleman, and his carriage was fine. He knew she was the new teacher for Burndale Academy, which likely meant he was some part of the local community. Did all that recommend him?

To some degree.

He huffed a breath, tapped his foot on the road, while in the distance thunder rumbled.

After a moment, he said, "You do like to mull things over, Miss Canham." He glanced at the sky. "Might I impose upon you to conclude your ponderings before the storm?"

It was the hint of amusement in his tone that decided it. She lifted her skirt and walked the few steps to his side. He handed her up onto the seat.

His was a lightly sprung carriage with room only for a driver and passenger, the design necessitating a closeness that made Beth a little uncomfortable. Once he took his place, Mr. Fairfax would be shoulder to shoulder with her. Thigh to thigh.

An unfamiliar flutter tickled her belly. Butterflies dancing.

Mortified, she was at a loss to explain her odd reaction. But she was not so mortified that she denied herself the intriguing sight of his long limbs pacing off the distance as he strode around to the other side of the carriage.

He did not climb up. Instead, he paused to stare at her in a most unmannerly way, his gaze lingering on her mouth, her eyes, and finally, longest of all, her hair.

Heat rushed to her cheeks, and she parted her lips to better draw air.

Instinct bade her raise her hand, smooth her wild curls, apologize for her shabby appearance. She thought she must look a fright, having sat in the stagecoach for so many days. Stubbornness and a little pride—both were sins she laid claim to—stayed her actions and her tongue. Instead, she gazed down at him steadily, her hands folded demurely in her lap.

His lips thinned. "Flax-pale and curled. They'd have been better to choose a dark girl."

Strange words, without context, and the soft way he said them made her shiver.

Chapter Three

Beth slanted Griffin Fairfax a glance from beneath her lashes as she held tight to her bonnet with one hand and the edge of the seat with the other. She thought they traveled far too fast for either safety or common sense, and she was stunned to realize that though a part of her was terrified, another part reveled in the excitement of their pace, the open carriage, the feeling of freedom. The wind snatched her breath and the countryside flitted past too quickly to see much of anything.

For his part, Mr. Fairfax spared her no further notice, instead focusing his attention on the pair of matched horses, his strong, blunt-fingered hands at ease with the reins.

He made no attempt at companionable discourse, and that was of no matter to Beth. She was just as happy to remain silent, for she feared that her tongue had been loosened by the fatigue of her lengthy journey. She would be hard-pressed to limit her discussion to polite observations of the weather. Likely, too many questions would find their way into her remarks, and without a doubt they would center about the odd comment he had made earlier.

What could he have meant when he said they'd have been better to choose a dark girl?

Had his intent been to disconcert her with that enigmatic observation? If so, he had succeeded.

A feeling of discomfort and disquiet chased through her as she recalled his tone and the alarming nuance of his expression as he had spoken. The way he had looked at her hair.

Beautiful he might be but, thus far, she had found Mr. Fairfax to be particularly confounding.

Beth twisted to glance over her shoulder as thunder rumbled in the distance. The heavy sky had grown more ominous still, a damp pewter blanket sitting low against the ground. She wondered if she would be caught in the rain, after all.

"Have we a long way to go, Mr. Fairfax?" She raised her voice to be heard over the pounding of the horses' hooves and the rushing of the wind.

"No."

Beth raised her brows. She had gone from Mrs. Beacon's verbose company to Griffin Fairfax's taciturn and discouraging society. She would find it a difficult task to choose the more annoying of the two.

He turned the curricle into a narrow lane, got down from his place, and went to open a pair of iron gates. Beth stared at them for a moment, nonplussed. There were neither stone walls nor ironwork fencing on either side, just two square brick columns and a pair of gates whose only discernable purpose was to block the road.

They resumed their journey once more, and Beth noted that Mr. Fairfax left the gates open behind him.

"I suppose they are ornamental," Beth observed, having no need to shout now over the sound of the horses, for their current pace was quite sedate.

Mr. Fairfax made a soft sound she chose to interpret as a huff of laughter.

"They serve no purpose but to block the road," he said bluntly.

She pressed her lips together against a smile, oddly pleased that he voiced her exact thoughts. It was a strange sort of connection, true, but her first in this new and foreign place.

With a sidelong glance, he caught her eye. Humor shimmered in his gaze, and for that instant, Beth thought they were in harmony, connected by some intangible accord.

He turned his face toward her, brows pulling together so a faint line appeared between them. Inquiring. Puzzled. His gaze dropped to her mouth, and he quickly looked away.

Again came that strange little flutter in her belly.

Hunger? Fatigue? Perhaps. An oblique glance at Mr. Fairfax, and the butterflies danced harder.

Unsettled, Beth turned her head to study the rows of trees that stood sentinel to either side, their line curving as the narrow road curved, their foliage blocking out all else. They had left the open fields behind, and here the forest grew dense and thick, separated from the road by only a narrow margin of long grass. Again, thunder rumbled, closer now, and she twisted at the waist once more to look behind her toward the source of the sound.

She curled her fingers tight round the edge of the seat, and held on to steady her balance as they rounded a sharp bend. To one side was a break in the trees, a flat field with long, swaying grass.

A moment later, Mr. Fairfax drew the curricle to a precipitous halt.

"Burndale Academy," he said, his tone strangely devoid of inflection.

Beth's gaze snapped forward and up. Before her was a long gravel drive leading to a massive house of two stories, framed on either side by a stretch of manicured lawn and then encroaching forest. The brick was red, the window frames white, the roof black with high, narrow chimneys that, in her fancy, appeared to touch the sky. A meager wisp of gray smoke curled from one chimney.

Eight large windows spanned the upper floor, and on the lower floor was a door in the center with three windows on either side. At the top of the house, a gable tented over a clock, and above that was a short tower with a bell. From the rear of the main structure, additional wings extended toward the woods beyond. From her current vantage point, Beth could only see a small bit of them.

"It is . . . large," she said, searching for some warmer observation and failing to find it.

This imposing structure was Burndale Academy. This was her new place in the world. A more unwelcoming façade she could not have imagined.

She shuddered, suddenly feeling inexplicably low. There was a frigidity, a barrenness about the place. The house appeared both looming and impersonal and, surrounded as it was by dense woods, so isolated as to make her shiver.

Perhaps it was the vast size, the isolation, or the sullen and dreary sky overhead that made her feel so. Or perhaps it was her fatigue and travel-worn patience. She thought it was neither; she thought Burndale Academy both grand and grim.

There was something . . .

Frowning, she noted three black and barren trees standing close to the west side of the building, their twisted, bare branches twining together like the clawed talons of three mythic beasts. Their presence only darkened her impression of the whole.

Foolish notions, she knew, but she could not seem to chase them away.

She started as the bell began to toll, a slow, mournful

noise. It tolled six times, the sound heavy and burdened, twisting about her heart and squeezing with a brutal fist.

"Does the bell toll all day?" she asked, turning to look at Mr. Fairfax.

His lips twitched in what might have been humor. Or disgust.

"It calls the girls to a light supper now. It tolls at dawn to call them from their beds, then to summon them to break their fast, to mark the start of lessons, and the end of them. So, yes, you could say it tolls all day."

Any uncertainty she had harbored vanished now. His expression was definitely one of disgust, his tone sardonic as he continued, "Nothing like order and regimentation to bring light to the day."

Beth thought of her penchant for neatness, for arranging her clothes according to color and shade, for lining her hairpins side by side like little soldiers. No, not merely a penchant, a *necessity* that *did* bring light to her day. She needed order and regimentation to stave off her ever-present fears.

"You prefer chaos, Mr. Fairfax?" she asked.

"At times." He shrugged, and his lips curved in a dangerous smile. "Disorder can be liberating."

He sent her a sidelong glance. Dark lashes, straight and thick and long. The ridge of his cheek, the stubble darkening the plane of his jaw. Masculine beauty.

She ought to look away. Instead, she simply stared.

His dark brows rose, and then she did look away, taken aback to have been caught ogling at him like a lack-wit.

Clearly reading her expression as one of dismay, he offered a paltry encouragement for what he must have thought was the cause, though his grim tone nullified any comfort his words might have offered.

"You can grow accustomed to almost anything, Miss Canham. A day or two, and your notice of the regimentation will lessen."

You can grow accustomed to almost anything. She thought of the pretty little house in South London, and of her father, laughing and teaching her to solve riddles and puzzles, and of her mother and her brother . . . then she thought of the ugly, rank flat they had been forced to and the noise and the smells and the rooms so small and tight and the terrible fear that chewed at her all the time—

Mr. Fairfax was watching her. She gave a nervous little laugh.

"Yes," she murmured. "I am certain you have the right of it. One can grow accustomed to almost anything."

He looked at her queerly, then set the curricle in motion once more, closing the last of the distance to the gloomy, forbidding structure that was Burndale Academy. As they drew nigh, the building seemed to grow larger, darker. Colder.

A fat raindrop slapped the back of Beth's hand, making her start just as the door of the school opened. A black-clad, white-aproned maid stepped out, hovering just beyond the portal with her palm pressed flat across her breastbone.

"Who's there?" she called timorously. Mr. Fairfax pulled the horses up, and when recognition dawned, the maid's features took on a wary and guarded mien. "Oh, 'tis you, sir." The observation sounded anything but pleased.

Beth glanced at Mr. Fairfax. He was watching her, his dark eyes shadowed, his expression intent. It was the strangest thing, the way he looked at her, pensive, his gaze dropping to her lips once more, and then jerking away.

Setting the brake, he climbed down from the curricle and went to untie her trunk. His dark hair fell forward, obscuring his expression.

Her movements as subtle as she could make them, Beth twisted in her seat and watched him. The cloth of his coat pulled taut as he bent and reached, accenting the breadth of his shoulders and the shape of his back. She found the sight both alluring and . . . disturbing. Confusing. She had the peculiar inclination to lay her hand on his arm, his shoulder, to feel the play of muscle, to test the strength.

The urge was terribly disconcerting.

Beth dragged her gaze away, took a moment to gather her thoughts. Alighting unaided from the curricle, she strode toward the maid.

"Good evening," she said. "I am Miss Elizabeth Canham, the new teacher."

The wind burgeoned, snagging the hem of her skirt and stray strands of her hair, snatching her words to carry them away. She was forced to repeat them, louder, and as she spoke the last, an eerie wail carried from above, raising the fine hairs at Beth's nape.

Her head snapped back, and she studied the windows overhead, but they were dark and blank, revealing nothing.

She swallowed and glanced quickly about, but neither the maid nor Mr. Fairfax gave indication of aught amiss. Perhaps it had been only the moaning of the wind.

The maid, a dark-haired girl with a frame as light as a bird's and enormous eyes that were slightly protuberant, blinked at her, and blinked again. Then her gaze slid over Beth's shoulder and she shivered.

"I'm sorry," the girl whispered miserably. "I have no liking for storms."

Startled by this greeting, Beth stared at her. She followed the girl's gaze, noting that she looked not at the storm-darkened sky, but at Mr. Fairfax.

Tipping her head, Beth studied the menacing sky, ash and pewter and, in places, almost black.

"Well, it is not so very dark yet," she offered placatingly.

The girl peered at her for an instant, her enormous, dark eyes flickering with an unsettling edge of fear.

"Is she ready?" Mr. Fairfax asked in clipped tones.

Thinking he spoke to her, Beth spun about, but she found his attention directed at the maid. Beside him was her canvas-covered trunk, sitting now on the gravel drive.

"She is *not* ready, sir." The girl shook her head. "She will not come!"

Mr. Fairfax made no effort to mask his displeasure. Two lines drew parallel furrows between his brows, and the corners of his mouth pulled taut. Sleek, long strands of dark hair fell across his brow, then whipped back, caught by the wind, making him look all the more forbidding.

In an instant, he leashed it, leashed the anger, the displeasure, and his expression turned cool, blank. He looked hard and cold, chiseled from marble, and again Beth thought of a panther in a cage, leashed by self-imposed bars.

He was angry still. Beth *knew* it, though no emotion played across his features now.

Why, he can lock himself away, as I do, she thought, surprised, the realization making her feel an affinity for him once more, as she had when they shared their thoughts about the gates that guarded the road to Burndale Academy.

Then she wondered if he was any more adept at this feat than she, if the walls he erected were impregnable. Hers certainly were not. Though she was far better now than she had been as a child, there were yet days that her anxious thoughts burgeoned and grew and overcame her best intentions.

"What has set her off this time?" Mr. Fairfax tapped his fingers against his thigh, a steady beat.

The maid made a choked sound.

"She had an awful afternoon, sir. Miss Percy could scarce settle her," she said, twisting the cloth of her apron with a desperate wringing motion.

Beth wondered of whom they spoke.

Letting go the now-wrinkled apron, the maid dropped her hands to her sides. The white cloth fell over her black skirt in creased disarray.

"Miss Percy says 'tis the storm," she said.

Griffin Fairfax pinned her with a hard stare, and his tone was silky soft. "Does she?"

The girl's hands moved nervously over her apron, smoothing in small, jerky strokes as she stared down at the ground for so long that Beth thought she would not speak again. At last, she whispered, "Will you fetch her?"

There was a terrible moment of silence, heavy with unease. Beth looked back and forth between the two, sensing there was some undercurrent of meaning to such an innocuous question. Mr. Fairfax looked hewn of stone, no trace of emotion to be read in his expression or posture.

"No," he said, abrupt.

Baffled by the peculiar exchange, and made wary by it, Beth wondered at the source of it. A memory came to her, of Mr. Fairfax offering her a ride and saying he was on his way to Burndale Academy, and now Beth understood that his errand must have been to fetch someone.

Someone who—according to the maid—would not come.

Mr. Fairfax looked at Beth then, his gaze fixed on her with focused intent, and her heart stuttered in her breast. Her breath came a little faster as he stared at her, his gaze inscrutable.

To call him lovely seemed absurdity, but it was nothing more or less than truth. Despite the hard cast of his features, or perhaps because of it, his face was incredibly appealing, his form equally so. She would be a liar to pretend she did not notice. To pretend that the sight of him did not make the butterflies dance.

There, she had acknowledged it, an inappropriate fascination with this man, an imagined connection to him.

An inexplicable urge to touch him, just for an instant. She could fathom no reason for it, yet here it was.

The moment spun out, like hot candy pulled from the pot, and then it spun too thin and disappeared. Beth felt the connection snap, and she was left to wonder if it had been there at all.

His expression told her nothing.

He made a slight bow and said, "It was my pleasure to make your acquaintance, Miss Canham."

With a glance at the sky, he turned and climbed up on the curricle once more. When she tried to catch his eye, intending to thank him for the ride, he did not look at her; instead, he lifted the reins. Strong hands. Confident grasp. He was so brutally controlled that he might have been held up by rods of iron.

Her body humming with sharp tension, Beth watched as the curricle rolled away and disappeared round the sharp bend, leaving her with a puzzling sense of loss.

"You mustn't . . . oh . . . you mustn't . . ." A glance found the little maid wringing her hands in distress, her gaze alternating in frantic rhythm between Beth's face and the ground, making her head move up and down like a bobbing cork.

Beth looked to the now-empty road. A quiet distress wove through her, a wariness.

Mr. Fairfax had come to Burndale Academy, and gone, and whatever errand had brought him here, he had not carried it out.

Because *she* had refused to come to him—whoever *she* was—and he had refused to fetch her. Something about the entire situation was not only odd, but somehow . . . dreadful.

Just as the pewter sky, and the great, looming face of Burndale Academy, and the three dead trees that stood like the bard's three witches swaying in the wind, were all dreadful and grim.

The maid shuddered once more, then seemed to come to herself.

"A poor welcome I've shown you," she said. "Miss Percy will not be pleased."

"I feel very welcome, thank you. There is no reason to tell Miss Percy otherwise," Beth replied.

The maid's shoulders, stiff and tense, sagged a little. "Will you come this way, miss?"

Resolutely navigating her thoughts away from Griffin Fairfax and his mysterious errand, Beth followed the maid up the front stairs and into the house.

Pausing, she looked around, dimly aware that the girl circled behind her, drawing into the shadows like a wraith. The entryway was large and rectangular, with dark paneled walls and a floor tiled in a geometric pattern of unglazed clay tiles.

There was no candle to light the way, the storm-cast gloom making the place less than welcoming. Beth stared at the wine-red tile; the shade had never numbered among her favorites.

A snick of sound issued at her back, and Beth looked over her shoulder to see the girl had turned the key in the lock of the front door.

"What is your name?" she asked.

"Alice, miss." The reply was whispered to the floor.

"What of my trunk, Alice?"

"Mr. Waters will see it's brought to your chamber, miss. He's a handyman of sorts. Keeps the place in repair. Our Mr. Waters was a sailor once. He says he has seen the whole world . . ." Her voice trailed off and she shot a quick glance at Beth. "He'll see your trunk brought to your chamber before the rain comes."

My chamber. That was a pivotal point that had drawn Beth to the position of teacher at Burndale Academy. She was promised a room of her own rather than one to share. A true luxury. Many positions required the teachers to share rooms, even beds.

Beth knew her numerous limitations far too well to imagine she could have borne that. She could just imagine what a fellow teacher would think if Beth bolted upright in the dead of night to light every candle in the room and throw the window open wide.

"Thank you," she said as Alice sidled past her.

They continued along a wide hallway, the walls bereft of adornment, the floors barren of carpet, more of the same red tile, the color reminiscent of dried blood. Again, Beth had the impression that Burndale Academy was chill and forbidding, and she felt a momentary pang of homesickness. A deep breath and a silent admonition chased those feelings into a corner. There was no sense wishing for what was no more.

Her home was gone. The little house with its sun-dappled garden was lost to her family, and the small, dingy flat they had been forced to was no more a home than this unfriendly place. Except that her family was there in that flat, their good society creating a home as it always had, regardless of how stained the plaster walls or how threadbare the carpet.

Pressing her lips together, Beth reminded herself that she—and her annual income—were now their best hope for survival. She thrust aside her sad musings and hastened her steps to catch up with Alice, who moved like smoke through the shadowy hall.

There came a loud clap of thunder that made Beth gasp, followed by an oppressive quiet, undisturbed by echoes of children's voices or squeals of laughter. That quiet weighed upon her, and she walked a little faster, following the maid down the dim passage.

The only sound was the tap-tap-tap of Alice's shoes on the wood, and Beth's a heartbeat behind.

Always, he cherished them.

Flipping open the lid of his ornately carved pocket

watch, he looked at his keepsakes, his treasures. Pretty golden locks of hair. They were his. His to touch. His to fondle. Soft and silky and smooth.

He had long ago torn out the workings of the watch to make room for these things of far greater import. The watch was quite full. Soon, he would add another trophy, and the time would come to remove some of the older ones and put them in the special box on the shelf. The box with the little bones. Such tiny bones.

Fat drops of rain touched his cheeks and brow as he turned his face to the wind. With a grunt, he lifted the reins and set the horses to a fast pace. He had no wish to be caught in a downpour with cold, wet rivulets snaking along his back, his neck, wending into his boots.

Rain had been his mother's weather. The rumble of thunder had set her on edge, tensed her shoulders, frayed her temper. She would tug strands of her long, curling blond hair from the knot at her nape, and her lips would move in silent recitation. Those had been the days he kept quiet as could be, hushing his brother, hiding them both away in an unused bedchamber or the attic. Sometimes they hid in the shed by the woods. Sometimes they found a small cupboard to wedge their bodies into, or a chest.

Invariably, his mother found them, and then she would fetch the strap, a belt, a wooden paddle. Once, she had used the leather bellows from the fireplace simply because it was handy. The leather had been dotted with iron studs.

She was dead now. They were all dead. His mother. His father. His brother. And so many pretty girls.

But not Sarah. Trusting Sarah, who had been bought with a handful of trinkets.

The rain was good for something. It would wash away the sticky mess she had put in her hair. Sadly, that would wash away her curls.

No matter. No matter. Her hair was straight, but silky smooth and a nice, shiny gold.

He smiled as he thought of touching it. Cutting away another lock for his collection. Cutting away parts of her and listening to her muffled screams.

Anticipation ratcheted through him as he thought of touching her. Stroking her. Hurting her.

He took a deep breath, and another, dragging his excitement under control, pulling back the urge to go to her now, to do the deed quickly and feel the rush of power, of lust, of aching, luscious release.

Slowly, slowly.

Long ago, he had possessed no finesse, killing them too quickly. There had been that time in Stepney, the tavern just off Ratcliffe Highway . . . and another in Covent Garden. He shook his head, appalled that those memories were painfully humiliating still. Such ineptitude. Like a green lad with his first woman, he had not held himself in check, had not known how to savor the experience.

Now he did his hunting much closer to home, took his time, enjoyed every nuance of the act.

Enjoyed their terror and their torment, those soft, sweet girls with their pretty gold hair.

He took the turn at a breakneck pace. The high, two-wheeled little carriage rocked to a halt as he sawed on the reins, and the grim sky broke open just as the stable boy rushed to his side.

Chapter Four

Griffin Fairfax paced the dusty, neglected Long Gallery that spanned the length of the upper floor of Wickham Hall, a hallway of ghosts and memories. If he closed his eyes, he could see Amelia here, dancing in a beam of sunshine, spinning faster and faster, dust motes floating about her . . .

"Bloody hell." The oath and his footsteps echoed hollowly against the backdrop of the howling storm that rattled the windows and whistled through cracks and crevices.

Above him arched the barrel ceiling, creating a vast and lonely space wide enough to drive a gig through. The roof and plaster walls had fallen in on themselves at the far end of the hallway, collapsing under the weight of disuse and disrepair, leaving an acrid pile of timber and rubble. The damage was done long before Wickham Hall passed to him, but none in all the years had seen fit to repair it. Including him. The collapsed section was boarded up, but the boards were half rotted and the air was heavy with a rank, damp smell. The smell of decay.

Rain beat upon the mullioned windows, a pounding

torrent, and for a single, frozen instant, he was tempted to run the length of the hall, to pause only long enough to throw open each window as he passed.

Let the rain come. Let a *flood* come in a violent flow to wash the blood from his hands and cleanse this place.

Of memories.

Of death.

He could imagine a great black wall of water cascading doggedly from floor to floor, destroying everything in its path. There would be a certain satisfaction in that, but there would also be an ember of regret.

Though unentailed, Wickham Hall and all it contained had been in his family for centuries, never changing hands by sale. Perhaps it was time it did. Perhaps he should sell it, leave here. 'Twould be the wiser course, rather than flinging wide the windows and letting in the storm.

All the water in the world would not make him feel clean, would not wash away the guilt or the scent of death that clung to him.

Leaning close to the window, Griffin squinted against the storm and the dark, and stared out into the night. At first he saw only his own face, hanging disembodied against the backdrop of black sky. After a moment, he saw beyond that to the shape of the gatehouse wall, its crenellated upper limit jagged against the murky, storm-laden heavens and the sheeting rain.

Then again, given the weather, perhaps he saw the wall only in his mind's eye, conjured it from memory and nightmare.

He should tear down the gatehouse, stone by cursed stone. Likely, he should have done that three years ago.

Should have. Should have. Regret was a pastime for fools.

Jerking back from the window, he turned away. He had not wanted to come here, had not intended it as he paced the halls of his home like a caged beast.

Or a madman.

Was he? Was he mad?

There were days he thought—nay, days he was *certain*—that he was.

With a snarl, he spun, flung out his arm to lash at the porcelain vase on the table by the window. In the last instant, he stopped, frozen, his breath heavy in his chest, the vase untouched, his emotion held in check by sheer will and determination.

She refused to come.

He had sat in the curricle by the front door of Burndale Academy and listened to the maid say that Isobel would not come.

Will you fetch her?

After what had happened the last time, he most certainly would not fetch her.

The maid—what was her name?—Alice. She had eyed him warily, as though she expected him to tear her head from her body.

Bloody hell.

Isobel was to come for dinner once each week. Usually she was there on the step waiting for him, docile. But once before she had refused to come. It had been a stormy day, like this one, like the one three years in the past.

Last time he had lifted her and carried her to the curricle. She had been a limp doll, unresponsive, her head lolling to the side. But as he had placed her on the seat, she had begun to scream and scream, bloodcurdling sounds that were horrific in their torment. His horses had shied and he had been hard-pressed to keep them from bolting with both the carriage and Isobel behind them.

He closed his eyes for a moment at the recollection, pinched the bridge of his nose. Isobel was better away from here.

Hell, *he* was better away from here.

Sometimes, he thought they were best off far away from each other. Perhaps she was the wiser of the two of them, given his current melancholy.

He ran his palm along the stubble that roughened his jaw, disturbed by this turn of his thoughts.

From the floor below him came the sound of the hall clock, echoing hollowly. He wanted to break that clock, to tear out the workings, to stop time—

No. He would not allow himself to free the rage. His anger was too close to the surface tonight, with the storm and the memories heavy upon him.

Footsteps sounded behind him, and he turned to find Mrs. Ashton, his housekeeper, standing at the far end of the gallery, shadowed but for the glow of her candle. Flickering fingers of light and shadow danced along the walls and darker doorways. Her hand shook, and the flame leaped and swayed, caught by the terrible draft that found its way through the boards.

He knew why she had come even before she spoke.

"Sorry I am to bother you, sir—" Her words caught on a sob. "'Tis my husband's niece, Sarah. She is gone. Never returned to her work at Briar House after her half day."

Briar House. Griffin tensed at her words.

"Perhaps she has run off with her beau," he suggested, forcing a casual tone.

"No." Mrs. Ashton shook her head. "No, I feel it. As soon as I heard, I thought of the other two, their hair shorn off, their fingers—" She shook her head again, and finished on a whisper. "I fear she is dead."

Not yet. Certainty clawed him, sharp and deep.

"Have searchers been organized?" he asked, though he knew they would not find her.

"Yes."

"I should like to offer—"

"No!" Mrs. Ashton cut him short, then continued in a quieter tone, though her voice shook and the words sounded clipped. "I beg your pardon, sir. I mean no disrespect. But I fear that were you to arrive at Briar House, even to offer your assistance, it would"—she drew a ragged breath—"it would . . ." Shaking her head rapidly from side to side, she exhaled in a rush. "I only ask leave to go to my husband's brother's home in Northallerton. To offer what comfort I may to the girl's family."

He knew very well what she left unsaid. His presence at Briar House would only make everything worse. Likely, they would have him dragged from the premises. He could not blame them. He could hardly expect Amelia's parents to welcome *him* to Briar . . . they had entrusted their only child to him in holy matrimony.

And he had killed her.

There was little else to be said about that.

"You must go to your family, Mrs. Ashton. Offer what comfort you can."

"Yes, sir. Thank you, sir." The housekeeper turned and walked away, her posture stooped, her gait pained, a middle-aged woman made ancient in the space of an hour.

Griffin closed his eyes, pinched the bridge of his nose.

And, inexplicably, thought of the teacher, Elizabeth Canham.

Her moon-pale hair.

Her wide, lush mouth.

The way she had made him smile.

The bell tolled at half past six the next morning, calling teachers and pupils both to the start of a new day. Awake and out of bed even before the summons, Beth stood by the heavy window curtains and looked out at hammering rain and an angry sky. A gloomy welcome to her new home.

She was a little surprised to realize that despite the

boom of thunder and the pounding of the storm, she had slept well, exhausted from her travels, grateful to have finally reached her destination.

Fatigued by her journey, she had been sorely tempted to fall fully clothed upon the bed the previous night. She had seen immediately that the linens and blankets on the bed were fresh, a circumstance that made her more comfortable than she might have been. But her nature felt uneasy with leaving her things packed in a trunk. She had a preference for order and neatness. So she had put her belongings away on the shelves of the large wooden clothing press in the corner, folding and organizing until she was satisfied. Everything in its place, organized by color and function.

That chore complete, she had nodded off quickly as she lay in bed, silently revisiting the things she had discussed with her mother before leaving home, preparing and planning for the next day's lesson, her very first. Unable to brave the full dark in this new and strange place, she had left the rushlight burning and drifted off to its small illumination.

The heavy curtains she had left open. She would have opened the window as well, were the weather even a bit friendly. Still, she had slept the whole night through undisturbed by dreams or nightmares. Unusual. It was rare for her to sleep so deeply.

Now there came a brisk knocking at her chamber door, calling Beth's attention from the dismal view beyond the windowpanes. As she turned, something caught her eye, a shadow, a shape at the corner of the back garden wall, curtained by the sheeting rain.

She paused, and leaned close to the cold glass, squinting into the gloom.

There . . . a shadowy form, barely discernable, a charcoal lump against the backdrop of the blackened trunk of the dead tree.

Shifting her weight, she tried to alter her position to

better her line of sight, but the three dead trees, and the man—if indeed it was a man—stood to the west, barely in sight, for the view from her window opened to the south.

The knocking came again, louder, the maid impatient to be about her duties. Beth cast a glance over her shoulder, and when she returned her attention to the window, the shadow was gone.

No man.

Only three dead trees lurking in the storm.

With a shake of her head, she crossed the room and opened the door to take the jug of warm water from the maid. The girl mumbled a morning greeting and scurried in to empty the chamber pot and wipe it clean. Beth carried the warm water to the stand in the corner and washed at the basin.

She cast the maid a surreptitious glance from the corner of her eye, feeling strange that someone had come to clean up for her. Of course, her mother had shared stories of her own childhood, when she had lived in a house with many workers—scullery maids and parlor maids and footmen and coachmen—but Beth herself had never known such a life. The only servant her family had ever employed was a step-girl to wash the front stoop on Saturday mornings, and even that had been a luxury in a time long past. Certainly they could afford nothing of the kind now.

Spurred by the early morning chill, Beth dressed quickly once the maid had left, then fixed her hair in two simple plaits. She worked deftly by touch and familiarity, twining and pinning one braid behind each ear. The style was easy and unadorned, and the best she had found for taming her wild and heavy curls.

Taking up a clean handkerchief, she brought the cloth to her nose and inhaled the scent. With a wistful sigh she tucked the square of cloth into her sleeve. It smelled like soap and a little like her mother's lavender water. It smelled like home, reminding her of the gift she was embroidering for her mother.

The gift . . .

She froze, looked around, lifted the lid of her trunk and peered inside, crossed to the clothes press and looked there as well, though she had the unpleasant suspicion that she would not find it.

Her embroidery bag was nowhere about.

Distress touched her. How could she have failed to notice? When had she last held it? In the stage? At the church?

She could not say with certainty.

Oh, the loss of it was a blow. The ecru linen bag itself had been a gift from her mother. The linen for handkerchiefs and the needles and colored threads, Beth had purchased with her own hard-earned and carefully hoarded coins.

She was frustrated with herself, saddened by the loss.

Then she shook her head, and a small ray of hope burgeoned. Perhaps she had left the bag not in the stage, but in Mr. Fairfax's curricle. She might yet see its safe return.

The thought of Mr. Fairfax brought a strange surge of emotion to the fore. She recalled the way he had looked at her, the way he had smiled, the rushing energy that roared through her when his gaze met hers.

After a long moment, she realized with sharp mortification that she was standing about, listless and dreamy, thinking of a man she barely knew.

Well, enough of that.

Busying her hands, thrusting aside all thought of Griffin Fairfax, she folded her nightdress and placed it beneath her pillow, her actions measured and focused. Then she tidied her bedsheets, though she suspected a maid might come at some point to see to the chore. She was accustomed to doing for herself, and saw no reason to change that.

There was nothing left to keep her in the room, and she could hear the echo of small feet and girlish voices from the hallway. The pupils were gathering. Excitement and apprehension warred in her belly.

On a slow exhalation she smoothed her hands along the plain twilled cotton and worsted cloth of her black bombazine skirt. The action served to steady her nerves and push back the concern that pricked her confidence.

Her place here at Burndale Academy had been earned by sleight of hand. She knew the truth of the matter, and she wondered how long before others recognized her for the fraud she was.

What did she know of teaching young girls?

She was educated by her mother, had never attended a formal school of any sort. Despite the purposeful, cultivated impression presented in her carefully worded letter of application, she had never *taught* anyone, unless helping her mother teach her younger brother and the three little boys who lived two doors down counted for something.

The character she had submitted was true enough, prepared by Mrs. Blackwood of Lyttleton Road, a widow Beth had helped on occasion, reading to her and sorting her embroidery threads. Mrs. Blackwood wrote of Beth's fine organizational skills, her moral fiber and rectitude, but made no mention of her teaching skill.

The headmistress of Burndale Academy had either failed to notice the omission or, being in desperate need of a teacher, had not cared. The guard's warning from the previous day leapt to the forefront of her thoughts, and the recollection of the gravestones she had read of two women who had died at this very school. A shudder chased up her spine, and Beth could not help but wonder if the ease with which she had acquired this position had aught to do with the two dead teachers.

What had happened to those women? How had they

died? She glanced about at the shadowed corners of her chamber, and a chill crawled across her skin.

Had they lived in this very room? Slept in this very bed?

She shuddered. The possibility was disconcerting.

Pressing her lips together, Beth rubbed her hands along her arms, then shook her head and shrugged off the cloud of anxiety that had descended upon her. She knew better than to conjure dark thoughts and suppositions, for to do so might open the floodgate to all her secret terrors.

She lifted her chin a notch as she prepared herself to face her day and the challenges she was certain would come. Blowing out a short breath, she forced aside her qualms and squared her shoulders as she reached for the door handle.

Today was her first day as a teacher. She intended to do her job well, despite her lack of experience.

In the wide, cold hallway, she found the girls already beginning to line up in pairs, whispering and giggling and occasionally daring to meet her gaze, only to look away quickly. She knew they speculated about her, and she thought that was fine. Were she a young girl, she might very well speculate about the new schoolmistress.

They were all dressed alike in matching uniforms. Inexpensive dark blue frocks, some threadbare in places, white pinafores, woolen stockings, and sturdy shoes with brass buckles. From the youngest to the oldest, they were very presentable, with scrubbed faces and tidy hair.

"You may proceed," came the command, issued in a firm tone by the dark-haired teacher who stood at the far end of the hallway. She caught Beth's eye and nodded, but there was no opportunity for proper introductions.

The girls began to descend the stairs, two by two, still whispering and giggling. Beth watched them go, aware of the other teachers—women whose formal acquaintance she had yet to make—positioned along the corridor at intervals, supervising the descent.

They were clothed quite like Beth herself, in serviceable and plain garb of neutral color, gray or black or brown. Beth was glad of that, and glad, too, that her mother had insisted she purchase these garments before she left, despite their rapidly dwindling funds. Her old dresses of brighter color and pretty ornamentation would have been very out of place here.

Moreover, those things were too young for her now in both style and frivolity. She had sold them to help pay for these more appropriate dresses, and she would not allow herself to pine for them. They were remnants of a different time, before her family had been forced to a dingy flat, before their circumstance had become so dire. A time of girlhood, gone now.

Gone long ago, really.

In truth, her childhood had been a poorly darned guise, filled with darkness and melancholy that no child should know. The seams had unraveled more than once, and at times they had torn asunder with brutal force. Hazy recollections swirled up like a choking miasma, leaving Beth's throat closed and tight.

Not now, she thought bitterly, resenting the intrusion of old fears. *Oh, please, not now.*

"Good morning, Miss Canham. I trust you slept well."

Startled, Beth spun, the dark wisps of her memories dissipating like smoke. A tall woman approached, brisk purpose and confidence in each step. She wore her russet hair scraped back from her face and rolled at her nape. Her forehead was broad and smooth, her gray eyes direct and keen.

Miss Gwendolyn Percy, the headmistress of Burndale Academy.

A woman of some four decades, she gave the impression of maturity, intellect, and inner strength. Beth had met her the previous afternoon upon her arrival at the school, and had liked her immediately.

Their meeting had been short and pleasant. Miss Percy had inquired after her trip, had a maid bring a small refreshment, and then outlined Beth's duties and the expectations on her time. Beth had found it all very civilized and had, in fact, been surprised and grateful to be treated with such consideration after her lengthy journey. Miss Percy was a woman of refined compassion.

Yet, beneath it all, Beth had sensed a vibrating tension, a distraction of thought and attention, as though Miss Percy's mind was somewhere else entirely, somewhere distressing. She had recalled Mr. Fairfax saying the headmistress was occupied by a weighty matter.

Good manners as well as an understanding of her position in the academy's hierarchy had prevented Beth from inquiring about that, or about why she had been left standing forgotten at the crossroads by the church, dependent on luck and the goodwill of Mr. Fairfax.

She had decided that to make mention of the headmistress's oversight would only set a poor tone for her employment here at Burndale. But in fact, it was Miss Percy who had raised the issue, offering an apology, but no explanation.

This morning, the headmistress looked far from rested, purple shadows marking the delicate skin beneath her eyes.

"Good morning, Miss Percy," Beth replied as she drew nigh. "Yes, I slept very well, thank you."

The girls continued their orderly, if not precisely sedate march, on best behavior under the watchful eye of Miss Percy.

"The rain did not disturb you?"

"Not at all," Beth demurred. "In truth, I did not even notice it during the night, so great was my exhaustion."

"You were not frightened by the storm?" Miss Percy

pressed, leaving Beth to wonder at her tenacious inquiry on the subject.

"I found the sound of the rain quite soothing." In that instant Beth realized that it was likely the sounds of the storm that had allowed her to sleep at all. Accustomed as she was to the riot and noise of London, perfect silence would be perfectly horrid.

Miss Percy spoke a few more words about the weather, the rain that yet beat upon the windows with fulminant vigor, and the likelihood that the girls would not go outdoors today for noontide recreation. Then with a polite request that Beth follow the last girl down, the headmistress strode off and, alongside the column of pupils, descended the wide stairs.

Beth stood to the side, watching the girls to make certain they continued on with appropriate decorum.

A moment later, she looked about to find the maid, Alice, walking swiftly along the hall from the opposite end, carrying a carpet brush. Her head was bowed, her shoulders hunched. She did not wear the black dress and ruffled apron of the previous afternoon, but a simple cotton print overlain with a heavy apron, her garments clearly suited for hard work.

"Good morning, Alice," Beth said with a smile.

The maid started and skittered to one side.

"Good morning, miss," she said, recovering. She cast a quick look at Beth, then at the dwindling line of pupils. Her gaze lingered at the end of the line before sliding away.

"Cleaning today?" Beth asked.

Alice stared at the carpet brush in her hand for a long moment, as though considering her reply. Finally, she nodded.

"Yes, miss. The carpets in the teachers' chambers need brushing. One of the upstairs maids is sick with the scarlatina. I'm to see to her chores until she returns."

There was a terrible melancholy laced through Alice's

words, and the unspoken hung between them. *If she returns.* The sick girl must be someone Alice valued.

"I hope your friend will recover soon," Beth said, then wishing to distract Alice, she continued, "Where are the girls roomed?"

"You mean where they sleep?"

"Yes. I believe each teacher is afforded her own chamber on this floor . . ." She paused, and Alice nodded her confirmation.

"Or the one above. Excepting Miss Percy, who has her rooms in the small house, and Miss Richards, who does as well, and Mademoiselle Martine."

"The small house?" Beth asked.

"In the back," Alice said, her explanation leaving Beth only vaguely more knowledgeable than she had been a moment past.

"And what of the pupils?"

"Two girls to a bed, ten to a room. Older girls in each chamber act as monitors for the younger," Alice said, turning to look down the long hallway. "They're the large rooms, at the far end of the hall, and two rooms upstairs, though there're girls in only one of them now. And another two in the east wing. The west wing"—Alice paused, pressed her lips together—"the west wing is mostly empty. Well, not mostly. It *is* empty. Best not to go there. The floor's rotted in places. Miss Percy says it's not safe. One of the girls fell through yesterday, wandering where she oughtn't, and was lucky she only came away with a scraped leg rather than a broken neck."

Likely the injured child was the matter that had occupied Miss Percy the previous afternoon.

"Thank you, Alice. I'm to take turns with the other teachers supervising prayers and overseeing bedtime rituals for the girls. And now I know where to go." Beth smiled. "And where not to go."

"That's right, miss. Best be wise and stay away from the west wing," Alice whispered, plucking at her apron.

The line of pupils had moved along now, and only a single girl trailed behind. She was pale and wan, with a fey and dreamy look. Her long, dark hair fell about her shoulders and down her back, the ends ragged and knotted. Her pinafore was askew. One woolen sock bunched about her ankle. She was by far the least tidy girl Beth had seen that morning. But it was something more that drew Beth's notice, something in the girl's eyes. She was shadowed by sadness.

Staring straight ahead, the girl walked slowly along the hall, alone, without a partner to giggle and chat with as the others had.

Looking at her, Beth felt a cheerless pang, and a whisper of terrible, cold memory, long buried. She well knew what it felt like to be alone, haunted by horrors others could not know.

Poor, sorrowful child.

"Except *her*," Alice said, her voice low but vehement. "*She* has a room of her own, when she stays. Can't have her in with the others. Can't turn her out, neither. So there you have it."

She gave a little shudder, and Beth stared at her in surprise.

A puzzle. Beth looked at the girl and then back to Alice.

"Why do you say that?" Beth asked, feeling certain that if she could only open her eyes a little wider, study the undercurrents of meaning just a bit more carefully, then she would discern the answer. She always felt that way when presented with a riddle. Layers upon layers of meaning, but eventually she would figure it out.

Her father had taught her that. He had held a great fondness for riddles and puzzles.

"Well, this is a charity school in part, isn't it?" Alice said. "Her father is generous with his money and very, very rich, they say. The trustees want her here, and so, here she is."

Beth looked at Alice in surprise. A charity school. She had had no idea. "What do you mean, a charity school in part?"

"Well, most of the girls come from families what pay, and some—a few—are local, from families what could teach them to read a little afore they came here. Those are supported by the good will and generosity of"—she pressed her lips together, lowered her voice, and continued—"Mr. Fairfax. And old Mr. Creavy and Mr. Moorecroft, and others. But mostly Mr. Fairfax. Miss Percy says this school is their experiment."

"I see," said Beth, though she really did not see at all.

Alice caught her lower lip between her teeth and her eyes widened. "I oughtn't have said that, miss."

No, she oughtn't. But at this moment, Beth's greatest interest lay with the odd little girl.

"And why can that child not be put in with the others?" Beth asked.

"Why, she's cursed, isn't she? Shadowed by death."

With questions chasing each other to the tip of her tongue, Beth drew a breath, held it, then asked in a moderate tone, "What do you mean?"

Alice shook her head and whispered, "Cursed and doomed, just like her father."

"Cursed and doomed? What . . . Who is her father?"

"Didn't I say? Mr. Fairfax, rot his black, murdering heart." Alice tapped the handle of the carpet brush against her skirt, her fingers curled so tight the knuckles were white. "A killer, he is. A killer." She pressed her lips together and shot Beth a wary glance. "I must go. I've said far too much already."

"Wait—" Beth cried, but Alice hurried off, leaving Beth alone in the hallway.

For a moment, she stood as she was, questions raining through her. *A killer, he is. A killer.*

She wrapped her arms about herself. A jarring chill touched her skin, as though a window had been thrown wide or some malevolent gaze locked on her with unerring attention. Beth spun, looking to the darkened doorways that lined the wall, to the shadowed and dim corners, but there was one there watching her. Each door was shut tight.

She recognized the fear lurking beneath the surface of her composure, an oily, fetid sludge. With determination, she thrust it aside. There was no place here for ancient terrors, no place for her to imagine dark things and malevolent intent. Alice's words were only words. They had neither substance nor power.

Squaring her shoulders, she followed the path the girls had taken moments past.

At the top of the stairs, Beth paused and watched the progress of that lonely little girl as she meandered down the last three steps, her hand trailing along the polished banister.

Suddenly, the child stopped and turned to look over her shoulder, her dark eyes locking with Beth's, sorrowful and far too wise for her years.

Griffin Fairfax was her father. And Alice had called him—called them both—cursed and doomed.

Again, a whisper of distress unfurled in Beth's heart, a dark and chilling thing held back by a weak, gossamer thread. She thought of the shadow she had seen earlier, the silhouette of a man outside in the storm, and she thought of the ugly cadence of Alice's words.

Chapter Five

Henry Pugh paced slowly along the hallway of the Black Swan Tavern, studying the bloody footprints that marked the killer's path. He moved carefully, pausing now and again, searching out the place where the ghastly trail began. The footprints led in the opposite direction of where Henry stood, *toward* the landlord's body.

Strange.

Halfway to the parlor, he froze, sickened and horrified by what lay before him.

The landlord's wife, Mrs. Trotter, was sprawled on the hallway floor, her skirt rucked up, her limbs in immodest disarray. The top of her head was gone, caved in, and most of her face, rendering her nearly unrecognizable. He could be certain it was she only because her dress—drenched now in her own blood—was the one she had worn that same afternoon when, smiling and winking, she had teased him as he had stood about, searching for any excuse to remain where he was.

He'd been at the tavern to hear the landlord's tale of a stranger in the shadows. It was a tale he had dismissed as unimportant. He had thought it all a ploy to bring him round to see Ginnie. Everyone knew the Trotters loved to meddle, loved to bring couples together and see them happily wed.

"Sweet on our Ginnie, are you?" Mrs. Trotter had asked, following his gaze to the maid, Ginnie George.

Henry had ducked his head, felt hot blood rush to his cheeks and the tips of his ears, for he *was* sweet on her. Raising his head, he had been helpless to stop himself from looking at Ginnie, with her Cupid's-bow lips and wheat-bright ringlets. He was very fond of her, and she of him, enough so that one night last week she'd let him steal a kiss behind the tavern.

She was the reason he'd signed on for a decent living and a decent wage. A man needed both if he was thinking to marry. Standing in the tavern, Henry had looked at Ginnie once more and thought he was not ready for that yet, not quite ready to marry. But Ginnie made him think that one day soon he might be.

A quick flash of her dimples and a coy look from beneath her lashes, and Ginnie had gone off to her chores, leaving Henry under Mrs. Trotter's watchful eye, with his pulse quickened and his palms damp.

Ginnie.

Henry battled his sorrow now as he looked at Mrs. Trotter dead on the floor. His one consolation was the knowledge that Ginnie had gone to see to her sick mother tonight, that she was nowhere near this hellish place.

Shivering now, and not from the cold, Henry battled the terrible nausea rolling deep in his belly. He could scarcely bring himself to look at the horrific scene before him, let alone crouch down and carefully look for clues. What had made him think he could do the job of parish constable?

He had not signed on for this, to witness the aftermath of foul murder and desecration of the dead. He had signed on at the Shadwell Police Office for a fine and honorable living, to break up a fight or look into a theft. Not to stand in a pool of blood, to bear witness to such heinous acts.

The stamp of heavy boots, male voices in the hallway, and the slam of the door against those who hovered in the street warned Henry he was no longer alone. Other officers had arrived. Glad he was of that.

Muffled exclamations echoed along the corridor, and the sound of approaching footsteps.

"What have we here?" Sam Loder asked as he stepped up, shoulder to shoulder with Henry. Sam was a seasoned officer, a man of experience. Still, Henry wondered at Sam's casual tone and seeming indifference to the brutality of the scene.

Clenching his teeth so tight he thought they might crack, Henry fought the urge to howl. A desperate animosity came over him; he barely managed to avoid snarling a reply to Sam's question, a demand to know if Sam had eyes in his head.

"What have we here?" Murder. We have murder.

Shamed by his thoughts, he scrubbed his palm over his face.

"We've sent men to seal off London Bridge, and the Bow Street Runners have been called in. We'll find him," Sam said. "Just as we found John Williams when he did foul murder at Timothy Marr's shop and again at the Kings Arms Tavern."

The murders Sam spoke of had occurred two years past, before Henry's time, but he'd heard the terrible tales repeated, and he'd seen the place where Williams was buried at the intersection with Cannon Street. 'Twas a place where four roads met. Some claimed that a stake had been thrust through the murderer's black heart to ensure he did not rise again, and that burial at the crossroad was meant to confuse and confound the evil ghost if he did rise from the grave.

Henry had never given much thought to ghosts.

A heavy hand landed on his shoulder, making him jerk. Blinking against the humiliating sting of tears, he willed himself to meet his duty as an officer. His gaze dropped to Mrs. Trotter's crushed skull, her ruined face, her blood-soaked dress.

To Henry's mind, one thing was certain. No ghost had done this deed.

Chapter Six

That evening the storm let up and the sky cleared. Beth walked along the road that led to Burndale Academy, following the curves and twists, having no solid destination in mind save the next step and the next. Hers was no sedate stroll, but a focused task that freed a measure of energy and emotion with each stride.

She had survived the first day of her employment without episode. No one had branded her an imposter, and she was grateful for that.

Moments past, when she had paused in the doorway of the small parlor and mentioned that she planned an evening stroll, the other teachers had looked at her askance and declined to accompany her. It was a circumstance that caused her no distress. She had no true wish for companionship, but good manners had led her to inquire if any would like to join her.

Miss Browne and Miss Doyle and Mademoiselle Martine and the others had seemed quite content to sit and sew and chatter amongst themselves, all lovely and worthy pastimes, but Beth could not bear to be still, to be confined in the small parlor with the four walls so close about her. A cage. A coffin.

She needed to walk, and since her duties of the day were complete, she had obtained Miss Percy's permission and set out.

Her day had been long, both trying and fulfilling. Now, as the wind slapped her cheeks and her blood pumped with exertion, she revisited frozen moments in time, sifting through recollections of her classroom performance, learning from them, using that knowledge to plan improvements to tomorrow's lessons.

Approached from the correct perspective, any puzzle could be solved, including a determination of how best to engage her pupils.

She did not stray far, only just around the sharp bend in the road, until the looming shadow of Burndale Academy disappeared behind the line of massive trees, their branches colored by the red-brown hues of autumn.

Beth found that the landscape, the trees, even the smells, were all strange and foreign in comparison to London. The only sounds were those of her own footfalls and the whisper of the wind. Accustomed as she was to the city, to buildings on either side and carts and people and the sounds of activity that almost never ceased, she had contradictory reactions to the countryside.

While the vast spaces were wonderfully appealing, the unfamiliar lack of noise was unsettling. Too quiet.

That quiet made the suddenness of a sharp sound all the more startling. Beth froze midstride and glanced about. What was that? The snap of a twig? A small animal skittering along a branch?

Wary, she turned right, then left in quick succession.

The hair at her nape prickled and rose. Prey to the eerie sensation that she was not alone, she searched for a glint of light, a reflection from unseen eyes that watched her from the depths of the copse.

Was it her imagination, or was something . . . *someone* . . . there?

She studied the foliage, feeling both wary and foolish as she did so. Imagination was a powerful thing, capable of conjuring all manner of ghosts and demons.

She huffed out a shaky breath. Of course she was alone. Did she imagine that some creature watched her with malicious intent?

The quiet only made her anxious, or perhaps the vastness of the heavens, unbroken by church spires and roofs, unsullied by the smells of city life. She enjoyed the open space, but she did not enjoy the sensation of feeling so solitary here beneath the saucer of darkening sky.

Beth twined the edge of her shawl through her fingers, then let the soft cloth slide free. Darkness would be full upon her soon. It was time to return to Burndale Academy.

Only . . . she could not completely dissuade herself from the certainty that there *was* something . . .

A last glance revealed nothing amiss. Nothing. Only her imagination.

Nonetheless, caution made her close her fist in the cloth of her skirt and raise the hem above her ankles lest she find herself in a position to bolt down the road at a tearing pace.

Now there was an image. It made her laugh at herself.

Gathering her emotions, she forced the tension from her shoulders. She could not allow the familiar terror to wriggle free, to swarm through her veins until her heart raced and her mind knew only fear. On that path lay only heartache.

No, panic was not welcome here, but reasonable caution was.

Retracing the steps that had brought her to this point, she walked quickly back along the road toward the school. The perfect beauty of the pink and orange sunset overtop the trees made her feel as though the evening sky had sprung to life, as though it breathed and sighed. The sight brought her quiet joy, but the reasonable caution she had deemed appropriate did not let her slow her pace, or tarry to enjoy the view.

As she rounded a bend, a movement caught her eye, a man in the distance walking parallel to her through the field. Turning, he cut across toward her.

Momentary alarm gave way to recognition when she saw it was Mr. Fairfax approaching. And then she had the thought that if Alice had her druthers, recognition of Mr. Fairfax ought to incite Beth to further alarm. Wry amusement touched her.

She watched his approach and wondered what he was doing, walking on this road. His curricle was nowhere to be seen and he was clothed for a warm day, not a rapidly cooling evening.

Her gait faltered and her heart twitched strangely in her breast. She turned and looked at the road behind her, then the lay of the field that blended with the copse at its far end. For an instant, she felt disoriented, and more than a little wary.

Had it been *his* gaze she sensed earlier, watching her from the woods?

She could not fathom it, for to be ahead of her here on the road he would have needed to sprint the distance from behind her, and he looked relaxed and comfortable, not at all out of breath or exerted. Still, she could not negate the possibility. She pulled her shawl tight about her shoulders, raised her head, and waited.

As he drew near, she studied him, taking in each magnificent bit of him, put all together in masculine perfection. That was the puzzle. What made him so attractive? The cut of his coat to his broad shoulders? The slight curl of his hair, dark against the white collar of his shirt? The way he tipped his head, just a bit to the right as he approached?

She could not help herself. Her gaze followed the line of his coat to lean hips, and lower, lingering on his muscled legs. He moved with the natural grace and elegance that she had noted the first time they met.

His stride was purposeful, his attention focused wholly on her person, and she had the odd inclination that he searched this road for *her*.

On a sharp exhalation, she looked away. Her heart beat too fast and her body felt flush and alive.

Had he known she would walk? Had he waited for her?

Impossible. She had herself not fully realized her intention or direction until she paused at the fork in the road.

So he did not—*could not possibly*—travel this way looking for her.

No sooner had the thought formed than he dispelled it.

"Good evening, Miss Canham. I had hoped to meet you," he said, inclining his head in greeting and offering a small smile. It was a strange and alluring beauty he had, harsh features, hard lips, handsome when taken in bit by bit, more than wonderful when looked at as a whole. She had never thought of a man as beautiful or wonderful, but Mr. Fairfax was.

"Good evening, Mr. Fairfax," she said, feeling breathless and silly and out of sorts.

He was near enough now that she could see his dark eyes, sparkling with an inner light, bright with a heat that was both disturbing and alluring. That look left her feeling as though his gaze touched her in truth, as though sensation brought life to her flesh.

Again her heart tripped over, and she was awash in an odd, hot ache that stole her breath.

The breeze caught her hair and pulled strands from her carefully placed pins, then sent the tendrils dancing, restless and free. She was grateful for the distraction. Raising her hands, she gathered the few wayward curls and held them still. As the wind abated for an instant, she quickly tucked the stray strands into her carefully pinned plaits.

Mr. Fairfax kept his gaze upon her, his expression thoughtful as he stepped closer. He looked both the gentleman and the ruffian at once.

When he was an arm's length away, he gave a spare smile that made her skin feel as though she had rubbed her feet on a carpet and caught a spark. She tingled with anticipation, with anxiety, with both dread and hope of . . . what?

The man flustered her to the extreme.

"Forgive me, Miss Canham. Do I intrude?" he asked.

She stared at him a moment, struck by the way the dying sun touched his dark hair, a bright halo, leaving his face in shadow. She dropped her gaze, anxious and uneasy, not in the way of fear, but in the way of . . . *excitement.*

The realization was disconcerting. Never had she experienced the like, but she was not so green as to play ignorance at the cause.

She turned her face away, having no wish for her heated—and surely reddened—cheeks to betray her thoughts. She *knew* what it was, this feeling. She had seen girls turn silly over it, laughing and twittering behind their hands as a handsome youth swaggered past.

But she had never been prey to such herself. Until now.

Mr. Fairfax had her blushing, but he would *not* have her sighing like a lovesick girl.

"There is no intrusion, Mr. Fairfax." She knew she sounded breathless. She could only hope that he attributed it to exertion.

"I believe this belongs to you," he said, and offered a small ecru linen reticule that she knew well. "You left it behind in my carriage."

Oh, the sweet joy that flooded her at the sight.

"You have my gratitude, Mr. Fairfax. With a heavy heart, I discovered the bag's loss this morning." She smiled at him, wanting to throw her arms about him and hug him for this, for the return of the bag's contents, the gift for her mother. Realizing she had half raised her hands to hug him in truth, she dropped them to her side, abashed.

He cast her a quizzical look, raising his straight, dark brows.

When he said nothing, merely looked at her in that intent way, as though he saw her right to the very core, she felt the awkwardness of the moment with piercing intensity.

"You are most gallant, sir," she said in a rush.

"Yes, I am the quintessence of gallant," he muttered, his gaze dropping to her mouth and lingering there. "Actually, I am not gallant at all." His tone grew warm, intimate, and he asked with deliberate care, "Shall I name my reward?"

"Reward?" A little tremor shimmered through her.

Stepping close, so his legs brushed the folds of her skirt, he studied her with a half-lidded look that made her heart race.

She had ascertained at their earliest meeting that Mr. Fairfax was an odd blend of gentleman and . . . something else. Now, the way he looked at her, his gaze gone hard and sharp, told her that the gentleman had gone into hiding.

Restlessness stirred inside her, something impatient and curious and eager. She could not think that these feelings portended anything good. She ought to step back, step away, perhaps even run away.

The scent of him carried to her, warm, a little musky, and . . . spicy. Like a dish she would like to sample. Lovely, lovely smells that tickled her senses and made her wish for more.

She held herself perfectly still, not daring to breathe, not trusting herself lest she succumb to the urge to lean close and press her nose to his coat. To breathe deep and full the scent of his skin.

Oh, what madness had taken hold of her?

With a soft sound, she stumbled back a step, searching for safety in physical distance, but finding only confusion.

The part of her that craved order, solutions, answers, felt overwhelmed.

Reaching out, Mr. Fairfax lifted a stray curl from her shoulder, slid the length of the strand slowly between his fingers. Her hair was pale and bright against his sun-bronzed skin. She gasped, raised her gaze, found him watching her with a hooded look.

Beth recovered both her common sense and her voice then. She batted his hand away and said with firm conviction, "I should be getting back. I do thank you for the return of my property, Mr. Fairfax."

He smiled a little, a dark curving of his lips that made her shiver, and she thought he would ask again for his reward.

She held up her hand, palm forward, forestalling him. "But though I have no desire to disappoint you, I am afraid that my words of gratitude will have to suffice as your prize."

"That *does* disappoint me." He gave a low laugh, making her breath catch in her throat. "But perhaps my reward will come at a future date. I am a patient man. Some things are meant to be savored."

The words were innocuous, but his tone was low and rough and intimate. Her skin tingled and sparked, as though he had touched her. Drawing a shaky breath, she rubbed her palms along her upper arms.

With a flourish, he offered her ecru bag. She murmured her thanks as she took it from him, then snatched her hand back as their fingers brushed. Even through her glove she felt the heat of that touch.

"I really must be on my way," she whispered, confused

by the strong emotions he engendered. And he knew that he flustered her. She could sense that.

Determined to gather her wayward emotions, Beth spun away and began to walk. Mr. Fairfax fell into step beside her, close enough that on one occasion his shoulder brushed her own. She swallowed, thoroughly unsettled, not so much by the contact, but by her peculiar, disconcerted reaction to it.

She actually *ached* to reach out and touch him, to know the soft feel of the cloth of his coat over the hard bulge of muscle that defined his arms and shoulders. She wanted to rub the thick strands of his hair between her fingers, to relish the texture, to lean close and know again the lush smell of him.

What lunacy had overtaken her?

Girlish whimsy had never been her natural inclination. Her nature was solemn and—for the most part—calm. Because she *willed* it so, *made* it so by sheer obstinacy and resolve. She liked everything neat and tidy, everything ordered, but the way Griffin Fairfax made her heart pound and her skin tingle was not tidy or ordered or even sane.

It was . . . it was . . . *absurd*!

Keeping her gaze locked on the ground before her and her fingers curled tight in the cloth of her bag, she walked on. She longed for him to leave her, to let her walk on alone, and in the same contrary instant, she hoped he stayed exactly where he was, by her side, matching each step to her own.

She cut him a glance through her lashes. Looked away.

Then lured by the hard, clean line of his profile, and the curl at the ends of his dark, dark hair, and the rather disreputable stubble that darkened his cheek and jaw, she wet her lips and looked again.

Was it soft, his beard? Rough?

What would it feel like under her fingers if she reached out right now and touched him?

Her mouth felt dry as sand, and her thoughts were an unwieldy and frightening mélange, so out of character.

"I have met your daughter, sir," she said. His expression grew closed and hard at her words, drawing forth memories of Isobel's haunted gaze.

He made no answer, and the silence stretched, seeming longer than minutes. Seeming like hours.

Well, that had certainly squelched her untoward fascination, Beth thought with a modicum of self-directed humor.

At length, Mr. Fairfax huffed a sigh and observed, "You prefer a brisk pace, Miss Canham."

"I do," she replied, and walked a little faster.

"Why?"

Such a simple question. Such a difficult answer.

Almost did she manage to hold her tongue and say nothing, but in the end she said far too much.

"When I was a child, Mrs. Arthur, the woman who lived next door, lost her husband. She ran screaming down the street when they told her. They dragged her back, and all the while she moaned and cried for them to let her run."

She glanced at him again, at the harsh and lovely profile of his nose, his cheek, his jaw, and then lower to where his hands were loose and relaxed at his sides. Strong hands, with squared fingers. She raised her eyes to find him watching her with quiet expectation, waiting for her to go on.

"My mother and I went to the widow's home every day for months to offer what help and comfort we could." She paused. "Mrs. Arthur never ran like that again. Instead, she took drops from a brown bottle until she could barely walk, or even sit. She would only lie on the chaise for hours, stroking the old, worn coat of a dead man and talking softly to his ghost."

Mr. Fairfax stopped cold, and Beth turned to look at him, her heart racing as their gazes collided and locked.

Her words had set loose something inside him, or if not set it loose, at least prodded it to life. His eyes, grown dark as a moonless night, reflected heartbreak and pain.

Or perhaps she saw only a mirror of her own torments.

"That is precisely the point of the brown bottle," he said, his voice a hard-edged rasp. "To drain away the restlessness, leaving a hollow-eyed shell behind."

Beth nodded. "In the end, Mrs. Arthur drank too many drops. They called it an accident and buried her next to her husband, but sometimes I do wonder . . ."

His expression chilled, and she fumbled for words, wondering what it was she had said that had brought such desolation to his eyes.

"I think it better to feel even dreadful things," she rushed on, the words tumbling free. "To feel even fear and pain, than to feel nothing at all."

His lips twisted in a cynic's smile, and a deep crease formed in his cheek.

"Do you? And what do you know of fear and pain, Miss Canham? What do you know of dreadful things?" he asked, his words almost a whisper. Intimate. Inviting her confidences. She thought he might charm souls from the devil if he had a mind to.

She shivered. The way he asked about dreadful things make her think again of Alice and her terrible intimations and accusations.

"Nothing," she mumbled when the silence had grown heavier than she could bear. "I know nothing at all." She spun away and began to walk, her blood rushing through her veins at a dizzying rate.

Oh, she knew far too much of fear, and quite enough about all manner of horrors. And she was wise enough not to say it.

Her fingers closed convulsively around the linen embroidery bag as she walked on, doubling her pace. She thought he would leave her, but instead, he matched his stride to her own.

Faster, dear heart. Walk until you are free of the terrors that chase you. Her mother's words came to her. So many times had her mother seen Beth's agitation, sensed her restless soul and bid her walk, *walk* until her heart pounded not with edginess, but with exertion, until finally she ran to exhaustion the secret fiends that gnawed at her.

There were days that to be still was a torment. Less often now. She had been far worse as a child.

Now she could pass weeks, even months, calm, serene, but eventually, from nowhere would come the memories, the terror, and she would feel the choking sludge closing her throat.

Her mother had understood, had found a way to channel off the fear.

Walk, dear heart. Walk faster.

Beth glanced at Mr. Fairfax. With a look in her direction that made her blood heat and a thousand questions race through her mind, he cast her a quiet, knowing smile. Then he quickened his pace and walked faster by her side.

Chapter Seven

Cold. She was so cold.

Sarah Ashton lay in the dark, shivering, her belly twisted in hunger, her fear near to driving her mad. There was nothing left now of the girl she had been, nothing left of hopes and dreams and fancies. There was only a fate she could never have imagined, not in her nightmares. Not ever.

She was soaked through, her clothes damp and frigid against her skin, her joints aching. Her arms were wrenched tight behind her, her wrists bound, her hands gone numb long ago. A fetid rag filled her mouth.

Hours had passed since he had left her here . . . hours? No, longer . . . days? She could not say. There was only the endless cold and the desperation and the jagged edge of terror. She was beyond tears, cast in a pit of fierce misery, vast and overwhelming.

She could see nothing of her surroundings, and now that the pounding rhythm of the rain had stopped, she could hear nothing save the steady thud of her own heart. She had taken to counting the beats to stave off the memories and the terrible suppositions that slunk from the darkest shadows of her soul. Then she lost count and the panic clawed at her, terror creeping to the fore.

With perfect clarity she recalled the length of his crop tap-tap-tapping his thigh as he stood, impatient, in the clearing. She remembered her eager steps, her girlish dreams, the scent of rain in the air and, finally, the metallic tang of fear burning her tongue.

He had overpowered her with ease, tied her wrists and her feet, muzzled her with a cloth tied so tightly that the sensitive skin at the corners of her mouth tore open. Her struggles had been pitiful in the face of his strength, and he had relished that. Somehow, she sensed that he had enjoyed her helplessness.

Then he had tied a rag over her eyes, and she had known only shock and dread as he hefted her like a sack of grain and moved her to a carriage. Bile had churned in her gut and up her throat, and she had fought it back, terrified that if she retched she would choke on her own vomit behind the press of the gag. The carriage had rocked and swayed and brought her here . . . wherever here was.

He had dragged her from the conveyance, his grasp bruisingly tight, hefted her once more to carry her a short distance before dumping her on the ground. Yanking off the blindfold, he had shoved her against something hard and unyielding. She had been too terrified to notice her surroundings. She remembered screaming into the gag, struggling as he touched her hair, a gentle stroke of his hand, then screaming again, more desperate as she heard the heavy slam of wood against wood.

Everything had gone dark, so dark.

Fighting her panic, she had struggled and squirmed and felt her shoulders bump against walls mere inches away on all sides. No matter how she turned and twisted, there was only the smell of damp wood and earth and the feel of unfinished planks close about her. Splinters pricked her fingers as she maneuvered her body to allow her bound hands to drag across the wood, searching for escape.

Dear heaven, a wooden box, long and narrow, smelling of earth and rot.

Sick with dread, she had bucked and jerked, slamming herself against the hard walls with whatever force she could muster, nearly driven mad with the fear that he had buried her alive.

Why . . . why . . . why . . . ?

After a time she had slumped in exhaustion and lost awareness of the passage of the hours, rousing at times to cry and wriggle and struggle, to rage and sob and plead with stifled cries, only to fall quiet once more when her efforts came to naught.

Now, she shivered and shook and waited in the choking miasma of her ever-present horror.

That was the worst part. The waiting.

How long had she been here? How long until she died?

She stiffened as the sound of horses reached her, the crunch of carriage wheels drawing nigh. She thought it a conjured notion, a dream, and then the horses nickered and she cried out, a dreadful muffled sound escaping her gagged mouth.

Every muscle and bone in her body protested in a riot of pain as she struggled anew, desperate to be free, torn between hope and horror.

There came a soft, scraping noise, booted feet against the ground, closer and closer still. Narrow optimism unfurled in her breast, then congealed into a glutinous mass that choked her breath and hung leaden in her lungs.

Likely this was no savior come to free her, but her captor, come to harm her, come to—

The lid of the box lifted away, and Sarah blinked

against the flare of light. She saw nothing but spots dancing before her eyes, glowing and bright. The light hurt.

"So, miss," he said quietly, his tone even, chillingly void of inflection. "You've soiled yourself."

She had, and now she was glad of it. Perhaps the stink would keep him away, perhaps . . .

He reached into the box, her coffin, and dragged her out as though she were a doll, then let her fall to the ground at his feet. Frantic, she looked about, the earthen floor cold and damp beneath her cheek, her eyes at last growing accustomed to the light.

Morning light. She could hear the birds.

Turning her head, she saw that she was in a small building with wooden sides and a wooden roof, and in the center was the simple wooden coffin set in a shallow trench. A terrible shuddering took her, to see it so, with only the top exposed that he might set the lid, and the remainder in the ground.

Buried alive.

She jerked and twisted and wriggled along the ground, digging her bound and numbed fingers into the hard earth, dragging herself away inch by inch.

He stood staring down at her, his expression perfectly benign, but something in his face made her stop her struggles, made her freeze in place and pray. Moaning, she flinched as he hunkered down beside her. Not even daring to breathe, she quivered, held in place, an insect pinned and studied.

"Yes, that's a good girl," he whispered, his voice a low caress that made her skin prickle and her heart slam against her ribs. "Be still. No tempests, now. No tantrums."

He never said what he would do if she was not still, but she knew. With brutal, lancing certainty, she knew.

Reaching out, he stroked the backs of his fingers along her cheek, and she lay rigid, frozen by the horror of it and the fear. She could not breathe. Her chest was tight, so tight, and the edges of her vision blurred and wavered. She thought she would fall into the blackness, the lovely, unknowing blackness.

"No," he murmured, and trailed his fingers along her cheek, her neck, the swell of her breast where he pinched her sharply. The pain chased away the promise of oblivion, reviving her.

And then she saw the gleam of the blade.

Leaning close, he spoke against her ear. "Be still." A lover's whisper, so soft.

She shuddered and squeaked as she felt a tugging on her scalp, a sting. He was cutting her hair, she thought, sawing at the length with his knife, gathering the golden tresses in a tail. His fingers stroked the pale strands of hair as he made low sounds of pleasure that chilled her to her core.

He was pulling too hard. It hurt. It burned. She cried out at a sharp pull, the sound swallowed by the gag.

Memories bubbled like a viscous brew, fevered recollections of two women found dead in the woods, mauled and bloody, their bodies gouged and slashed by some unnamed beast's claws.

Sarah began to struggle, despite his whispered urgings that she be still. Fresh horror chewed at her, and she knew then that he had killed them, Helen Bodie-Stuart and Katherine Anne Stillwell, the two young teachers from Burndale Academy.

Everyone had thought them mauled by some wild beast, but shivering here on the cold ground, with her tormentor crouched overtop her, his knees pinning her shoulders flat and the feel of his blade scraping against her scalp, Sarah *knew*.

He had killed them, and now he would kill her.

"Not yet," he whispered, his voice hard with excitement as he leaned close to let his breath touch her ear. "Not yet. First, we have things to enjoy together, you and I."

* * *

The afternoon was miserable. A fog had settled, obliterating the morning sun, leaving the air clammy and cold. Griffin trudged along the road to the Red Bull Inn, one of four coaching inns on Northallerton's main road. His business of the morning had been less than satisfying in its conclusion. The exertion had stoked his appetite; the unfulfilling outcome had fouled his temper. He was of a mind to find a meal and a drink before setting out for Burndale.

He paused, listening to the town bell strike the hour. The sound was muffled, as though the clapper was shrouded and dampened by the fog.

On the far side of the thoroughfare, out of the cloying mist, loomed the rambling, dark outline of the Red Bull Inn. Out front was an entrance porch, and Griffin knew that just inside the front door was a parlor. He had warmed his hands before a glowing fire more than one night when he had chosen to stay in Northallerton rather than take the road to Wickham Hall.

A ill-preferred highway that was, even in the sunshine. The road to London always beckoned, or the road to the coast, or the road to anywhere that was not Wickham Hall.

Griffin scrubbed his hand along his jaw. There were days, like this one, where he had a wish to choose a different path, one that led to a new and heretofore untraveled place, one that would see him unburdened by responsibility and regret. On those days he wished to be the ne'er-do-well lad he had been a decade past.

But there was Isobel to consider. The lad he had once been was no fit parent.

The thought brought a dark twist to his lips. The man he had grown into was no better.

He had miserly success at fathering her. He ought to hire a nurse and a governess and leave her to more capable hands. That thought both appealed and re-pelled. *Ought to* was a far distance from *would*.

Having been so thoroughly abandoned himself, he found he could not do the same to her.

Interestingly, she had no similar qualms, choosing to abandon him at will, to stay at Burndale Academy for lengths of time that varied as to her disposition. A week, a day, a month. In the beginning, he had been baffled as to why she chose to stay there. But she had only stared at him with her great, dark eyes and her body stiff and still. He had quickly come to understand that she would not leave there. Too, he had come to understand that she chose to stay there because it was away from him.

At first, he had visited her daily, the two of them facing each other, awkward and silent in Miss Percy's office before the mullioned window. Isobel would sit, unmoving, her gaze locked on the floor, her body rigid. After a time, he realized that his visits only made it worse, and so they became less frequent and they fell into a pattern where he would fetch her once a week to come home for dinner to Wickham Hall.

Sometimes Isobel refused to come at all. Usually when the weather was foul, reminiscent of the night—

No, he would not let his thoughts wander that path.

Isobel. She was the sole fine thing in his blackguard's existence, and he knew not how to reach her.

What did he expect? She bore witness to his crimes, dark deeds that they were, her memories reflected in her too-wise and haunted eyes.

With a whispered oath, Griffin returned his attention to the Red Bull and strode forward. Off to the side of the porch was a separate entrance to the bar, and it was toward that doorway he headed, wanting a meal and a drink and a moment to gather his thoughts.

Gather them?

Nay, bury them.

He paused to let an elderly man with a black slouch

hat and a hunched back pass by. He was about to walk on when, with a swish of skirts, two women emerged from the fog, walking arm in arm.

Griffin started and stared, seeing only the black dress and the glint of fair ringlets peeking from beneath the bonnet that shadowed the taller woman's face. For a heartbeat he thought it was the teacher, Elizabeth Canham.

Inexplicably, his mood turned expectant, only to scuttle back to surly when he saw it was not she. This woman was of middle years, her hair more silver than gold.

With a polite bow, a lift of his hat, and a step to the side, he let them pass.

Elizabeth Canham. She fascinated him, though he could not precisely mark the why of it. She was pretty, but not beautiful . . . until she smiled. And then her beauty stabbed him like a shiv in the gut.

The pure oddity of his thoughts struck him, and he felt a surge of annoyance at himself. He wondered what he was doing, staring at a stranger, thinking of Miss Canham. He had exchanged only a handful of words with her, and those in two brief conversations . . . though one had been of an oddly intimate nature.

What *had* they spoken of? He frowned. That first day, he had found her waiting on the road, calm and cool despite the fact that there must have been a seed of fear sprouting in her heart as she waited and waited for a cart that did not come.

Ah, yes, he recollected . . . they had discussed fencing and the weather. And the ridiculous brick columns and iron gates that guarded the road to Burndale Academy.

He recalled the way she had pressed her lips together against a smile, the light of humor in her eyes, and his own rare huff of laughter. A moment of affinity.

Their meeting of yesterday had only strengthened his feeling that there was a communion of thought between them. Their discourse had been fraught with a loaded tension, circling topics of death and personal distress. Yet he had found their interaction oddly soothing, had felt that she understood him to a depth and richness that was surprising.

In those strange moments of kinship, Miss Elizabeth Canham had definitely piqued his interest. She would likely run screaming if she knew it, for he was not a fit companion for one such as she. He was a man responsible for his ample share of gross deeds, and villainous ones, deeds that destined him for eternity's fires.

What matter? The things he had done could not be undone, even if he wished it. And in truth, he did not.

One thing he knew for certain: she harbored a secret. As a man who guarded a goodly share of his own, he was attuned to the fact in others.

Reaching his destination, he pushed open the door of the Red Bull and stepped inside. Paltry daylight—a weak gray even under the open sky—grew dimmer still as it leaked through begrimed front windows to fall across the handful of patrons sitting at tables. The air was peppered with puffs of smoke and the sounds of conversation. At the bar a lone man sat straddle-legged upon a chair, a full mug of ale in his hand, his back to the room.

Griffin studied the set of the man's shoulders, the shape of the back of his head, the scar on the hand that held his ale.

Here was the unexpected, slithering out from his past.

Turning, he made his way to a shadowed nook and the empty table that waited there. He chose the chair that would see his back to the wall and his face to the room. Reaching down to his boot, he slid free the blade he kept there always and laid it flat across his thigh, ready.

In short order, the barmaid brought him ale and a meal, boiled beef, oat pudding, and pickled salmon. He sampled the fare and found it adequate. He had eaten far worse in his time and, often, he had eaten nothing at all. Little effort was required to recall the nuances of deprivation, the sensation of his belly knotted with hunger. Those memories made this meal all the more appreciated.

When the serving maid crossed his path again, he sent her a close-lipped smile and a nod, then flipped her a coin that she caught with a swipe of her hand and a grin. She preened as though she'd slaved over the preparation of the food herself.

Turning his attention to his plate, Griffin ate, but always he was aware of the atmosphere in the pub, the ebb and flow of conversation, the play of light and shadow as the sun peeked out for a moment from behind the heavy clouds. Griffin knew when the man at the bar rose and moved, sensed him drawing nigh. He looked up as a blunt, scarred hand slammed a fresh glass of ale before him, sending the amber liquid sloshing over the sides.

"I woke this morning like a boar with a sore head," came the gruff statement. "Likely too much ale drunk in the wee hours. A hair of the dog, hmm? What say you, Griff?"

The voice, rough as a file scraping to and fro on iron links, was recognizable for the tone and pitch, and for the use of a familiarity that Griffin had not heard in a good long while.

"Hullo, Richard," he said, gesturing with his right hand to the free chair on the opposite side of the table, though he felt little inclined to welcome the man. His left hand he slid beneath the table. "Been a long while since our paths crossed. What? A year now?"

Not a full year. He knew it perfectly well. The frozen ground had been buried beneath a January snow last he'd seen Richard Parsons.

And they'd both seen the girl's blood that stained the snow dark crimson.

"*Richard*, is it? When did you become so formal as that? Were we not boon companions, *Griff* and *Dick*, the two who could drink any other man under the table and still weave upright from any pub"—he grinned—"with our pockets heavier from the coin we lifted to make his lighter."

He grabbed the chair, dragged it from the table, and straddled it. Then he cast a wary glance toward Griffin's obscured left hand. "Do you greet an old friend with the threat of a slit throat?"

"A man can never be too careful." Not about his enemies . . . or his friends.

With a laugh, Richard held his hands out, palms up, and only raised his brows when Griffin reached out to shove the sleeves up above the wrists and take a look for good measure.

"No, it's not been a year since last we met, my friend," Richard said, watching with narrowed eyes as Griffin leaned down and shoved his knife back into the sheath set in his boot. "Mayhap nine months. Since that girl—a teacher, was she not?—was found at the edge of the woods, killed by some . . . beast."

Griffin gave a small nod. The reference was meant to unsettle, but he'd long ago learned to show none of the strong emotion that burned in his gut, to hide his temper behind a bland mask.

The silence dragged. Richard shifted on his chair, toyed with his watch, cleared his throat. Finally, he spoke.

"Glad I am to find you here, Griff. 'Tis good to meet a friend along the way. Why, I do remember . . ." He laughed, and launched into a tale of their shared exploits, though to Griffin's recollection the telling leaned far across the line between truth and imagination, and bore little resemblance to actuality.

Taking up his fork and knife, he returned his attention to the remains of his meal. He murmured appropriate responses to Richard's anecdotes and comments, letting the other man fill the silence. At length, he pushed the empty plate aside and rocked back in his chair.

"So what do you do in Northallerton, Richard?" Griffin asked, sipping his ale and studying his companion over the rim of the glass.

Richard was handsome enough, dark haired, dark eyed, with a touch of arrogance to his features, and a touch of brutality. He dressed the part of the gentleman he ought to have been had life and poor choices not set him on a different path, but careful perusal showed his coat to be threadbare at the cuffs and not quite right in the fit of the shoulder, as though the garment had been made for another and then poorly altered.

From a distance, or in meager light, he looked of an age with Griffin. Closer examination proved the fallacy. Richard's jowl was beginning to fall and heavy pouches sat beneath his eyes, testament in part to the start of middle age, and in part to a life of debauchery and excess. But his smile was as ever it had been, wide and infectious, inviting the unwary companion to murmured confidences and shared good humor.

Unless that companion knew a little of Richard Parsons. Of his past. Of the barren place that might once have been his soul.

Griffin knew. He had such a place at his own core.

"Business drew me to Northallerton, dear boy," Richard said. "Business, and perhaps a little pleasure."

Griffin nodded. "Honest trade?" he asked, his relaxed posture and tone maintained by will and not by natural inclination.

Honest trade. He thought not. Which left only the dishonest kind. There had been a time when they had shared both the enjoyment and the profits of such.

With a wink, Richard laughed. "What would be the fun in honest trade?" He lowered his voice and leaned his forearm on the table. "A question, dear boy. Do you know of a . . . well, no way to be delicate . . . a woman who might ease a man, lad? I've been here six full weeks, and though the inn is clean, there's a certain lack." He shifted closer still. "Of the female persuasion, if you understand me. What I'd not give for a sweet blond whore, young, mind you, and up for a bit of rough play."

Griffin took a long, slow pull of his ale. Swallowed. Said nothing. Six full weeks. Parsons had been in Northallerton an inexplicably long while.

Hunting, or hunted?

"Well, I'll take your silence for a no." Richard waved a hand. "So we'll talk of what's on every mind in Northallerton, and likely every village for miles around. No doubt you've heard of the missing maid, a blond girl from the telling of it. Speculation as to her fate is on every loose tongue."

Griffin heard an undercurrent to the casual tone, a challenge. "Do you join in the speculation, Richard? Do you present your thoughts and suppositions on her whereabouts?"

"Do *you*, Griff?" Richard's fingers drummed a staccato beat on the table, slid to his waist to toy with his silver watch, then strayed to the buttons of his waistcoat. "I say she ran off with her lover." Then he laughed, the sound low and menacing. "Strange how history repeats and repeats, eh? Wonder what the local constabulary would say to know of a fifteen-year-old tale from Ratcliffe Highway . . ."

When Griffin made no reply, Richard laughed again, an ugly sound. He slapped his knee, relishing the private joke. "And here we are again, the two of us, so many years on, sitting in a pub, speaking of butchered blond whores."

"The girl was no whore, but a maid at Briar House." Griffin held his neutral tone with effort. "And the niece of my housekeeper's husband."

"At Briar, you say?" Richard made a tuneless whistle. "Well, that is a thing. Can't imagine you would find a welcome there." He paused, nodded slowly, watching Griffin for any hint of reaction.

Griffin said nothing, merely drank his ale. No, he would find no welcome at Briar House, the home of his dead wife's parents. He had married Amelia Holder, and he had killed her. Little more to be said on that.

With a pull of his mouth, Richard leaned back in his chair and needled further. "And the niece of your housekeeper. Hunting a bit close to home, dear boy?"

Still Griffin said nothing, and Richard's expression grew crafty and mean.

"Someone's scratching at an old wound, Griffin. Making inquiries in London about bodies and ghosts best left buried. You wouldn't know aught about that, would you?"

"Not a thing," Griffin replied, his mask in place, though emotion churned beneath his surface calm. Someone was stirring up old venom, poking at things best left buried. Who? Why?

"You know nothing about that, hmm, but you *do* know something about Briar's little missing maid. You say she *was* no whore. Interesting choice of words and tense . . ." Richard's gaze grew sharp. "So she is dead, is she, Griff? She *is* dead."

Tossing some coins on the table, Griffin rose and stood staring down at Richard, his once boon companion.

"She is dead," he said softly, his blood running cold as a winter stream.

She was dead. They both knew it.

Just as the two missing teachers had been dead, and the whore at Covent Garden, and the barmaid in Stepney, and so many others in between.

Turning away, Griffin strode from the Red Bull with the sound of Richard's dark laughter biting at his back.

He hummed as he worked, running his fingers through Sarah's long blond hair.

Yesterday, he had made a liniment: an ounce of vinegar, an ounce of powdered stavesacre, a half ounce each of honey and sulfur, and two ounces of oil, all in a mix. He had rubbed the treatment along her scalp and the roots of her hair, taking care to work it in well.

His mother had used this recipe. Repeated it again and again to rid the hair of vermin. She had sworn that he and his brother were crawling with vermin. He had never seen a one. Not on his own head and not on his brother's. But he'd quickly learned not to gainsay her when she was in a mood, or she would beat them both until they were bruised and bloody.

Once, she had said he might not see them, but they were there, crawling on him, in his hair, in his ears.

More than once, in a frenzy, she had scraped his scalp with a dry blade, her movements jerky and unsure. She had drawn blood, and then the knife grew slick and red, while he and his brother sobbed and pleaded.

He shuddered at the memory.

Again, he ran his fingers through Sarah's hair. Shiny and glossy from the oil. He wanted it soft and pretty.

With a frown, he wondered if the liniment had done its work yet, if the vermin were destroyed. He could not recall the length of time required. It had been so long ago.

His frown deepened.

Surely a full day was long enough. Leaning close, he peered at her hair. He saw no vermin, no nits, no crawling things.

Bright gold. So pretty. Her hair was almost perfect.

He raised his head, stared out the window. His preference ran to lush curls, thick, coiled ringlets that gleamed like moonlight.

Sarah's hair was a shade too dark, and the curl was missing. Nonetheless, she would do. She would most certainly do.

Lifting the pitcher, he turned his attention back to his task and poured water into the basin before him, immersing all that lovely hair. The water was cool on his hands. He closed his eyes, ran the strands through his fingers, worked a lather with a cake of soap, allowing himself to savor the tactile pleasure.

After a time, he opened his eyes, set the soap aside, rinsed her hair, once, twice. He wanted no residue to dull the color.

With a smile, he added a splash of vinegar. The pungent scent wafted up to tickle his nose. His mother had always said that a splash of vinegar brought out the fairest lights of her hair.

He wanted that for Sarah, wanted to draw out the fairest lights.

When he was done, he squeezed out the water and stared at the long tresses. Wet as it was, Sarah's hair looked dark, almost brown. Dry, it would be soft gold once more.

He sighed. He *did* regret the lack of curl. Her hair was so straight, he wondered how it had ever held a pin.

With a final twist, he wrung out the last drops of water, wrapped the length in a large square of linen, and pressed until the cloth dampened.

An evening breeze carried through the open window, fanning across his face. It was less than perfect weather, cloudy and damp, though it had cleared a little since he had been in Northallerton earlier in the day. He thought that with the breeze, it would take her hair less than an hour to dry.

Whistling tunelessly between his teeth, he set aside the damp linen, crossed the room, and stood by the window, looking out. There was nothing to see but trees. A veritable sea of them.

He pushed the window wide, breathed deep. The scent of fall was in the air. With a grin he turned to the nail he'd hammered in the wooden window frame and hung Sarah's severed scalp to dry, watching as the damp strands of her hair danced in the wind.

Chapter Eight

Burndale, Yorkshire, September 6, 1828

Beth found that the routine of Burndale Academy varied little from day to day. First off were prayers and hymns in the largest schoolroom, with Miss Browne playing the piano in accompaniment.

Hymns read and done with, the girls whispered and giggled as they marched into the refectory, a great, long room that spanned the entire depth of the building. Narrow tables were neatly placed throughout, with low benches alongside and stout stools at either end. The room was lit by large windows along one side, with an enormous hearth on the other. No fire burned there now, for the morning—Beth's third at Burndale—had dawned mild and bright. Still, Beth thought she would be glad of the hearth's warmth during the cold winter to come.

In groups that were arranged by age, the pupils went each to her assigned table, and the teachers sat at the head and the foot. Each teacher was expected to sit at a different table each day.

Ignorant of that rule, Beth had mistaken her place on

the second morning, going to the exact seat that she had taken on the first.

That, it seemed, was not the Burndale way.

She had felt her cheeks heat as Miss Browne stood over her, tapping her foot against the ground, heavy arms folded across the ample shelf of her bosom. For a moment, Beth had imagined herself the wayward pupil, caught in Miss Browne's displeasure.

She had not enjoyed the experience.

Wiser today, Beth made her way to a different table, the one in the far corner. As she passed a small group of teachers, Miss Doyle, Miss Hughes, and Mademoiselle Martine, she heard snippets of their whispered conversation.

". . . missing since her morning off . . ."

"They'll find her. Find her dead, mind you . . ."

". . . thinking Sarah Ashton ran off with a man . . ."

"I heard she has guinea-gold hair like the others . . ."

As Beth approached, they broke off, looked away, their faces drawn, their expressions wary.

Miss Doyle looked back, and her gaze slid to Beth's, narrowed, expectant. Beth had the sensation that there was something they were keeping from her, while at the same time they wanted her to overhear it. They wanted her to wonder. To ponder. To be afraid.

The thought made her shiver.

Turning away, she guided her charges onto the benches, encouraging both promptness and decorum.

Steam rose from great kettles that were set on the tables, and the smell of porridge flavored the air. Plain fare, but well-prepared, generously ladled into bowls and passed out amongst the girls. Inhaling the scent of the porridge, Beth recalled the pallid gentleman from the coach—the one who had left the stage in Grantham, but whom she had thought she caught sight of as the coach passed through Northallerton—and his horrid stories of beatings and starvation. As she watched the girls take their places, she felt very glad that his morbid insinuations had proven far from the truth. There were no hungry bellies here, no bruised and beaten children.

"Silence!" The cry, loud enough to be heard over the general commotion, was accompanied by much double hand-clapping. "To your places!"

Finally, all were settled and the bowls passed round to each place. Miss Percy led grace, after which a buzz of conversation hovered in the room, ricocheting off the walls and growing in volume by the moment.

A maid brought tea to the teachers, and the girls drank water poured from a pitcher set in the center of the table. There was one cup for each side of the table, and they passed it from girl to girl, refilling as necessary.

Turning her attention to her meal, Beth sampled a spoonful of porridge, and another, before realizing that the lively discussion at her table had trailed away to furtive whispers. She glanced up to see Isobel Fairfax, the pale little girl from the first morning, her dark hair tumbling about her shoulders, her eyes wide and dreamy. She stood a little to one side, making no move to join the others at breakfast.

"Good morning, Isobel," Beth said, and smiled.

The child made no reply, but something, perhaps a sharpening of her gaze or a flicker of recognition, made Beth certain that she acknowledged the greeting.

"She don't talk. Not once since I've been here," said a girl with mud-brown braids and a plain and open face. "Come on now, Isobel"—the girl, Lucy, patted the bench at her side—"you may as well sit here, because none of the others will welcome you."

Isobel sidled a step closer, but did not sit.

Beth had the odd notion that the child had come to this table because of her. Though consumed by the newness of Burndale Academy and the demands of her duties for the past days, Beth had been aware of Isobel clinging to the shadows like a wraith, watching her with eyes wide and solemn.

Their communication had been limited to a nod or brief greeting, but Beth had made certain to meet Isobel's gaze and murmur a kind word when the opportunity presented. The other teachers seemed inclined to disinterest, letting Isobel sidle along the cool walls, always an outsider, always watching. Even in the classroom, Isobel was silent, though she did write a lovely hand, and her ciphers were without flaw or error.

Looking at her now, Beth felt a twist deep in her heart, both sadness and affinity for this eerie, quiet girl.

She rose, ladled a bowl of porridge, and set it at the place beside Lucy, to her own left. Isobel stepped closer, hesitated, then slid onto the bench, shifting to the farthest possible reach, away from her neighbor.

Lucy made a sound of disgust.

The girls were not kind to Isobel. Beth had seen them pinch or poke or pull the child's hair, just to see if they could make her squeal.

She never did. And that was the thing that saddened Beth the most.

Though she watched the world around her unfold, Isobel seemed to react to very little. Beth wondered what had driven her into the shadows, what tragedy had marked her in such a way. Of course, there was the possibility that Isobel had simply been born with her peculiarities, but Beth thought not.

The memories of her own past, locked tight away, made her recognize terrible heartbreak in another.

Isobel Fairfax kept silent to hold her secret demons at bay.

What was it that Alice had said? That both father and daughter were cursed and doomed. Beth held no belief in curses, but *something* had happened to this child, something tragic.

She recalled the way Griffin Fairfax had looked as

they stood on the road in the light of the fading sun, the silky sound of his voice as he asked her about her knowledge of dreadful things, the cynical curve of his lips and the dark secrets in his eyes. Those recollections only served to solidify her conviction that all was not right in this small family, that tragedy had struck them a vengeful blow.

Finishing her breakfast, Beth glanced up and saw Lucy's hand snake toward Isobel's, sly, furtive. Lucy's face was turned away as she chatted with the girl on the opposite side. She pretended interest in conversation while she edged her fingers closer and closer, carrying out a clandestine attack.

Annoyance pricked Beth, and something else, something stronger. Pressing her lips together, she shot Isobel a look, and laid her hand flat atop the little girl's. Lucy's questing fingers came close, gathered the skin of Beth's wrist, and twisted hard.

"Lucy!"

At Beth's sharp reprimand, the girl turned and instantly realized her error. She had pinched her teacher. Her face turned white.

Isobel's hand shot out, and she caught the skin of Lucy's wrist and squeezed, short and sharp, until Lucy cried out. Beth gasped. All the times that Isobel had been cuffed or pinched, she'd done naught save draw away, or scamper a safe distance to the shadows. Yet now, she returned the insult with vigor, seeking to avenge Beth's hurt at Lucy's hands.

"Well," Beth mused softly. "It appears, Isobel, that you can be roused to defend another, if not yourself."

The child made no reply, her expression unreadable, her dark eyes veiled by her lashes.

Every eye at the table was trained on Isobel, every girl's face a mask of surprise. For her part, Isobel stared straight down at her lap, retreating into the misty, dreamlike expression that was her norm.

The other girls dropped their gazes and concentrated on their bowls, but Beth knew they listened and watched, waiting to see how the scene would unfold.

With her voice pitched low, Beth spoke clearly and directly, determined to see the matter to an acceptable conclusion. "Lucy, Isobel, there shall be no more pinching. Of anyone. By anyone."

She let her gaze wander along the table then, waiting until each girl in turn met her eyes. They knew she included each of them in this edict.

"Please, Miss Canham," Lucy whispered, her voice clogged with tears. "I didn't mean it. I didn't. I thought . . ."

"You thought to pinch Isobel," Beth said quietly. "And that makes the deed no better. Perhaps far worse."

In that instant, Beth recognized that Lucy was trembling, genuine fear painting her countenance a stark white.

"Will it be the strap?" The child raised her gaze at last, her eyes damp, her jaw set, and Beth felt a momentary horror. She had never raised a hand in violence to anyone. The thought made her ill.

What to do now? What punishment to decree? Oh, but she had so little knowledge of such things. She thought of her mother and the way she had handled sibling spats between Beth and her brother.

Lucy and Isobel both stared up at her now, and Beth spoke slowly, carefully, choosing her words as ideas spiraled through her mind.

"You shall . . . mind Isobel . . . and watch over her, Lucy. Make certain that no one pokes her or pulls her hair. Or pinches her. For the . . . week. Yes, you shall be responsible for Isobel for an entire week. That is no punishment, Lucy, but a task that matches the strength of your character."

"The strength of my character?" Lucy blinked, and blinked again. "Watch over her? You mean like I do my little sister?"

"Yes, exactly."

"For a week?"

"She is in your care," Beth said. "And I have every confidence that you shall watch over her as you would your sister."

Lucy shot her a look of mingled fear and incredulity, as though pondering the merits of taking a beating in favor of this odd and daunting task.

"And . . ." Beth continued. "Lucy, Isobel, you shall both weed and tend the garden in your free hour every day this week. Perhaps if you learn to busy your hands with productive tasks, you will not busy them with pinches."

"Yes, miss," Lucy whispered, her head bowed.

In that moment, the bell tolled, marking the end of the morning meal. The girls rose and trooped out of the refectory, along the wide, dark hall to the school-room. Isobel lagged at the rear, dragging her feet with slow, heavy steps, and as she passed the place Beth stood, she reached out and ran her fingertips along the back of Beth's hand, a butterfly stroke, there, then gone.

Afternoon found Beth outdoors in the walled garden, supervising the two girls as they carried out the chore she had set them. They had both come to the garden of their own accord, and she was glad that she had not been forced to fetch them.

Her gaze strayed time and again to Isobel, who pulled weeds from the earth with sharp, aggressive tugs, her brow wrinkled in concentration. After a moment, Isobel raised her head, met Beth's gaze, her eyes solemn and wide. Then she cast her attention back to her task, and Beth was left with an odd, warm sensation in the center of her chest.

Turning away, she looked around the garden, then

beyond the tall, surrounding wall to where the leaves of great trees formed a canopy of yellow ocher and rich brown. She wandered to the end of the yard where a large verandah ran across the back of the house. There, Beth sat on the stone bench and watched as the girls worked at their task. Satisfied that they were well occupied, she drew forth a handkerchief and needle and thread from her ecru embroidery bag.

How grateful she was that Mr. Fairfax had returned it to her. Pressing her lips together, she thought of him, of his eyes and his hands and the way he walked. There was something dangerously enticing about him. Something exciting and dark and forbidden.

She thought of his smile, his lips, his mouth. Were his lips soft?

Her breath caught.

With a start, she jerked her head up, realizing where her thoughts wandered.

In dismay, she stared at the square of white linen in her hand, and the hash she had made of stitches that should have been small and neat. This would not do. A sigh escaped her and she began to pick out the stitches that she had only just put in.

A faint sound—odd and out of place—carried to her. Not a rustle of the leaves, or the breeze in the trees. Something . . . else.

She looked up, her gaze traveling along the high brick wall. She could see nothing amiss, but a strange quiver of unease made her skin crawl. The feeling passed, and she looked down once more, intent on her task.

When three-quarters of an hour had gone by, she called a halt to her charges' activity. "Well done, girls," she said, tucking away her embroidery. "Go and wash your hands before afternoon lessons resume."

Lucy straightened and took two steps, then paused and turned back.

"Come along, Isobel." She took the younger girl's hand in her own and led her away.

With a flicker of hope, Beth watched them go. Perhaps her words to Lucy about watching over Isobel had brought about a permanent change.

Perhaps.

She shook her head and thought of her own childhood, of the girls who had pinched her and poked her and pulled her braids, and she had the suspicion that the benefits of her solution might be short lived.

As the girls turned the corner and disappeared from view, Beth picked up her bag and rose from the bench. A gust of air swirled about her, making the dry leaves dance and crackle at her feet. They tumbled end over end, then drifted away.

She hunched her shoulders, noticing a sudden nip in the air as the sun slid behind a cloud and the breeze gathered strength to tug at the ends of her shawl.

Unease slithered up her spine, an oily chill.

Slowly, she turned to face the empty garden. With the kiss of sunlight gone, the leaves she had thought so pretty only moments past now looked dried and brown. The thick green hedge that followed the wall suddenly harbored menace, offering any number of shadowed places to hide—

"There is no one there."

Even as she breathed the words on a whisper, she knew them for the lie they were. There *was* someone there, watching her from the shadows.

She took a step back as her gaze slid along the hedge, searching for any glint of light, any sign of movement. Nothing stirred for a moment, and then she thought something did.

Her heart raced in her breast; the sound of her blood rushed loud in her ears.

There, to her right. Rustling leaves.

She spun but could see nothing. Heart pounding, she took a step back, and another, not daring to look away.

Again, a sound reached her of leaves shushing against each other and branches creaking and sighing.

The sharp snap of a twig.

She turned and narrowed her eyes, even as she sidled to her right, around the stone bench. Her fingers clenched the material of her skirt, and she lifted it above her ankles lest she find herself tangled and stayed when she wished to flee.

As quickly as it had gathered, the wind died, leaving all still. Too still. Heavy with malice and threat.

A moment later came a muffled thud, distinct and solid, as though feet hit the ground on the far side of the garden wall.

Beth exhaled on a sharp breath, her belly knotted with genuine fear. Panic clawed at her, a torrent fighting to rip free of her control. No. *No!* She *would* hold it back, no matter the cost, for she knew from vast experience that to set her panic free would cost her far more.

Trembling, she battled for control, and her thoughts focused on a single truth. Someone had watched her from the trees.

Why?

She took three quick steps, intent on summoning Miss Percy and telling her—

The tenuous reality of her situation slapped her. She stopped short, her heart pounding a rough rhythm.

Summon the headmistress and tell her what?

Someone watched me. No, I did not see him. I only know he was there because . . . because . . .

Therein lay the difficulty. Without proof, or even a glimpse of the hidden menace, there was nothing for her to say. Her only proof was her belief that he had been there, and the sound she had heard as his booted feet hit the ground. Even to her own mind, her case was weak, indeed.

She might jeopardize her situation if Miss Percy thought her some excitable and fainthearted fool, jumping about at every shadow or gust of wind. And she could ill afford to lose her place here and the generous income it provided.

She looked around once more, rubbing her palms against her upper arms. Had she imagined it? Had she conjured an evil watcher where none existed in truth?

'Twould not be the first time her fretful nature had led her to fruitless worry.

Narrowing her eyes, she considered the possibility.

No. She *had* sensed a malicious gaze, but she could not risk the likelihood that no one would believe her. She had too much to lose.

What would she do if Miss Percy determined her cotton-headed and excitable, a poor example for the pupils? What would she do if she was dismissed from her post? How would her family survive?

Her mother had warned her to have a care what she revealed, to trust no one, to present only a calm and capable façade.

No one here must know . . .

Beth closed her eyes and filled her lungs with a breath so deep she felt the stretch right in the center of her chest. Turning, she strode forward, tempering her pace as she left the garden, a deliberately sedate promenade. The squeal of the gate set a knotted tension to her shoulders and neck. Her teeth clamped tight together.

Some intangible certainty made her pause, her hand resting on the iron scrollwork. She heard it then . . . the unmistakable sounds of a bridle, and horses' hooves clopping against the road, and wheels creaking and turning as they rolled away.

With a shudder, she yanked the gate closed behind her, lifted her skirt, and bolted around to the front of the school. Heart pounding, she skidded to a stop and saw the back end of a vehicle disappear around the bend.

She had seen him.

No, not seen him, not precisely. Perhaps *sensed* him.

Closing his eyes, he felt a quiver of excitement deep in his gut. There was a connection there, a link that made her search for him though she could not possibly know he was there.

Soon, she would be his.

The sweet, perfect bow of her lips. The silky strands of her hair. The pounding of her heart, her terror and pain.

All his.

He had watched her several times before. Once, before he even knew who she was, he had spied her as the stagecoach rolled through Northallerton. She had leaned out the window to study her surroundings offering him a fine view. Once from the woods as she walked on the road. He had watched her tip her face to the sunset, seen the flash of appreciation in her gaze. And he had watched as she walked along the road, her black skirt swaying with each step. No sedate walk. Not Elizabeth Canham. Hers was a purposeful stride, full of life and vigor.

He wanted to taste that life, to feel it drain away in a pool of hot, wet blood. Ah, but he loved the blood. The smell of it. The rushing in his own veins as he watched it pump from severed vessels.

The first time, so many years ago, had been too quick, a brutal taking that lacked all finesse, all beauty. He had been confronted by the landlord and then the landlord's wife. Unexpected and disturbing. But he had dealt with them, and then he had slit the girl's throat, so deep she had been dead before her body slumped to the ground.

A pity and a waste.

But he had learned from that. Perfected his approach. Now he savored every moment. The terror of his prey. The muffled screams, muted behind a gag that stifled all but the most desperate moans.

Perhaps someday, he would find a place so private that he could enjoy the music of the kill, a place where he could listen to the screams rise and crest, toppling one over the next in a storm of terror.

He drew a slow breath, shifting on the hard seat as the reins looped through his fingers, the horses drawing the high-sprung, two-wheeled carriage at the pace they chose.

Would pretty Miss Canham cry out with the same strength and passion she showed as she walked? Would she struggle and rage?

He smiled at the thought of Elizabeth screaming and screaming while he cut away her lovely curls, bright as the sun. Cut away her scalp. And then her fingers.

Treasures. His treasures.

Letting the horses have their head, he slid his right hand to the pocket of his coat to draw forth a cloth-wrapped little bundle. He brought it to his nose, inhaled deep and long. The metallic scent of old, dry blood filled him, and through the cloth he felt the fingers, delicate little fingers. Sarah's fingers.

He would take them home. Put them in a jar with maggots. In the end there would be only the bones.

Treasures. Perfect little white bones for his treasure box.

Oh, how Sarah had cried and struggled and screamed against the gag. She had died too quickly for his taste.

But Elizabeth—

"Beth." He whispered her name aloud, feeling the thrill of it shoot straight to his groin.

—Elizabeth would die slowly.

Chapter Nine

Stepney, London, January 15, 1813

Henry dared not breathe too deeply. The scent of blood, sharp in the cold, thin air, mingled with the stink of tallow that wafted from Sam Loder's candle. The rank combination made his gut clench and bile crawl up his gullet.

Raising his hand high so the light of the flame dipped and plunged, Sam peered along the dim and gloomy hall, then brought the flame low and stared at the bloody footprints. They led from the black recess at the end of the hall to Mrs. Trotter's still form, painting a macabre trail.

Henry followed Sam's gaze, then drew up short, shook his head. The footprints were wrong. Going the wrong way. They ought to be heading from the dead landlord to his murdered wife, not from the parlor to the taproom as they did. That would mean . . .

A chill of premonition twisted up his spine. With a shudder, he battled the terrible suspicion that wormed through him.

No. He must be wrong.

"Look here," said Sam as he moved the candle to

better view the crimson marks, his head bowed and eyes cast down. "These footprints . . . I think he went first there"—he jutted his chin toward the darkness that swallowed the far end of the hall—"and then here to the hall where he met Mrs. Trotter." Sam tapped his index finger against the floor. Once. Twice. Henry wanted to scream. "He killed her here, and continued on, met the landlord, murdered him last."

"Yes," Henry said, the word like dust in his mouth.

Ginnie was safe. She was not here in this place of horror and foul murder. She had gone to see her sick mother and take her a mince pie.

Even as he silently recited the litany, he wondered why he did not rush down the hall, did not look in the parlor, did not see for certain that she was not there.

But he knew.

Oh, vile coward that he was, he knew. If he did not go to the parlor, he could not see that which was too terrible to consider.

He stood, a shadow of a man, turned inside out and barren. He thought that to feel anything right then was to feel a dread so profound that he would die from it. And so, he hovered, frozen, looking down at Sam Loder where he hunkered beside the landlady's dead body, seeing the whole of it as if in a muddied dream.

Sam rose and started cautiously along the hall.

Henry closed his eyes, then opened them, willing himself to follow, one foot before the other, his gut twisted so tight he felt like he was sawed in two. In his mind he ran, reached the parlor door, found the room empty.

In reality, his feet were made of lead, dragging and heavy, each step more effort than he could bear, his legs flaccid and weak.

As they came to the parlor door, sick certainty bubbled in his gut, an acid brew.

Sam made a sound, turned toward him, his hand held

up with the palm forward, a paltry barrier to Henry's forward movement.

Too late. Too late.

With a cry, Henry stumbled back a step as the room swam and his heart twisted into a cold, black knot. He slammed his eyes shut. If he did not see her like this—with her throat slit so wide her head was almost all the way off, and the blood a dark, shiny puddle all around her—then she would not be here, lying like a broken doll on the parlor floor.

Not Ginnie. Not his sweet Ginnie with her bouncing golden curls.

Not Ginnie.

He opened his eyes. There was only blood, glistening blood.

Where was her hair?

Chapter Ten

Burndale, Yorkshire, September 13, 1828

Beth sat on the stone bench in the shade of the verandah on the south wall of the school, watching Isobel and
Lucy at their gardening tasks as she had each afternoon
for a week. Her embroidery bag lay by her side, and a
square of linen was open in her lap. She had rolled and
hemmed the edges, and had begun to sew her mother's
initials in the lower right corner. Staring at the cloth,
she tried and failed to summon more than listless interest in colored thread and tiny, neat stitches.

Edginess rippled through her, a powerful tide. There
was no true reason for her unease, no particular trigger.
There was only . . .

She shook her head, glanced over her shoulder, her
skin prickling.

The school was not three feet behind her. She studied each window in turn, and saw . . . nothing. No one
watched her, yet the fine hairs at her nape rose and her
pulse raced as though someone did. She ought to have
grown inured to it by now. Each afternoon this past
week she had sat in this garden watching the girls, certain that someone watched *her* from the shadows. Each

afternoon she rose and paced, and each afternoon she failed to find him.

She was beginning to wonder if she was sliding back toward the terrible episodes that had punctuated her life, the overwhelming fears, the secret terrors. Not a particularly pleasant possibility.

Her fingertips tapped a random pattern against the stone as she made a last slow perusal of the garden.

Drawing a deep breath, she stilled, determined to rein the scrabbling agitation under her will and control. Based on what she had observed of the women she had met here at Burndale Academy, she imagined that all teachers were calm and genteel and sanguine. She supposed that if she was meant to maintain her employment, she would be best to present the exact same mien.

With a glance at the girls, who worked side by side at the far end of the garden, she placed her embroidery in her lap. Lucy and Isobel appeared content enough, even happy. That gave her no small measure of satisfaction.

She turned her gaze to the sky, the vast, open sky. Small, dark shapes—swans, she thought—glided through the clouds in the distance, their flight beautiful. The open space, the freedom of the birds, the sound of Lucy's laughter . . . these things made the unease in her heart settle a bit, and she was glad of it. She must not allow her control to crack, must not let her anxious temperament slide free. She knew where that would lead. Her heart would race, her chest grow tight, her palms grow slick with sweat. The world would fade away and there would be nothing but cold and bitter fear, a black pit of despair.

She had spent years learning to master her terrors.

How many doctors had she seen? A half dozen? More? Her parents had sacrificed so much to afford the exorbitant fees. Once, they had even taken her to a German doctor who was reputed to be a worker of miracles.

Beth could remember well the concern that had laced her mother's words as she sought the opinion of those experts. *She does not sleep, Doctor. Night after night, she prowls, or tosses about on her bed. She cannot bear the dark or closed spaces. Throngs of people near send her to fits.*

Oh, she bitterly regretted the money her parents had wasted on those consultations. The doctors had invariably suggested that she would be best off in Bedlam or some similar place, that her condition was a weakness of her feminine nature, that she was inclined to hysteria.

And perhaps she was.

But now was not the time to indulge in it. Now her family was relying on her income, and she would not allow herself to fail in this.

Over the years, her mother had expressed hope that she would outgrow her peculiarity. That had proven a fallacy. But at least Beth had learned to master her terror to some small degree, to lie in the dark though she *knew* it would smother her, to stand in a close crowd and imagine a barrier of distance between her body and others, to travel in an enclosed carriage and not fling open the door and throw herself from the horrid, tight little box.

She had learned to funnel the powerful unease into tasks that busied her hands and her mind.

And she had learned to hide her secrets.

Her terrors had not faded, but they came upon her less frequently, and she learned to control them rather than allowing them to control her. She had worked so hard to master them and, until now, she had thought her success quite remarkable. But that success had been achieved within the safe confines of her parents' home, where everything was known and familiar. With the horrific change in their circumstance—her father succumbing to apoplexy that left him confined to a bath chair, unable to walk or speak, the subsequent loss of their home, their dire financial straits—Beth had found the waves of panic grew ever stronger, more difficult to hold at bay.

And it appeared that Burndale Academy, vast and remote and cold, brought out the very worst of her anxious nature.

Returning her attention to her embroidery, she raised the handkerchief and frowned at it, irked by the series of uneven stitches. Again. That was the very reason this gift would be so precious to her mother: because she was well acquainted with Beth's inability to sit still long enough to form anything remotely resembling fine stitchery.

With a little shake of her head, she began to unpick what she had only just put in. Yet again. How many times had she repeated these same actions? At this rate, her mother's gift would never be complete.

Lucy's voice carried to her, and Beth glanced up at the sound. Ever bossy, Lucy was instructing Isobel in the proper way to squat in the gravel, and the correct angle for her bonnet, and the best way to turn the earth. Isobel stared straight ahead and listened. Or perhaps not. Perhaps the words only washed over her like the tide.

Watching the two for a moment, Beth smiled. Yesterday had been the last day of the punishment she had imposed on them. No, *punishment* was the wrong word. Both girls had appeared to enjoy their gardening duties and had brought themselves here today, though no requirement constrained them. Their presence this afternoon was no longer mandated, but was purely their own choice. Beth found a quiet satisfaction in that.

As though sensing her regard, Isobel paused and raised her head. She met Beth's gaze, then turned to study the top of the high garden wall. Seconds ticked past, and the girl did not move, her shoulders hunched with tension, her body tight as a bowstring.

Wariness trickled through Beth's veins. Was Isobel subject to the same eerie sensation that ruffled Beth's calm?

Her gaze slid to the trees beyond the wall. There was nothing to see, save greenery and turning leaves, but . . .

Was there a sound out of place? The faint crunch of gravel? No . . . but . . . *something* . . .

She could not say with certainty. She only knew the suspicion that swam at the edge of her thoughts.

There is someone out there, watching, waiting.

Tucking her embroidery away in her bag, Beth rose and walked the perimeter of the garden, feeling twitchy and jittery. Her every sense was attuned for a clue, an indication of any sort that her wariness was justified.

Again, she scanned the surrounding trees, their red-brown foliage forming a thick barrier to her questing stare. She looked back to the girls. Lucy hummed quietly as she worked, but Isobel was still, frozen like a rabbit stalked in an open field, as though she, too, sensed a strange current in the air.

The child stared hard at a tree that grew on the far side of the wall at the corner of the garden. She tipped her head slightly to the right. Her brows rose and the ever-dreamy expression she bore sharpened and changed.

She smiled, open and bright, joy radiating from her in a way that Beth had not seen before.

Startled, Beth stilled and stared.

The moment passed too quickly. Isobel's smile disappeared as it had come, in an instant. Then, dropping her chin, she went back to turning the soil.

Beth glanced at the tree and saw nothing. She sifted through the limited information she had, lining up bits and pieces until she was satisfied with the result. Certainty chased through her, and she strode to the corner of the wall.

With her back to the tree and her arms folded at her waist, she spoke, her tone conversational, though too low to carry to the girls.

"Why do you hide in a tree to watch your daughter?"

Silence greeted her query, and then sound: the rustle of leaves followed by the dull thud of booted feet hitting the ground. She turned to find Griffin Fairfax an arm's length away.

Her heart jerked and plunged.

Tall. Broad. Darkly intriguing. She had thought it was only wishful memory and imagination that painted him so in her thoughts. But here he was, more alluring in the flesh than in her private recollections.

He was disreputable. He wore no hat, and his dark hair, long and thick and shiny, curled over the white collar of his shirt, a vivid contrast. His brown riding coat was square cut, finely tailored, and perfectly respectable, as were his tan waistcoat and cord breeches. But the open neck of his shirt was not respectable in the least.

She stared at the vee of sun-kissed skin revealed there, the hollow at the base of his throat.

Wild, she thought. For all that the cut and fit of his clothing screamed quality, he was feral beneath a thin veneer of civilization.

The realization made her shiver.

He studied her, his expression both quizzical and intent, and she felt a warmth run from her belly to her arms and her legs, a rushing heat. The way he looked at her—absorbed, thoughtful, a little puzzled—left her breathless.

"How did you know I was there?" he asked, his tone laced with a cynical and self-directed humor. He gestured at the canopy of changing leaves. "The foliage obscured your view."

She heard it again, the odd shade to his vowels, the clipped, round tones that spoke of a gentleman, and the coarser underlay that hinted at something else.

Swallowing, she glanced at the tree he had so recently vacated, and said, "Isobel knew you were there."

The low, breathy quality of her voice made her feel ridiculous. Did he hear it?

"Isobel . . ." He cut a sidelong look to his daughter,

and Beth was uncertain of the emotion that crossed his features. Love? Hope? Regret?

With her head bowed, Isobel worked away at the weeds and did not look in their direction. After a moment, whatever sentiment Mr. Fairfax had allowed to surface faded away, and the silence hung like a damp fog, heavy and cloying. Uncomfortable.

"And you made a sound. In the tree. You . . . *crunched*," Beth said in a rush, compelled to fill the void, to explain the answer to the riddle. She looked pointedly at his left hand, where he yet held an apple core, his fingers long and dark against the remains of white flesh. That had been the sound she had heard, not the crunch of gravel, but the faint noise of his teeth breaking the skin of the apple.

She could not imagine why the thought of that made her mouth feel so dry.

"You are most observant, Miss Canham." He lobbed the apple core over the wall.

Turning back to her, he raised a brow and smiled a little, enough to flash bright teeth against the stubble that shadowed his jaw. It was not a wide smile, or an open one. Not a *nice* smile.

That smile was for *her*. Her alone. Hinting at secret thoughts and private entertainment.

It made her shiver, made her wonder about forbidden things.

Dangerous things.

Her fingers dug into the material of her skirt, crushing and releasing in an alternating pattern. The silence pricked her like an itch she was desperate to scratch. Words tumbled out to fill the void.

"I suspected there was someone there . . . in the tree." Had she said that already? "I assumed . . . given that I have seen you at Burndale Academy at least once each day . . . that is . . ." Her voice trailed away as she real-

ized that her disjointed observation implied that she
had watched for him each day.

She *had*, from the upstairs window or a shadowed
doorway, and once from beside the privy where the net-
tles grew thick. Each time the sight of him had sent an
odd little thrill through her veins, and she was mortified
that because of her loose tongue, he *knew* it.

"Do you watch for me, Miss Canham?" he asked, the
words smooth and soft as satin.

No reply came to her. What to say? That each day she
waited for some glimpse of him? That each night when
she walked on the road, she watched for him? She shook
her head, glanced away, but her gaze was drawn back to
him like metal shavings to a magnet.

A peculiar and foreign euphoria rushed through her,
like that she had felt when they had walked side by side
on the road. She was hot inside, butter melted in a skil-
let, warm and liquid and finally, sizzling. She looked
away, torn by the strange emotion.

What was it about this man that she found so fascinating?

She thought of their conversation on the road, when
they had spoken of the widow, Mrs. Arthur, and her
little brown glass bottle of laudanum. Mr. Fairfax had
understood exactly where her thoughts lay. They knew
each other not at all, yet he appeared to understand her
as well as anyone ever had.

With sardonic humor, she wondered what he thought
of close spaces and crowded places and the deepest,
darkest hours of the night.

Unnerved by the direction of her thoughts, she
glanced at the girls. Neither Lucy nor Isobel paid them
any heed; they were busy still. Though they needed no su-
pervision, Beth continued to watch them, her heart beating too quickly. She was afraid to look at Mr. Fairfax once
more, at the thick, long lashes that made his eyes so extraordinary, at the high curve of his cheeks, the hard line

of his jaw. The tiny white scar that she knew marked the right corner of his mouth.

She thought she would like to lay her fingertips against that scar. To ask him how it had come to be.

She made herself look at him then, determined to see only a man, to feel none of the cascading emotion that had drowned her each time she encountered him.

But determination, however strong, was not strong enough.

There it was again, the warmth and the heady rush of elation, the ache that was not an ache.

He was watching her with a taut, hard expression that only fueled her heated thoughts. Common sense bade her look away, run away, but some abominable perversity made her choose to stay.

A huff of air escaped her and she dropped her gaze to his mouth. What would it feel like to have those hard lips on hers? She had never before kissed a man. Never *been* kissed. She wondered . . .

With a jerk of her head, she looked away, appalled by her imaginings, but stimulated by them, too. There was a riot in her belly that felt like a thousand butterflies fluttering for freedom.

Did he know her secret yearning?

She thought he might.

She thought he *must.*

That in itself was enough to make her flushed and dizzy.

The faint scent of turned earth reached her, and the smell of autumn in the air. Leaves swirled about her feet, caught by the wind, their chorus a dry, crackling sound. She glanced down and frowned, remembering another day in this very garden when dead, brown leaves had danced at her feet.

A day when someone had watched her, veiled from sight.

Apprehension skittered across her skin and through

her veins, to lodge like a lump of clay in her belly. Her gaze shot to the man before her once more. He was no longer looking at her; instead, his attention had turned to his daughter.

The trees rustled as the leaves caught in the strengthening wind. Beth tensed. She was certain that a week past there *had* been someone watching her from those trees, and she thought it had been so every day since.

Today, that someone had been Mr. Fairfax.

She pressed her lips together and frowned.

Suddenly, she thought that standing alone with him in this garden, with only two little girls as chaperone, was reckless and imprudent. Though she had not even considered it a moment past, now she wondered if she ought to be afraid of him. She knew next to nothing of this man, save that he had a pleasing face and form, a silent, sad daughter, and a haze of monstrous rumors that hung about his head.

Alice's accusations tumbled through her mind. The maid believed Mr. Fairfax capable of murder . . . no, not just *capable*. Alice believed he had done murder.

Whose?

Questions. Questions.

Had it been Mr. Fairfax watching her on those other occasions? Had he been outside her window, a shadowy figure standing in the rain? Had he watched her that day on the road and again here in this garden?

Perhaps. But if so, why?

Queries and uncertainties circled her thoughts, crows after carrion. Now there was a lovely image.

With a little breath that was more sigh than mere exhalation, she looked at Mr. Fairfax once more.

She chose her words with care. "Do you sit in that tree and spy upon us very often, sir?"

"Every day," he replied, sardonic.

"In truth?" Beth blurted, aghast.

He merely shot her a closed look and said no more.

The sunlight touched him, and he was incredibly handsome, so dark against the bright glow of it. She was . . . attracted to him. A bee to pollen.

Oh, dear. Her cheeks heated at the thought and at the fact that he was now watching her once more with perfect concentration, his eyes warmed with a light that spoke to something deep inside her and made it roar to life.

She let the first words that came to her mind trip from her tongue. "Why do you spy? Why do you not simply play with Isobel? Talk to her?"

"I know little of children's games." He paused, grim, then added in a low, rough tone, "She never speaks."

He sounded . . . sad. Beth could summon no rejoinder.

"She never laughs. She never *plays*." He shrugged, the blithe action out of synchrony with the intensity of his tone and the sudden starkness of his expression. "And I have none but myself to blame."

Then he blinked and his mouth tensed, as though he was surprised—and perhaps none too pleased—that his words revealed so much.

"Why do you say that?" Beth asked, her heart pounding a hard beat. "Why is the blame yours to bear?"

For a moment, she thought—*prayed*—he would answer, would share some secret. She could not think why he should entrust his confidences to her; she only knew that she wanted them, that in this frozen moment, she *coveted* his secrets, his trust.

She, who could trust no one.

She held his gaze, noting that in this light his night-dark eyes were rimmed by a rich and verdant green. Noting, too, that he suddenly looked severe and remote and cold. Despite the sunshine and the shawl that draped her shoulders, Beth felt chilled.

"That is a tale for another day," Mr. Fairfax said shortly, then he slanted a sidelong look at the looming back wall of Burndale Academy. "Or perhaps you have already heard hints of it."

"I—" What to say? That she had heard he was a killer, a murderer? Alice's whispered accusations could have no possible basis in truth, could they? If, in fact, Mr. Fairfax had actually killed someone, surely he would have been brought to justice.

As though he read her thoughts, he said, "So you *have* heard something." Then he laughed, the sound soft and smooth . . . and infinitely appealing despite the tinge of darkness.

"Yes, I have," Beth replied after a long moment. She cast a warning look toward the girls. Lucy, the farther of the two, was at a great enough distance that she could not likely hear their exchange. Closer to them, Isobel stared at nothing, her fingers buried in the dirt, quiet and still.

When Beth turned her face to Griffin Fairfax once more, she found him staring at his daughter with contemplative longing. For a moment, she just watched him, *saw* him, and felt something inside her shift.

Mr. Fairfax was a man faced with an odd, eccentric daughter, a girl who was fey and wan and eerily quiet. Most would have simply seen her confined to a madhouse.

What did it mean about this man's character that he did not pursue that very avenue? And why did it please her so very much that he did not?

Walk, dear heart. Walk faster.

Beth's heart gave a sharp, quick twist.

It pleased her because she knew very well what it meant to be a fey, wan, eerily silent child.

Chapter Eleven

Griffin watched the play of emotion that crossed Beth's face. Clearly, she knew not what to make of him. As she walked a few steps away and went to stand by Lucy and Isobel, he had the thought that at the moment he knew not what to make of himself or his inexplicably strong attraction to her.

He had thought her merely pretty. He remembered that as he stared at her now. Her hair was tumbling loose in a half dozen places, curling moon-pale tendrils that escaped and fell free of the plaits she had twined, light against the dark cloth of her bodice.

She glanced at him, and away. Dusty blue eyes rimmed in dark lashes.

Not coy. Wary.

Wise girl.

He found her smart and intriguing and far more than merely pretty. Lovely. Fascinating. Full of contradictions, and strengths and vulnerabilities that combined in a heady mix.

He found it interesting that she had deduced his presence in the tree. She was an exceptionally observant individual.

"Watch the wasps," he said, stepping forward to bat

one away from Isobel's cheek. "They can be aggressive at this time of year. The threat of the coming winter drives them to a frenzy."

Not a flicker of emotion altered Isobel's bland expression. He had expected nothing else, but hope and expectation were not the same thing.

"Lucy, Isobel, time to wash your hands," Beth said, the sound of her voice calm and even.

Isobel glanced at her and nodded. *Nodded!* Elizabeth Canham had reached past the broken places that tormented his daughter, the first person to do so in three endless years.

Elizabeth. *Beth.* He wanted to whisper her name, to watch her eyes widen and her lips part as he said it. He wanted to touch her calm center and ruffle her a bit.

More than a bit. He wanted to bring a flush to her cheeks and a darkening to her eyes.

She had her back to him as she watched Isobel and Lucy gather their gardening tools. Her hand lifted, and with a languid movement, she shooed away a wasp. The sun caught her hair, bright, dazzling. A nimbus.

"You mention the threat of the coming winter," she said, her gaze meeting his, open and frank. "Do you see winter that way? As a threat?"

"Not at all," he replied, smiling a little at her tone. And that surprised him. He thought he had not smiled so much in three years as he had smiled since meeting Elizabeth Canham. A poor reflection on his life, or a wonderful reflection on her. Either way, he was nonplussed. "I have a fondness for winter, for a crisp, sunny day. For a fresh fall of snow."

As he said the words, he recalled the stain of dark crimson against a blanket of white snow. He folded the image away. That memory had no place in this sun-dappled garden.

Beth nodded, a graceful tip and tilt of her head.

He tried to determine what it was about her that so piqued his interest. Her face. Her form. Her bright-as-the-moon hair. She *was* lovely, with her delicate features and her wide, lush mouth. When she smiled, she was truly beautiful.

Her physical attributes tempted him. Of course. All those feminine things drew a man, and he was perhaps more base than most.

The truth of it was, as he looked at her sweet round bottom outlined by the black cloth of her dress, and the tempting swell of her breasts where they pushed against her bodice, he wanted to touch her, stroke her, pull his knife from his boot and slit her wretchedly ugly dress straight down the front, baring her smooth, soft skin to his touch.

Bloody hell.

But there was something else, something more. A different connection. He frowned, pondered, caught an idea. It was that she *saw* to the heart of the matter. That each time they met, spoke, she said something that left him feeling as though she saw him, *knew* him, and found his company pleasing nonetheless.

In turn, he knew things about her. He knew she was intelligent, observant. She was acquainted with fear, but chose to face it rather than cower. That made her both wise and brave.

He knew she could not bear to be still, to be confined. He had sensed a nervous edge in the way she stalked along the road and set her gaze to the horizon, the way she put stitches in her handkerchief, then ripped them out, again and again.

He knew she had suffered.

Or perhaps he only painted her with attributes and quirks where none dwelled in truth.

Perhaps. But he thought not.

"Come along now, Isobel," Lucy said, her tone mimicking a schoolmistress's as she took Isobel's hand. "We must wash our hands."

Isobel allowed herself to be led away by the other girl, docile, looking neither to the right nor the left. Then, as she passed Griffin, she reached out and touched the hem of his coat. Just touched it with the very tips of her fingers, before she moved on.

He stared after her, astonished.

A long moment passed. Slowly, he turned his head and met Beth's gaze.

She had seen it. Seen Isobel's touch, the first that had been granted him voluntarily in the years since his daughter had witnessed his darkest sin.

And she understood.

He wanted to shout to the heavens. He wanted to grab Beth and drag her close and kiss her, revel in the hope and exultation that rocked him.

Her eyes widened as she held his gaze, and her breath hitched, a soft, sensual sound that reached inside him and made him think of other sounds he'd like to draw from her lips. Cries. Moans.

A surge of fierce, hot longing twisted him tight.

Christ.

He stepped forward, close enough that she was forced to let her head fall back in order to meet his gaze. Her lashes were not very long, but they were thick and curled and dark for one so fair.

Inches separated them. Mere inches.

He could smell the scent of her hair, subtle, faintly floral. And the scent of her skin. Feminine. Arousing.

"What do you want of me?" she whispered.

Sweet innocent. It made him smile.

She was breathing quickly, the swell of her breasts rising and falling and he wanted to touch her, taste her, *take* what he wanted of her in silent answer to her query.

Almost did he reach for her.

Trembling, she stumbled back a step, jerked her gaze away to look down the now-empty path. She meant to flee, to follow the children. Griffin sensed it in the distant, close-lipped smile she cast his way and the angling of her body to shift around him. When he failed to move from her path, she frowned.

"Please let me pass, Mr. Fairfax," she murmured, her chin raised high, her tone almost steady.

Of course, a nice man would not have accosted her so in the first place. A *gentleman* would step to the side and offer a bow or doff his hat and politely let her go on her way.

He did neither, but rather shifted his weight to more completely block her escape.

"Sir," she said, her voice quite calm. "I must go."

In her words and tone he discerned the clear expectation that he would let her, and the faint tremor that belied her pretense of control.

A dark smile twisted his lips.

"Beth." He spoke her name like a caress. *Beth.* His Beth, with her delicate appearance and her core of forged metal. "You must realize by now that I make no claim to politesse. I barely graduated from short pants when I wandered onto the path of villainy, and though I now find myself back in the guise of an upstanding fellow, highborn, well-bred, the image is deceiving." He shifted closer, their chests almost touching.

She stared at him, eyes wide and dark with emotion. A pulse beat swift and hard in her neck. He wanted to lean in and press his lips to the spot, feel the tempo of her lifeblood, know the taste of her skin.

"I am neither a nice man nor a gentleman," he whispered, a clarification lest she had misunderstood his meaning. A simple truth. No matter the clothes he wore or the fine, pretty façade he conjured, he had long ago acknowledged that he was no scion of chivalry, that his was a heart of darkness. Or perhaps no heart at all.

"You are a villain, then?" she asked, low and breathy.

"I am."

She nodded, unsurprised. Studied him. A disconcerting thing, the way she looked at him, as though she could delve deep and see parts of him that even he did not know.

"A villain who issues pretty warnings," she observed, making no move to look away.

He remained as he was, blocking her path, far too close for their interaction to be deemed appropriate, breathing in the scent of her hair, unapologetic. Hot lust ground through him, and images of wants and needs. He wanted to drag her against him, push her thighs apart with his knee, feel her writhe as he pressed his fingers deep into the softness of her buttocks and held her tight against him—

On a sharp exhale, he stepped back.

"What—" She pressed her lips together, shook her head, her confusion apparent, as was her attraction to him. She was innocent, yet he had little doubt that she knew what he thought, what he wanted.

What he meant to have . . . eventually.

His gaze slid to her hair, pale as flax. The wisps that had come loose from her plaits, so sweetly curled, made him ache to drag out all the pins, to let the whole of the curling mass tumble free, to dig his fingers in and weave them through the silky strands.

With a desperate little gasp, she edged to one side.

He had no desire to let her go, but he realized with a bolt of clarity that he had no wish to frighten her, either. He merely wanted to . . . *to what?*

Be with her. Listen to her voice.

So he did the unacceptable and closed his fingers on her wrist, not tight or hurtful, but enough to stay her impending departure. Her skin was warm and soft and smooth.

With actions instinctive and swift, he drew her wrist up, breathed deep. She gasped and twitched but did not pull away.

Pressing his mouth to the soft skin on the inside, he ran his tongue along the crease, tasting her. *So sweet. Christ, so sweet.*

She froze, trembling in her place. He could feel the pulse at her wrist pounding wildly.

"Mr. Fairfax," she whispered. "You overstep the bounds of polite company."

Without raising his head, he cut her glance through his lashes and swirled his tongue over her skin, a luscious taste of her, before offering his reply against her skin.

"Yes, I do overstep. You see, I have little care for the bounds of polite company. Make no mistake about the sort of man I am, Miss Canham."

"No." The word was less than a whisper.

With care, he licked along her wrist, sank his teeth into the fleshy part at the base of her thumb, a gentle bite. She made a sound, of shock, of pleasure, a sharp exhalation that sank through his gut straight to his groin.

"Please," she gasped, and tugged briskly once, then again, harder.

Dropping his gaze, he studied her slender wrist, her skin pale against his own where he held her. Then he looked up once more.

Brows high, eyes wide, the dusty blue color darkened to purple, she stared at him for a tense moment, holding his gaze, never wavering.

Brave, but not unafraid. A woman of valor, or perhaps a woman who had known—and faced—her share of fears.

She took a step back, pulling on her wrist once more, and this time he freed her with a slow, lazy uncurling of his fingers and a lingering caress to the back of her hand.

She looked down, her lashes veiling her eyes, her head bowed as she stared at her wrist, and the seconds trooped one after the next like a line of ants. At length, she raised her head.

"Is it your intent to distress me?" she asked, her eyes narrowed now, sparking blue fire, her successful withdrawal leaving her anger stronger than her fear, and her passion lacing both.

She took another half-step around him.

Studying her face, reading the nuances of her expression, he let her sidle away. Her lips, full and lush, were drawn taut at the corners.

She was an intriguing enigma, strength and fragility.

He noted that she had asked only if he meant to distress her, not if he meant to harm her. Was she such an innocent that she did not realize that he might well do just that? They were alone here in the garden and he held her back from escape.

Anger roared through him, at himself for his precipitous actions, at her for not screaming and running. He had warned her, and still she did not seem to grasp exactly what he was.

A villain. A monster.

He was grateful that she did not see it; he was furious that she did not see it.

Unreasoning anger, as usual.

He mastered it quickly. Long years of practice had taught him the way of it.

She took a deep breath, and he thought she would flay him with her words. Instead, she wet her lips, stared again at her wrist, and ran the tip of her index finger over the base of her thumb. He found her actions sensual.

Innocence held a powerful allure.

Flashing him an unreadable look, she sank her teeth

into her lower lip, gave her skirt an irate twitch, and stepped the rest of the way around him. She stalked to the stone bench on the verandah without looking back, retrieved her ecru bag, then strode on toward the garden gate. There she paused, and he saw her shoulders stiffen, her body tremble just a little, and she ran her fingers along the inside of her wrist once more.

Her actions gave her away. She had liked it, his tongue and teeth on her skin.

In that instant, Griffin found himself wishing that he could rip both his anger and the stain of his crimes from the black, roiling void of his soul, that he had something better to offer her than what he was.

"Miss Canham," he called. She froze, her back to him, one hand resting on the iron grillwork of the gate.

He had tantalized her, but he had also distressed her. A part of him was glad. He wanted her to be wary, careful. His actions ought to have done more than cause her distress; they ought to have terrified her. But they had not. He thought of the irate way she had flicked her skirt, and he was puzzled, intrigued.

From whence did she draw her courage, her strength? 'Twas a well of great depth.

"My apologies," he said, and meant it, but not for the reasons she likely imagined.

Not for the fact that he had detained her, touched her, tasted her in a way most sensual.

No, he was sorry that he would not be noble or kind or good, that he would not be able to stay away from her.

He was sorry that he was not, at his core, the man he was on the surface, a man without demons and ghosts and dark secrets.

She yanked open the gate, and the hinges cried out in protest, a strident noise. A wasp buzzed by her cheek, and she waved it away, then again and again, but it came at her once more.

A few steps and he was by her side, his hand shooting out, faster than hers. He closed his fist, leaving the wasp trapped inside. A sharp flick of his wrist and fingers, and he set it free to fly off in the opposite direction with an angry buzz.

Beth spun to face him, lips parted, eyes wide.

"You did not kill it."

He studied her, intrigued. "You are pleased by that. Pleased that I let it live, that I set it free."

"I am," she said. "To kill it would have been a simple matter. A sharp swat and the danger is gone. But to control the urge, to risk a sting . . . well, there is valor in that."

The way she looked at him, bright and honest. *Bloody hell.*

"You choose to label me as something I am not."

Her pretty lips compressed in a tight line, then released. She opened her mouth. Closed it. Looked to the ground.

He wanted to kiss her in truth, to pull her hard against him and drag the pins from her hair until the wild mass of her curls tumbled free. To gather the golden strands tight in his fist. To put his mouth on hers, push his tongue inside her, rough, ungentle, to kindle a flame in her blood that matched the burn in his own.

Christ. The tiny sample he had stolen was not enough; it had only whetted his appetite, stirred the beast to life.

"There are rumors . . ." she said, hesitant, pulling her gaze from the ground.

Of course there were. "Yes," he agreed.

"Do you know what they say?"

She was brave; he had known it all along. And she liked to seek answers, to solve puzzles. Here was most definitely a puzzle. Rumors branded him a killer. Her own observations might suggest to her that that he was not.

"The rumors?" He inclined his head. "Yes, I know what they say."

Her knuckles had gone white where they yet clutched at the gate.

"Whom—" Just a single strangled word. She could not manage the rest of the query. He could not blame her.

"Go on, now," he said softly, reaching around her to pull the gate all the way open, then resting his splayed fingers at the small of her back to give her gentle direction. The contact and the urge to slide his hand lower, to the tempting curve of her bottom, made his groin ache.

She took a handful of steps, then stopped and looked back at him over her shoulder, her blue eyes bright and intent. She held his gaze, waited, waited.

Her sharp, shaky intake of breath almost stayed his next words, then he thought, *Tell her.*

Tell her all? No, not yet. But tell her part. She would only hear it elsewhere if he did not. Still, he found himself reluctant to offer the ugly truth.

In a low, emotionless voice, he said, "My wife, Miss Canham. The rumors state that I killed my wife."

That night, Beth unlocked her chamber door and stepped inside. Already confused and dismayed by the events in the garden, by Griffin's touch and the press of his mouth to her wrist, she had been further confounded by his quiet admission. What was she to make of that? Of his assertion that he had killed his wife?

Only, that was not what he had said. He had not admitted murder. He had admitted only that the rumors *claimed* he had killed her.

Griffin Fairfax was full of contradictions. A puzzle.

Recollections and images teased her: His expression as he looked at his daughter, filled with such bewildered yearning. His movements as he caught the wasp, then set it free. The sound of his voice, warm and seductive, then coldly emotionless as he unveiled the darkest of his secrets.

My wife, Miss Canham. The rumors state that I killed my wife.

The rumors *state* . . .

Rumors. Rumors.

They hung about him like a choking miasma.

Was that his darkest secret, then? That there were suppositions and whispers that dogged him, or was there a darker secret still, a truth she could not wish to know?

Had he killed his wife?

The part of her that was her father's daughter looked to the rationality of that and decided that if he had, he would be incarcerated now. The part of her that was purely herself was disinclined to believe his guilt.

With a sigh, she turned, locked the door behind her, and took the key from the hole. She paused, took a long, slow breath, and forced herself to bury the urge to fling open the portal and free herself from this confined space. The time she had spent with Griffin Fairfax had befuddled and confused her, a situation that boded ill for her continued emotional constraint, and made her acutely aware of the small, restricting box her chamber had become.

She knew herself well enough to recognize the danger signs.

Taking a deep breath, she glanced about. For a moment, she simply stood in place, then she moved into the room, set her candle on the small table, and crossed to the bed. There, she reached for her pillow, intent on retrieving her nightdress.

Her heart slammed against her ribs as certainty slapped her, swift and brutal.

Someone had been here, touched her pillow, moved it.

Her hand trembled as she reached out and clasped the edge of the pillowcase, gingerly dragging it to one side. Her nightdress was there, folded yes, but not the way she had left it. The hem faced the head of the bed rather than the foot.

She was ever meticulous in her organization. She would never have left her nightdress so.

Who—

Spinning, she went to her wooden keepsake box, a treasure that her father had gifted her with in a better time. She lifted the lid, her breath frozen in her throat, and then exhaled in rushing relief. It was there. The small pearl brooch that had belonged to her grandmother and passed to Beth was still there.

Which implied that her clandestine visitor was not a thief, for the brooch would have been easy pickings.

Slowly, she made a circuit of the room, noting the details as a tugging dismay pulled at her. Strange, how she imagined she could hear the sound of her father's voice, patient, calm, cataloguing each finding.

It appeared that nothing was taken, though many of her things had been disturbed.

Oh, the evidence was subtle enough. A few hairpins turned the wrong way. Her brush shifted a hairsbreadth to the right so it no longer lay perfectly aligned with the edge of the table. Her small pile of handkerchiefs, folded neatly in her press, rearranged so the top square had its edges misaligned.

In all likelihood, most people would have noticed nothing amiss. But Beth was not most people. From the earliest age she had been determined to maintain order over the small things in her life because so many things were beyond her control. Large things. Frightening things.

She closed her eyes as memories crept forth, rank and ugly. With a shudder, she thrust them aside and focused her thoughts on the question at hand.

Who had been in her room, touched her belongings? A maid, to straighten up?

Of course, that was the likely explanation, but something nagged at her, something that made her think otherwise.

With nervous energy, she ordered and tidied every article of her clothing, aligned her brush and comb and each and every hairpin, smoothed the bedsheets until they were free of any crinkle or crease. Finally, she prepared for bed.

As she slid between the cool sheets, restless agitation left her hot even in the chill of the autumn night, and she knew her suspicions of an intruder were only partly to blame.

She could find no peace because he had kissed her.

Griffin Fairfax had *kissed* her. Not the sort of kiss she had innocently dreamed of in the past, as girls were wont to do. Not a soft, safe brush of warm lips on her own. No, his had been a kiss of decadence and magnificence, a kiss meant to lure desires she had never imagined she possessed.

And, oh, he had succeeded.

The recollection made her anxious, uneasy, her limbs liquid, her senses flooded with awareness. His mouth had been warm on her wrist, the damp trail of his tongue drawing a flood of heat, the sharp press of his teeth sinking into her flesh leaving her weak and panting.

A shaky sigh escaped her. She brought her hand to her mouth, dragged the base of her thumb back and forth across her lower lip, recalling every nuance of Griffin's touch. Inexplicably, she wanted him to do those things again, to her wrist, to her mouth. She wanted him to press his lips to hers, just as he had on the skin of her wrist, to stroke his tongue over her mouth, to bite her lips as he had her thumb.

She felt such *wanting* of him, such *yearning*.

She was afraid and enticed and confused. She needed to be free of it, free of such dangerous desire.

But a part of her wished to be chained by it.

With a gasp she flung herself from the bed and began to pace.

Spinning sharply, she strode to the window and yanked back the heavy draperies. The back garden was a mass of shapes, slate and pewter and black, washed in paler gray moonlight. She raised her eyes to the moon and the onyx sky.

In London, her family would see that same moon. That same slice of beautiful moon.

She took some comfort in that, in the familiarity of her thoughts of them and her memories of home. She thought of her mother, humming softly as she prepared a meat pie with rich gravy. She thought of her brother's laughter when he won at chess. She thought of her father . . . but no, to think of him as he was now—trapped in a wheeled chair and a body that did not do what he wished—was a road too painful to travel. Instead, she thought of him as he had been years ago, taking her hands in his and dancing a jig while they laughed and laughed.

She missed them horribly, and longed to write a letter home. Well, that was out of the question. As the recipient, her mother would be expected to produce the postal rate of three pence, an amount she could ill afford. But, oh, to be able to unburden herself, to pour out the details of her long journey, her arrival at Burndale, the experiences she had had since coming here.

Her encounters with Griffin Fairfax.

She ran her fingertips along the crease of her wrist, remembering the powerful emotion his touch had engendered, then jerked her fingers away. Perhaps she would not wish to share *every* nuance of those encounters.

Closing her eyes, she imagined his face, his windblown hair, the lean, hard line of his cheek. The way his eyes lit with a secret amusement that lured her into a feeling of kinship. The way he moved. The way he smelled.

Her skin heated and her eyes popped open, the wayward turn of her mind leaving her confused and dismayed.

Worse than her unfortunate and inappropriate attraction was the fact that she *liked* him, enjoyed him. Not only his physical allure, though that certainly swayed her. She found him fascinating and frightening and reassuring all at once.

Earlier, in the garden, when he had put his mouth on her wrist, tasted her, she ought to have been terrified. She shivered.

Yes, that was what he had done. *Tasted her.*

And instead of feeling frightened, she had been tempted. Enthralled.

Beth curled her fingers in the heavy curtain and rested her forehead against the cool glass. The quiet wrapped close about her, smothering her like a shroud. In that instant, she found the silence awful and she longed for the street sounds of home. Not the loud cacophony that always boomed outside their horrible little flat, but the softer sounds of the house in south London. The morning call of the milkmaid or the baker. The wheels of a carriage and the hooves of horses ringing on the cobbled road.

Here, there were no such sounds, and no familiar city sights. There were only the sky and shadows and the black shape of the trees in the distance. For an instant, the moon hung bright and clear, and then the wind moved the clouds across its face, leaving the view beyond her window murky and forbidding.

Beth wrapped her arms tight about her waist.

In the now-muted light, the back garden seemed grim and frightening, dotted with ghostly shapes, the high wall that surrounded it sinister somehow. And there, at the far edge of what she could see, the three dead trees with their twisted branches. They only added to her unease, lending an awful, eerie nature to the place.

A general distress settled over her, a clammy shroud. She was faced with all manner of frightening things, the surge of new and unfamiliar emotion, the anxiety of her separation from her family, the worry that all was not right in this place. That someone stalked her, watched her, and now came into her own sanctuary to touch and move her things.

Or was she fashioning dark and threatening mountains where only tiny hills existed?

'Twould not be the first time.

She shuddered. Old fears blended with the new, and suddenly the room felt close, stuffy, the walls moving in on her until she thought she would be crushed. The suddenness and strength of the assault was overwhelming, far stronger than it had been in many years.

The box was tight, barely big enough to hold her, and she pressed at the lid and sobbed until her throat was dry and sore. Dark, so dark. Please . . . please . . . Someone come. Someone save me.

Trembling, battling the horror of her memories, she leaned close to the window and stared out at the night, pretending there were no walls, no darkness. Pretending she did not feel the bite of ancient terrors.

Suddenly, a flicker of movement in the garden caught her eye. She shifted to one side, peering through the glass, trying to see beyond her own reflection, but in the moments that followed she saw nothing out of the expected.

She had almost convinced herself she had seen nothing in the first place, that it was only her anxious nature that conjured ghosts and goblins, when the shadows changed once more and a dark shape separated itself from the trees beyond the wall.

Broad of shoulder and narrow of hip. A man.

His hair was dark, or mayhap he wore a dark cap. The contrast made his face pale in the night, tipped up toward her. With a gasp, she drew back. But he was too far away for her to see his features clearly, which meant he was too far away to see hers.

Mr. Fairfax? She could find no reason to think so, other than the wayward meanderings of her imagination.

She leaned close to the cold glass panes once more. He was as he had been, frozen in place, his face turned to her window. *Watching.*

An ugly swirl of fear uncurled in her belly.

She was about to move away, to draw the curtain, though it would mean she would have to burn a rushlight the whole night through, when she caught sight of someone moving swiftly across the back garden.

The moonlight illuminated the figure but a moment, and Beth saw it was a woman, garbed in a dark cloak with a scarf or hood pulled over her hair. Her stride was confident, her form lean and tall, and though Beth could see nothing of the woman's features, she recognized her as Miss Percy.

How odd. What could Miss Percy seek in the late hour of the night, slinking about without lantern or light? Did she go to meet that man who lurked and . . . watched? The thought made Beth shudder.

Peering into the darkness, she squinted against the night. She could see the heavy hedge of the back garden, a dark, blocky shape, and beyond that the outline of the trees, black against a blacker sky. She searched for the man she had seen earlier, but he had melded with the night and she could see him no more.

Then, she thought she *did* glimpse him, almost obscured by the trees, the pale shine of his skin, the glint of his eyes, looking not at Miss Percy, but at Beth.

A fist closed about her heart, tighter and tighter still.

Was he the same man she had sensed watching her on the road? In the garden? Who was he? What did he want?

Had he been here, in her room, touched her possessions? Or was she feeding the spark of her own unease, seeing a wolf where there was only a lamb, allowing her anxious nature to spin fancies and fears?

He stepped back, his form blending with the other shadows of the night.

Miss Percy had reached the hedge now. She paused, looked cautiously about, drew her scarf closer about her face.

And then she too was swallowed by the darkness.

Chapter Twelve

Stepney, London, January 15, 1813

Ginnie. Dead. Oh, God, she was dead, torn and cut, her blood a dark, glistening pool. Henry wanted to touch her. To gather her in his arms and keep her safe, hold her safe. Too late. Too late.

Who had done this? And why?

Why? Why? Why?

Sam Loder stared at him in mute sympathy, his normally ruddy color gone to ash.

"Henry," he said, his voice gruff. "This is no place for you now."

No place for him.

He swallowed and almost choked on the mad cackle that ached to spring free of his chest.

There would never be a place for him.

His heart, his hope, his faith had died here today.

He had loved her, more than he had realized.

Seeing her here, gray, lifeless, her hair matted with blood, her clothes saturated with it . . . her blood . . . the horror of it was a jagged wound inside of him. Carefully he squatted low, mindful not to step in the blood, and he reached out to lay his hand on her shoulder. How long he stayed crouched by her side, he could not say, but after a time he became aware of a high keening sound, tuneless, terrible.

And he realized the sound came from him.

Blinking, he battled with himself, but the tears slid free and scalded his cheeks. He shook his head, rose, stood staring down at her.

He was cold, as though he'd been dropped in the Thames in the dead of winter. A bone-deep ache made him feel he could die, close his eyes, lie down on the floor in the pool of Ginnie's blood, and die. He thought of her, all alone in the darkness, and he felt sick.

Tearing his gaze away, he stared straight ahead at a thin crack that ran down the wall, and a smudged handprint beside it. A small handprint, like a child's.

Something nagged at him, breaking through the haze of shock and horror. Something . . .

He forced himself to follow the thread of his thoughts. The girl.

"The child," he croaked, distress scrabbling through him to lodge like a rock in his chest. His heart beat a frantic tattoo, horror and overwhelming grief clouding his mind.

Ginnie. She was dead.

But the girl . . .

His gaze slid to Ginnie's body once more. He wanted to gather her in his arms, kiss her sweet lips, feel her breath on his cheek.

Nevermore.

He shuddered.

Ginnie, with her golden ringlets . . . Gone . . . Gone . . .

Where was her hair, her beautiful hair?

The girl—

"Where is the girl?" Henry asked, turning to the others as he spoke. He forced himself to concentrate though he felt as though a tempest raged inside him, whipping about, screaming to get free, tearing all rational thought from his mind.

He ached to break something. The wall. The lamp. He wanted to beat something until his fists were raw and bloody.

"The Trotters' granddaughter," he rasped. It hurt his throat to speak.

Sam was in the parlor with Robert Seymour, a seasoned officer who had arrived some moments past and immediately set about searching for clues. Neither man even glanced at Henry, and he realized that he had spoken so low that they had not heard him, not a word.

What was the child's name? He tried to recall, and failed. A surging sadness so acute that it was almost pain tore through him. She deserved to have a name.

Spinning around, he peered down the darkened hallway, his heart pounding a hard and brutal rhythm.

"Look here," came Robert Seymour's voice from inside the parlor, tight with excitement. "There's blood here on the windowsill."

Henry glanced back and saw Robert lean out the open parlor window, his hands braced on either side of a dark smear.

"And I believe I see a footprint there in the dirt."

What good was it, such a find? Would it make the dead rise again?

A footprint. In the dirt.

Henry looked down at his boots, then looked at Sam's, and finally Robert's. Three very different pairs of boots.

"The footprint," he said, and because he spoke louder, they heard him now, despite the hoarseness of his voice. "Measure its length. And then trace the shape to a paper." He paused, his thoughts muzzy, his stomach clenched in a sick knot.

"Whatever for?" Robert asked and turned to stare at him.

Yes. Whatever for. It would not bring her back. She was never coming back.

"To compare to his boots. To show his guilt. If"—Henry swallowed, forced himself not to break down and sob. He looked back and forth between Sam and Robert—"*when* we find him."

They were dubious of his suggestion. He could see it.

He knew the way things worked. Talk to witnesses. Survey the scene. Surmise and make a guess as to what had happened. It was the way things had been done for a very long while. Sam and Robert were seasoned officers, while he was green as new grass. They had no reason to value his opinion.

Sam frowned, long furrows marking his brow, and finally he nodded and headed toward the front door. Henry wasn't certain where Sam went. Perhaps to measure the boot print.

Turning away, he looked down the long, dark hall. Numb and nauseous, battered by a cold fury, he could not divert enough emotion to care if they listened or not. Ginnie was dead. Dead. Dead.

But the girl . . . the girl . . .

Feeling bleak and sick and terribly overwhelmed, Henry backed away and followed the hallway to the far end where he found the staircase to the second floor. Bending, he touched his finger to the edge of the stair. It came away dark with blood.

His stomach heaved and rolled. He ought to run, ought to tear up the staircase and see with his own eyes that the child was there, asleep, unharmed. Instead, he could only drag his feet up, one step and the next, weighed down by fear and loathing of what he might find.

The child *was* up there. Alive?

The wood floor of the landing creaked and groaned beneath his weight. He shoved at the first door on his right, and it flew open to hit the wall with a sharp crack.

The room was dark, empty.

Turning, he tried the first door on the left, with no better results. The faint stink of tallow lingered in the air, but the room was unoccupied. In a frenzy, he returned to the hallway and shoved at each door, thrusting them open, until at the end of the hall he pushed open the last, the creak of the hinges strident and harsh, the rasp of his breath loud in his ears.

A rushlight in a tin waged battle with the darkness, the meager illumination crawling across the walls, the floor, the bed. The scent of blood was strong, like tarnished silver.

He froze, shaking, hands fisted at his sides. In horrid contrast, crimson flowered against the white bed linens, a massive, dark stain right in the center of the bed.

Dear God.

On shaking limbs, he walked forward, hands outstretched, touched the child's pillow, the small rag doll. Finally, he turned his gaze to the crimson blot.

His breath stopped. His heart stopped.

Dear God. Dear God.

With a great, gasping breath, Henry Pugh sank to his knees and began to sob.

Chapter Thirteen

Burndale, Yorkshire, September 14, 1828

Beth lay in the dark, her limbs shifting restlessly under the covers, her emotions knotted and snarled like a ball of yarn tossed about by a cat. She had slept in fitful snatches, haunted by a multitude of disturbing things: thoughts of Mr. Fairfax, his mouth pressed to her wrist; the certainty that she had seen someone lurking in the back garden last night, standing in the dark, his face tipped up to her window; the conviction that someone had been in her room, touched her books, her clothes, even her nightgown where it lay folded beneath her pillow.

Alone, each thought was distressing. Combined, they multiplied and swelled, and the secret terrors she had thought well under her control oozed free of the confines she set.

Exhaustion and worry combined to weaken her defenses. Over the years, she had learned to recognize the signs of her fraying control. The walls she had constructed around her quirks and peculiarities were only as strong as her will, and this morning she felt poorly suited to the task, her panic threatening to slide free in a greasy torrent.

The dawn was not yet upon them, but she rose from her bed, prepared herself to meet the day, performing her morning ablutions and dressing with all haste. She had come to a determination. She must seek out Miss Percy in her office first thing this morning. The headmistress was fond of routine, and she regularly worked at her desk for an hour before breakfast.

Taking up her candle, Beth made her way through the dark passage and down the stairs. A damp chill seeped through unseen cracks to touch her skin with clammy fingers.

She quickened her pace, pausing once to shift to the right and avoid the place on the stair that creaked.

Corridors fanned from the main vestibule, and she chose the one she sought, though it was as dark as a pit, with shadowed doorways on either side. The flame of her candle was a pallid warrior against the gloom.

She passed a partially open door, and with a hissing sound, the wind seeped through, catching the flame, making it dance and finally, snuffing it altogether.

Freezing in her place, she felt the press of darkness heavy upon her shoulders, her chest. With a shake of her head, she fended off the tide of dismay. There was a bit of light, the first whisper of morning. It was enough. She willed herself to believe it was enough.

A scratching sound, quick and light, came to her. A mouse? A draft, come through a crack? It mattered not. She had a task, and she would see it done, and so she walked on.

Once, she stopped, fearing she had taken a wrong turn, only to continue on, uncertain of her way until her destination appeared out of the shadows before her.

The door to Miss Percy's office was slightly ajar. A finger of candlelight and a murmur of sound slipped free.

Beth stepped closer, her hand raised to knock, and

then the sounds became a low-voiced conversation that made her stay her movements, made her stand and listen, her pulse speeding up with each word.

". . . not at all the sort of woman we wish to employ at Burndale." Miss Percy's voice, sounding perturbed and blunt.

"I quite agree. But we need her for the time being. Perhaps an admonishment to temper her ways?" Beth could not be certain, but she thought the respondent was Miss Browne.

The sound of china touching china made Beth think they were taking tea in the office, that a cup had been set on a saucer.

"She is barely competent in the classroom, and her overblown emotions hardly serve the students well," Miss Percy pointed out, the words an icy dagger plunging deep in Beth's breast.

Dear heaven. She thought they must be speaking of her, and she felt sick and terrified, horrified that she might lose this position, her family's one hope. She had come here, to the headmistress's office, to share terrible suppositions and fears, things she had no proof of, things that would only serve to underscore her failings.

Oh, what had she been thinking?

Slowly, she backed away, feeling the heavy thud of her heart and the sick swell of her despair. She dared not tell Miss Percy anything. Not after overhearing such a damning exchange.

They spoke of overblown emotions. Surely spouting suspicions of watchers in the night and unseen intruders would only solidify their worst opinions of her.

Spinning, she retreated down the corridor, making her steps soft and quiet, little caring where she went. She knew only that she must get away from here before her presence was discovered, before she added eavesdropping to the headmistress's list of her failings and gave her further cause for dismissal.

She thought to return to her chamber, then she thought she could not bear it, could not bear the confined space.

Perhaps she would go to the refectory and await the girls. The room was large, with a bank of wide windows. She would not feel so very confined there. She thought for a moment, mentally mapping the way from Miss Percy's office to the refectory. The halls and passage were a labyrinth, and she had no wish to lose her way.

Unfortunately, with her worries and unease crackling like a raging fire and her exhaustion from her restless night leaving her prey to her secret despairs, the way was less than clear to her.

Lifting her skirt, she began to walk, choosing a vaguely familiar passage with floors of red clay tile and walls of paneled wood the color of oversteeped tea. The walls felt like they were closing in upon her, and she pressed her palm over her heart, willed herself to settle.

With a shudder, she turned through a doorway into a wider hallway, paused, backtracked, and finally chose the same path she had started out upon in the first place. There was a little light now as the dawn seeped from beneath closed doors to paint the walls gray and mauve.

Her footsteps echoed hollowly in the empty space, the sound ricocheting back and forth, until she began to wonder if it was merely the residual noise of her own steps that followed her, or something else entirely.

She froze, spun, her heart thudding against her ribs.

The sound of a shuffling step carried to her, unmistakable. Frightening. The suspicion that someone followed her shifted to certainty.

"Hello? Who is there?" She could not help but think of the man who had stood in the back garden, watching her window. A man she suspected had been in her room, touched her things. The thought horrified her, terrified her. "Is anyone there?"

A thin, shallow reflection of her voice bounced back at her. Then, into the silence came the scrape of a footstep.

Chilling tendrils wove about her heart, and her gaze darted along the hallway, pausing at every shadow. She was *not* alone. She felt the icy certainty of that close about her chest and squeeze tight.

She spun, looked behind her. To the right. To the left.

How far to the refectory?

Even as the question formed, she recognized her folly in allowing her distress to cloud her thoughts.

She recognized the pattern from multitudinous episodes in her past, the episodes her mother labeled attacks of dismay.

She was amplifying the danger, stoking the flames of her fears, feeding them with the truth of dark memories and the distress over her present circumstance. She was succumbing to hysteria, though the rational part of her knew her reaction was overblown.

It was early morning. There were people about. Teachers. Students. Maids. Perhaps it was one of them she had heard, and even if it was not, even if someone *did* follow her along this corridor, surely someone else would hear her and come if she screamed.

A sharp sigh escaped her, and she pressed the back of her hand to her forehead, angry at herself for how far she had allowed this to devolve.

Dropping her hand to her side, she looked about, getting her bearings. The passages and rooms were a dim maze.

Her thoughts in turmoil, she began to walk down the corridor, her heart racing, her heels tapping out a rapid pace. She fought the urge to glance back over her shoulder to make certain she was alone.

Walk, dear heart. Walk faster. And she did, her pace quickening with each step until she was running, her hand fisted tight in her skirt, her hem held high.

A part of her recognized that she was unreasonable, her reaction extreme. She tried to slow her gait, to measure her tread, but she felt as though her skin would burst, as though needles and pins poked her and gouged her. Her heart twisted with a sharp and bright pain, as though a mighty fist reached deep inside her and crushed the palpitating organ.

She tried all the tricks she had taught herself over the years: counting her breaths; counting her steps; slowing each breath by force of will.

To no avail. Her heart pounded like a smith's hammer.

Oh, this would not do. Not at all—

"Miss Canham!" Mr. Fairfax caught her as she slammed against him, steadying her as she stumbled and swayed.

She stared at him, trembling, her heart racing. She wondered if she had conjured a mirage, or if he stood here in truth.

"Beth," he said gently, his gaze locked on hers, his hands about her arms. "Beth," he said again, stronger, and she felt a hard lump choking her, a lump of tears and fear and humiliation.

Confusion buffeted her. What was he doing here at such an hour? What happenstance had brought him to this hallway at exactly this time? Or was it happenstance at all? Did he follow her, watch her, hunt her?

She jerked, but he held her arms, though his grip lightened.

"The color is gone from your face," he said. "What is it, Beth? What has frightened you so?"

Mute, she shook her head rapidly from side to side. What was she to say? She dared not trust him, his convenient presence here, or the possibility that it was he who tormented her.

She found she could not bear it, not the confines of the passage, or the grip of his hands on her arms. She needed to run, she needed to breathe—

Catching her wrist, he drew her hand up, turned her palm forward. With no concern for propriety, he pushed her fingers inside his coat and his vest, against the thin linen of his shirt. Against his heart.

Warmth flooded her, the heat of his body. The heat of his gaze, so focused, so intent.

"Feel my heart, Beth. Feel the beat of it. Let my heart beat in time with your own."

He *knew*. He knew what she thought, what she felt. But how? How?

He pressed her palm tighter against him, and she did feel it, the steady, steady beat. Strong, slow, even. A metronome setting the pace for her own pulse.

Rocked by confusion and dismay she stood, battling the inappropriate urge to fling herself against the warm, solid strength of him.

"Trust me, Beth," he said, a low murmur that lured and beguiled. "Let me be your anchor."

She exhaled sharply, and was left deflated and confused. Trust him? She could trust no one.

For a long moment, he studied her, his eyes narrowed in contemplation, his pupils dilated, leaving his gaze dark and unfathomable. Then he smiled, a faint curve of his lips, enough to offer a glimpse of the crease that carved his cheek.

"Better?" he asked.

Oddly, she did feel marginally better. Like phantoms, her worries and secret fears shadowed her every thought, her every breath, but somehow, they felt distant now. Bearable.

Lowering her lashes, she studied her hand where it disappeared inside his coat. She could feel his heartbeat. Feel his warmth. She ought to draw away. It was the proper thing to do. But for this frozen moment, she only wanted to pull what small comfort she could from him, to steal just a little of his calm demeanor and drag it about her like a cloak.

She raised her gaze to his and nodded, and he winked at her then. Not as though to make light of her, but as though they were in collusion, as though he understood.

Because he did. She knew that. Griffin Fairfax boxed his emotions up so neat and tidy, held them back behind a solid reserve.

They *were* in collusion. He *did* understand.

She knew what demons she battled, what horrors tormented her soul. She knew exactly why she must fight to hold them back. Which left her wondering . . . What monsters ate at his?

The following morning Griffin rose with the sun, met with his land steward, answered a stack of correspondence, and scrutinized his books before riding to the village of Burndale on a small errand. The day was fine, the dawn chill giving way to a milder morning.

He knocked at the Widow Gormley's door and was greeted cordially, if slightly warily. Mrs. Gormley, like most of the villagers, regarded him with a modicum of concern and suspicion. With just cause. The circumstances of Amelia's death were ugly and twisted as sin, and the telling and retelling of it over the years, the story whispered behind cupped palms, had made the thing uglier still.

Patiently, he waited as Mrs. Gormley folded his shirts—she had darned the hem of one, and replaced the buttons on the other two—wrapped them in waxed paper, then bound the whole with string. As the widow tied a neat knot, Griffin looked around the shabby parlor of her small cottage, enjoying the scent of fresh-baked bread that flavored the air.

They had food, then, he thought. She and her younger son, Elliot, were not going hungry. Smooth relief settled over him.

Though he barely knew her, the woman's dire straits

had caught his attention last fall when her husband had dropped dead for no reason at all and left her a widow with two young children. Before the man's death, Mrs. Gormley had often been seen with her face beaten black and blue, her lip split, her eye swollen shut. Once, in Griffin's hearing, the chandler had wondered aloud if perhaps Mrs. Gormley's widowhood had been hastened into being by a dose of poison. For some inexplicable reason, Griffin had found himself compelled to engage in discourse with the man out back of his shop, and that rumor had died a timely death.

He could not say what touched him about the woman's circumstance. Kindness was a virtue he laid no claim to. But Mrs. Gormley's plight *did* touch him. He thought it might be because of her sons, because of the way she looked at them and cared for them and stood in front of them to take their father's blows. Or perhaps it was because she reminded him of himself in a time long past, weak and small and forced to endure, determined to survive nonetheless.

Or perhaps it was merely a whim. *That* explanation sat best with him.

Accepting the package from her, he thanked her for her fine stitches. Mrs. Gormley made a small smile in that shy way she had, with her chin dipped low and her face turned a little away.

He could not help but think of Beth Canham, her direct gaze, the way she met everything head-on. Even her fears. She was a mystery. And she drew him as no one had in a very long time.

Thinking of her, the way she had looked in the dim passage the previous morning, pale and fearful, her breath coming in rapid little pants, made him wonder about her all the more. He wanted to peel away her layers, peel away her secrets.

"I thank you for bringing the work to me," Mrs.

Gormley said, and he glanced at her, drawn back to the moment.

Her words elicited a rising discomfort. Bloody hell. He had enough money to buy the entire village if he'd been of a mind to. An easy enough matter to share a small measure with this woman.

He had originally offered charity, arriving on Mrs. Gormley's doorstep with a little bag of coins three days after her husband was buried. That offer was immediately and firmly rebuffed. He had been wise enough never to repeat it. So he took her elder boy, Thomas, a lad of twelve, to Wickham Hall to work at the stables. And he found ways for Mrs. Gormley to earn a little extra, as well.

In return, he had clothes that were always in the finest repair.

"'Tis I who thank you, for unless I wish to purchase a new shirt each time I lose a button, I see no way around it."

Her gaze flicked to his, then skittered away. "There are a dozen maids at Wickham Hall you might have set to the chore, Mr. Fairfax," she said.

With a nod, Griffin passed her the payment for her sewing.

"True enough," he replied, then lowered his voice, sharing a confidence. "But the maids at Wickham never seem to put the buttons exactly where I want them."

Her dark, finely arched brows rose and she shook her head, clearly unconvinced. She might have been beautiful once, before her husband's fists left her nose twisted and her right cheek lower than her left.

"Can they not match the buttons to the holes?" Her fleeting smile flashed again, then disappeared. "A daunting task, that."

He nodded gravely. "Precisely."

A soft huff of air escaped her.

She was right, of course. Any maid—one of an army of

servants he had to see to his needs—might have darned his shirts. He was used to having servants. As a child, he had known a life of riches. But there had been a time between childhood and manhood when he had had only himself to see to his needs, when he had known far too intimately the twisting ache of an empty belly, the worry and fear over where the next meal was coming from, or if there would even be a next meal.

Was it that kinship, that empathy, that motivated his largesse?

The possibility appalled him. He chose to tell himself otherwise, that it was because Mrs. Gormley's stitchery was unsurpassed.

He glanced at her then, noted the thimble on her finger. The sight of it summoned a recollection of Beth sitting on the stone bench in the back garden, her head bowed, her needle flashing. She had made a sad hash of her embroidery, but with tenacious determination she had picked out the stitches and put them in again and again.

He thought of walking with her on the road, and their meeting in Burndale's back garden. The taste of her skin. The catch of her breath when he kissed her wrist. It was more than attraction. He enjoyed her company, her wit, her intelligence. He valued the way she cared for his daughter. He valued *her*. A disconcerting realization.

"Mr. Fairfax!" Mrs. Gormley's tone, laced with surprise, pricked the bubble of his imaginings. "Oh, I'm sorry . . . I never meant . . . it's just that I have never seen you smile like that—" She broke off, looked away, clearly abashed by her presumption.

He shook his head, uncomfortable at being caught out in his private musings.

"No, I do not suppose you have." He paused, tucked the packet of shirts beneath his arm. "I will be sending young Thomas home to do the heavy chores on Saturday," he said, and Mrs. Gormley's head jerked up, her expression brightening.

"I have little in the way of heavy chores, but my heart gladdens at the thought of seeing my son."

Her words brought a twinge of pain. His mother's heart had never gladdened at the sight of him. Instinctively, his fingers traced the small white scar at the corner of his mouth, and then he noted his action and dropped his hand to his side.

Impatient with himself, he drummed his fingers on his thigh and looked away, noting the broken chair tied together with twine, and the long crack that snaked down the wall. He brought his gaze back to the widow.

"I have been weighing the need for new aprons for the upstairs maids," he said. "If you would be so kind as to cipher the cost and provide me with a list of requisite materials, I will have what you require delivered from Northallerton"—Mrs. Gormley shook her head, but Griffin cut off any protest—"within a fortnight."

In a rare and unusual action, she raised her gaze to meet his own dead-on.

"Within a fortnight, Mrs. Gormley," he repeated softly.

She hesitated a moment longer. "Yes, sir. Thank you, sir." And with that, her gaze slid away.

Taking his leave, Griffin stepped out the door and strode down the street.

The main thoroughfare of Burndale boasted a tavern with three rooms above for weary travelers, and a small assortment of shops, including the draper, the baker, the chandler. Northallerton was larger by far, but Griffin liked to visit the local vendors, not from generosity, but perversity.

They always watched him as though they expected him to sprout horns and cloven hooves and a forked tail.

He found it mildly amusing that none dared confront

him directly with their suspicions and dire imaginings.
Of course, they all knew of his actions, knew he had
killed his wife. He was certain that they were horrified
by that, but it was the deeds they knew nothing of that
were darker still.

He crossed the road toward the chandler's, only to
draw up short as a man emerged from the tavern, the
sun hitting him full in the face, leaving no doubt as to
his identity.

Richard Parsons saw him immediately—they were the
only two people in the roadway—and raised a hand in
greeting. In his other hand, he held what appeared to
be a folded handkerchief, marred by a dark reddish
brown stain. Furtively, he shoved it in his pocket and
swaggered forward.

"Ho, Griffin!" he called.

Griffin waited, forcing himself to maintain a relaxed
posture.

What the bloody hell was Parsons doing in the village?

Bad enough to know he was slinking about in Northallerton, but to have him here in Burndale, virtually on
Griffin's front drive, was . . . dangerous. The man knew
too much, had stories to share that Griffin had no desire
for others to hear. And Parsons knew it.

Drawing near, Richard shot his cuffs and straightened
his shoulders. His fingers strayed to the buttons of his
white waistcoat, fumbling across the empty front. Empty
because his watch and chain were not there.

Griffin raised his gaze to Richard's face and caught
his unguarded expression of concern. Where was the
watch? Lost? Sold off? He could not recall ever seeing
Richard Parsons without his pocket watch. Richard and
Griffin had each obtained one in Stepney more than a
decade past; they were common enough there, a fa-
vorite among sailors who put in to port.

Though Griffin's watch no longer told the time, he
wore it still. Perversity, or habit.

Clearing his throat, Richard dropped his hands to his sides, curled the fingers into fists, only to uncurl them an instant later. He cast a glance at the package Griffin carried.

"I've a tear here"—he indicated the place, a worn patch on his sleeve near the elbow—"small, but bothersome. I have need of a seamstress. Can you offer a recommendation, dear boy?"

Griffin weighed Mrs. Gormley's monetary need against the certainty that sending Richard Parsons through her door would not be an act of kindness. Not for her. Not for himself.

"I'm afraid not," he said, silently vowing that Mrs. Gormley would spend the next weeks sewing new aprons for the upstairs *and* downstairs maids of Wickham. That should be enough to see to her needs for months.

Richard's brows rose, but he made no effort to force the matter.

"What do you here, Richard?" Griffin asked, tired of the game.

"Ah, a bit of this and a bit of that."

"A bit of *what*?" Griffin prodded. "Here? In this tiny village?"

Purposefully misunderstanding Griffin's remark, Richard grimaced and blew a snort of air down his nose.

"Yes, yes. 'Tis a pedestrian place, to be sure," he said, then paused as a wagon approached and the sound of hooves and rolling wheels grew loud, only to fade as it rolled on. "Little in the way of entertainment. Even less in the way of business. But I have a concern here of an entirely different nature."

"And what concern might that be?"

"An affair of the heart?" Richard ventured, his tone ironic.

"That I doubt," Griffin mused. "Unless the heart is one you wish to rip, still beating, from a bloodied, carved breast."

Richard cleared his throat, a choked sound, and slapped his open palm to his chest. "You wound me, dear boy."

Griffin narrowed his gaze. "Then the heart you speak of must be solid gold encrusted with jewels, a heady lure for any thief. Offhand, I cannot call to mind such a treasure." He drummed his fingers on the side of his thigh, and continued, darkly soft. "Richard, there is no one hereabouts worth robbing . . . save me. And I warn you against that."

"For shame, dear boy." Richard reared back. "Do you think so low of me, then, that I would stoop to thieving from a friend?"

"We have both sunk that low at times. And lower," Griffin replied, blunt.

"Aye, well, those were hard times that called for hard measures. We are different men now, are we not?" Richard waited a heartbeat, and then laughed, an ugly, mocking sound. "Or perhaps we are exactly what we have always been, eh, dear boy? Exactly the villains we have always been."

"How much will you take to leave?" Griffin wanted Richard gone. Gone with his secrets and his vile knowledge of their ugly shared past.

He wanted what paltry peace he could find in the daylight, for the nights offered no serenity, haunted as they were by guilt and ghosts.

"Leave, dear boy? I would not think of it." Richard's expression hardened. "There are fine, sweet pickings here. Fine, sweet pickings, indeed. But you already know that, don't you, dear boy? You already know."

Chapter Fourteen

Burndale, Yorkshire, October 4, 1828

Beth stood in the large schoolroom, reading lines of dictation and waiting as the girls wrote the words in their copybooks. The room housed three groups of students and their teachers. At the far end, Miss Doyle read aloud a rather ridiculous poem in her high, girlish voice, the sound carrying above the general din of the schoolroom.

At the opposite end, near the door, Mademoiselle Martine drilled her class on French verbs. The ever-present cacophony seemed amplified today, loud and distorted, coming at Beth from all sides.

Bending her head to the book she held, she read aloud in a modulated tone another line of dictation, her thoughts jumping about in distraction.

Over the past two weeks, she had seen little of Mr. Fairfax. Once or twice, she spotted him from a distance, and her heart danced and sped. She told herself she was foolish, for there was no good place for her fascination with him to lead.

His relationship with his daughter captivated her. He was so handsome he stole her breath. He was so interesting that she found herself thinking of every word they had exchanged, over and over. He was strong and intelligent, and he had shown her only kindness.

And he might well be the person who stalked her from the shadows and watched her in the night.

Did she truly believe that? No. But she would be a fool to discount the possibility.

In truth, she knew nothing about him save that he named himself a villain, and that he was conveniently present at Burndale Academy each time she felt she was being watched.

Since the morning she had met him in the corridor, the morning after someone had snuck into her chamber, she had become careful and wary, taking her evening walks only within sight of the school. But she took every care to let no one see her distraction, to present only a calm and sanguine demeanor, to teach her lessons to the best of her capacity, to draw no attention to herself.

She could not chase the memories of Miss Percy's overheard words from her thoughts, the implication that she would be let go for her lack of skill and her emotional behavior.

A letter had come from her mother, and though she tried to put a cheerful turn to her words, Beth could read the truth in what she did not say. The situation at home had only grown more dire. There was little money, little food, little coal. And there was no improvement in her father's health.

Losing her employment at Burndale Academy was out of the question.

Glancing up at the girls, then down at the book, Beth finished reading another sentence of the dictation and waited while they labored over their letters. She opened her mouth to resume, only to stop as rapid footsteps echoed from behind. Turning, she found the maid, Alice, approaching.

"I am to fetch you, miss," she said, each word running

rapidly one into the next. "Miss Percy said you are to come at once."

Alice's words delivered a brutal blow to Beth's fragile control.

Glancing about, she saw that the girls watched her with wide eyes. Not once had she seen Alice in the school-room prior to this day, and since coming to Burndale, Beth had witnessed no other teacher called away from her duties in such a manner. The peculiarity of the sum-mons left her distinctly uneasy.

The headmistress had come to watch Beth teach sev-eral times in the past fortnight, leaving after a few silent moments of observation. Twice, she had brought two men with her, one very old and one of middle years, and their observation of her teaching methods had brought expressions of mild dismay to their faces.

An inauspicious outcome.

Beth knew her methods varied from the other teach-ers', and she had wondered if Miss Percy's benign ex-pression hid approval or dissatisfaction.

Now the headmistress had summoned her, mid-lesson, an unheard of and unpromising circumstance.

The time had come. Miss Percy meant to dismiss her. A cold knot of dread choked her, and she stared at Alice in mute dismay, her pulse leaping and bounding, her heart pounding in her chest.

She could not bear to fail. She could not *afford* to fail. Her family depended upon her income for the meanest necessities: food, shelter, coal.

"Lucy," Beth said, grateful that the tenor of her words gave no indication of the tumult of her emotions. "Please continue reading, here"—she showed the girl the place in the book, then turned to the others—"and the rest of you continue to write out the passage. Mark that you use a fair hand. Upon my return, I shall evalu-ate your work for both penmanship and spelling."

She remained only long enough to ascertain that her

pupils did as she bade, and then she turned and followed Alice toward the door of the large classroom.

Delving deep for her reserves of composure, Beth willed her racing pulse to slow. Now was a poor time for this dark, oily swell of panic to surge.

Why, oh why, must it come now? Save that one morning when Griffin Fairfax had held her hand over his heart and helped her rein in her dismay, she had been so very adept at controlling her panic since coming here.

Feeling as though the eyes of both pupils and teachers were upon her, Beth clasped her hands together to still their shaking.

No, she must not allow this, must not allow her nervous imaginings to feed the dread growing in her breast. She knew where this would lead. Having spent her life subject to the horror of her attacks of dismay—the wash of clammy fear, the numbing thud of her heart—she could not mistake the signs now of the terrible and overwhelming tide.

She followed Alice, feeling as though she traversed the distance to a gallows.

Beth's heart gave a hard thud.

She glanced to the right and found Miss Doyle peering at her over the top of a book, and the group of girls that surrounded her casting sidelong glances and whispering to each other.

"This way, miss," Alice said when Beth stepped through the door and turned right. Sending Beth a quizzical look, Alice walked left.

"Yes, of course," Beth murmured, the surge of unease growing and pulling at her. She could not control it.

She *must* control it.

"Miss Percy said you must wait for her in her office. She will be with you shortly." Alice paused and frowned, peering at Beth closely. "I'll leave you now, miss. You know the way."

With that, Alice went off in the opposite direction, leaving Beth alone in the dim hallway.

For a moment, she simply sagged against the wall, angry and frustrated that it had come to this, that her will and control had failed her so miserably. With a sigh, she rallied, forced herself to walk the long corridor, and in her thoughts she began to prepare her arguments, her defenses.

Perhaps the headmistress could be swayed.

Reaching her destination, she found the door open, the room empty. Mindful of Alice's words, Beth stepped inside to await the headmistress's arrival.

Blowing out sharp little huffs of air, she turned a slow circle, cataloguing the contents of the room in an effort to maintain her control over her emotions. There was the mullioned window, the heavy draperies, the little wooden desk with its scrolled legs. Two straight chairs before the desk and one behind. A room designed for work rather than lounging comfort.

She stared at the top of Miss Percy's desk. A tidy desk, with not a single speck of dust to mar the surface.

Resting her palm flat against the base of her throat, Beth slid down onto the seat of a hard-backed chair. She perched there for a moment, panic lurking like a scavenger at the edge of her control. Nausea churned in her belly.

Well aware that her emotion far exceeded what was appropriate for the circumstance, she was nonetheless caught in its violent thrall. As she had been caught so many times over the years.

A sound carried from the hallway, and Beth twisted to look behind her through the entry. Beyond the open portal, the hallway was poorly lit, a gray and dim domain. Again came the scrape of a boot along the tile, and a shadow fell across the floor.

Pushing against the narrow wooden arms of the chair, she surged to her feet, rushed to the door.

Mr. Waters, the handyman, stood some ten feet away, hammer in hand. On the floor lay the splintered re-

mains of a doorjamb, and beside them, a fresh cut piece
of wood.

Hammer poised mid-strike, he turned his head to
look at her, and she realized she must have made some
sound.

"Miss," he said, and bobbed his head.

"Good afternoon, Mr. Waters." Beth looked past him
down the dim corridor. For an instant, she wondered if
it could have been he who followed her that morning
two weeks past, who lurked in the garden and on the
road. Then she cast aside such ponderings, for what
reason had she to think it?

Turning to his work, he set a nail and brought the
hammer down in a sharp blow. The sound made Beth
jump.

Mumbling to himself, he scratched his head, looked
about him, then ambled off.

Beth backed into the office, paced across the rug to
one wall, then the other and back again, keeping her
eye on the open door and her ears attuned for Miss
Percy's footsteps. Midway through her third mad dash
across the small room, the door swung shut with a solid
bang.

She froze. A half turn and she faced the door once
more. The closed door.

Panic swelled, and Beth looked about sharply. She
stood, trembling, her arms wrapped about herself, mortified and horrified that she had allowed her emotions
to sink her to this place, to carry her so deep into the pit
of her attack of dismay that she felt as though she might
not claw her way free. It was like a murky bog, sucking
her under, filling her mouth and her throat and her
lungs until she could barely breathe.

The walls grew dark and darker still, pressing in upon
her until they seemed to crush the very breath from her
chest.

No! She could not bear to be closed in.

The tiny box. She felt as though she were trapped in the tiny box of her nightmares, pushing and pushing at the lid, but it held fast, refusing to budge.

She looked about, frantic, seeing not the headmistress's office, but only cloying gray fog. Unable to trust her senses, to trust herself to know what was truth, she wrapped her arms about herself and fought the thick tide of her panic.

She was *not* back there. She was *not.*

Frowning, she dropped her hands, clenched her fists tight at her sides, and willed herself to see Miss Percy's desk, her chairs, and not the wooden box from her memories.

On jellylike limbs she crossed to the door, yanked on the handle. With a creak, it swung open. The hallway was empty, but she could swear she heard the rapid retreat of booted feet.

Had someone followed her, watched her, waited for Mr. Waters to leave? Slammed the door? To what purpose? What end?

Who could know that it would distress her so?

Extending her arm, she pressed the flat of her hand to the wall, bowed her head, and struggled to master herself. This would not do. She knew it would not do. If Miss Percy came upon her like this, in a frenzy of nerves and emotion, she *would* have cause to dismiss her.

Dear heaven, she knew better than to allow herself such delusions.

Turning, Beth walked at a sedate pace—oh, the effort she put into holding herself back—to the mullioned window that overlooked the front drive. A band of iron closed about her ribs, squeezing tight. Her hands shook. Beads of sweat gathered on her upper lip. She laid her trembling palm flat against the cool wall and stared out at the late afternoon sky, a clear, blue canvas with only a single wispy cloud far, far in the distance.

Distance. Wide open space. Relief touched her, cool and sweet.

There. That was better. She could breathe a little now. She could breathe. The sky was vast. Vast and endless and open.

There was no reason for her to feel distress. So she told herself over and over.

No one followed her.

No one watched her.

And she must believe that the headmistress had not summoned her to dismiss her. Perhaps she merely wished to discuss a particular pupil, or some aspect of the lessons.

Dragging a handkerchief from her sleeve, Beth patted her lip, her brow, then tucked the cloth away once more.

In the next instant she heard them coming, footsteps and voices, Miss Percy and a man.

". . . to dinner . . ." came a low, masculine murmur. Beth thought the voice belonged to Mr. Fairfax. A strange flutter echoed through her veins, a leap of her pulse that had nothing to do with her fears and dismay. Her emotions tangled one with the next in a twisted knot until she thought it would take a patient hand indeed to pick the strands apart.

"I am not certain that it is appropriate," Miss Percy remarked, her crisp tone carrying along the hallway into the room.

"Likely not, but the devil take that. I want her there, and so I will have her. Isobel will like it, and she is my sole concern."

"I, too, have concern for Isobel, but I must also exercise responsibility for Miss Canham."

They were speaking of *her*, Beth realized with a jolt.

"Then I must point out that Miss Canham, as Isobel's teacher, is of the same ilk as her governess. And I sat across the table from Isobel's last governess every night for two bitter months. Does that moderate your concerns?"

"It—" Miss Percy stopped abruptly in the doorway as she caught sight of Beth standing by the window.

Beth attempted a smile. Her face felt stiff, like starched linen. From Miss Percy's frown, she gathered that she might look as sickly as she felt.

"Ah, Miss Canham, you are here," Miss Percy said. "How fortuitous that I also happened upon Mr. Fairfax in the hallway."

Beth's gaze snapped to Mr. Fairfax, who stood just behind Miss Percy.

Their gazes met across the room, locked, and Beth thought that Mr. Fairfax's dark eyes missed nothing, not the sheen of sweat on her lip or the way her palm pressed hard against the wall by the window or the shudders that racked her frame though she wished them away.

He was intense, unsmiling, his attention focused wholly on her.

In some vague part of her thoughts, Beth recognized the charged tension in the small room. An awkward triangle they made, Miss Percy and Mr. Fairfax and Beth.

She ought to drag her gaze away. Ought to speak, to fill the void of silence. But she did nothing. Only stared at him, the hard, captivating beauty of him, and wondered again if perhaps she was going mad.

After a long moment, Miss Percy stepped deeper into the room. Mr. Fairfax followed. Beth studied the two of them, her back rigid, her hands trembling, her belly twisting and writhing like a nest of snakes.

Her gaze flicked to the open door, then to Miss Percy, who had turned and reached for the handle. Beth's throat grew tight. She could not bear it if they closed the door.

Mr. Fairfax continued to watch her, his expression bland, his dark eyes shadowed.

"I find the air a bit stuffy, Miss Percy," he said, his gaze never leaving Beth's. "Would it trouble you to leave the door open?"

There was only silence for a heartbeat, and another.

"Not at all," came Miss Percy's delayed reply. Walking briskly, she rounded her desk and sat.

Beth shifted her stance, clasping her hands tight together behind her back, uncertain if she should be grateful or wary.

Mr. Fairfax seemed to see to the heart of her. Had he requested that the door be left open for her comfort, or for his own? Had he seen her fear, somehow divined that she felt uneasy in this small, closed space?

Uneasy. She almost laughed. Such a gift for understatement.

Not for the first time, Beth had the thought that she shared some odd affinity with him, that he somehow knew her secrets, her passions, her fears.

A far from reassuring notion.

Miss Percy's voice poked through her reverie. Realizing that she had been invited to sit, Beth did just that, unclasping her hands as she perched once more on the edge of the hard-backed chair.

". . . so you see, Mr. Fairfax and I both feel that Isobel would benefit from your presence. You seem a calming balm to her, and it can only be for the good."

Beth blinked, started, the words coming down a long tunnel to her, and she realized she had missed the beginning of Miss Percy's explanation, and only heard the tail end. The headmistress was watching her with a marked frown as she spoke, and Beth thought it best that she not request a repetition. Instead, she tried to use the bits she *had* heard to fashion the whole. A puzzle.

But one thing seemed clear. She had been granted a reprieve. She was not being dismissed. In fact, this meeting had nothing at all to do with her classroom skill.

"I see," she said, grateful that her voice, at least, sounded calm. "I would be pleased to be of assistance. When . . . ?"

There. That should garner her a clue. Perhaps Miss

Percy would say enough in reply that Beth could understand what it was they had asked of her.

"Isobel comes to dinner once each week." Mr. Fairfax spoke from his place behind Beth's chair. She swiveled to look at him and found him positioned in the corner, in the shadow where the light coming through the window did not reach. "At least, that is the preference I have. The unfortunate truth is, there are times she simply refuses to come."

The memory of the day of her arrival at Burndale Academy tugged at Beth, the recollection of Alice's words. *She is not ready, sir . . . She will not come!*

"And my role?" Beth asked, curious now, curious enough that the racing of her pulse slowed a little.

Focus on the riddle, not the fear.

Yes, there, her panic snuffed a little more, and she knew now that she would come through this episode without disgracing herself. Relief was sweet and clear as water from a spring.

"Isobel appears to feel some affinity for you," Miss Percy said. "Mr. Fairfax is of the opinion that your presence at the weekly dinner would both encourage Isobel to attend and ensure her enjoyment of the experience."

Startled, Beth looked back and forth between the two, an action that necessitated her twisting about at the waist, given their opposing locations in the room. With a breathy sigh, she tapped her fingertips on the spindly arm of the chair.

The corner of Mr. Fairfax's mouth twitched, and he stepped forward to take the seat on her right. So close. Too close. She could smell the faint scent of spice, and of *him*, so enticing.

Despite the turmoil that tugged at her, she noticed that and other things about him. The simple white stock tied at his throat. The wind-tousled fall of his hair. If her preoccupation with him, despite the panic that yet threatened to swell, was not proof that she was fit for Bedlam, then she could not imagine what *would* be.

She looked away, focusing her attention on Miss Percy.

"So you wish me to accompany Isobel to dinner once each week?" She found the proposition unsettling, not for the dinner itself or the role of companion to the child, but rather for the prospect of sitting at a table with Griffin Fairfax.

Oh, she could well imagine it, the two of them, cozy over dinner, with the silent child between them.

"If you do not find the inconvenience too great, it is truly the best solution for the child," Miss Percy said. "She has formed an attachment to you. It is most unusual. She has never behaved so before."

Because she has never before encountered a soul matched to her own, strange and fey and burdened with all manner of private terrors, Beth thought, but she said nothing, merely bowed her head and nodded her understanding as Miss Percy turned to Mr. Fairfax and discussed the arrangement for his carriage to come for Beth and Isobel on Thursday next, a week hence.

A pang of regret echoed inside her that it would be the closed carriage that fetched her and not the open curricle that flew along the road, letting the wind sting her eyes and tear her hair free of its pins. She had liked the curricle very much, the freedom of it. Like flying.

The idea of the closed carriage was far less appealing, especially in her present state of fatigue and heightened distress. At this moment, she found the prospect of such a small space infinitely ghastly.

As though he read her thoughts, Mr. Fairfax said, "If the weather is fine, I shall come myself with the curricle. Isobel prefers it, and she takes not much space. I suspect we can wedge her between us."

Raising her eyes, Beth found him watching her, his frame relaxed on the chair beside her, his gaze unreadable.

A shaft of sunlight sliced across him, painting him in bronze and gilt, the contrast playing over his hard features like a gift. In this light, his eyes were not so very dark, the whisper of green more apparent.

His thick lashes swept down, then up. In his gaze she read shrewd awareness, a knowing understanding that left her feeling as though he stripped her secrets bare.

The way he looked at her was . . . *unsettling*. Her pulse fluttered, then raced, as it had earlier in her panic. Only now, both the sensation and its cause were different. A prickling awareness made her mouth go dry and her limbs restless. Her gaze dropped to his lips, hard, well formed.

Oh, she was a regular pendulum, swinging to and fro between panic and . . . *what*? Apprehension? Anxiety?

No . . . *attraction*, hot and sharp.

Tension knotted her shoulders, and Beth was grateful when a knocking at the door drew their attention.

Alice. A distraction. Oh, thank heaven.

A glance at Mr. Fairfax showed he had leaned back in his chair, behind the beam of light. The shift in his position left his face in shadow, veiling his expression from her sight.

"Excuse me, Miss Percy," Alice said. "The stonemason is here to speak with you about the wall."

Beth knew the part of the wall she spoke of, near the gate of the back garden. There was a crumbling section that was both unsightly and a danger. Miss Percy rose, excused herself, and left the room.

Left her alone. With Griffin Fairfax.

Chapter Fifteen

Sitting rigid in her seat, Beth stared at her lap for a long moment. The silence was unnerving. She slanted a glance at Mr. Fairfax, caught his eye for an instant, then dropped her gaze to her lap once more.

He had haunted her these past weeks, haunted her secret dreams that surfaced in the midnight hour, and now he tormented her in the full light of day. Not by any particular action, but by his mere presence, the way he looked at her, the subtle scent of him, the way he moved. He had risen as Miss Percy rose, and now stood tall and solid, broad of shoulder and narrow of hip, filling the space.

Just the two of them in the tiny room.

Beth said, "I had best return to the schoolroom."

"Wait," he ordered, his voice resonant and low.

She froze in her seat, her head falling back to watch him as he moved to stand above her. His gaze held her pinned, enthralled. She felt a sharp click of connection, like a key in a lock.

There was yet some small physical distance between them, but it was no barrier. The look of him, unsmiling, mysterious and handsome and vaguely frightening, sent shivers through her.

"What is it you fear, Miss Canham?" he asked, low voiced.

He knew. He had seen what she hid, perhaps today or in one of their encounters in days past, something that had revealed her secrets. Her heart banged against her ribs, and she stared at him in mute dismay.

She would not say. She could not.

She folded her hands in her lap, closing one tight about the other so their shaking would not betray her.

With an oath that was soft and slurred—she heard only the tone but not the word—he jerked away from her. In three strides he closed the distance to the door and pulled the portal shut with a firm tug.

Feeling trapped, Beth half rose, appalled.

"Sit. Please." His voice was little more than a whisper. It did not need to be more. She sat, her heart thudding ever harder, a dull, steady rhythm, too fast for comfort.

"Tell me, Miss Canham. Tell me your greatest fear. Closed, tight places? The dark?"

She was frozen in place, unable to follow the shift in his mood. Where was the tug of amusement that he often showed at the corner of his mouth? Where was the gentleness she had witnessed in the garden when he had opened his hand to free the wasp, unharmed?

He was not that man now. He was hard and implacable and chillingly calm.

Dear heaven, she was caught in his grasp as surely as that wasp had been, but she doubted in this moment that she would escape unscathed.

"I will scream," she whispered, her voice hoarse and cracked.

Of course, she would not. In truth, he had done nothing more than close the door. What had she to scream about, other than her myriad terrors? And those she should have long ago learned to bottle in the depths of her soul.

"Then scream." He shot her a sardonic look and strode

to the window to jerk the heavy draperies closed, blocking out the sun, blocking out the light, leaving the room small and closed and dark. "But I think you will not."

In that instant, she hated him. Hated him for the meanness that made him choose to torment her so.

"Yes," he said, his gaze caressing her face. And he smiled ironically. "Be angry. Fill yourself with fury. Rage will chase away the dread."

She stared at him. He sounded so certain, as though he *knew*.

"Tell me your greatest fear." He spoke each word with precise, sharp diction. There was no question that it was an order. "Tell me."

"I fear—" What was she thinking? To tell him all? Nay, that was sheer folly.

With a strangled gasp, she pushed herself up from her seat, but he was faster than she, moving on limbs stable and sure while hers were weak and trembling. In a heartbeat, he crossed the distance between his place at the window and her seat.

Strong, blunt flingers closed around the arms of her chair, and he leaned his weight down, caging her with the solid lines and planes of his body. He bent closer, until she could see each dark, curling lash, and the fine white lines that converged to form the scar at the side of his mouth.

Not one scar. A network of little lines, like a star. Some darker, some fainter.

This near to him, she could see that now, while before she had seen only the deepest lines that, from a distance, appeared as a single white mark.

Half standing, half sitting within the steely circle of his arms and his chest where he bent over her, she hovered, frozen. A deep breath, and the tips of her breasts brushed his chest, sending a sharp jolt to her senses.

Trapped. She was trapped. By his physical presence, and by her own volatile emotions.

"Tell me," he whispered.

Her heart pumped so hard and fast that she was sick with it, dizzy from it, and the walls were so close, the light so dim. She hated it. Hated the closed space, the dark. The fear.

"I fear small spaces. I fear the dark." Piteous words that made her as angry as she was afraid. She let them fall free, tumbling through the silence where the only sound was the harsh rasp of her breath, and his.

She prayed those words—an admission that cost her much—would make him step back, step away, let her free. She had given him what he asked for. Nay, what he demanded.

The warmth of his breath fanned her cheek. Her hands tightened round the arms of the chair, holding her up. She dared not sit once more but he—with his hands next to hers, bearing his weight—prevented her from fully rising. And so she hung suspended in the space in between, her thighs burning and screaming in protest.

But to sit once more was to capitulate, to leave herself vulnerable.

Arching a little, she drew back and met his gaze.

In the absence of sunlight, his eyes were night dark, turbulent.

"You fear those things . . . closed places . . . the dark," he rasped. "But here you are in a tight little room with the shadows eating the corners, dim enough that I must be this close to truly see your face, and you are fine. Do you see, Miss Canham? *You are fine.* You have given them voice, your worst fears, but they have no power. You sit here in the midst of them, and in the end, you have survived with no greater consequence than a racing pulse."

"I—" Dear heaven, it was true. He had forced her to speak of her terror, forced her to sit here and face it, and though her heart pounded like the hooves of a runaway beast, her breath scoring her with a sharp pain, she *had* survived it.

As she always survived it.

"And if you were locked in a tiny box, in a space so tight that your shoulders bumped each side, you would not die from it. Your fear has power only if you let it."

In a rush she exhaled, and she was left weak and trembling. She sank down on the chair, no longer able to maintain the odd, crouched position she had held.

Locked in a tiny box with my shoulders bumping each side. Memories tore at her. *How did he know? How could he know?*

"You are intelligent and courageous, Miss Canham, stronger than all your terrors combined. You can master this. You *have* mastered this."

She understood then. He did not know about the box, but he *did* know about unreasoning terror.

His words—little more than a vehement whisper—did make her feel brave, strong. Why? Because she could hear the secret knowledge in him.

Griffin Fairfax was well acquainted with the power of fear.

Dragging in a shaky breath, she wondered how she could think at all, with her emotions so raw and ragged. Comprehension hovered just beyond her reach as she puzzled it out. She was afraid, yes, but where was the mindless panic that had overwhelmed her earlier? The walls were as close as they had ever been, the shadows as frightening, but as Griffin Fairfax loomed over her, his breath ruffling her hair, the strength of his body surrounding her like a cage, she thought that what she feared most was *him*.

Unbidden came the image of his strong fingers closing about the wasp, a trap. As she was trapped by him now. But he had set the insect free, unharmed . . .

She stared at him, at the stubble-darkened plane of his jaw and the hollow of his cheeks, the shadowed depth of his gaze. He overwhelmed her, his presence, his intensity and energy.

Had that been his intent? To give her something even greater to fear?

Or perhaps only something greater to fill her thoughts. Him. *He* filled her thoughts.

"Tell me what you fear now," he whispered, leaning close enough that his nose touched her cheek.

The scent of his skin, his touch, his nearness, they made her limbs feel sensitized, and her lips, and her breasts. Every part of her lit with heat, a liquid glow deep in her belly. She was left quivering with something far more complicated than fear.

A realization, an awakening of sorts.

It was not him she feared most, but *herself*. Her reaction to him. To Griffin Fairfax. Even in the wretchedness of her distress she found him beautiful. Alluring. Fascinating.

She thought that if he touched her, drew her close, wrapped her in the shelter of his embrace, she would not be afraid.

He was warm and hard and solid.

Dear heaven, what madness was this?

He moved his head so he drew his nose down, along her cheek, her jaw, the side of her neck. The sound of his soft inhalation shimmered through her, and the even softer sigh of his appreciation.

Emotion buffeted her, a storm of confusion and dismay. The room had not changed. It was still small and close and gloomy. But she could not see that now.

She saw only him, felt only him.

"Tell me," he whispered again, drawing back so his gaze snared hers. There was hunger there, such hunger, feral and stark. The strength of it touched her, lured her.

"You. I fear you." A half-truth. She feared the frightening urge to turn her face to his, to breathe the scent of his

body as he breathed hers, to touch her tongue to his skin
and know the taste of him.

"Then you are a wise woman." A dark whisper, his
words made her shiver.

She had no wish to be wise at this moment. She
wanted to be reckless, wanton, to press her open mouth
to the side of his neck and lick his skin, to sink her teeth
into the swell of muscle where his shoulder began.

Why? *Why* did she feel this?

Arrow-sharp yearning speared her, straight down the
middle to her most private place, between her thighs.
She reeled with the shock of it, from excitement and
mortification and a slew of emotions mixing together in
a heady brew.

Kiss me.

The madness of her thoughts made her gasp. She
wanted this, wanted him, his mouth pressed to hers,
here, in the dim, small room, where there was nowhere
to hide but in the feel of him, the taste of him.

He would be her anchor.

A sound that was barely a sound escaped his lips. He
closed his fingers round her upper arms and dragged
her to her feet, then hard against him. Genuine alarm
touched her, mingled with pounding anticipation.

Such a formidable thing, attraction.

He moved, and she had little choice but to move with
him, a step backward, and another and another until
the cold wall was at her back and the hard length of him
at her front.

His weight pinned her, burning heat.

Breathless, panting, she absorbed the sensation, con-
flicted. Her heart thudded and jerked.

With a groan, he turned them both, so it was *his* back
against the wall and she was pressed full against his
front, pinning him, holding him, her weight on his.

She was free. Free to want. Free to choose. Free to flee.

For an instant, nothing held her but her own desire.

Then the flat of his palm eased down to the small of her back, while the other hand cupped her chin, his thumb dancing over her lower lip. He did it again, a stroke of his thumb, dragging the soft flesh, and she felt as though every part of her tingled and hummed.

Her legs felt weak, shaky, and as he stroked her lip a third time, dipping the tip of his thumb *into* her mouth to touch her tongue, her knees gave way altogether until she was held up only by the corded strength of his arm at her back.

Solid, contoured, he felt like a wall of pliable stone layered in coat and shirt and breeches. The clothing did nothing to hide the shape of him, the feel of him. She was full against him, thigh to thigh, belly to belly.

The sensation was foreign and heady and wild.

She had the shocking, tempting urge to run her hands over him, over the solid muscle that ridged his chest, and lower, around to the small of his back, to the tight swell of his buttocks. To stroke him. To know the impression of him.

The heat of his body passed through the layers of cloth between them, and the scent of his skin surrounded her, luscious, spice and man, sending a thrumming urgency coursing through her.

His gaze dropped to her mouth.

Hunger roared to life inside her, stronger, brighter, a burrowing need that left her reckless and aching. The suddenness and power of it nearly undid her.

She was mad with it. Mad with the need to press closer still, to wind her hands round his neck and pull his mouth down until she could taste him at last.

At last. At last. She had dreamed of him, woken restless and confused more than one night with her sheets tangled about her limbs. She had dreamed of the way he had kissed her wrist, the memory so real, so powerfully stimulating.

She had nurtured this secret yearning all along. She realized that now.

Some part of her had been waiting for his kiss since first they met, since he had smiled at her and teased her about her indecision that first day on the crossroad before the church.

"Beth," he rasped, and then he dipped his head and took her mouth, took the kiss, his lips solid and insistent against her own, his tongue pushing into her, hot and wet and so luscious that she moaned at the pleasure of it.

Dark, rich pleasure.

She had not imagined . . . she could never have imagined . . .

He bit her lower lip, gentle and rough at once, exactly the way he had nipped at her thumb. The sensation was wonderful. Heady. Thrilling. Urgent shards of need, ardent and primitive, radiated to her belly. She made a soft sound, capitulation, lust, and he shifted his mouth on hers to kiss her deeper still.

A sweet burning turned her limbs weak. She could not think, could not breathe, and she could not find the will to care. She only let herself *feel*, the rough stroke of his tongue. The sharp nip of his teeth. The ache in the tips of her breasts where they were pushed tight against him, so sensitive. She rocked her hips forward, wild with the urge to undulate, to sway.

The *wanting* of him was a living, writhing thing, powerful, lush. A drowning of sorts. A madness in her blood, both alarming and pleasing.

Wriggling in his embrace, she gave in to temptation, rubbed her hips against his, lured and fascinated by the hard round ridge that prodded her. *Him.* So different than her. She did it again, shifting from side to side, reveling in his sharp intake of breath and the pounding of his heart against her own.

He liked that.

Fascinated, she had the thought to touch him, to

touch *this*, the evidence of his need, and she slid her hand along the curved bone of his hip to the flatness of his belly, and lower.

"Bloody hell," he rasped.

Steely fingers closed about her wrist, and his warm lips left hers. She could feel his body straining, taut as a bow-string, and then he loosed her wrist and put his hands at her waist, shifting her from him just a little.

In the dim light, she saw him close his eyes, lower his head, his breathing ragged. His elbows were locked as he kept his hands at her waist, holding her from him.

Beth watched him, confused and dismayed, bereft at the loss of his heat and the feel of his mouth on her own. Her entire body thrummed with the need to touch him, stroke him, rub herself against him like a cat.

With a tentative touch, she reached out and caressed the long, silky strands of his hair, following them along the back of his bowed head to where they curled at his collar.

His shoulders tensed. An instant later his lashes lifted and his head came up. She thought he would kiss her again.

She prayed he would kiss her again.

Instead, he eased to the side, away from her.

Befuddled, she stared at him, and then she understood. He did not wish to kiss her anymore, to pet her, to hold her. There was now a bitter tinge to his expression, a coldness that chilled her. For an instant, she felt ashamed, somehow lacking.

Then his gaze met hers and in it she read all the self-recrimination, the guiltiness, the remorse.

He believed the lack was *his*.

"Mr. Fairfax—" she began, but his low huff of self-mocking laughter stopped her.

"Griffin," he said. "After what we have shared, Beth"— he said her name slow and sultry, as though savoring the flavor of it on his tongue—"you must call me Griffin."

She stared at him. He had kissed her and she had kissed him, twined her tongue with his, felt the hard proof of his desire press against her belly. And she felt shy to use his given name.

Now, *there* was another peculiarity to add to her already lengthy list.

Confusion buffeted her, and she came to a sudden sharp awareness of where she was and what she had done.

She had kissed him. *Here*, in Miss Percy's study, where any might happen upon them.

What madness had caught hold of her?

He had touched her, pressed his mouth to hers, and she had been lost. Lost in sensation. Lost in the feel of him and the taste of him. Everything else had faded from her thoughts.

With folded arms, she stood, her thoughts in turmoil, her face half turned from him, her gaze flitting from him to the drawn curtains to the door, and back again. For once, the confined space was not her greatest concern, but rather the knowledge that she had kissed Griffin Fairfax, and that even now, faced with the realization of what she had done, and where she had done it, she wanted to do it again.

In the aftermath of the most stirring moments of her life, she knew not what to say, what to do.

Because she wanted to step back in time, step back to the moments past, when he had held her and drawn such passion and sensation from deep within her.

All her life, the most powerful emotion she had known was fear. In essence, her fear had controlled her.

But with Griffin she had discovered something more powerful.

Desire. Ardor. Delight. A fervor so strong, she shook with it still.

"Why did you do this?" she asked, and she was very

aware of the sound of her voice, hearing the desperate cadence as though through a muffling fog.

His chest expanded on a slow, deep inhalation.

"Shall I tell you pretty words?" he asked. "Compare your hair to moonbeams and your eyes to the sky? Never trust a man who whispers such pretties as his hand rucks up your skirt and his cock stands to attention."

The crudeness of his words made her gasp.

He stroked her cheek, such a gentle touch. "Do not look at me so, sweet Beth. I warned you that I am a villain."

She blinked, unsure of how to reply. He *had* warned her.

Yet even his coarse words seemed somehow laced with caring.

He made a low sound. Frustration. With her? She glanced at him, caught his frown.

No, with himself.

"I had no right." His tone was tight, clipped. "And yet, I could not resist."

She thought he might say more.

Instead, he turned to the door and had it open in a trice.

"What do *you* fear, Griffin?" she asked, certain that he did, that he feared something terrible and grave. That he had offered such crude advice as a means to hold her at bay. He had recognized her fear too easily not to have firsthand knowledge of his own. "What shadows and torments gnaw at you in the night? What drives you to despise yourself so?"

He froze in the doorway, the light from the hallway haloing him, a nimbus. The muscles of his back tensed under the impeccably cut cloth of his coat. She thought he would not speak, that he would walk away, leaving her with her kiss-swollen lips and her pounding heart and her dreadful curiosity.

Miss Percy's mantel clock ticked loudly in the quiet.

Finally, he spoke, the words torn from him, his voice as rough as a metal file.

"I feared that I would become exactly the man I am." His admission was so soft she could barely hear it.

From his place in the doorway, he looked back at her. A glance over his shoulder, no more. Enough to let her see the darkness in his soul.

"The truth of it is, Elizabeth . . . *Beth* . . . I have become exactly the monster I feared I could be."

Chapter Sixteen

Night rolled in like a fog, coming early at this time of year. He stood in the corner of the garden, hidden in the growing shadows of dusk. An easy thing to climb the tree and lower himself to the ground inside the wall. He had done it myriad times before, stood in this exact place, watched the bedroom window on the second floor.

There was a chill in the air this evening, a scent that was fresh and clean. Fall was full upon them, and soon, winter.

He liked winter. Liked the snow when it fell. Cold and white.

A crimson splash on white snow.

He liked the look of that, fancied himself an artist.

He thought that maybe he would wait for the first snow. For Elizabeth. *Beth*. She deserved a perfect setting. Pale hair. Porcelain skin. Hot, dark blood spurting over white, white snow.

A surge of excitement raced through him, stimulating, arousing.

Yes, he would wait for the first snow. And in the meantime he would play with her, a cat with a mouse.

His gaze slid to the window on the upper floor. Not

to *her* chamber, but to the larger one that held the little girls. He could see her through the window, overseeing the nightly ritual, a black-clad form with moon-bright hair, moving, gliding. Sometimes she stopped and leaned low. He thought she might be speaking to a child, but from this distance he could not say with certainty.

No matter.

He just liked to watch her. To think of the things they would enjoy together.

Soon. Very soon.

The twilight deepened and the light that shone through the window, a warm glow of candle flame, was rich against the darkening night. She came close and paused by the glass, a silhouette.

He wet his lips, the tip of his tongue sliding to the corner of his mouth. His body thrummed with heat and tension.

With her face close to the glass, she was looking out at the garden. He could see the pale oval of her face.

His breath caught, and a thrill of alarm shot through him.

She was looking *at him.*

Blood pounding, he froze, then inched back, blending with the shadows.

Of course she could not see him now. Not here in the dark garden. So far, she had seen him only when he let her. She thought him a far different man than he was.

Beth. Beth. His sweet, pretty Beth with her innocent face and her valiant heart, braving all manner of terrors. Oh, he knew all about those terrors. Yes, he did. He had known who she was since the second he saw her, heard her name, though she had looked at him many times now without a spark of recognition.

The irony of finding her here, in Burndale, was poetic.

She was his. She had always been his.

He would not take her yet, though the wait was an agony.

But soon. Soon she would see him in the darkness, know him, know his smell and his touch, the rough stroke of his hand, the sharp kiss of his blade.

Her face turned from the window, and he saw a little girl come to her side. Then she drew the thick curtains, shutting him out. Gone from his sight.

Irritation bloomed. He was not done with her yet. He wanted to watch.

His gaze slid away, to another window, dark and empty.

Beth's bedroom window.

She liked to leave her curtains open the night through. A smile twisted his lips. So generous of her to invite him to watch.

He had taken the invitation further still, creeping into her room, touching her comb, her pins, her hairbrush. That had been delicious ecstasy. With infinite care he had untangled several silky strands and wrapped them in a square of cloth. Perfect strands, flax pale and curled.

Beneath her pillow he had found her nightdress. Pressing the garment to his nose, he had inhaled her scent, stood there for a moment wrapped in the pleasure of it. With care, he had folded the nightdress once more and placed it exactly where he had found it.

Beth liked things neat and tidy. She liked order. It made him want to laugh. Did she think there was safety in her precious neatness and organization? That by ordering her life she could stave off chaos?

Well, she might delude herself a little longer. Perhaps until the first snow. He would let her live until the first snow.

In the meanwhile, he had taken a little something for himself. A token she would not miss. Not yet. And soon, he would leave her a gift. A small gift.

Slowly, he returned his gaze to the little girls' window. The curtain remained drawn and after a moment, he turned away.

Setting the toe of his boot to a chink in the wall, he began to climb.

"Soon," he whispered, a breath, a promise, caught and carried away by the wind. "Soon."

Having heard the girls' evening prayers and seen them to bed, Beth left the dormitory and proceeded along the hallway together with her companion, Miss Eugenia Doyle. She was glad that her evening had been consumed by her duties, glad that she had had little time to think.

The events of the day haunted her. She had lost her poise, her rigid control, succumbed to the worst of her terrors.

And she had succumbed to Griffin Fairfax, reveled in his touch, his kiss, kissed him in return with wanton and heated abandon. She was appalled by her behavior, her lack of control, her inability to rule her emotions.

Melancholy lay upon her, a heavy weight.

She wanted to believe it was because Griffin had pushed her to acknowledge the fearful, anxious places in her heart. Or because the sensation of his lips on her own, his tongue twined with hers, his body flush against her, had drawn a tide of emotion from her soul that she had not imagined she possessed.

But she knew those evasions for the self-deceptions they were.

Her disheartened and glum mood came not because he had kissed her, but because she yearned for him to kiss her more. What sort of woman did that make her?

Warily, she cast an oblique glance at Miss Doyle. Did she know? Could she tell?

No, of course not.

Beth gave a sharp exhalation and dragged her thoughts away from such dangerous musings.

Moonlight cut through the windowpanes at the far end of the long, drafty corridor, splashing bright lines across the dark floor. The tallow candle Miss Doyle carried sent a pungent odor wafting in its wake and shadows plunging along the walls and hollowed doorways, lending the environs a menacing cast.

A strange, fraught silence hung between them.

In the time that Beth had been about her duties at Burndale Academy, she had made every effort at cordiality with her fellow teachers. Some, like Miss Percy and Mademoiselle Martine, had warmed to her overtures with readiness; others had held themselves aloof. Miss Doyle was such a one, and the past hour spent in her company had effected little change in that circumstance.

Beth found it interesting that Miss Doyle was quite effervescent when in the company of Miss Maclean and Miss Hughes. Three peas in a pod, they were, laughing and gossiping behind their hands. But when Beth drew near, they grew quiet, and she sensed a tense undercurrent, an unease she could not explain, one that left her wary and watchful.

The candle flame danced and flickered and Miss Doyle made a nervous little catching noise in her throat. The wind howled, rattling the panes and seeping through unseen cracks on a low, eerie moan. A shiver crawled along Beth's spine.

With a soft, huffing exhalation, she marveled at her own imaginings. What was it she feared now?

The past. The memories. The truth.

Had the lessons she had learned been for naught?

She must not let fear chase away her common sense. Surely nothing threatening dwelled *here* at Burndale Academy. True, she had heard things since her arrival, whispered snippets that only stoked any wild imaginings she might conceive, but she had seen no real evidence of evil lingering in these corridors. There was no tangible threat.

The closest she had come to finding true cause for distress was the suspicion that someone had been in her chamber, touched her things. On closer consideration, she decided that her reaction might have been overblown. Likely, the maid had come and tidied, and in the process moved her hairbrush a little. There was no cause for alarm in that.

Which left only the rumors to fuel her anxious suppositions. Were rumors enough to justify her unease?

Alice's ramblings of curses and doom, her aspersions against Griffin Fairfax, his own admission of the rumors that dogged him . . . these were not the only troubling things Beth had heard. She might have dismissed the maid's words, supposing her to be of nervous temperament, but she had quickly found that Alice was not the only inhabitant of Burndale leaning to morbid thoughts and blatant suspicions.

She had overheard the other teachers whispering amongst themselves about a maid who had run off from her place at a house in Northallerton. They seemed to place some significance on that, make some connection between the missing girl and Burndale Academy.

She glanced again at the woman who walked at her side.

Catching her gaze, Miss Doyle pursed her lips and said in her high, girlish voice, "Do you have"—she paused, frowned, then brightened and continued—"some hairpins I might borrow until I can go to town on my next half day?"

Beth blinked at the odd request. Pausing at her chamber door, she turned fully toward her companion, noting that every strand of Miss Doyle's straight nutbrown hair was scraped back from her pale moon face and pinned with neat precision.

How many hairpins did a woman require?

Raising the candle high, Miss Doyle peered back at her. The flame leaped and sputtered. Miss Doyle gestured at the nearly guttered stub.

"I do not like the dark," she said, and Beth stiffened with a momentary wariness as she wondered if Miss Doyle had sniffed out her own secrets. But the woman only gave a high, short giggle. "I am forever burning a candle until it is nothing more than a puddle. At night, I do not set pins to extinguish the rushlight, but let it burn and burn. Especially now, with . . ."

She widened her eyes and clicked her tongue against her teeth and let her words trail off, a dire implication that hung unspoken.

Beth was certain then that Miss Doyle knew nothing of her private fears. The woman's words were a transparent ploy, the trailing insinuation a thinly masked invitation. This interlude in the dark and drafty hallway had little to do with hairpins or candles and everything to do with secrets.

Forcing a polite smile, Beth studied her companion. She was heartily tired of veiled suggestions and overheard snippets.

All the years she had spent trailing behind her father, learning the joys of a riddle solved had taught her that a direct inquiry was, at times, the best course. Here Miss Doyle offered a clear opportunity for answers.

"The dark can be unsettling," Beth agreed. "Or welcoming. I suppose it is a matter of perspective." She closed her fingers about the door handle, then continued in a voice made soft with an invitation to familiarity. "But tell me, my dear Miss Doyle . . . is there aught amiss? I cannot help but sense your distress, though you are most brave and stoic in your mien. I have wondered these past days . . ."

Miss Doyle preened at Beth's praise, then made a great show of peering along the dim hallway in one direction and then the other, before venturing to whisper, "Do you know of Miss Stillwell?"

The name seemed vaguely familiar.

"Or Miss Bodie-Stuart?"

Beth frowned as the names teased her, tweaking a distinct unease. She drew a short breath as recollection came upon her.

Katherine Anne Stillwell. Helen Bodie-Stuart. The names she had read in the graveyard. The two dead women.

"Ah, I see you have some knowledge. A terrible death they died. Terrible." Miss Doyle's small eyes glittered with barely suppressed glee as she pressed her fingertips to her lips in a false show of dismay.

"You horrify me!" Beth exclaimed. "How brave you are to speak of it. But, please, do not distress yourself to bring forth the entire tale."

Miss Doyle was almost trembling with eagerness, clearly oblivious to Beth's ironic tone.

"I do feel a most grievous distress," Miss Doyle agreed, her voice breathy with excitement, her smirk unctuous. "But the telling must be done, for your own protection."

"I thank you for your kindness."

Miss Doyle inclined her head like a queen to her subject, and whispered, "'Twas a murderous assault upon their persons—"

She broke off and reared back to ascertain the effect of her disclosure.

The mention of murder made Beth's heart clutch.

"—a murderous attack by creatures unknown . . . creatures never found, though they were hunted near a sennight each time," Miss Doyle said with macabre relish. "Both ladies, poor souls, were sorely wounded, their flesh torn, their clothing in tatters. Two bloodied bodies, separated by years, but not by deed. Their deaths were so very similar, runnels gouged in their skin and their hair slashed from their very heads . . . along with their"—Miss

Doyle's small, pale eyes glittered, and her voice lowered still more—"scalps."

Beth gasped, but Miss Doyle was not done with her chilling tale, her body fairly vibrating with excitement as she relished the telling.

"And each had their fingers hacked from their hands," she finished on a whisper.

Beth had expected to be apprised of death by tragic disease, consumption or scarlatina or the ague. She could never have expected such brutal tidings. The hair at her nape prickled and rose, and a sick horror overtook her, doubly so because she could not mistake Miss Doyle's pleasure at sharing the horrific account.

"Oh, my dear, you have paled to chalk!" Miss Doyle observed, her tone rife with barely suppressed delight, dripping with false concern. She squinted at Beth in the flickering light, her gaze razor sharp.

"I am well, truly," Beth demurred. "Please, do go on."

"Little more to add, save that they both were chambered here"—Miss Doyle leaned very close and made a vague gesture at Beth's unopened door—"and none has since occupied this room. Until now." She paused. "Both ladies were fair of hair and skin, as you are. Strange, is it not, that nearly two years apart, the beast took two women so similar in appearance and coloring, and now, here you are? Why, you even sleep in their bed . . ."

Certainty slapped Beth like a cold, wet rag as her private suspicions proved true. Behind the guise of friendliness and genuine camaraderie, Miss Doyle intended to rouse alarm and horror.

Hard resolution bolstered her. If her companion was hoping to see a fit of hysteria or a terrified swoon, she had chosen to impart her secrets to a disappointing listener. Having failed to master her emotions earlier, Beth had no intention of letting her terrors have free rein once more.

She had quite exhausted her store of fits and frenzies

for the day. She would not allow herself to descend into such madness a second time. She had great practice at battling her panic and tamping down her hysteria, and she meant to employ every trick at her disposal to ensure that her manner remained calm.

Whatever she might feel in her heart, she would offer no glimpse of it for Miss Doyle's entertainment.

"Yes, here I am," Beth observed dryly in response. "Sleeping in the same bed that once held Miss Stillwell and Miss Bodie-Stuart." Then throwing caution to the wind, she sacrificed any pretext at politesse. "What pleasure you take in the grisly sonata you sing, Miss Doyle, each note designed to elicit both fear and dread. In truth, you have brought such dissertation to the level of art."

A moment of silence passed as Miss Doyle digested Beth's words and finally drew the conclusion that she had been maligned.

"Well," she huffed, drawing herself to the fullness of her meager stature, watching Beth with cunning eyes. "You are clearly overset by anxiety, Miss Canham. I had best take my leave of you now, and *you* had best lock your door. Did you not notice that we have no fair-haired teachers at Burndale? With good reason." She paused for effect, a nasty little smirk turning her lips. "They are all dead."

She took three steps forward along the gloomy hallway, then paused to look back at Beth over her shoulder. Shadows licked at her hem.

"Oh, dear, just one more small thing . . . Do you know who found them, there in the woods, all bloody and savaged so their own mothers might not recognize them? Why, it was Mr. Fairfax, dear Miss Canham." She gave an ugly laugh, high and trilling.

Rearing back, Beth sucked in a sharp breath. Miss Doyle retraced her steps, drawing nigh, crowding Beth back against the door.

"Do you think we have not noticed the way you cast your moon eyes at him, watching him every time he is about?" she asked, her eyes narrowed with malice. "Oh, *do* watch him, Miss Canham. *Do* feel your heart flutter for him, just as Miss Stillwell did, and Miss Bodie-Stuart. And perhaps he will stumble upon *your* body, as well, just as he happened upon theirs"—she paused, long enough for Beth's heart to plunge and twist and her wariness to escalate, then she finished in a harsh, malicious rush—"and just as he happened upon the ravaged and broken body of his poor, dead wife."

In the dark hallway, with the flame of the candle casting light up from below, Miss Doyle's features took on a monstrous cast. Shadows danced and dipped along the walls.

"Some say he killed her, right in front of Isobel. 'Tis no wonder the child never speaks. She is deranged from the horror of it."

Beth felt the blood drain from her face in a rush. She leaned against the door for support, shocked and distressed not only by Miss Doyle's revelations, but by the woman's twisted delight in sharing them.

A dead wife. Two dead teachers. All discovered by Griffin Fairfax.

Her stomach dropped, and in the center of her chest was a tight, sharp pain. Miss Doyle's words and insinuations oozed through her thoughts.

'Twas a terrible thing, to have such a spiteful heart.

"Well, I believe I am done here." Miss Doyle laughed, a burbling, childish giggle.

"Yes, I believe you are," Beth replied shortly, uncaring that her tone was rude, her words clipped and tight. "Good evening, Miss Doyle."

"And to you, Miss Canham," came the reply. "Sleep well."

With her breath coming in short, shallow pants, Beth stood in the hallway outside her chamber door and watched the other woman walk away. After a moment,

Miss Doyle disappeared down the stairs at the far end of the hall, taking the meager light of her candle with her.

For a time, Beth simply stood, alone in the dim, moon-dappled hallway.

Better alone than in Miss Doyle's bilious company.

Opening her door, she went inside, then paused to turn the lock behind her. She checked the key a second time and drew it from the keyhole. There was a coal fire in the hearth, set by the maid. Beth was glad of both the warmth and the light.

Aware of the lingering disquietude in her heart, she drew the curtains and made quick work of preparing herself for bed. She hesitated, then hurried across the room and dragged open the heavy draperies once more.

She could not bear to sleep with the curtains pulled shut. Not tonight. In truth, not any night.

Moonlight touched the room with a purple-gray cast, and Beth sighed with relief. Even that small amount of light was welcome, as was the sight of the open space beyond the window.

She stood for a long moment staring out at the night. Three dead women . . . *murdered* women . . .

She had only Miss Doyle's word as to the veracity of Mr. Fairfax's presence at each horrific scene, and to the violent nature of the women's demise. Not an especially unimpeachable source.

Pressing her lips together, she thought back on her day and the emotions that had carried her up, then down like breakers crashing on the shore.

Cold fury rolled through her.

Enough. Truly enough.

With a sharp yank, she dragged the curtains shut. She *would* face the small, closed room tonight, and the darkness. She *would*. And not only face them; she would master them.

Stomping across the room, she tossed back the sheets and blankets, then paused. Sighed. And lit a rushlight.

So much for her best intentions.

A moment later, she lay in her bed, her blankets drawn to her chin. Silence, thick and heavy, shrouded the room, and she strained to hear any sound, anything that would serve as a reminder that she was not completely alone here in the gloom. She glanced at the rushlight, a weak and pallid soldier staving off the darkness. It would have to serve.

Closing her eyes, she massaged her temples and tried to gather her riotous thoughts. To no avail. She could think of little save Griffin Fairfax, of his dark beauty and his enigmatic words.

Of the way she had felt that afternoon when he laid the flat of his palm against the small of her back and dragged her tight against him until she felt every ridge and prominence of his hard body.

His kiss had been forbidden ecstasy, a pleasure she had never imagined, his mouth open and hot, his tongue stroking her until she moaned and writhed.

The recollection sent heat flaming in her cheeks, roused a singing in her blood that left her breathless.

Her limbs grew restless and she shifted beneath the cool sheets, overheated and twitchy. She could *feel* the rushing of her blood, *hear* the pounding of it, and each thought she had of Griffin only made it surge stronger, wilder.

She rolled to her side, biting her lip as she revisited every moment of their time in Miss Percy's office, right to the moment he had left her.

I have become exactly the monster I feared I could be.

The recollection of his words and tone haunted her, distressed her. Made her think of the vicious poison Miss Doyle had spewed moments past.

She trembled in her bed, despite the warmth of the

fire and her covering of blankets, a chill taking her from
within.

Sounds carried from somewhere far off in the vast,
sleeping building. The bang of a door. Footsteps on the
wooden stairs. And then there were no sounds at all.

Rolling onto her back once more, Beth lay in her bed
and waited for sleep. It must have come, for at some
point in the night she jerked and started and sat bolt upright. Wide awake.

The rushlight had burned down. The room was very
dark, and for an instant she felt only stark, icy terror, a
cold rush of fear. Clammy palms, rapid breaths, pounding heart. Then she recalled that she had purposefully
drawn the drape.

She heard the rapid, harsh gasps of her own breathing cutting the silence.

Resolutely, she lay back once more, determined to
overcome, determined to see out this night without a
light.

Griffin walked the outside of the wall that surrounded
the back garden of Burndale Academy. Chilly tonight.
Much colder than the daylight hours. His breath showed
white as he exhaled, a cloud. No matter. He had lost
count of the times over the years that he had been far
colder, shivering and blue with it, feeling nothing save a
numb deadening of his limbs. This night's autumn chill
was little enough.

Reaching up, he brought his collar higher about his
neck and walked on.

A moment later, he paused, turned, studied the three
ugly, dead trees that always made him call up an image
of Macbeth's three witches. Again, he turned, this time
toward the school, toward a particular window, silently
counting across until he reached the one he wanted.

The curtains were drawn, but the faintest line of light showed from between the panels of heavy cloth.

Beth. He thought of her lying in her bed, her glorious ringlets free and wild, her eyes heavy lidded and slumberous.

A deep breath expanded his chest, filling him with the sharp bite of frigid night air and the scent of the woods. He leaned his shoulder against the thick, gnarled trunk by his side and settled in to wait.

To watch.

In time, the rushlight failed, its life extinguished, leaving only darkness.

Stirring from his place, he moved, silent as fog, blending with night and shadow. This was territory known and familiar, the darkness a place he far preferred to the light.

He skirted the garden wall, reached the little-used door to the yard, and turned the knob slowly, then pressed with the flat of his hand.

Locked. He slid his hand into his pocket, pulled free a thin metal pick, and eased it noiselessly into the lock.

A twist, a turn, all quiet and quick, then a push and the door swung open with only a faint creak of its hinges to reveal a corridor, very black, very silent.

Dropping the pick back into his pocket, he paused to listen for any telltale sound, then leaned down to draw his knife from his boot. Moonlight danced along the blade, only to be eaten by shadow as he stepped into the school and shut the door tight behind him.

Chapter Seventeen

Perhaps she dozed . . . a minute? An hour?

Disoriented, Beth lay quiet in her bed.

A sound came to her then, and she raised her head, listening, tense. It came again, the creak of the floor-board outside her chamber door. Once. Then yet again, moments later.

Jerking upright, she fisted her hands in the blankets, staring at the closed door. She had locked it, checked it twice. She plunged her hand beneath her pillow, felt the distinctive shape of the key. Closing her fingers around it, she drew the key forth, clenched tight in her fist, and pressed it to her breast.

In that moment she could not say what was the stronger emotion, the fear evoked by the knowledge that she was locked in this small, dark chamber with the walls so tight on every side, or the relief that she was safe behind a locked door.

The irony was not lost on her.

A muted, shuffling step sounded from the hallway, and the crack at the bottom of the door showed a shadow that momentarily blocked the narrow strip of moonlight eking through.

Beth forced back her fears and distress, and called

upon her rationality and reason. Who could be in the hallway outside her door, and why?

Miss Doyle, returned to play a prank? She could not imagine it.

Frowning, she recalled her own nocturnal wanderings as a child, her night terrors and her need to leap from her bed and pace through the house. *Of course.* Likely, one of the girls had stumbled from her bed in the aftermath of a dream.

The thought of a child, alone and afraid, made her brave.

She rose and crossed to the door, her hand trembling as she slid the key in the lock and turned it with care. Easing open the door, she curled her fingers around the edge of it, waiting, listening, hearing nothing at all.

She peered into the hallway. The moonlight shone through the large windows at the far end. Fingers of pale purple light stretched straight across the floor, illuminating the empty corridor.

There was no one there.

Stepping back, Beth was about to close her door once more when something caught her eye. She frowned and paused. Lying on the floor in the middle of the hall, centered in a band of moonlight, was a cloth. White. Neatly folded, as though carefully placed there rather than dropped by accident.

Chilling tendrils of fear curled about her bones and crawled up her spine. She scanned the corridor, her gaze lingering on each shadowed niche. Her pulse galloped, her mouth grew dry, but even after she counted off a full minute, nothing stirred.

With a shake of her head, she hurried forward, bent and scooped up the cloth, then backed toward the open door of her chamber. Reaching behind her, she felt for the handle, cool, smooth, and closed her fingers about it.

She glanced up one last time and froze, stunned.

A man stood in the shadowed niche of a doorway halfway along the corridor. Her fingers crushed the square of linen in her hand, and her heart bucked hard in her chest.

No, not just any man. Griffin Fairfax.

He was dressed in dark clothing that blended with the night, and he watched her, dark eyes glittering.

She could not comprehend it. What was he doing here? What—

A cloud shifted across the face of the moon, and the gloom deepened. There came a scratching sound to her right, and she glanced that way to see a small shadow moving across the larger. A mouse running along the wainscoting.

She made a sharp, huffing exhalation and jerked her head back toward Griffin Fairfax. Except . . . he was not there. There was no one there.

On legs weak and trembling, she backed into her room and shut the door. Locked it. Tried the handle just to be certain.

Slumping against the wood, her thoughts stumbling one against the next, she tried to make sense of it all.

Had he been there, in truth, watching her door? Or had she conjured him from the darkest corner of her dreams?

She could not imagine a man moving so quickly, so silently, that he would be gone in the space of a heart-beat. Closing her eyes, she rested her head back against the door, heard the rushing of her blood pulsing hard and fast in her ears, and knew she was afraid. Very afraid.

Was that why she had conjured him? Imagined Griffin standing outside her door, a sentinel to hold her safe?

She thought it might be so, for just the thought of him brought her comfort, and that realization both amazed and confused her.

He was a dangerous man. She had no doubt of it. In fact, she felt the certainty of that deep in her marrow. Yet she could not believe he was dangerous to her.

Whirling, she unlocked the door, jerked it open. But there was only an empty hallway to greet her, and a cavernous and vast silence. The school was quiet now, quiet as a church. There was no sound inside her room, no sound without, just the beating of her heart pumping a sluggish river of blood.

With a shudder, she drew the door closed once more and locked it.

Slowly, she unfolded the cloth in her hand, frowning. A handkerchief, white, but not pristine, for a dark blot marred the corner.

She thought she knew exactly what she looked at, but could not be certain, for the room was painted in shades of gray and slate and pewter, with only a frugal measure of moonlight filtering from beneath the door and through the thin crack left between the curtain panels.

Crossing to the window, she dragged open the heavy draperies. Moonlight spilled through the windowpanes, bright enough that she could see now with certainty exactly what she held.

Not just any handkerchief, she realized, but one of the ones she was embroidering for her mother. But it was *wrong*. There, in the corner where she had worked her mother's initials, her stitches were obscured by a dark blot.

A moment past, when she had first unfolded the cloth, she had thought the blot was ink, but now a faint scent of copper and rot touched her nostrils, and she knew.

Not ink.

Blood.

The corner of the cloth was stained with blood, and in the opposite corner was her own name—*Beth*—done with lovely flowing letters and neat, perfect stitches. Not *her* stitches. She had never sewn such embroidery in her entire life. Someone else had put her name on the cloth.

With trembling hands, she set the handkerchief aside and lit a candle, blinking as the light flared.

Someone *had* been in her room, touched her things. Stolen the handkerchief to play this hideous trick.

Why? Why? Why?

She pressed her open palm to her breastbone, panting, dizzy.

Someone had been in the hallway earlier, outside her door, and they had left this for her to find.

Griffin? Was he that someone? *Had* she seen him there in truth, or conjured him, a dark protector, from the deepest well of her fear?

Beth wrapped her arms about herself and battled to stay the tide of burgeoning dread. She had spent her life wrestling with her secret terrors, bottling her memories and her panic so they would not surge free and overwhelm her.

But she carried them with her always, had carried them here, to Burndale Academy, all the horrid things that dwelled in her memories.

They were here.

They were real. The monsters from the dusty corners of her mind.

Swallowing, she looked out at the garden, let her gaze fall on the place she had seen someone lurking before. And there he was, a wraith, wrapped in coal-black shadows.

She gasped, and her thoughts went wintry white and blank.

Walk, dear heart. Walk faster.

Only, there was nowhere for her to walk, nowhere for her to run.

* * *

Beth took care with her appearance the following morning. She knew her black dress made her seem pale and wan, and so she chose the more becoming brown and pinned her grandmother's pearl brooch to the collar for ornamentation. As she dressed and fixed her hair, her gaze strayed again and again to the blood-stained handkerchief that sat on her table, the sight of it scrabbling across her raw nerves like a rat's clawed feet.

Lying sleepless in the hours before dawn, she had determined that she must speak with Miss Percy, must tell her all. But the sun had yet to rise, and so there was time still before that unpleasant conversation must take place.

Beth thought that a walk on the front drive for a few moments would allay her anxiety and calm her distress, and perhaps bring a healthy flush to her cheeks. She would need to hurry, though, if she meant to have the time to herself before returning to supervise the girls' procession down to breakfast.

She made her way down the flights of stairs, out the front door and along the gravel drive. With each step and each breath and the sight of the vast, open sky above her, she felt her anxieties become, if not weaker, at least more controllable. Dew glinted on the grass, catching the new-risen sun, and the smell of trees and freshening morning flavored the air.

Walking briskly down the road, she reached the fork in the path. There, she paused, turned, and sighed. She wanted to walk on, to walk to the village of Burndale, or perhaps to Northallerton.

Or perhaps all the way home to London.

Worry gnawed at her, but she thrust it aside, determined to maintain a calm and detached demeanor. She took a step and another, walking back the way she had come, and all the while she recited again and again in her mind the words she would choose to share with Miss Percy. She would not share the image of Griffin standing in the night-sketched shadows, but she *would* tell the headmistress about the sensation that she was being watched, and about the handkerchief with its sinister stain.

She could no longer deny the threat, or the need to divulge her suspicions to the headmistress. She had proof now, in the form of the handkerchief, and if someone was slinking about the school in the dead of night, then they all might be in danger.

Beth knew from experience that such revelations carried a note of risk. She might be believed, or she might not. In fact, she might be viewed askance and accused of all manner of things.

Only once had she dared tell a stranger her secrets, dared to share the fears and anxious thoughts that chased her, snarling and growling like hounds after a fox. She had confided in the little girl who lived next door, who in turn had dreamed terrible things for many nights and had finally confided in her mother.

The result had been a lost friendship—one of the few Beth had managed to form as a child—and the burgeoning of dark and ugly rumors that circulated through the borough like a plague. Beth recalled how the neighbors began to view her askance and whisper to each other as she passed. One loud and belligerent woman whose cat had died a sudden death had accosted Beth's mother from across the street, calling out that Beth was a danger, a mad child who might murder them all in their beds and who most certainly had murdered the cat.

With a sigh, Beth folded away that dusty memory and hurried up the drive, then took the steps with unladylike haste. Pulling open the front door, she barreled through only to find Mr. Fairfax exiting at the exact moment she entered.

She gasped and pressed her palm to her breastbone, her pulse racing far too fast, her blood rushing loud in her ears.

"Miss Canham," he said, sounding not at all surprised to greet her here.

"Mr. Fairfax," she replied in a breathy rush. "What are you doing here?"

In the thin rays of the morning light his hair gleamed, coffee dark, and his eyes, brown and green and gold, watched her as she made to step away.

He was not dressed in black. She almost laughed at her expectation that he would be. No, he was handsome in fawn trousers and a white shirt and waistcoat, with a blue coat overtop. He looked every bit the gentleman, and nothing like a man who had prowled darkened hallways in the night.

"I am here to see Miss Percy," he replied, and then queried, his tone faintly amused, "Is there aught amiss?"

Her gaze shot to his. She should ask him if he had been here last night. If he had stood in the hallway outside her door. But how? How to phrase such a bizarre and outlandish inquiry?

With his head tipped slightly to one side, he studied her, and his brows arched just a little.

Just that. Just a look, and her pulse fluttered like a trapped bird.

Speechless, she shifted to her right as he did the same. To her left, and he followed.

Again, a quick shuffle of bodies, to the right, to the left, and with a soft laugh he put his hands on her arms and held her still while he stepped aside to let her pass.

His fingers were warm, even through the cloth of her sleeve, and his touch sent a fleeting jolt through her veins, a shock of pleasure.

"A fine morning," he said, smiling, feral, a wolf's smile. Dropping his hands away in a slow, languid manner, he let his palms run down along her arms. "The weather is unseasonably warm."

Beth stared at him. His touch evoked a wild cascade of wanton thoughts and emotion. She murmured a reply though she knew not exactly what she said—some pleasantry about the weather and the unseasonable heat of the early October days. And all the while, she was aware of the unreasonable heat in her blood, brought on by just the sight of him and a mere touch, by the sound of his voice and the dangerous curve of his smile.

She wet her lips, a quick roll of them inward and a swipe of her tongue, and she wondered if she was losing her mind that Griffin Fairfax fascinated her so. That she dreamed of him in the night, even conjuring him in waking dreams.

His gaze lingered on her lips a moment, then dropped to her collar, and a faint frown creased his brow.

Reaching out, he lightly ran his index finger over her brooch.

"An interesting design," he said. "Where did you get it?"

There was something odd in his tone, a tense under-current.

"It belonged to my grandmother," Beth replied. "It passed to me when she died."

The bell began to toll just then, reminding her of the need for haste, and she realized that she had dallied here, inane and mindless, while the minutes ticked past. She must hurry if she was to be in place to supervise the girls, and to catch Miss Percy in the hallway.

She took her leave, a rushed tumult of words that made Griffin's eyes light with secret amusement. Not mockery, but pleasure, as though they shared a joke. The thought of that warmed her.

The last toll sounded, reminding her that time was short. With a last glance, she zipped away, her boots tapping a rapid beat on the tiles as she rushed off.

A thought nagged her, a realization, and she paused, froze. The watch on Mr. Fairfax's chain . . . she had noted it only absently, but something about it bothered her . . .

Frowning, she turned, but he was gone. The foyer was empty. He had melted from sight without a sound.

She wondered why the sight of his watch nagged at her so. Wondered, too, what he had been doing at Burndale Academy in the new hours of the breaking day, and if he had been there last night after all, in the hall . . . in the garden . . .

Watching.

"Show me," Miss Percy said, her normally smooth brow furrowed in an uncharacteristic frown.

Beside them, the procession of girls walked two by two along the hallway, sedate and orderly under the watchful eye of the headmistress.

Beth and Miss Percy walked against the tide toward Beth's chamber. She had bottled her apprehension and corked it tight, and she was composed now, ready to tell the whole of her story once she showed the handkerchief.

At the far end of the hallway Mr. Waters worked to repair a jammed window. The rain had soaked into the wood over innumerable years, making it swell and split and hold the panes tight so only one side could be pushed free. He pried the warped piece of wood and it broke away with a sharp crack, splintering in the process.

Pausing in his task, he turned his head and watched them for a moment, and Beth felt a flicker of unease. There was something *unseeing* in his gaze, something blank and cold, as though he looked at them but saw nothing. Then he turned back to his work and Beth thought that her mood had set her to painting all manner of distressing things where none existed in truth.

As if there was not enough to distress her without adding more noxious ingredients to the bubbling cauldron.

They were at her door now, and she reached for the handle only to draw up short.

"What is it?" Miss Percy asked.

Beth shot her a glance. "The door is open," she replied. "Though I am certain that I closed it and locked it earlier."

"Perhaps the maid did not draw it all the way shut after she tidied the chamber," Miss Percy suggested in a tone benign and bland.

Pushing the door fully open, Beth stepped inside and looked about. The bed was unmade. The basin where she had poured water to perform her morning ablutions was unemptied.

"The maid has not come." Beth looked about the room once more, putting her palms together and pressing them tight, counting to three with each breath, in and out, determined to let none of her dismay show. Something was wrong. Something was—

Her gaze cut to the small table where she had left the handkerchief, the only true evidence to support her tale.

Her heart sank.

The table was empty, the bloodstained cloth gone.

And with it the sole proof that might have made her bizarre tale even remotely believable.

Turning to stare at the headmistress, Beth was tempted to raise the issue of Miss Doyle's horrid stories of dead women with their scalps torn away, her assertions of Griffin's involvement when the bodies were discovered. She ached to unburden all her suspicions and fears.

But even as she thought of it, her tongue twisted on itself. Because she dared not forfeit her position here. And because in the absence of proof, with her assertions listed so simply, so linearly in her thoughts, the facts seemed ludicrous, even to her.

She knew herself prone to displays of her anxious temperament. Perhaps the whole of it was a story woven with threads of pure malice by Miss Doyle, and by Beth's own overactive imagination.

Even if she had the handkerchief to show, in the bright light of day she was hard-pressed to say what threat lay in a crumpled bit of linen. In the darkest hours of the night, it had seemed terrifying, but then, she was terrified of *everything*, which made her a rather poor judge of the matter.

Miss Percy watched her with a quizzical look, faintly incredulous, the silence spinning out like thread from a wheel.

Beth's gaze dropped to take in the headmistress's dark gown. She blinked, recalling that she had seen Miss Percy moving through the back garden without candle or lamp in the darkest hours of the night.

Wetting her lips, she held her tongue, suddenly painfully aware that both Burndale Academy and Miss Percy appeared to hide as many secrets as Beth herself.

Chapter Eighteen

Stepney, London, March 14, 1813

Time healed all wounds, even a broken heart. So the well-meaning told Henry Pugh again and again. He'd heard it enough times in the past months that he'd long ago stopped answering, or even nodding in reply. He just stared straight ahead, stone-faced, and wished that if their assurances were true then time would march faster, for the wound still ached and bled and screamed.

Today, a coroner's inquest was called at the King's Arms Tavern, across the street from the Black Swan. Henry had paused outside as the first rays of dawn painted the street a pale gray. He had stood at the door of the King's Arms, just looking at the Black Swan. Looking and wishing. But wishes were no better than bad coins; a man could spend neither.

Now Henry sat on a hard bench at the back of the room, letting the sounds swirl around him. Someone coughed, a dry, hacking sound that seemed to go on and on for an eternity. The place smelled of ale and smoke and too many people in too tight a space.

There was a witness speaking now, one Jeremiah Skirven. He claimed that in the wee hours of January 15, he had heard the sound of running steps on the cobbled road. He remembered the sound of the nails on the sole of the shoes ringing out in the cold night air, distinctive and clear.

Henry pressed his lips together. The boot print in the dirt outside the Black Swan's parlor window had made an imprint that clearly showed no nails.

Two men, Hartwood and Jackson, regulars at the Black Swan, spoke next, one after the other. They each described a black-coated stranger who had drawn their notice because he lurked by the back window of the parlor, not entering the establishment, just watching it. Waiting. Both witnesses described him as a young man, broad of shoulder, tall of form. They thought he had been dark-haired, but mayhap it had been a dark cap he wore. There had been a dark-haired Yorkshire lad taken in and questioned, but a witness had attested to seeing him elsewhere and he'd been set free.

Whoever he was, Hartwood and Jackson both thought they had seen him speaking with Ginnie George outside the front door of the tavern the day before the murders.

Henry's heart plummeted to hear Ginnie's name bandied so casually. He shifted on the hard bench, staring straight ahead at the broad back of the man in front of him. He could not bear to think of her, saucy and smiling, speaking to that stranger outside the front door of the tavern.

Speaking to her murderer.

That thought haunted him. That, and so many others. Had she known him, the man who had killed her?

There was nothing to prove it one way or the other, but Henry thought she had. He thought the man had sat at the bar of the Black Swan, had quaffed ale, had exchanged a quip with the landlord. That piece of the puzzle was missing, but Henry felt it in his gut.

The killer had wanted Ginnie. He had watched her. Hunted her. And the Trotters had merely been in his way.

Henry only wished there was some way he could prove it. Especially now that another woman was dead, found just two mornings past.

The most recent murder was not exactly the same. Not in a tavern, and no bashing of skulls. Only one victim, and she was young and pretty. And blond. The woman's body had been found in Covent Garden, her throat slit so deep that her head was nearly hacked right off. She had been found lying in a great pool of blood, with her hair cut away.

Nay, not just her hair. For Henry that was the proof. Her scalp was shorn clean off. Gone. And the fingers of her right hand.

Henry sat here recalling the way Ginnie had looked, the way he had wondered what had become of her beautiful hair.

'Twas the same killer. He would swear it. The vile slaughterer was one and the same. But he had no way to prove it, and he knew neither the name nor the face of the man to accuse.

No one agreed with him.

Sam Loder thought the Trotters' death was burglary gone awry, with Ginnie only caught there by happenstance. After all, she was to have gone to her mother's that night with a mince pie. Who could have known that she would be delayed?

Who indeed, Henry mused. For him, that question only set the conviction stronger that she had known her killer, that he had sat in the tavern and listened as Mrs. Trotter bade Ginnie stay back an extra hour.

But Hartwood and Jackson both swore they were the last to depart that night, that the bar was empty once they took their leave.

Henry had considered Sam's theories of burglary, but if Sam had the right of it, then why had they found Mrs. Trotter's pearl brooch on the floor of the hallway, kicked to one side against the wall, and found, too, a bag of coins in the bar? And why had the thief left behind the little gold watch pinned to Ginnie's bodice?

Funny, Henry could not recall her ever having worn a watch before.

The killer had not cared for money or jewels. His goal had been the thieving of human life.

Dr. Cornelius Patch came up to testify now. He had examined the bodies, and he now set about giving his report. Henry swallowed and battled the urge to leap up and flee. He knew how Ginnie had died. Every night, he dreamed it, saw the blade bite deep, slashing her throat with such force that her head nearly rolled free.

He was shuddering now, his limbs quaking and his teeth clacking together so he was forced to set his jaw tight to stop the men on either side from glancing at him with narrowed eyes.

He could do this.

He *must* do this.

He must sit here to the bitter end. Because he himself had a question for this inquest. A matter of life rather than death.

Chapter Nineteen

Burndale, Yorkshire, October 6, 1828

As it often did by late afternoon, the girls' interest in their studies was flagging. Deliberately choosing an activity that would engage them, Beth placed a large round globe on the table and waited as the monitors collected the little clay inkwells and set them on a tray. They had completed their dictation, and there was no sense inviting a spill.

Watching the monitors with listless attention, Beth found her thoughts wandering a tortuous path, revisiting again and again the events of the previous days. She could almost convince herself that she had imagined the whole of it: the unseen eyes that watched her on the road and in the garden, the man who had lurked outside her chamber in the quiet hours of the night. Even the bloodstained handkerchief.

Except . . . when she counted the squares of linen in her embroidery bag, one was missing.

She pondered the situation from all possible perspectives. Was there true threat to her, or only some malicious intent to frighten?

Perhaps Miss Doyle . . . But even as that possibility

flitted through her thoughts, Beth disbelieved it. Eugenia Doyle was a woman who enjoyed witnessing the fruits of her spiteful actions at close association. She was not the sort to carry out a convoluted plot that would take her any distance from her prey. No, Miss Doyle had not left the handkerchief that night for Beth to find, and she had not crept into Beth's chamber to steal it back.

But *someone* had.

With the inkwells safely collected, Beth gave permission for the pupils to leave their small desks and move closer. Murmuring and whispering and bumping shoulders, they organized themselves around the table and the globe.

As she waited, she idly traced the ocean and then the outline of a country.

"Italy," the girls chorused as one.

Startled, Beth let her hand drop away.

"Why did you say that?" she asked, astounded.

"Well, you pointed to Italy, did you not, Miss Canham? You pointed and we recited," Lucy supplied, her expression wary, her tone faintly belligerent. "That is the way we learn our geography. We recite the countries on the globe, again and again and again."

This being the first time since her arrival at Burndale that Beth had incorporated the globe into their lessons, she had no firsthand knowledge of how it was routinely used. Recalling her own wonderful and fascinating studies of the world, Beth thought that the method of education Lucy described sounded both bland and sad.

She had intended to use her mother's fashion of teaching geography by employing riddles and puzzles that would catch the girls' interest. She had not thought to merely have them speak a litany of names, but now that it had been pointed out to her, she realized that that was the exact methodology she had seen Miss Doyle employ with her pupils only the previous afternoon.

"We will try something new today," Beth said, and

spun the globe a half turn, so the continent she wanted faced toward the group of girls. "I will offer a clue, then another and another, as necessary. The first girl to solve my riddle must raise her hand and name the place of which I speak. Then I shall ask her to show us all where it is located on the globe."

Blank stares greeted her announcement, and then a spark of interest. One girl at the front raised her hand.

"Yes, Jane?"

"Miss Canham, that sounds like a game," the girl whispered. She tugged on her left earlobe, then brought her dark brown plait to her lips and chewed on the end of her hair.

Beth reached out and gently disengaged the strands from between the girl's teeth and fingers, then let it drop over her thin shoulder.

"Hair is not meant to be chewed, Jane, unless you wish to cough up a disgusting hairball, like a cat," she murmured.

Jane grimaced, clearly appalled by the thought of the hairball. "Yes, miss," she said. "May we play the game now?"

The game.

Tell me a place that is shaped like a boot, a place that was once home to great emperors . . . Beth remembered how eager she had always been to give her answer to her mother's riddles, and the proud praise she received when she made the correct response. *Well done, dear heart. Show me here on the globe. Now, tell me a place that boasts a rich delta, a vast river, and great pyramids. Yes! Egypt. Now show me.*

She studied the girls before her for a moment. Some looked eager, others wary. From the edge of the group, Isobel watched her with eyes bright and focused. That variance from the child's normally dreamy and fey expression made Beth glad she had chosen to bring out the globe. She had captured Isobel's interest, and that brought a warmth to her heart.

"'Tis not precisely a game, Jane," she said with a smile. "The study of geography is serious and important work. But there is no reason we cannot enjoy it. Now"—she let her gaze roam her group of pupils—"tell me a place of emperors and silk and spice . . ."

As she spoke, she beckoned Isobel closer to turn the globe, and was secretly pleased to see the child do as she was bidden, interacting in the lesson though she did not speak.

The girls laughed and grew enthralled by their task, even volunteering to take turns offering the clues. As she watched them and listened to the riddles they fashioned, Beth wondered if her mother was employing this very method to teach her brother right now.

A stab of homesickness, potent and sharp, caught her unawares.

Lost in thought, she slowly became aware of a change in the large schoolroom, a subtle tension. There was a dampening of volume, a quieting of all sounds. She glanced up, toward the door, and her whimsies and fancies and wishes for home scattered like dust.

Griffin Fairfax. Here.

The sight of him assaulted her. There was no better description, for she felt as though she had been dealt a sharp slap that left her skin prickling and tingling in the aftermath, and her breath coming shorter and faster than it ought.

Only . . . a slap was a most unpleasant thing, while the sight of Griffin Fairfax was pleasant in the extreme.

She had not seen him since the previous morning when she had encountered him in the foyer. Now he was standing across the room from her and she ached to look her fill, to drink in the hard angles of his face, the dark mystery and beauty of him.

Finding his gaze locked upon her, she tensed and her

heart twitched like a hooked fish. He was watching her with a focused intensity, a heat that made her shiver.

Memories buffeted her. The scent of his skin, spicy and masculine, so lovely. The feel of his mouth, tantalizing, drawing on her own until she thought she would give up all to him, anything, everything.

She did not want to feel this sudden thrill at the sight of him, this vitalization of her skin and nerves and heart. She did not want to feel as though he brought the light of a thousand candles to the room.

A flush of exhilaration warmed her and a strange play of emotion—discomfiture, awkwardness, elation—swirled up like eddies of mist to curl through her. He watched her from his place near the door with that absorbed, intent gaze she was coming to know.

Attraction.

Inappropriate, at best.

Dangerous, at worst.

Flustered, she dropped her gaze to the globe, only to feel an undeniable lure. She raised her eyes once more and, for the first time, realized that others accompanied him. Miss Percy and two other gentlemen. She knew them by sight, had seen them before.

Mr. Creavy was ancient, short and painfully thin, with a few white wisps of hair at the edges of his pate and heavy, white whiskers on his face. A dull, black broadcloth suit hung on his rush-thin frame.

Beside him was Mr. Moorecroft, a youngish man, perhaps five-and-thirty, bland as oat pudding. Beth knew that as soon as she looked away, she would be hard-pressed to say a single feature of Mr. Moorecroft's that she had noticed. Or perhaps that was only because he paled next to Mr. Fairfax.

The two trustees had visited the classroom before with Miss Percy, had stood in silent judgment as they observed Beth teaching a class. And now they were back.

Understanding dawned, and with it a tense wariness.

Mr. Fairfax—Griffin—was here for a specific reason, as were his companions.

He had come to evaluate her. They had all come here today to judge her, to determine her suitability for her position. Beth knew it, though they took their time coming to her side, pausing first to listen to the pupils who recited French verbs with Mademoiselle Martine, and then to watch the girls scratch their dictation into their copybooks as Miss Doyle read aloud.

How could she not have realized? Griffin Fairfax held her fate, and that of her family, in his hands. Had Alice not said that Mr. Fairfax gave money to the school? That he was a benefactor and a trustee? Alice had named the others as well. These two men, Mr. Creavy and Mr. Moore-croft.

Beth swallowed, dropped her gaze once more to the globe, idly noting that a bit of Germany had flaked away, leaving a bald patch. She pressed her finger to it.

Anxiety drilled deep, a frigid ooze in her veins, in her mind, but she held her outward façade of calm and continued the lesson as though naught were amiss. And all the while, she was aware of their meandering approach through the room.

At length, the sound of their footfalls announced their proximity. They were upon her now, her observers. Her judges.

Her stomach rolled and her limbs quaked and she only prayed they did not know it. She felt anything but composed and secure. A part of her imagined that at any moment her deceit would be discovered and they would know her for the fraud she was. Know, too, that her temperament was horribly ill suited to her role, that she believed Miss Doyle's tall tales of murder, that she was spooked by a shadow in a dark corridor.

Recalling the conversation that she had overheard outside Miss Percy's office door, she thought that they already suspected she was not what she claimed, that they already marked her for dismissal.

Resolutely forcing herself to behave as though Miss Percy and the trustees were not there, Beth posed a riddle and nodded to Isobel, who turned the globe once more. All the while, she silently admonished herself to stop this useless self-castigation. Her performance of her duties was perfectly acceptable. She knew it was.

But the question nagged at her, was *acceptable* enough, or need she be *exceptional*?

She waited for the anxiety and dismay her insecurities invariably elicited, and was surprised by the emotions that came upon her. Defiance. Pride. She had engaged these children, evoked a love of learning. What matter that her methods were unorthodox?

"Why do they not recite the countries?" the old man asked with querulous humor, his voice pitched low enough that Beth surmised he did not ask the question of her, but rather of his companions. "They should recite the countries."

"Let us watch and see, Mr. Creavy," said Miss Percy, her tone placating.

But he was not to be appeased. With a hard stamp of his wooden cane against the floor, he spoke again, louder, more shrill.

"She is not doing it correctly. They must recite the countries."

"Let Miss Canham teach the lesson, if you please," Griffin said, polite.

"I beg your pardon," came Mr. Creavy's high, thready response. "I'll have you know—"

"Be *silent*," Griffin said in a different voice, low and soft and polite still, which only made it all the more threatening.

And Mr. Creavy *was*, instinctively obeying the command that cut the air like the sharpest blade. Confused

by her reaction to the exchange, by the current of anger
she sensed beneath Griffin's cool veneer, Beth realized
that he acted the part of her protector. She was uncertain if that relieved or distressed her, uncertain how she
felt about the emotion he held on such tight rein just
beneath the surface.

Griffin made a small gesture toward the globe.

"Please continue, Miss Canham. My apologies for the
disruption."

Miss Percy and Mr. Moorecroft said not a word.

There was a swish of sound as Isobel spun the globe,
and Griffin turned his gaze upon his daughter, loving,
yearning, that same bittersweet expression he wore each
time he looked at her. Beth's heart skipped, and then
she felt the eyes of the others upon her. Realizing that
the moment had spun out too long, she turned her attention back to her duties.

Closing her thoughts to their presence, she kept on
with the lesson until it was done and the last toll of the
bell echoed through the room. She dismissed the girls
and watched them leave, but held herself to her place.

Mr. Moorecroft looked thoughtful as he bit on his
lower lip, his brow drawn low. Then he pulled in his
cheeks, and Beth thought that there *was* something she
noted about him. He looked like a fish, bulging-eyed,
and with his mouth sucked in and opening and closing.

Giving a loud huff that drew her gaze, Mr. Creavy
stood for a moment glaring at her, then walked off, mut-
tering under his breath about upstarts and new ways.

Beth felt as though she had lost her place in a book,
as though she was flipping pages and scrambling to find
the lost words. She longed to rub her damp palms on
her skirt, but she held herself back, determined to show
a placid and calm mien.

"A novel approach," Miss Percy said in a dry tone.

Beth's heart plummeted. Her methods had disap-
pointed.

For a moment she was too alarmed to do more than stand, mute and unhappy. Then she fell a surge of irritation.

Modulating her tone, but determined to present her reasoning, she said, "I thought to stimulate the girls' interest. Recitation by rote is . . ." She hesitated, unwilling to offend.

"Boring," Griffin supplied.

"Less than stimulating," Beth continued, not daring to look at him. "Just because a method of instruction has been in place for any number of years does not necessarily mean it is the best method. One may always hope to improve."

The entirety of her explanation was delivered with her gaze locked on the globe, and when she was done, she took a deep breath and raised her head.

Miss Percy was watching her with approval.

"An emotional argument," Miss Percy said. "But not, I suspect, without merit. Thank you, Miss Canham."

With that, she inclined her head and invited the remaining gentlemen—Mr. Moorecroft and Mr. Fairfax—to her office. The old man, Mr. Creavy, had already made his way across the large room and waited impatiently by the door. Now Mr. Moorecroft joined Miss Percy, and the three of them departed, leaving Beth alone with Mr. Fairfax.

She could not look at him, for she thought that her expression would surely give her away. She wanted him to touch her, to close his hands around her arms as he had that morning in the foyer, a warm and human connection. To draw her close in his embrace, chest to chest as they had been in Miss Percy's study.

Reaching for the tray of clay inkwells that sat on her desk, she drew it closer and lined the little pots up in three perfect rows.

No, she could not look at him. He would surely read the emotion that clawed through her despite her best intentions to hold it at bay. The yearning to be held by him, to be buffered in the shelter of his arms. To touch him. Hold him. To press her lips to his. To soothe him, to take his secret pain, and let him take hers, a burden shared.

Oh, what was she thinking?

Heart hammering, she pushed one of the inkwells into perfect linear alignment, stared at it for an instant, then lifted her skirt and prepared to leave.

"A moment, if you please, Miss Canham," Griffin said. The sound of his voice, low and intimate, made her shiver.

Her gaze shot to his. Dark eyes. Beautiful. Brown and gold and green. Clever eyes. He saw far too much.

Would he kiss her again? Here? The thought made her tremble.

She recalled every nuance of their kiss. The press of his smooth lips. The sweep of his warm tongue. Wet and deep and lush.

He made a hushed sound, a low chuckle. Her breath caught.

"You defended yourself," he noted.

"I have been known to speak out when I feel passionate," she replied, both amazed and amused, for the truth was, she never spoke out in her own defense. The moment spun out as she held his stare and he said nothing more. Then her amusement died as heat sparked and flared in his gaze.

"And do you feel passionate?" Rough, hushed, his tone stroked her like a caress.

Oh, he knew she did. He *knew.*

She huffed a short breath, looked away and then back again.

He stepped closer. The scent of him washed over her, so tantalizing. She wanted to breathe in and out until she was filled with him, glutted with the lovely smell of his skin.

How was it that she could be attracted so strongly and wary of him all at once?

Brisk footsteps sounded in the hallway. Miss Percy?

Beth jerked away and set about tidying the lines of inkwells once more, her heart pounding, her hands shaking.

"Meet me." A low whisper against her ear. Tempting. Seductive. "Meet me this evening on the road."

Without waiting for her reply, he turned and strode off, leaving her with the knowledge that though common sense bade her flee to her chamber, lock her door tight, and not come out until morning, she would go to the road as she did almost every evening. But tonight she would not stay in sight of the school. Tonight she would go round the sharp bend, out of sight of Burndale Academy. Because though she was afraid of many things, Griffin Fairfax was not one of them.

As though he heard her thoughts, he turned and looked back at her, his close-lipped smile wicked and sinful and full of promise.

He wanted everything perfect. With an artist's eye he studied the small clearing. It was close to the road. Not so close that any carriage or passerby would see his beautiful tableau, but close enough that Beth would feel safe if she strayed this far.

And she *would* stray. He would make certain of it. He had only to decide *when*.

Perhaps not tonight, not yet. But soon.

A small niggle of regret wormed through him. He hated to part with his treasures, so lovingly and painstakingly gathered. Hated to leave them where others might find them. He enjoyed the visits, the private delight of coming again and again, touching skirts and petticoats and little cloth-covered buttons. The lobe of her ear. The tip of her nose.

Two others he had left in the open. Not this place. Another. But he dared not go there now, and besides, this clearing was well placed, close to Burndale Academy. Close to Beth.

The treasures he had put out before had not been found for many days. He had come to visit them often, hanging in the shadows to make certain no one else was about, then creeping forward to squat by their sides. To touch them, fondle them.

Katherine had looked lovely, laid out on the ground with the sunlight peeking through the autumn leaves, painting a dappled pattern on her body.

Helen had been lovelier still, sleeping on a blanket of white snow. He had taken her to his special place, alive, bound and gagged, her blue eyes wide with fear and horror.

Huge, fluffy flakes of snow had fallen from early morning to early evening that day. Lovely, lovely snow. That night, the moon had come out full bright, washing the clearing in moonglow and silver.

He loved the snow. He could recall entire winters where there had been the barest flurry that melted as soon as it touched the ground. But last January, one perfect day had been a gift to him, layering a thick blanket of snow to act as his canvas.

Helen. Her blood had been warm and thick and red.

He had killed her right there, on the snow. Let his blade kiss deep. Watched her blood spurt and spread like a flower.

She had been so beautiful.

His. She had been his. Never to leave him. *His.*

He looked down at the girl before him, at her faded blue cotton dress, dark and stiff with her blood. Sarah. Pretty Sarah. He had taken her from the treasure box in the ground and brought her here.

Because Beth was coming. The thought sent a sharp thrill to his groin.

How he wished there was snow to act as his canvas. There were only flowers, yellow wildflowers. Yellow flowers to take the place of the yellow hair he had shorn. It was all rather poetic.

Reaching out, he touched the small watch that was pinned to Sarah's dress. The watch he had given her. *Tick. Tick. Tick.* Time ticking away, counting down the moments until her turn.

Carefully, he unpinned the watch from her bodice and pinned it to the inside of his coat.

Tick. Tick. Tick. Sarah's turn had come and gone, and now was Beth's time. Beth's special time.

Chapter Twenty

Beth walked in the fading light of dusk, enjoying the breeze and the sky and the rustling of the leaves.

Flanking the road were rows of trees a short ways off, and patches of grass closer in, bald in spots where the dark, damp earth showed through, long in places, thin green blades that trapped the fallen leaves like fish in a net. The wind stirred the blades and the leaves fluttered free, then settled, trapped once more.

She thought she was like a leaf, caught by the wind and tossed to and fro, and trapped in places she had no wish to be.

Dark places both real and imagined.

Frightening places that never set her free.

Except right now. Right now, on this road, she had chosen to be free.

A heady feeling of independence suffused her. She felt a measure of pride in herself for the way she had taught the class today, and more than that, for the way she had defended herself, explained her methods and stood by them. Whatever distress had twisted her in knots, she had presented a calm and controlled mien.

Where had such bravery come from? She had never considered herself strong or courageous, and now she did. Courage lay not in the lack of fear, but in the facing of life's challenges despite it. Griffin had made her see that in the dark, tight room that was Miss Percy's office. He had made her see not her fears and her failings, but her strengths.

In this moment, she thought back to her choices in the past months, and realized that she *had* been brave. Brave to come to Burndale in the first place. Brave to face the unknown.

She had faced the fear of that, the fear of failing in her task, of being sent home to her family with no income, no way to keep them safe. She had felt the dark tide of it wash over her. But she had not drowned.

She had seized the freedom to choose, to defend her choices, to walk as fast as she willed, to escape the confines of Burndale school and meet Griffin on the road.

The thought of him, of the intensity she read in his gaze, of the heat there and the passion, filled her with shimmering expectation. Oh, she was not so naïve that she could not see the hunger in his eyes, that she did not know it for what it was. He *wanted* her, and that knowledge was heady and luscious and ripe, bursting inside her like a juicy berry with a sharp, tart tang.

The choice she made here was not without danger.

She knew she invited attentions that no unmarried girl ought invite. But there was the crux of the matter. She had always been honest with herself in regard to possibilities, and she had never counted marriage as a likelihood.

What man wanted a mad wife who woke screaming in the night, her eyes wide, seeing terrors that no other could see? What man wanted such a mother for his children, a woman who would likely taint them with her own anxious temperament?

That honesty made her acknowledge that here was an opportunity she wanted. Craved. She ached for Griffin's touch, his embrace, his kiss.

Was it madness to want it? Of a certainty. But it was a madness that made her burn, and she yearned, just once, to take what she wanted and not be afraid.

And so she walked on, knowing he would come. Knowing precisely what he wanted.

She reached the fork in the road and chose her path, following the curve of packed earth, a ribbon of road that carried her to places both familiar and unknown.

Pausing, she turned her face to the heavens. The sky was awash with color, apricot and cherry and buttercup yellow. Beautiful. She stood for a moment and let the sight fill her heart.

There was a faint chill in the air, the herald of a cold night. On a whim, Beth pulled off her glove, bent low to the ground, and put her palm on the road. It was warm to her touch, holding the last vestiges of the day's sunlight.

Meet me this evening on the road.

He would come to her soon. She knew he would.

He would kiss her. Beth was certain of that.

Wanted that.

Wanted him. Griffin.

He had not played the gallant when he had spoken in her defense earlier, silencing Mr. Creavy with whip-sharp words. No, he had not *played* the part. He *was* gallant, though he would be pained to know she thought it. He would tell her she was mistaken.

But she thought of the way he had taken her—a girl stranded by the churchyard—up in his curricle that first day on the road. The way he had caught the wasp to protect her from a painful sting, then set the creature free though it might have stung him in turn. The way he struggled to engage his daughter in some way, coming to Burndale Academy almost daily just to see her, be near her.

He had seen to the heart of all Beth's fears, known her secret terrors though she had not given them voice.

He had pulled her into his arms and kissed her, not trapping her with his weight, but turning her so it was she who held him in place. She who chose.

That memory made her shiver.

Lifting her hand from the road, Beth straightened and walked on, her thoughts full of him, full of the knowledge that she could love him if she dared. Or perhaps she would love him regardless, whether she willed it or not.

She thought that, like a plague, love chose its victims where it would.

She had come as he asked. Atop a low rise, Griffin watched her from a distance, the sway of her hips, the angle of her shoulders, the way she tipped her face to the sun.

Beth did not walk with her eyes on the ground, with small, mincing lady's steps. Not his Beth. She walked as though she meant to go somewhere, with her arms swinging by her sides. He found that incredibly appealing.

For all her fears, she was brave and brazen. A contradiction. A conundrum. He found that appealing, as well.

The wind caught her skirt, made the hem rise, the cloth billow before it settled once more, flowing about her like water.

What did he want of her?

The thought held a sardonic edge. Yes, of course, he wanted *that* . . . but there was something more. Something intangible, almost indecipherable.

He wanted to hold her safe.

He wanted to take her fears. To know what had birthed them and steal that darkness from her. Make it his own.

Admiration swelled, warm and filling as fresh-baked bread. She was the bravest woman he had ever known,

for she faced each day with optimism and light despite
the shadows that nipped at her heels and dogged her
every step.

What was it like, to know such fear each moment of
each day? What had she lived through to shape her so?

Whatever it was, she saw its reflection each time she
looked at Isobel. He read that affinity in every interaction he observed between Beth and his daughter.

What would she think to know that *he* was the source
of his daughter's darkness, that he blocked the sunshine
from her life?

He thought perhaps she had disbelieved him when
he told her he was a villain, perhaps she thought he
spoke in jest. Soon, she would know the truth of it.

As he watched, Beth paused, bent low, and touched
the road. Why? Of course. To feel the last vestiges of the
sun-warmed day.

Then she straightened and walked on, disappearing
from his sight round a bend in the road.

With a grin, he ran lightly down the hill and set himself a course meant to intercept hers.

She did that. *She* summoned his smile whether he
willed it or nay, had done so since that first day on the
road by the church. She made him feel he ought to grab
what joy he could, as she did.

He was halfway to the road when he heard her scream.
Short. Sharp. The sound died almost before it began.

His gut clenched and his heart twisted, and Griffin
began to run in earnest.

Beth knew that smell. She thought that once encountered, it was a memory that dwelled close to the surface
forever, a scent never forgotten.

Blood and death.

Pressing her hand to her mouth to hold back any further sound, she scanned the clearing and then the shad-

owed wood. In her shock and horror at the sight of the dead girl lying amidst the yellow wildflowers, she had screamed once, quick, the sound truncated, sliced off as soon as she realized what she did.

She knew better than to scream, but the shock of seeing the girl—

Hide in the dark. Don't make a sound. His footsteps coming closer, and the wet rasp of his breath.

No! She slammed the door on her memories and thought only of *now*, of survival, of a way to be safe. Panting, she fought to stem the tide of terror, to freeze like a rabbit in a field.

Do not see me! I am hiding. Hiding. The pain in my belly is so sharp, and the box is so small.

Slowly, she turned a full circle, watching for anything that did not belong. A sound. A scent. It might be here still, the thing that had killed this girl. If she screamed she might lure the beast back. If she ran, she might run to her own death.

Her heart slammed against her ribs and she was choked for breath, dizzy with it. Dizzy with stark terror.

Breathe. Breathe.

She dredged up every bit of discipline she had taught herself over the years, forced herself not to scream, not to run. Those were the worst things she could do.

Panic was a choking smog, coating her every thought with a brown, greasy sludge that oozed and dripped.

With the back of her hand pressed to her mouth and her lips closed tight, she retched and retched again, her gut churning, her throat burning with the sting of bile.

Was the monster lurking in the shadows?

She spun, her gaze darting frantically about, but she saw only thick brown tree trunks and high branches, heard only the sigh of the wind through the trees and the rustle of leaves.

Swallowing, she listened again for any sound out of place, the crack of a twig, the flapping of the wings of a startled bird. Nothing. Nothing. Only her own breath sounding harsh and loud in the quiet.

The monster might still be about, watching, waiting. *Oh, dear God.*

She ached to run screaming from the place, to sob and cry and run down the road, to let her panic surge free.

And that was exactly why she stayed where she was. Because she would not give in to her fear. She would *not.*

Logic told her the beast was long gone, the girl long dead.

Her gaze slid back to the dreadful scene before her, drawn against her will by pity and dismay, and by the need to *know.* She was her father's daughter, raised to think as he thought, and so a part of her catalogued all she saw even as the shock and fear threatened to overwhelm her.

Breathing shallow little puffs of air through her open lips, Beth drew her shawl from her shoulders and stood staring down. A woman. She knew that by the attire, a pale blue cotton print dress, muddied and soiled and stained with old blood.

The woman was dead. But not recently. There were maggots crawling in the holes that had once been her eyes and nose and mouth, and flies rising and landing.

Her flesh was gnawed away in places, showing glimpses of white-yellow bone. The fingers of her right hand were gone. And her hair. She had no hair.

Beth shuddered. Had the girl been killed here? Or dragged here after her death?

Why? Why?

She knew that only seconds had passed since she had stumbled upon this macabre scene, yet she felt as though she had stood here for hours staring down at the decaying corpse.

A swirling maelstrom threatened to drag her deep into the sucking mire of her panic and despair. Trembling so hard she could barely stand, Beth draped her shawl over the remains of the girl's face, feeling as though she must offer at least that small show of respect, must cover this poor girl and shield her from unkind eyes.

She backed away then, step by step, keeping a careful watch on her surroundings. Her gaze moved rhythmically from left to right, and then she paused and checked behind. Again and again she did this, one step and the next, carrying her away from this place of horror.

She knew now that Miss Doyle's stories of the dead teachers were not a far-flung tale fashioned to instill fear. They were real, and the beast had been here . . .

Do you know who found them, there in the woods, all bloody and savaged so their own mothers might not recognize them? Why, it was Mr. Fairfax . . . Perhaps he will stumble upon your body, as well, just as he happened upon theirs . . .

Griffin. She had meant to meet him here on the road.

Heart hammering, she whirled and ran now, toward the road, away from this place. Away from death.

Griffin. Griffin. Griffin.

Wrong. Everything felt wrong. And she was drowning in dread and confusion.

She was to meet him on the road. *This* road.

He had asked her to come.

To find this horror? Was that what he wanted?

Even as the questions battered her, she found them obscene.

She stumbled, her right foot slipping into a shallow hole in the ground. With a cry, she fell to her knees, her palms scraping across the ground, damp leaves and damp earth, the smell rising up to fill her senses.

Frantic, she surged to her feet, swayed, and ran on, skirting trees and brush, and there . . . the road. Sweet relief.

She burst from the line of trees, slammed into something hard, and went down, kicking and screaming now, clawing at the thing that held her.

"Beth! Beth!"

Strong arms closed tight about her and she was sobbing, shaking, struggling against the bands that held her fast. Free. She must get free.

"Bloody hell!"

Hands grabbed her own. Griffin, she realized. Griffin held her fast. Still, she could not stop shaking, struggling.

His warm fingers closed about her own and, holding her hands, he crossed his arms, bent his elbows, guiding her hands until she closed them about his forearms.

"Hold fast to me, Beth," he rasped. "If you cannot bear for me to hold you, then *you* hold me."

He loosed his grip, set her free.

Sobbing, she dug her fingers into the muscles of his forearms, holding fast, shaking so hard that her teeth chattered and her bones rattled. But she held on to him. Closing her fingers as tight as she could, she held on to him.

He let her sob, making no move to drag her close, no move to hold her, and she was grateful. So grateful. She could not bear it now, to feel anything confining. Even her dress felt tight. Her bonnet.

With a cry, she undid the ribbons and tore her bonnet free, then raised her gaze and found him watching her.

Griffin. Just watching her, so calm and patient.

He rose, staring down at her, his eyes night dark here in the shadows. In that instant, there was no logic to her thoughts, no rational bent. There was only gut certainty.

Griffin was her one safe place.

Memories slammed her.

Hands lifting her out of the box. The flare of a rushlight, paltry and weak. A scent. The sound of a man's voice. And then darkness.

Taking her hand, he drew her to her feet, the sensation familiar. Another time. Another place. With the stink of blood heavy in her nostrils.

Clinging to him, she swayed, finding her footing and her balance. The memories faded, and she was here, in this place, with the wind cutting through the cloth of her dress. In that moment, she was grateful to feel the cold. Grateful to be alive.

"Come," he said, and then he drew her to him, closing his arms around her. She stiffened, expecting a cage and finding only comfort.

"I cannot"—she gave a hiccoughing breath, her throat sore from her crying, her head pounding, and all she could think of was the flies, the maggots—"I cannot simply leave her there like that. Alone. I cannot—"

Griffin drew back to study her. With his gaze locked on hers, he reached out and stroked the back of his hand across her cheek. She turned her face into his touch, her heart sick with all she had seen, her emotions aching for this small bit of human contact. Human warmth.

No, not merely human contact. She wanted Griffin. Only Griffin.

"I will send people to fetch her. I shall take care of her now," he said. "And of you, my Beth. I will take care of you."

He meant something more than the words implied. She sensed that. She shook her head, opened her mouth to protest.

Griffin cut off any sound with a kiss, a hard press of his mouth to hers, and no other part of him touched her. Just his lips, warm and smooth, his breath blending with her own.

Alive. She was alive as that poor girl was not.

He lifted his head, his gaze locked on hers, and bent to scoop her in his arms. Carrying her high against his chest like a child, he walked along the road, she supposed toward his horse, or mayhap his curricle.

"Where do you take me?" she whispered, her cheek against his coat.

He said nothing for a moment. She could feel his heartbeat, steady, solid, pounding in time to the cadence of his stride.

She snuggled her cheek against his shoulder, let his warmth seep into her.

When at last he spoke, the words were a mere whisper, a breath. "Home, Beth. I take you home."

Chapter Twenty-One

Hours later, Griffin found Beth in the bedchamber next to his own, wrapped in nothing more than a white sheet, the folds gathered and draped about her slender frame. She was sitting at the foot of the bed with her knees bent to one side and her feet tucked up. Flickering firelight danced over her, gilding her hair and her skin, accentuating the swells and dips of her body. He wanted to trace his fingers along each shadowed hollow.

He looked about the room. The bath things were gone, cleared away. While he had dealt with the sending of messages, the gathering of men, and the dispensing of a wagon, Beth had been tended by the maids. He had already been told that she seemed appalled by the attention and had shooed the girls out, insisting that she be left alone to bathe.

Griffin had refused to let the magistrate question her tonight. He had told Squire Spencer that there would be time enough for that in the morning. For tonight, he would see Beth sheltered and quiet and safe.

Her clothes had been taken to be laundered, her boots to be shined. Having no wish for the garments to draw bleak memories in the future, he would have preferred to see everything burned or buried. He would have preferred to buy her a new dress—a dozen new dresses—but Beth had protested to the maid and, occupied elsewhere, he had not been present to argue.

Still and quiet, he stood in the doorway, a voyeur, watching as she ran a comb through her hair with slow, languid movements. The long tresses were damp from her bath, just beginning to dry and coil up into ringlets.

Flax-pale and curled.

Such beautiful hair. This was the first he had seen it down, tumbling free over her shoulders and along the curve of her spine. The sight was sensual, alluring, enticing him to bury his fingers in the heavy mass, to feel her soft curls against his skin.

The fire cast shadows and light to paint her naked shoulders, her arms, her face, dusting her with a golden glow. He wanted to press his lips to her smooth, pale skin, taste her. Mark her as his.

Temptation. The fever of wanting her rose and swelled, a pulsing ache.

She glanced up, saw him in the doorway, and paused in her movements. Dropping her chin down, she turned her eyes aside, her lashes casting small crescent shadows on her cheeks.

"Isobel will be distressed," she said, not looking at him, her voice very soft. "We take breakfast together each morning, and I cannot bear for her to be dismayed by my absence on the morrow. She does best when there is order and routine."

Her words, her tone, poured through him. She cared for his daughter, perhaps loved her a little. Of a certainty, she knew Isobel better than he did, for he had not known that she did better with order and routine.

He recalled a conversation on a long ago day, Beth's first in Burndale.

You prefer chaos, Mr. Fairfax?

At times . . . Disorder can be liberating.

He knew himself for a man who held his emotions

under rigid control, but who decried any other limitations. No schedules, no planning, no organization. He found such things confining, restricting.

Given his own penchant for mayhem, he had not even considered that Isobel might not favor it. Instead of liberating her, perhaps chaos caged her all the more in her world of silence. The thought pained him no small degree.

But he would learn. With Beth to teach him, he would learn.

"Isobel is here, at Wickham Hall," he said. "She is even now ensconced in her chamber with a maid sleeping on a trundle by her side. I sent a footman to fetch her the moment we returned. She came readily once she knew you were here." He paused and then braved the remainder of the thought. "I needed to know she was here, under my roof. Safe."

Beth exhaled and her shoulders slumped. "I am greatly relieved to hear that she will not search for me in vain tomorrow."

Still she did not look at him. He wanted very much for her to look at him.

"And what of my absence? What did you have the footman tell Miss Percy?" she asked, tracing the tip of her index finger in small circles on her sheet-covered thigh.

"That you would remain at Wickham Hall for the night to supervise Isobel and return to the school some time on the morrow. I begged her indulgence in making do without you for a short time. I suspect that she will think nothing of it, given our conversation regarding your attendance here at dinner."

She exhaled at his reply, sharp and quick.

"It feels as though a month has passed since we spoke of my accompanying Isobel to dinner," she murmured. "Has it only been a day?"

"Only a day. And I suspect that Miss Percy will be

forgiving of your absence in light of what you have lived through this day." The words came hard to him, seeming paltry comfort. He wanted to tease and cajole her, make her smile, but in this laden moment, he could not think how.

With deliberate care, she leaned to the side and placed the comb on the small table near the bed. Then she turned her gaze up to meet his, her eyes wide and blue as the heavens, solemn and wise.

"I have been put through little enough when one takes all in context," she said, and her tone turned fierce. "I am *alive*."

Three small words, spoken in a manner that said all. Brave Beth. *His* Beth, shining like the brightest star in a dark sky. He felt something inside him give way, like a dam succumbing to the brutal assault of a storm-swollen river, and he balked at the tide of emotion.

Did he love her?

He thought he might, and that brought a bitter twist to his lips. His affection was a poison she would be better off without.

He had loved Amelia, and he had killed her.

He loved Isobel, and he failed her again and again.

Better that he not love Beth. Better that he *want* her, and let that be enough. He knew what manner of man he was, charming when he wished, deadly when he chose. He had no right to love her, for his love only brought destruction.

But he could not control the flicker in his heart, the insistence that his best plans and rigid control might not be enough to hold back the emotion. Unwelcome. Unwanted. There, whether he willed it or nay.

"And if Miss Percy *does* think something of my absence?" Beth asked.

"Then the devil take her," he said. Seeing Beth's eyes widen in dismay, he added in a milder tone that hid his deeper inclinations and contemplations, "Miss Percy will say nothing."

He wanted to tell her that he had no intention of letting her return to Burndale Academy. That she was meant to stay here with him from here on.

She was *his*.

His to treasure.

But such thoughts were outlandish, perhaps even obscene. She deserved better than to have him think of her as a possession, and in truth he did not. It was only . . . no, he would not visit the root of his peculiar preference to hold her by his side, to never let her go, to keep her safe.

He had no right to say those things, and such words would only frighten her. He had no wish to do that. Fear had no place in what he intended for this night.

Pulling the door shut, he turned to her and took a step forward, then paused.

"Do you prefer that I leave it open?" he asked with a gesture at the door, uncertain of her mood.

Her lips curved, and when she spoke, her voice was low, husky. "Do you prefer an audience?"

He blinked, laughed, taken aback by her reply.

Beth smiled. She couldn't help it. He had a . . . *wicked* laugh. Unself-conscious. Deep. The sound fascinated her, wove through her, making her blood pump in an eager rush and her pulse trip over itself.

He prowled the room, paused to stir the fire with the poker, moved to the washstand. There, he paused, frowned. Reaching out, he traced his finger over the pin Beth had left there, her pearl pin from her grandmother. He studied it for a moment, and moved on.

Holding the sheet tight about her, she put a hand to one of the carved oak bedposts and rose, his prowling igniting her own need to move, to walk. A fine pair they were, two caged cats.

She went to the window, her back to him, her gaze

directed out, into the night. With eyes closed, she just stood there, thinking that she should be afraid of the dark, of the closed chamber, of the horrific memories that threatened to surface and swallow her whole.

But she felt nothing like that. In her heart and her mind, there was only a sweet swell of gratitude.

She was alive. She was here, with Griffin. She was not that poor girl lying on the forest floor with yellow wild-flowers about her and maggots crawling from the holes that had once held her eyes.

That girl would know nothing more of life.

But Beth still had a chance, an opportunity to taste what she could, and she meant to do that. Meant to grab hold of the possibilities and sample them as she might, to tamp down the insidious wave of her secret dismay. No more would she let terror be her prison.

She meant to *live*, even if in doing so she flouted convention and rules of appropriate behavior. What care had she for such things? Despite the life her mother had once led, pampered and proper, it was not the life Beth had been born to.

Earlier, when she had left Burndale Academy, she had already taken the first step on this path, intending to meet Griffin on the road, to let him kiss her and hold her, to sample a sip of forbidden joy. Now, she would sample all he offered. She meant to enjoy this moment, for who knew when there would be no moments left.

She knew that better than most. Had always known it, since she was a child. It had only taken this to make her remember.

And her position at Burndale? The income she guarded so carefully? Well, she had seen enough now to know she was not in danger of losing her place. Foolish girl that she had ever thought otherwise. Who would come here to re-place her?

People talked. Rumors traveled. She remembered the stagecoach guard that first day by the church, his warnings and his look of apprehension. People *knew* of the women who had died here, and now there was yet another dead girl.

Who would come to a place where foul murder had been done, not once but thrice?

No, her fear of dismissal was gone now. Burndale Academy had as much need of her as she had of it.

She opened her eyes then and studied the window, searched for the moon, the stars. But she saw only Griffin's reflection in the glass, behind her and slightly to one side, his eyes dark and shadowed as he watched her.

Patient man.

He moved then, his feet shushing across the carpet, and in the glass she watched him draw near, patient no longer.

"The girl . . ." she whispered, and let her voice trail away, unable to finish her question.

"Her name was Sarah Ashton." His voice was cool, devoid of inflection, and in the night-hued panes she saw that his expression was as dispassionate as his tone. A mask, hiding much. His fists, clenched tight at his sides, belied his detached demeanor. "She was the niece of my housekeeper's husband, and she is returned to her family now."

"For me, there is no comfort in that." Beth pressed her lips together, shook her head. "And I suspect little enough comfort for them. *She* is not returned to her family, only her empty shell."

No comfort. Only sadness. Such a terrible waste. She reached out to splay her fingers against the window. Cool, smooth glass.

Hesitating, she watched his reflection, quiet and still, and then words slid free, sentiments and certainties that were pulled from the depth of her soul. "He has done this before. Will do it again. He likes it more each time. He likes to kill."

She wondered what he would think of them, think of

her and her knowledge of such things. She had shared more of herself with Griffin than she ever had with anyone else.

"Yes," Griffin agreed, and she said nothing more, for he knew it as well as she. A monster walked in the night, or perhaps in the light of day. A human beast with a taste for human blood. The thought left her cold and shaken. Sarah Ashton was not the first and she would not be the last. Not unless he was caught.

Griffin stepped closer. She could feel him now at her back, the heat of him, the rise and fall of his chest, barely touching her. His slow exhalation ruffling her hair.

"When I heard you scream," he said, bending his head so his breath fanned her skin. "I thought"—he paused—"I felt . . . concern."

'Twas not what he said that made her heart leap, but what he left unspoken. *Concern.* Such a mild word, but for a man such as he to say it seemed monumental somehow.

He lowered his head a little more and ran his lips across the swell of her shoulder.

Slowly, he gathered the damp curls that tumbled down her back, swept them to one side. Warm fingers brushing her naked skin. She inhaled sharply, and the fine hairs on her arms prickled and rose.

Reaching around her, he caught the edge of the curtain, drew it closed, blocking out the night. Beth held her breath, waiting for the tide of nervous dismay, the horribly familiar sensation of being locked in a box. But it did not come. Perhaps it was the size of this chamber—large enough to accommodate six beds—that held her fear at bay.

Or perhaps it was Griffin, the way he made her feel. Safe. She let her head fall back until it touched his shoulder. *Safe.*

The thought shimmered through her, and with it a

realization. Faint. Hazy. *What?* It slid away, smoke in the night, and she let it go.

Griffin brought his face to the nape of her neck, inhaled slow and deep. Then his tongue traced her skin, a warm, damp trail. Her knees gave way beneath her.

Wrapping one arm about her waist, he caught her tight against him, her back sealed to his front. He held her upright, his forearm pressed to her belly, his lips on her skin, and then his teeth.

The breath left her in a rush, a sob, and his free hand closed about hers, drawing her fingers from where she clutched the sheet to her breast. The cloth glided away with a susurrus of sound, whispering as it slithered down to pool at her feet, white as snow. She was appalled and awkward and secretly thrilled to be naked before him with his hands on her skin.

"You are beautiful, Beth." A low murmur. "So beautiful."

She moaned as he brushed his hand along her buttocks, up the curve of her hip, the dip of her waist. He traced the puckered scar at her side, and she froze, but he only outlined the shape of it with the tip of one finger and moved on to skim the side of her breast.

There was a sinful pleasure to this, to standing naked in his arms while he was fully clothed, to reveling in the feel of his hand on her body.

A shiver took her, working through her until it grew and changed, leaving sharp anticipation and a kind of inundation, a hot, dark throb that spread through her blood and filled her lungs, her veins, her heart.

It was terrible and terrifying and wonderful all at once, to want him so.

He was right behind her, his chest to her back, close enough that she could feel the press of his waistcoat buttons, cool and hard against her skin, and lower, the feel of his trousers and the heavy ridge of his erection pressing against the curve of her bottom. Cupping her chin, he turned her face to the side so he could kiss her lips, deep and wet, his mouth open, his tongue pushing inside her until she trembled and gasped.

The taste of him was foreign and fine, like wine or chocolate . . . or both at the same time. It left her dizzy and giddy, and hungry for more. She followed his tongue as he withdrew, sucking on him, earning a low, rumbling groan for her efforts.

That touched her, touched something deep inside her and made it flip over and over, an endless spiral.

Turning, she brought her hands to his shoulders, feeling muscle and strength, and the soft cloth of his shirt beneath her fingers. He was so . . . hard . . . like supple stone, his chest, his shoulders, his arms, all hewn and solid and firm, so different than her.

"Beth." He brought his mouth to her jaw, her ear, her throat. "Let me tell you what to expect. I want you to understand—"

She rubbed her lips across his, then kissed him deep, gripping the loose material of his sleeves as she poured all she was into him.

"I know," she whispered against his lips. "My mother is a most unusual woman. She explained all to me long ago."

That admission earned her a startled huff of laughter.

"A conversation for another time," he murmured. There was a smile underlying his words, and something else, something tense and urgent.

He kissed her neck, nudging her head to the side so she was arched away, exposed, held up only by his strength. His lips and tongue and teeth burned a trail along the column of her throat, her collarbone, the rise of her breast, to her nipple. His mouth closed around her, a gentle tug, and she cried out, astounded, shocked. Ensorcelled.

Panting, she twined her fingers in his hair, believing she meant to drag him away, but instead she pulled him close, wanting more, needing more. She could never have imagined this, the feel of his mouth on her breast, sucking, pulling, nipping the sensitive flesh until she gasped and arched and felt the hot storm of desire swirl up, stronger and stronger.

With a sound of pleasure, he lifted his head from her breast. In the firelight, she saw that her nipple glistened, swollen and wet.

Scooping her in his arms, he crossed to the bed and laid her there. The mattress was soft at her back, an embrace of feather-stuffed cloth. The sheet that had covered her was left in a puddle on the floor. She glanced at it, murmured a protest—"Let me fold it."

Her words earned her a hushed laugh and the press of his palm against her breastbone, holding her in place.

A thrill chased through her, his action both arousing and slightly distressing.

Griffin stood over her, his eyes never leaving hers, and slowly, slowly, he slid the buttons of his waistcoat through the holes and shrugged off the garment, tossing it aside to land where it would. More clothes followed, neckcloth, shirt, stockings, trousers. Tossed about. Haphazard. Chaos.

Embarrassed, she looked away from the sight of him, gloriously unclad. Then she looked back, enticed.

He wore only his smallclothes now, nearly as naked as she, but his nakedness was different than her own. Shoulders so wide and hips so narrow. Muscled legs and forearms. Hair on his chest, dark, crisp, arrowing down the center of his taut, flat belly in a neat, tapered line.

The sight was unsettling and appealing. Beautiful. He was so beautiful. She wanted to touch him, with her fingers. With her tongue.

To lick the planes of his chest and his nipples, as he had licked hers.

The thought made her shudder.

A three-quarter turn to the side and he tugged off his smallclothes. She had only a glimpse of his penis, thick, heavy, jutting out from a dark nest of hair at his groin, the tip rounded and smooth. The sight of him interested her, aroused her, made her a little wary.

He came down on her then, down from above, heat and solid weight, pressing her into the bed. She had never known a sensation like that. She was surrounded by him, held by him, his arms on either side, his body above.

Barely breathing, she waited for it, for the feeling of terror, the need to wriggle free.

A heartbeat, two, but it never came.

There was only his warmth around her, and deep, deep inside her a glowing heat that swam outward, tendrils of pleasure through her belly, her limbs.

She liked it, the weight of him upon her.

Because she knew in her heart that if she made even the smallest sound of distress, he would open his hand and she would fly free.

Tipping his head to hers, he kissed her, pushed his tongue into her mouth and the sensation of that cycled through her, lush and rich. His knees were between hers, nudging her open, spreading her. She let him. Liked what he did. The feel of the hairs on his thighs brushing her skin. The rasp of his beard against her jaw. The thrust of his tongue, tasting her as she tasted him.

Shivery hot, she moved beneath him, undulating slowly side to side so her skin rubbed against his. Delicious. Her hands ran along his back, his buttocks, hard muscled and taut, and she closed her fingers, kneading. She knew he liked it from the way his hips shifted against her own, not just warm now between her thighs but feverish hot and hard. *Him.* His penis, the rounded, smooth head she had glimpsed in the firelight. Pressing into her, a foreign stretching, stinging a bit, but somehow right.

Between her thighs, she felt strange, exotic, moist, and aching.

She moved, gasped. He moved, back, then forward. Slowly, so slowly. A stretching and burning, a feeling of invasion, odd and a little painful and stimulating all at once.

"Don't move, sweet Beth," he rasped. "Christ, don't move."

She froze, her body arguing against that, trembling with the urge to piston her hips closer to his, to slide her heels around his back. A different sort of embrace.

Instead, she lay panting beneath him, trusting that he would take her where they were meant to go. *Trusting*. How odd.

Bending his head, he licked her breast, took her nipple in his mouth and sucked. Gently at first, then harder. Hard enough that she gasped and squirmed, the pleasure so keen she arched up off the bed.

It came quickly then, the fitting of bodies, his hand gliding down between them, his fingers touching her and stroking her, *there*, where the smooth head of his penis pressed a little deeper and again, deeper into her.

Into her. A frightening and strangely scintillating concept.

Again, he stroked her, a lush, moist glide of clever, clever fingers until she *did* move, could not help but move, an urgent jerk of her hips forward, followed by a gasp.

Quick, sharp pain. Smarting. Stinging. And a feeling of fullness, of stretching, of accommodating him.

Her maidenhead, gone.

A dark angel gilded by firelight, he held himself rigid above her. So beautiful. Despite the discomfort, there was something lovely about joining with him, feeling him inside her. She arched up, ran her tongue along his throat, then fell back, smiling, letting the taste of him melt on her tongue.

He stayed very still, his weight balanced on the length of one forearm, his free hand between them, stroking, caressing, The sensation—only pleasant at first, and then fuller, stronger, more than pleasant—became delight, winding in an ever-tightening coil. With a moan, she moved, following primitive, driving instinct, but he shifted his hip, his thigh, holding her still.

Moving his mouth along her jaw, her neck, her ear, he kissed her and murmured softly, things she could barely hear. His breathing was raspy, his body taut with tension. He held himself in check, and she wondered at that. Wondered why.

She ached to move. She *needed* to move.

Panting, she shifted beneath him, but he held them both still, only his hand working its sweet, aching magic. Pleasure drove her. She closed her fingers tighter and tighter in the hard muscle of his buttocks, writhing beneath him as much as his weight allowed.

Bright pleasure, almost beyond bearing. She trembled and ached, until the liquid stroking of his fingers made her shatter, scream.

Closing her eyes, she let the waves crash over her, through her, casting her high and floating her back to the ground.

She thought she hung suspended for an eternity.

"Oh," she breathed.

"Oh," he whispered in return, the sound colored with a smile.

Which made her smile and bury her face in his shoulder, and lick the salt of his skin.

He was still there, barely inside her, hard and full, pulsing, his hips moving just a little. She understood then that he had not pushed himself as deep as he might go, that he had not floated on that same wave. What he had given her was a gift.

One she wished to share with him.

Tipping her hips to bring her as close to him as she could be, she gasped, the sound of her cry caught in his mouth as he kissed her, hard and deep. His hips pressed forward, back, a little deeper, a little faster, and she moaned, tension tightening her limbs. Lovely, seductive tension. A pleasure that built in sharp layers.

She moved as he moved, a dance of sorts, and she thought she had been right, that long-ago day on the road. He moved like a dancer, a fencer, all grace and leashed energy.

No, not leashed. He was less controlled now, a wild excitement coloring his thrusts as he drove deep and hard, very slick, very wet. At his urging, she wrapped her legs about him, her heels pressed tight to his back. She knew now where this would carry her, and this time she meant to take him with her.

Tightening her fists in his hair, she pressed her face to his neck, inhaled him, bit him. It was the same as before, only different, better, deeper and stronger, a spiral winding her until she thought she would cry, scream, if she could only—

Oh, God.

He thrust into her, hard, and again, and her insides clenched on themselves. She could feel the pulse of him inside her, or was that her own pulse? Her own wild, sweet contractions, together with his. He came to shuddering release, and she followed him into the maelstrom by seconds. And they held on and on, together, straining *against* each other and *with* each other until with a gasp, Griffin let his weight down to her side and rolled her until she was confined in the circle of his arms, his legs.

Held.

Warm and replete.

And not afraid.

Chapter Twenty-Two

Stepney, London, March 15, 1813

Henry ran his finger around the inside of his starched high collar and glanced at the sparse and sad posy he had bought for a penny from the flower girl at the corner. 'Twould have to suffice, for it was the best he could find, and his task had a powerful urgency behind it.

A mizzling rain fell, cold and damp. The cold ate at him. He thought he had not felt warm since that night at the Black Swan, since a chilling horror had gnawed clear to his bones and never wormed free.

He was not the man he had been before, but he was still a man with a conscience and morals. He knew what needed to be done.

Making his way along the gloomy alley that led to the back of the shabby little house, he pondered the words he ought to choose, the best way to approach the matter. He had practiced it a dozen ways, and he supposed that any of them would do. He had thought of going round the front door today, for his errand seemed to demand it. But he knew Miss Smith would be in the kitchen, bent deep over the tubs of hot water, mangle in hand, scrubbing and dipping and wringing, sweat rolling down the sides of her face.

Miss Smith. Before today, he had not bothered to wonder if it was her true name. For months, he had brought her his shirts and picked them up a day later, paid her what he owed, and gone on his way. Now he did wonder. Smith was no gentrified name, and she was definitely quality. Or had been, once, though hardship had landed her here, working as a laundress in a tiny hovel.

She did not belong here. Her mannerisms and mode of speech gave her away. But she was here and he was here. She, with her scarred face and body. He, with his scarred heart. Together they might do some good.

The sound of his own footsteps thumping up the stairs seemed painfully loud, and Henry paused a long moment before raising his hand and knocking hard at the door.

He heard the scrape of the bolt. The door dragged open, slowly, slowly, and the strong smell of laundry soap carried through the crack on a waft of hot, damp air.

"Oh! Mr. Pugh! Are you back already? I hadn't thought you would come until next week." Miss Smith barely met his gaze before glancing away, dropping her chin and tipping her head to the right to hide the side of her face. Not that her efforts were particularly effective.

Many times had he noted the burn scars that marked her face, puckered and painful to see. She wore a cap each time he saw her, but he thought her hair on the right might have been burned away. Her sleeves were rolled back, and her right arm was red and marked with the badges of her suffering.

'Twas no brilliant deduction to know she had been caught in a fire, but anything more than that was a mystery to him. From her pattern of speech and some innate elegance of manner, he felt certain that she had been beautiful and wealthy, pampered and cared for at some point in her life. So how had she ended up here, in an alley just off Ratcliffe Highway?

Before today, he had not wondered. But now, given his purpose here, he intended to ask her.

"Mr. Pugh?" she prodded, and he realized he had been standing about like a dolt for a very long time.

"These are for you," he said, and shot his hand forward with the small posy clutched tight.

She looked from the flowers to his face and down again, her expression almost comical in amazement and disbelief.

"Why?" she whispered, extending a hand toward him, then dropping it back to her side where she scrubbed her palm up and down against her skirt. "Why?"

He stared down at her in mute dismay. He had planned this, every word of it, but now that he stood here, he knew not what to say.

Swiping the back of her hand across her forehead, she huffed out a breath.

"Do you play a nasty trick on me, Mr. Pugh?" She raised her gaze to his then, such a depth of pain and emotion in her huge brown eyes.

"No trick, Miss Smith." He glanced beyond her into the kitchen that served as a laundry. "May I come in?"

She shook her head, and he thought she would decline, but in the end, she dragged the door open enough that he might enter.

Henry's pulse quickened, and he felt a spark of hope. He could make this work. He *must* make this work.

A memory slapped him, sharp and unkind, terrible recollections of the bed in the child's room at the Black Swan Tavern, and the great crimson blot in the center of the white sheets. Of his own emotion and sick regret, and the salt taste of his own tears.

Miss Smith went to the fire where she was warming a flatiron. She pulled it free, and with a self-conscious glance in his direction, she spat on it to test the heat. It sizzled and popped and, satisfied, she began to press and fold a shirt.

That glance tugged at Henry's heart, proof in his mind that she was from a different world, a place where ladies did not spit. She had built a life here, Miss Smith, but Henry wondered what ashes of her old life she had left behind.

"Uh . . . the . . . uh . . . posy . . ." Henry offered it to her once more.

With a sigh, she set the flatiron back in the fire and turned to face him, but made no move to accept the flowers. Henry stepped to the side and set the posy on the small table in the corner.

"Out with it, Mr. Pugh," she said.

Henry felt as though his breath was caged in his chest, trapped there, unable to tear free. Finally, he exhaled in a noisy rush.

"Well," he said, and rubbed the back of his neck awkwardly. "I find myself in need of a wife, Miss Smith, and I was hoping you might see your way clear to accept the position."

She stared at him so long, he wondered if he'd actually said the words or only thought he'd done so.

"I am scarred. Not only my face, but my arm, my back, my leg. Why do you want such a wife?" Her tone was steady, calm.

"You are available . . . er . . . convenient . . . That is, you are unlikely to receive an offer from—" He paused, ran his finger along the inside of his collar. It was exceedingly warm in here. Exceedingly warm.

"You are a businesswoman," he tried again. "And my proposition has somewhat of a business bent—" He broke off once more, thinking that none of his words were stringing together in the way he had imagined. He was making a terrible hash of this.

"And you think that to marry a laundress is as good as a fortune?" she demanded. "Then you are a fool, sir. I survive on my earnings, but am far from wealthy."

"No, no! You misunderstand. 'Tis not your money I want, but you." Her brows rose so high they almost disappeared under her cap. Suddenly, a thought came to him, one he had not considered before. "You are not already married, are you?"

Dark and derisive, a low puff of laughter escaped her. "No. Nor did I ever think to be. Not since the fire. Those dreams burned with the pretty dresses and the dolls . . . all the trapping of the girl I once was."

Henry nodded, and gentled his voice to ask, "How did you end up here, Miss Smith?"

"Well, you are full of strange and unexpected questions today, Mr. Pugh." She exhaled delicately, then shrugged as though it was of no matter to her, though he suspected the memories tore at her still. How could they not?

"The fire took everyone," she said. "My mother. My father. My three brothers. Only I escaped. The title and property went to my father's cousin, a twisted old man who thought my scars an abomination. A punishment for unspecified sins. He wanted me consigned to a madhouse for the remainder of my life. One night, I heard him speaking with two gentlemen who run a private asylum. They were there to *examine* me and take me away."

Pressing her lips together, she glanced at the posy, then asked in a low, weary tone, "Have you ever been to a madhouse, Mr. Pugh?"

"No." He cleared his throat. "No, but I have heard tales . . ."

"And I suspect that what you have heard is better than the reality. They are dark places. Evil places. Even the private asylums which are supposed to be better than most." She shuddered. "I suspect they are worse. My brother's wife was . . . unable to bear children. He put her there, in an asylum. I think she was not mad when she went there, but she was quite far gone by the time she died there."

Finding that he had nothing of value to say, Henry held his silence and listened.

Miss Smith sighed, and squared her shoulders. "The cook took pity on me. She had her brother help me sell what jewelry I had left. 'Twas all done very quickly. Very efficiently. My mother's pearls. My father's watch. There was little enough left, for my father's cousin had taken almost everything. But the cook's brother got enough to satisfy."

"Ah." Henry met her gaze and cast her a sardonic smile. "For a price, yes?"

"Of course." She did not smile in return. "Half the money was their fee, and there was little enough paid for the pieces. They were not diamonds or emeralds or rubies, after all. But there was enough to satisfy his greed, and my need." She gestured about her to encompass the kitchen. "I had no skills, no training for this life. My skills lay in polite conversation and the choosing of a menu and the best seating for a dinner party. Excellent skills for a lady. Worthless skills for a scarred girl who wants to survive. But I was lucky enough to have taken a fancy when I was small to the laundry maid, Molly. I used to follow her about and sit on a stool watching her while she worked. So, I had money to purchase lodging and enough knowledge to wash clothes."

"A hard life," Henry said.

She shot him a genuinely amused look. "Yes, but I should think that life in a madhouse would be harder still. Given my choices, I do not regret the path I took." She folded her arms across her waist and stared at him, full in the face. Slowly, she reached up and drew the cap from her head, showing the place above her ear that was bald and puckered. No more hiding. She let him see the whole of it.

He thought her incredibly brave.

"So I have told you my sad story, Mr. Pugh," she said. "It is your turn to tell me yours."

Chapter Twenty-Three

Wickham hall, Burndale, October 7, 1828

Beth opened her eyes, aware of a thin stream of dawn light leaking in from a gap in the curtains. Dust motes danced and swayed, and she frowned, disoriented. *What—Where—*

All of a sudden, all rushed back at her like the contents of a bucket sloshed in her face. She recalled the sad and terrible tragedy of the girl in the woods.

Griffin, finding her, bringing her to Wickham Hall, to a chamber that adjoined his, drawing the sheet from her body, making love to her.

She closed her eyes, a wash of confused emotions swamping her. Everything felt so *normal*, and yet so different. Outside, birds chirped, and behind her, the sound of Griffin's breathing, even and smooth. Her back was against his chest, her buttocks cradled in the crook of his flexed hips. He was *sleeping* here. With *her*.

And they were both entirely naked.

That was definitely outside her usual morning routine. Perhaps he still slept. Perhaps—

"Good morning," he said, his voice gravelly, his breath

tickling the back of her neck. His erection stirred against her bottom.

She closed her eyes, judged her options, and chose the one that most appealed. The lure of him was like strawberry tarts in the baker's window. And just as she would plaster herself to the window to be close to the tarts, she wriggled in his embrace, pressing her bottom and back against his hardness, his warmth, the contours of him that so fascinated her.

"Good morning," she whispered back, and smiled as he moved closer against her to ease his entry, settling his penis between her thighs, prodding her, and finally pushing inside her just a little, withdrawing, pushing in a little more, rocking slowly.

She angled her hips in what she hoped was an encouraging manner. But he was lazy in his thrusts, unhurried and relaxed, and though each stroke brought him closer to filling her, she was impatient. Lustful. With a moan, she arched her buttocks back and took all of him in a lovely, smooth surge.

The feel of him stretching her, filling her, was bliss. He made a sound in the back of his throat—pleasure, approval—that shimmered through her to lodge in the pit of her belly.

Slowly and languidly, he made love to her, shallow thrusts, his lips and tongue on her neck, her shoulder, and his fingers on the peaks of her breasts, gentle strokes, until she could bear it no more. She wanted all of him, all his passion, all his need.

"I want—" She broke off, bit her lip.

"Tell me. Tell me what you want." A rough whisper, heavy with desire. The sound stroked her already inflamed senses.

She wanted to tell him. Wanted to demand that he pump hard and deep, faster, like he had last night. But somehow, the words caught on her tongue, and so she showed him instead.

Reaching back to hold his side, she drove her hips against his, working them both to a frenzy. *She* determined the pace, the depth. *She* drew the feral sounds from low in his throat.

It was a heady power.

Lush, rich enjoyment spiraled through her.

Griffin stroked her breast, kneaded the fullness of it, took her nipple between his fingers, pinched lightly, then harder.

"Yes," she whispered, the word little more than a hiss of delight. *That.* She wanted that and more.

Taking her breathy word as the plea it was, or perhaps as capitulation, a relinquishing of control, he altered the rhythm, thrusting deeper and faster, and—*oh!*—moving his hips in a lovely swivel that dragged a hoarse moan from her. He ran his thumb across her nipple, back and forth, then took the sensitive flesh between his fingers and pinched again.

"Yes," she whispered again, lost in sensation, such pleasure. She had never thought to search for it, never imagined it existed.

He pinched a little harder, setting off a clamor in her blood. She clutched at his forearm where it wrapped across her, dug her fingers into the hard, corded muscle. Arching her back, she offered her breasts to his touch, while her bottom curved back, opening her more fully to his thrusts.

Close. So close. She felt the wild tempo beat through her and knew he was as close as she.

His lips moved on her shoulder, a damp kiss, and then his teeth.

Sliding his hand along her belly, into the curls at the juncture of her thighs, and then lower, to the folds of her sex, he touched her, a hard, pressing stroke that shoved her past bearing.

She shattered, crying out as he thrust once more, hard and smooth and deep, his body both frozen and shuddering, the breath escaping him in a harsh rush as he joined her in release.

Moments passed, and she lay in a pulsing reverie, a cycle of slowly fading delight, while he stroked her hair, her shoulder, her back.

Replete, drowsy, she lay in Griffin's embrace. Such a lovely place to be.

She dozed, and awoke sometime later to a tentative tapping. The light was brighter now. Past dawn. How long had she slept?

Glancing over her shoulder, she saw that Griffin lay on his back, arms and legs spread wide, his face relaxed in slumber. So handsome, a dark bandit with his tousled hair and the shadow of his beard shading his jaw. She liked the look of him. No, more than liked. She *adored* the look of him.

The knock came again and Beth rolled from the bed, retrieved the sheet that had spent the night tossed aside on the floor, and wrapped it about her naked body. Crossing to the door, she opened it a crack to find that a maid had brought a pitcher of warm water along with Beth's dress and stockings and petticoat, all freshly laundered and pressed, and her boots, cleaned and shined.

Clutching the sheet, Beth wondered how best to guard her modesty and to hide the fact that Griffin was sprawled across her bed. She opened the door only enough to take the pitcher, then, bidding the maid wait, she closed it and crossed the room to set the pitcher on the washstand. Returning to the door, she opened it once more and accepted her clothing, struggling to maintain her hold on the sheet and the door and the clothes all at the same time.

As Beth closed the portal for the second time, the sound of Griffin's laughter came from behind her, and she turned to see him propped up on the pillows, with absolutely nothing covering him.

"You are wicked," she said, glancing away and draping her garments over the back of a chair.

"Yes," he agreed, jovial. "Are you not the least bit curious?" He paused. "Not even a bit?"

"No!"

"Liar." He laughed again.

"Oh! Not only wicked, but arrogant!" She cut him a glance through her lashes, then away, tantalized and mortified at once, and amazed that she felt so easy with him. So free.

"Guilty as charged," he agreed and then said nothing more, the silence and her curiosity growing apace.

Curiosity won, as he had obviously known it would, and she spun toward him to take in her first full sight of him in all his naked glory, hard muscle and taut golden skin, laid out like a sumptuous feast.

Tipping his head to the side, he held her gaze for a long moment, then uncoiled his tall frame from the bed. Supple muscle and tendon, sinew and grace. She could not help but stare, could not help but move her gaze down his broad, beautiful chest, his lean waist, the dark hair at his groin. Lower, to the bulge of his thighs and the well-built curve of his calves.

"I never knew a man could be beautiful," she murmured.

He gave a strangled huff of laughter, and her gaze shot to his.

"Beauty is in the eye of the beholder, Beth." He lowered his voice then, a soft admission. "And my eye beholds you."

Not flowery or lush, the compliment was all the more lovely for its simplicity.

"Thank you," she whispered.

With a dark, knowing smile, he lifted his arms out to the sides and spun a slow circle. So she could look at him. Her pulse bucked and raced.

He came about to face her once more, and with a

lunge he caught the edge of the sheet, tugged, then tugged again, harder, when she resisted his attempts to divest her of it.

"Turnabout is fair play, Beth," he cajoled, a thread of laughter woven with his words.

Narrowing her eyes, she hesitated, then raised her brows. "Is it?"

She let the sheet fall and turned slowly, then faster, around and around with her arms held wide and her head tipped back until he caught her to him and hugged her, just hugged her, his arms wrapped tight about her, trapping her own arms at her sides.

Resting her cheek on his chest, she waited for it, for the sensation of confinement. For the fear. For the world to cave in on her in a black wall of terror.

Her heart raced from her reckless spinning. Her breath came a little faster than normal. But there was no tide of panic. No fear. Only a pleasant sensation of connection. Affection.

He held her with such gentle care.

More than affection. She had known she could love him if she dared. Known she might love him whether she wished it or nay.

Oh, on this road lay terrible folly. She knew it. What good end could come of this?

Drawing a slow breath, she pushed those thoughts aside. She would not spoil this fleeting joy by worrying about what would come when it was over.

Instead, she let herself enjoy the feeling of his arms wrapped around her, and that was a new and strange thing. Even her mother's hugs had distressed her at times. Yet all she felt in Griffin's embrace was safety and warmth and . . . *physical interest.* Again. Already. It seemed he was subject to similar emotion if the stirring of his penis against her hip was any indication.

Flustered, she pressed her lips together and dropped her chin. She could not recall a time when her secret terrors had not hovered just below the surface, ready to burst free without warning. Yet, standing here, held in Griffin's embrace, those fears seemed, if not fallen by the wayside, at least paled to a less glaring shade.

Why? Because she was alive? Because she had come so close to the Reaper, not once but twice, and lived to tell of it?

A measure of self-reproach came to her then.

How was it that she stood here now, with a vision of poor Sarah Ashton still so clear in her mind, and in the face of her horror she could still enjoy the sensation of Griffin's touch, enjoy the pleasure of being alive in this moment and being with him?

Griffin kissed the top of her head, and somehow read her confusion.

"You have come through a horror, Beth, not unscathed, but undaunted," he said. "Your curiosity, your intellect, your bravery are all far stronger than your fear. And to let me make love to you is an affirmation of life."

His words resonated with her, such simple truths. All these years, she had survived her memories, her nightmares, her fear. They were there, always there, eating at her like burning acid, but she had never given in. It would have been far easier to hide herself away, to sit by a window day after day and stare out at the sky. To never put herself in a position that triggered the crashing waves of terror. Never mingle with a crowd. Never go out past dusk. Never leave her home at all.

But that would have meant that she yielded. Surrendered. Admitted defeat.

She would never do that. Never.

She had escaped from the box once before. She would never allow it to lock her in again.

And she would not take Sarah Ashton's tragedy as her own, though her heart bled with horror and dismay.

Why did she see this so clearly now? Was Griffin her crutch, offering her false confidence?

Snuggled against him, she felt the weight of his arms tight about her, and she thought that he was no crutch. Rather, he was the catalyst. If she was a cake, he was the powder that made her rise. And she thought that perhaps she offered a little of the same to him.

After a moment, Griffin kissed the top of her head once more and swatted her lightly on the bottom, an action that both pleased and affronted her.

"Isobel will be wanting her breakfast, and wanting to see you," he said, stepping away from her. "Best dress with all haste."

Dress? Beth froze, sinking her teeth into her lower lip as she glanced at the privacy screen in the corner of the room and then at her pile of clothing. Finally, she looked at Griffin once more.

"Shoo," she said.

"I beg your pardon?" His dark brows lifted.

"Shoo," she repeated, mortified that he would think to remain here while she performed her ablutions or used the chamber pot. She flapped her hand at him, genuinely distressed by the thought. "Shoo, shoo, shoo."

Laughing, he sketched her a graceful bow, the propriety of the action marred by his naked state. Then he turned toward the door that led from her chamber to his dressing room. Enticed, Beth leaned forward and swatted him lightly on his buttocks, then scooted behind the chair, putting it between them, a barrier.

"Turnabout is fair play!" she insisted, laughing, and when he made to walk toward her once more, she shook her head, wagged a finger. "Uh-uh-uh. Best dress with all haste. Isobel will be wanting her breakfast."

He stared at her for a long moment, his expression solemn and pleased and puzzled all at the same time, and then he said, "You are the oddest woman, Beth. There is no other like you."

Her heart flipped over, not for the words. The simple,

silly, mundane words. But for the *way* he said them, carrying a wealth of emotion in inflection and tone.

She gasped, looked away, and barely managed to hold back her own emotions, her own words.

I love you.

To say them aloud would make them too real. She could barely comprehend the depth of her feelings for this man, She was not ready to divulge them. They were too new, too raw.

Wetting her lips, she dropped her gaze. After a moment, she heard the door between their chambers close with a soft snick, and she was left to her privacy and her confusion.

Hours later, Beth walked by Griffin's side under the midday sun. The air was fresh, perhaps too fresh, for she felt the bite of it through her clothing.

They had breakfasted with Isobel. The girl had smiled at Beth, and her gaze had not been distant and dreamy but sharp and pleased, her eyes shimmering. There had been untold pleasure in that moment, a wealth of hope released like a thousand butterflies to flit about the room on gossamer wings.

The only bittersweet moment had come when Beth had glimpsed the yearning in Griffin's expression and realized that he ached for his daughter to smile at *him*. Not for the first time she wondered what tragedy marked this small family, what horror had driven Isobel so far into herself and so far from her father.

After breakfast, the magistrate, Squire Spencer, had come with four men, and Beth had told her story with Griffin standing close behind her, his hands closed over the back of her chair. There had been comfort for her in that, in his mere presence, in the unspoken implication that he would let none distress her. In the end, she had answered all their questions, even the ones that made

her heart twist with aching horror and her eyes burn
with unshed tears.

The sad part of it was she doubted anything she told
them would be of use in finding the killer. It was clear
to her by the time they left that Squire Spencer and his
men were still harboring the idea that all three killings
were the doing of some wild beast.

How could they not see it was the work of a man . . .
a monster in human guise? She had made every effort to
suggest it to them, but they had simply stared at her, chal-
lenged her, asked for proof of her suppositions. Of course,
she had none . . . not without revealing too much. Revealing her secrets, her fears, her past. And that, she would
not do.

Shaking her head now, Beth pushed aside the memory
of the squire and his men. She glanced first at Griffin,
and then at Isobel, who walked ahead of them pushing a
miniature pram with a porcelain baby doll inside.

"I almost forgot," Griffin said, and drew forth a
folded, sealed note. "This came for you earlier."

Frowning, Beth took it from him and scanned the
contents.

"'Tis from Miss Percy," she said, glancing at Griffin to
judge his reaction. "She bids me rest this day, and she
will send Mr. Waters with the cart this evening to fetch
me back to Burndale Academy. She writes that I am
sorely missed."

His expression remained bland, but Beth detected a
slight tensing of his shoulders.

"I see," he replied, and turned his gaze to a point
behind her. "I suppose you are indispensable to the
headmistress."

"I suppose I am." Beth tried for a jaunty smile and
cheeky tone, but she suspected she fell flat on both
counts. What had she expected? That he would ask her
to stay here at Wickham Hall? In what capacity? Governess? Mistress?

No, in truth, she was far too pragmatic to have expected anything of the sort, but expectation and hope were not at all the same thing.

Still, it made leaving him no easier.

He continued to stare at something behind her, Beth turned to see what he saw. There was only the looming bulk of Wickham Hall, the windows catching the sunlight, the brick adorned by creeping ivy, thick and green and strong. The front of the house was higher than the rear, lending the whole a somewhat romantic air. But there was something unsettling about the place, as well.

Not precisely grim, just . . . unsettling.

Frowning, she realized that one part of the roof was lopsided, covered by dark green moss, and the chimney there had toppled so all that remained was a jagged outline of tumbled brick.

"Why does the roof look so strange?" Beth asked, pausing to turn fully and study the line of the house.

Griffin shrugged. "The ceiling of the Long Gallery collapsed more than a decade past. Almost no one goes there now. 'Tis a dusty, neglected place, boarded over by slats of wood."

There was something in his tone that gave Beth pause.

"Do *you* go there?"

"At times," he replied. A heartbeat, and he continued, "To brood."

Beth might have laughed at that, but his words were not said in a tone that implied humor. She thought he offered them more as a warning, a glimpse into a part of his nature she had yet to see. They conjured an image of Griffin, sitting alone in a cavernous, disused hallway, brooding over his sins, staring out a window, thinking moody thoughts. She wanted to scoff, to disbelieve him inclined to such melancholy, but there *was* a different side to him she sensed, an element of darkness. He made no effort to hide it.

In fact, he named himself the villain quite readily, as she recalled.

The wind swirled down, and she drew close the blue cashmere shawl that draped her shoulders, her fingers sliding over the soft, fine weave. Griffin had handed the garment to her as they left the house, his expression strangely flat.

"This shawl is heavenly," she said, and glanced at him to find him watching her with a tight, controlled look.

"It belonged to my wife."

"Oh . . . I . . ." She had suspected it might but had not dared to ask, had not thought to hear him speak of her. Her curiosity surged, and given that he had opened Pandora's box, she had every intention of asking what questions she could. "What happened to her, Isobel's mother?"

"Amelia. Her name was Amelia."

For a time they simply stood on the lawn, side by side in the sunshine, their breath forming little white puffs before their faces as they watched Isobel walk her baby doll in its pram. Beth thought he would say nothing more, and then he did, his words a gift where she had expected none.

"I warned you that I am a villain. Do you recall?"

"Yes." Beth pressed her lips together to keep from pointing out that she had seen nothing of his villainy and much of his kindness. He would not like her to say it, and she would do nothing to preclude his telling of this tale. She felt an urgency to know him, to understand what had shaped him.

"Amelia's death is part of my villainy." He stared down at her, and something in his expression shifted. Hardened. "Her death. My family's deaths. And more than those."

He cut a glance at Isobel, and then returned his dark, shadowed gaze to Beth. "I must tell you that I was ever a disappointment to my parents. They had their perfect son. My brother, Ethan. Older by eleven months. He was the golden son, and I"—the smile he offered then was laced with disgust—"I was the child they regretted. By the time I was eight and ten, I was a wastrel, reckless, profligate. I lost a fortune at gaming, enough that my father swore I would not see another guinea of the family wealth, and that was the best of my deeds. I was caught in the dark of night in other men's houses, caught in the bed of a wife or a daughter. More than once. More than twice. So many times I lost count. I dueled with one poor sap, a man I had cuckolded, and I shot him dead in the first light of dawn."

He stopped abruptly, and she held her breath, the weight of his admission heavy upon her.

"Let us walk," he said.

She nodded, understanding the need to move, the need to walk, the need to stay a single step ahead of memories that haunted and pained. They followed Isobel across the courtyard and the lawn and finally stepped over onto a wilder place where the grass was not so carefully trimmed, the hedge not so square. In the distance were the woods, dark and dense, the trees growing close together.

Beth shuddered. Was there a clearing in that wood, with yellow wildflowers?

"Are you cold?" he asked, but did not wait for an answer.

Shrugging out of his coat, he laid it about her shoulders, and so she was warm and he was not. She protested. He rebuffed.

Finally, he walked once more, his hand at her elbow.

"You are most chivalrous," she said, and smiled.

But he offered no smile in return. Instead he replied, solemn and quiet and somehow sad, "No, I am not. That is exactly my point, sweet Beth."

She stopped, glanced at Isobel, who had taken the doll from its pram and now sat on the grass some distance away, rocking it in her arms. Turning to face Griffin, she laid her hand on his arm, then stared at her hand. She wondered how in the space of a night she had come to a place where she dared touch him so freely.

"That man you shot . . . did you mean to kill him?"

He stared down at her, his dark eyes transformed from the laughing amusement she had seen there often to shadowy contradiction.

"Does it matter?" he asked, bitter.

"No. But it makes you less a villain," she murmured.

"Ah, and you would like that. For me to be less the villain." He paused, and she felt frantic, her heart beating too fast for a simple conversation here under the sun. She wanted him to tell her he had not meant it. She needed him to tell her that.

"No, I did not mean to kill him," he said, and his reply made her let go her breath, though she had not realized she was holding it. "The pistol was his. From a matched set. I had never shot it before. I aimed high on his right shoulder and hit him where I aimed." He stopped, rubbed his hand along the back of his neck. "He was never meant to die."

"But he did."

"He had a bleeding sickness. The wound bled and bled no matter what was pressed to it, no matter what was done."

"He *knew* it. He must have," Beth pointed out. "He knew he could die if your shot even grazed him, and still he insisted on pistols at dawn. Does he not bear some of the burden?"

"I slept with his wife, and I shot him. Where is his burden of guilt in that? I am the villain. I alone."

She nodded, his words proving him a man who would always judge himself harshest of all. "What happened to his wife?"

A lopsided smile twisted his lips, more disgust than humor. "She married a viscount in need of funds. There were whispers that it was a love match."

She realized then that she still had her hand on his arm, and she drew it away slowly, reluctantly. Before she could withdraw completely, he caught her wrist and pressed a kiss to her palm, then closed her fingers into a fist before letting her go.

"For safekeeping," he said, and slanted her a glance through his lashes, before raising his gaze to Isobel. He stood there for a long moment, saying nothing more, watching his daughter with his expression carefully remote.

"Can you not forgive yourself?" she whispered.

"No," he said, blunt, still looking at Isobel. "Not for that, and not for all that followed. Not for the years when my parents washed their hands of me and I lived on the street by my wits and my crimes."

Shocked by that, she gasped. He turned his gaze to her then and went on, talking slow and smooth, unhurried in his telling.

"I was disowned and poor and little suited to any honest labor, and so I made my way by theft and sizing up the mark, by dodging and passing off snide as real"—he paused, frowned—"Do you know what that is?"

She recalled then that he likely thought her some well-bred miss fallen into genteel poverty, taken to teaching as a respectable means of support. She opened her mouth to tell him where she came from, to tell him she likely knew as much of dodging and snide as he, but in the end, she held her tongue, deciding not to distract him from the telling of his tale.

There was time enough for her story when he was done.

So she merely nodded and he nodded in return, though she read the question in his expression, the wondering of how a girl such as she—genteel, a teacher—would know words such as those.

He drummed his fingers on his thigh, short, staccato taps, and then slapped the whole of his palm flat.

"None of those things matter but two. The first is that my brother died of consumption. My parents were killed in a carriage accident shortly thereafter. On their way to London. To find *me*, their sole remaining son.

"Upon their deaths, I was summoned home by the family solicitor. It turned out that despite my father's avowal that I would have not one guinea more of the family fortune, he had neglected to make it official. I was the heir, and all came to me."

He fell silent then and Beth felt the heartache beneath his coolly even words, the anger and turmoil that roiled inside him still. His cadence was too perfect, too controlled, and she had lived far too long inside self-imposed cages not to recognize such confining bars in another.

"And the second?" she asked, amazed that he would confide in her so. What did it mean that he trusted her with his secrets? She wondered if she dared trust him with all of her own.

His brows rose, and he said, "The second is that I married Amelia Holder, the girl I had loved since I was a lad. The girl whose father had chased me off, who had sworn never to allow me near his daughter. Much changes when one inherits vast wealth." His lips curled in a sardonic smile that held no warmth. "A year later, Isobel was born."

They both looked to Isobel then. She yet sat on the grass with her baby doll, smoothing its hair and rocking it. The sight warmed Beth's heart. She could not help but wonder if in weeks past, Isobel would have played thus, or if she would have sat staring at nothing, locked in her own thoughts.

"For a time, we were happy," Griffin said. His expression was cast in stone and he continued in a flat, dark tone. "But Amelia was headstrong and spoiled. If something took her fancy, she meant to have it, regardless of consequences. There were the sugar swans she had made for an outdoor picnic in damp weather. Her temper knew no bounds when they melted into little oozing lumps. There was the high-spirited gelding she demanded for her mount, and then demanded I shoot it when the mount proved more than she could control."

Beth gasped, horrified, and Griffin shook his head.

"I sent the horse as a gift to a friend. Amelia was contrite the next day. She knew I would not harm it. She had a temper and no limitations.

"One evening, she determined to take Isobel up to the top of the gatehouse, to watch the sunset from the crenellated wall. There was a storm brewing, the clouds dark. In truth, there was no sunset to see. As the first drops of rain fell, I let them go. The two of them, alone. I never thought to check on them. I never thought to join them. I simply let them go.

"You see, I was in a foul temper that day. My best bay had thrown me, bruised my shoulder and arm so they were swollen and numb and useless. I was not fit company for anyone save a brandy glass. Certainly I was in no mood to argue with Amelia when she had her heart set on going."

He turned then and looked toward Wickham Hall. The gatehouse stood sentinel on the front drive, and the bulk of the house hid it from view now. But Beth knew it was there, as Griffin knew it was there, and she sensed that it played a terrible role in the story he shared.

Should she distract him? Take his mind from these memories and guide their conversation to a less painful place?

A part of her thought she ought to do exactly that, to protect him from the demons that ate at his soul, but a part of her believed he would be more at peace if he would only set them free. And so, she let his tale develop as it would, saying nothing, only shifting a step closer so her arm pressed to his.

"I know not how long they were up there. I only know that my dinner was ready and Amelia was not there, and that I stalked out the front door in a temper. At first, I saw nothing, and then I heard a cry, faint and piteous. Isobel, calling for her father, for *me*.

"I ran then, to the gatehouse, and there they were, the two of them clinging like barnacles to the side of the rain-slick wall. Fallen or climbed over . . . I will never know. I called for the footmen even as I took the stairs two and three at a time. I remember little from that point except crushing desperation and fear and horror."

Beth felt them now, those emotions he described, her heart twisting in empathy.

"I leaned over. I yelled Amelia's name, and Isobel's, and they looked to me, two terrified faces." His voice dropped to a whisper. "She bade me save Isobel, her gaze locked on mine. I had only one arm worth anything, and I had only a second to choose. My wife or my daughter. One to live, the other to die. I grabbed Isobel with my good hand, winding my fingers in the cloth of her dress and dragging her up even as I dropped my weakened limb to Amelia, hoping she might grasp it, hoping she might hold on for just a moment more. And she did, she clung to the wall with one hand, and locked the fingers of her other about my wrist.

"I could feel her grasp sliding away as I hefted Isobel over the wall. Sliding farther and farther down my wrist, to my hand, to my fingers, and then away. I lunged forward, as far as I could, caught her *shawl*, her damned pink shawl, and still she slipped away. I could not hold her. Could not save her. And as I straightened, there was Isobel, staring at me with her great dark eyes. Accusing. Knowing. And she has never spoken since.

"You see, Beth. I killed her. My own wife. Isobel's mother. I killed her right before my daughter's eyes, and she has never spoken since.

"She has never forgiven me. And I have never forgiven myself."

Chapter Twenty-Four

That night, Beth settled Isobel in her bed at Wickham Hall, tucking the covers close about her and singing her a lullaby that Beth recalled her own mother singing to her. The girl squirmed free, pushing back the sheets to her waist, and for a long moment she simply stared up at Beth, her eyes very dark, her skin painted gold by the lamplight.

She looked so much like her father. Her hair, the same rich brown-black as Griffin's, the shape of her eyes, dark lashed and tipping up a bit at the corners. But her mouth was different and her chin. After a moment, Beth realized that Isobel was studying *her* in an equally assiduous manner.

Reaching up, her small hand casting a shadow across the white sheets, Isobel touched Beth's cheek and smiled. Then she sat up, the covers falling away, and pressed her lips to Beth's cheek.

Emotion surged, sweet and clear as a spring brook, and so unexpected it took Beth's breath.

For a moment, she hovered, frozen in shock and delight.

On impulse, she leaned in very slowly and wrapped

her arms about Isobel in a careful hug. Nothing confining. Nothing restricting. Just a loose touch.

The child stiffened, then relaxed, and when Beth drew back she saw Isobel's lids droop as she snuggled against her pillow. Her breaths grew deep and even, untroubled, and her limbs shifted until they were flung wide in slumber. Like her father. The sight touched something deep in Beth's heart.

How long she sat on the edge of Isobel's bed she could not say, but after some moments the clatter of hooves echoing on the drive drew her attention.

She rose and crossed to the window and looked out, but saw nothing save a night-dark expanse of manicured lawn and beyond that a glimpse between the trees of the pale ribbon of road where it curved from Wickham Hall toward Burndale Academy. From this vantage, there was no view of the cobbled drive, for Isobel's chamber was to the east side of the house, not the front.

A wise choice to house the child in a chamber that did not face the gatehouse. After what Griffin had told her earlier that day, she imagined that to look out the window and spy the crenellated wall of the gatehouse would be a horror for Isobel.

Griffin's words, the harsh self-recrimination in his tone, broke her heart. *You see, Beth. I killed her. My own wife. Isobel's mother.*

No, she did not see that at all. She saw something else entirely, and she finally understood the root of Isobel's silence, the torment in her young soul.

Griffin thought Isobel blamed *him*, but he was so very wrong.

Isobel blamed herself.

The child believed that *she* was the cause of her mother's death. To survive when a loved one died brought a terrible guilt, a crushing self-evaluation and castigation. Poor child. She locked herself behind walls of silence, in penance, in guilt, in terror of bringing down some further tragedy on her family.

Oh, Beth understood that. She understood Isobel as she understood herself. All that was left for her was to find a way to make Griffin see the truth, to find a way to heal them both.

Because she loved them. Father and daughter.

How could she not?

Griffin, her lover. The man who had scaled her walls and dropped over them with the same ease that he dropped into the back garden at Burndale Academy. The man who had offered her the only moments of real peace she had known since she was very small. In his embrace, the demons that stalked her were held at bay, not by him, but by *her*, because in his eyes she saw a reflection of her braver self, her better self.

And Isobel, the child who mirrored her own heartbreak and pain. The child of her lover. Her love.

There. She had admitted it. No more pretending that she would love him only if she dared.

She loved him despite her fears. She was afraid to love. Afraid to lose. But more than that, she was afraid to *not* know this beautiful, wonderful emotion, and so she dared to love him, and dared to open herself to what might come.

She had loved him a little right from the start, despite her demons, and his. In a way, she loved him because of them, for his secret torments allowed him to recognize hers. An excellent basis for a love match.

The irony was both dark and amusing.

Moving away from the window, she took up the candle, cast a last glance at the sleeping child, and exited the chamber. Her tread was soft as she walked the dim corridor, muffled by the carpet, pale shades of yellow and rose and blue.

She was anxious to find Griffin now, to tell him that Isobel had smiled and kissed her. His would be a bittersweet gladness, but perhaps she could help him with that. She could tell him her thoughts on Isobel's silence. Perhaps share her own secrets, make him understand.

Drawing up short, she stood staring at the candle flame as it writhed and coiled, a thin, dark stream of smoke winding up from the tip.

Did she dare tell him of her love?

That she had yet to decide.

With a shake of her head, she walked on.

At the main staircase, she hesitated, staring down into the dark well of it, then up at the heavy, thick frames of the great portraits that lined the wall. She wondered if she would be best to seek the servants' stairs.

Griffin would be appalled by that.

She was *not* a servant. The closest she could come to defining her place here was a sort of makeshift governess.

And her place in his life? She was his lover, but did he feel some greater emotion for her?

He had not said. But she was not such a fool as to imagine that he shared the story of his wife's death with just anyone. Despite her inexperience in the ways of men, she was wise enough to recognize that there was a link between them, a bond that was not felt solely by her.

Just then, she heard a sound and turned to see a maid—the same girl who had brought her dress and boots that morning—coming along the dim passage toward her.

"Do you know where I might find Mr. Fairfax?" Beth asked.

"Yes, miss. He is in the library with Squire Spencer and his men."

"Squire Spencer has returned?" So she *had* heard horses on the drive.

"Yes, miss."

Beth frowned. What matter of import had brought them back here so soon? What weighty issue could not keep until the morning? Inexplicable apprehension rode her, not an unreasoning panic, but a gut-deep certainty that something was wrong.

"Might you direct me to the library?" Beth asked.

"Oh, yes, miss. Down these stairs, then the next flight and the next, then take the gallery to"—she broke off mid-direction, likely reading Beth's bafflement in her face, and offered—"I will show you the way, miss."

The maid took her as far as the gallery, then left her on her own to take the last set of stairs to the hall below and then the library. Beth felt a pang of dismay for poor Isobel, left alone in the dark so high in this empty, echoing house.

As she descended the last few stairs, she could hear the sound of men's voices, low at first, then a little louder, then louder still until she could hear not only the tone, but the words.

"I have it here in the letter, sir"—a strident tone, confrontational and somewhat nasal—"written by the constable in charge of the investigation of the Stepney killings, one Samuel Loder. And the circumstances described are horrifyingly akin to the killings of three women right here in Burndale!"

Beth thought she knew that voice. She frowned, paused, her hand resting on the newel post at the base of the stairs.

The man spoke again, louder, more insistent.

"Mr. Fairfax," he said, "do you deny any knowledge of the events at the Black Swan Tavern on the fifteenth of January, in the year of our Lord 1813? Do you deny that you were taken to the Shadwell Magistrate's Office and there interviewed the day after the crime?"

She *did* know that voice. It was Mr. Moorecroft, the school trustee. She felt both shocked and amazed to hear his tone so strong, his words so forceful. She had

found him bland and mild each time she had met him
at Burndale Academy.

"Tell me you deny knowledge of the Black Swan
Tavern," Mr. Moorecroft demanded, his voice rising.
"That you deny knowledge of the landlord, William Trot-
ter, and his wife, both butchered in cold blood. And
Ginnie George with her scalp cut from her skull. Tell me
you were never seen at the Black Swan Tavern."

In the utter silence that followed his interrogation,
his words echoed through Beth's thoughts, louder and
louder, the *content* of his attack buzzing and snapping.
A chilling distress bobbed up like a cork.

He was speaking of murder. Those in Burndale, and
others from a time past.

The Black Swan Tavern.

Beth closed her fingers tight about the newel post,
struggling for balance as Mr. Moorecroft's words sent
dismay thudding through her veins, cold and slick and
greasy.

William Trotter, and his wife, both butchered in cold blood.
And Ginnie George with her scalp cut from her skull.

Dizzy with the suddenness of the choking black wave
that crashed through her, Beth stood there, sick with
what she heard. She swayed, the world caving in on her,
crushing the very breath from her, until her chest knotted in a tight, agonizing ball.

. . . butchered in cold blood . . .

The accusation in Mr. Moorecroft's tone, and the
things he said . . . to *Griffin.*

To her lover. Her *love.*

"I deny nothing," Griffin replied, his tone calm and
chill as the grave.

Beth's knees gave way beneath her and she sank to
the floor at the foot of the stairs.

. . . butchered in cold blood . . .

She was choking, dying, her heart slamming about in
her chest like a feral creature desperate to tear free, her

vision dim, her thoughts muddled. Panic roared through her, surging and plunging.

Suddenly, she was back there, in the horrid little box, dark as tar, the sides close about her, the fear thick and sharp enough to cut.

She was full to the brim with terror, so strong she could taste its bitterness, so strong that she breathed it in like air, smelled it and touched it and knew naught else.

. . . butchered in cold blood . . .

They had come for her, the things she was always afraid of. The memories. The dreams.

The truth.

"I deny nothing."

Griffin met the gaze of each of the men assembled in his library. Squire Spencer, who served as the local magistrate. Four of his men. James Dover, Ian Pinn, Mick Christie, Charles Price, all from Northallerton. They hung back, hats in hands, frowning as though they knew not what to make of Mr. Moorecroft, who stood before Griffin's desk and in the wake of Griffin's quiet assertion, began to reread passages from a letter that he had received from London in reply to inquiries he had made. Moorecroft had been very careful to explain it all to them at the outset, before he began his recitation.

"This passage here is of great interest . . ." In a monotone he read on, a litany of villainous crimes. He finished the letter and asked again about Griffin's presence in Stepney the day of the Black Swan Tavern murders, and the presence of Richard Parsons, as well.

With his patience grown thin and his hospitality strained, Griffin sliced through Moorecroft's sonorous tone to ask, "Is there a specific question you wish answered, a specific accusation you make, sir? Not one buried a decade in the past, but something current and relevant to the moment."

From the corner came the sound of someone clearing his throat.

"You were in Stepney the night of the murders on New Gravel Lane. And you were in London the night that a girl was found dead in Covent Garden," Mr. Moorecroft said, belligerent, his cheeks reddening.

"Yes, I was." Griffin drummed his fingers in a slow roll over the top of his desk. "I was there, and I was interviewed and questioned in both incidences, as you are well aware from the content of the missive you are so taken with." He let the silence hover, then said in a low tone, "I was interviewed at length, and I was declared quite free to go."

Rage churned in his gut, a lush and tempting thing. How long since he had given free rein to his anger? How long since he had felt the enveloping heat of it, the power? Both too long, and not long enough. A cool head would better serve him here. He nodded at the letter clutched in Mr. Moorecroft's hands. "I recall Samuel Loder. And another man . . . Seymour . . . Robert Seymour. They were competent and thorough inquisitors."

"And they recall you, sir, as well as your companion, Mr. Richard Parsons. The letter states that a witness saw one of you drinking at the Pear Tree Inn on the night of the murders, but he could not be certain which of you it was. He stated that there was a similarity of hair color and build, and he was a bit in his cups."

"Yes, you have read that part," came Squire Spencer's voice. "Is there aught else to add?"

Mr. Moorecroft turned and looked at the other man over his shoulder, then spun back to Griffin and said, "The letter further states that you and Parsons vouched for each other, claimed to have been together the entire time. Combined with the witness's testimony that placed at least one of you at a location other than that of the crime, you were removed from the list of suspects."

"There, you see," said Squire Spencer. "This is a waste of time. I told you that from the outset."

"Is it?" asked Moorecroft, his eyes never leaving Griffin's. "And what if I were to tell you that Mr. Richard Parsons was in Northallerton at the time Sarah Ashton disappeared, and that he is here, in Burndale, now that we find her dead. Do you see no relevance in that? I say there is no beast killing these women, unless it is a beast in human guise. And I say that it is no single monster doing the deed, but the two of them, in cahoots."

Griffin rose then from his place behind his desk, let his gaze sweep the men who stood in his library. Men he knew. Whose families he knew. For the most part, men who were levelheaded and even, who had not been inclined to judge and gossip when Amelia died. Each met his gaze, and in their eyes he read no judgment. Not yet. They were not convinced of Moorecroft's accusations, but with enough rhetoric, even intelligent men could be swayed.

His gaze swept the room. A shadow shifted in the hallway, stretching through the open door. Someone there. Someone listening.

Moorecroft cleared his throat, and Griffin's gaze jerked from the library door to the man's face. He blinked, startled by what he saw etched in his features. Malice. Perhaps even hate.

For a moment, Griffin was taken aback. He had always seen Jeremiah Moorecroft as a mild man with little fervor or flame, a man of bland features, bland temper, bland intellect. But now, something different shone in his pale eyes, the zeal of a man on a mission, determined to see the end of his quest, regardless of the cost.

Someone said, "We must find this Parsons. Hunt him—"

"No." Griffin kept his tone low and flat, though he felt

the rising anger, a crushing wave, felt the need to snarl
the order. Which was precisely why he did not.

It was happening again, his life spiraling out of his
control, and he had no intention of letting it. Not now
that he had found her, found Beth.

He knew who she was, had probably known on some
level ever since he first saw that pearl pin on her collar.
It was a unique piece, one he had fleeced a fellow of in
a card game at the Pear Tree Inn fifteen years in the
past. He recalled it because the pearls were strangely set
in the shape of a square, and because he had used it to
pay his bill at the Black Swan Tavern on the very day of
the murders there.

The vagaries of fate had brought her to him, his brave,
brilliant Beth. She was his. She was meant to be his. And
no bumbling moron like Jeremiah Moorecroft was going
to set in motion a chain of events that would rip her
from him.

Griffin was no longer a stripling lad thrust into a circumstance he could scarce fathom, green as new grass
and twice as trusting. He was versed in life's darkness
now. He knew what to do.

"I say—" came Moorecroft's offended protest, and
Griffin almost laughed, not with mirth, but with incredulous fury, with the dark rage that swelled and bulged.

"*I* will hunt him," he said, polite, smiling, in control.
His anger was alive, a writhing, snarling beast, and he
held it by the tail. He let the smile fade and his tone
grow cold. "I know his ways. I know his thoughts. He was
my boon companion for nigh on a decade, and I *will*
find him. Any who would gainsay me, speak now."

Bloody hell. Whatever Richard Parsons was, Griffin
could not believe him a murderer of innocent girls.
But a swarm of men bent on finding a killer might not
listen to reason, might allow vigilante inclinations to
rule. For the years they had spent together in Stepney,
for the times Richard had kept him fed and safe, for

the lessons on how to use both his fists and a knife, Griffin owed him.

His gaze slid once more to the open library door, but there was no shadow now, no movement, no sound.

Shifting his attention, he looked at Squire Spencer and each of his men in turn. Their eyes met his, but they said nothing, though each wore a troubled frown. Did they lend credence to Moorecroft's accusations, or did they frown at the tension they sensed hovering in the room like a fetid mist?

It mattered not.

He must do this alone, and do it now, face the demons in his soul, in his past. Face the things he had done, the choices he had made. They had leaked into his present where he had no liking for them.

At length, he looked to Moorecroft, to the pale glitter of his eyes and the sweat-beaded paleness of his skin.

"We are in accord, then?" Griffin prodded, a warning woven through the question.

Moorecroft swallowed, once, twice. Finally, he nodded.

Griffin inclined his head and gestured to the open door. "Then I shall bid you gentlemen good evening."

He came round his desk and strode past them into the passage.

Glancing about, he crossed to the newel post and stood for a moment before reaching out and closing his fingers in soft blue cloth. Draped over the post was a dark blue cashmere shawl.

Beth.

Bloody hell. How much had she heard?

Beth climbed into the cart, grateful for Mr. Waters's helping hand. She was woozy and ill, her belly turning over and over until she thought she would be sick on the cobbled drive.

"You're shaking, miss." Mr. Waters squinted up at her, then reached into the back of the cart and dragged forth a thick blanket. With a flick of his hand, he shook it out and tossed it across her skirt. "That should help."

"Thank you," Beth whispered, her mouth dry as sifted flour.

She had forgotten that Mr. Waters was to come fetch her back to Burndale Academy. It was only happenstance that saw her in his cart now.

Overwhelmed by what she had overheard outside Griffin's library, she had managed to gather herself from the floor by sheer force of will. Her thoughts in turmoil, she had fled. Oh, she was honest enough to admit that she could not bear to face those men if they walked from the room and found her trembling on the floor.

She had wandered through the halls, sick at heart, and found herself in the front entry, just standing there, her arms crossed and held tight about her waist, as though she could hold in all the horrible thoughts and memories and confusion that buffeted her like a winter storm.

How long had she stood thus? A minute? An hour? She had no recollection of the passage of time.

She only knew that a footman had come to her and said that the cart had arrived to take her to Burndale. She thought she must have made some reply, though she could remember none of it.

Like storm waves crashing on the shore, doubts and questions buffeted her.

Griffin had been at the Black Swan tavern fifteen years past.

How was that possible?

He had been questioned in the Stepney murders, and the murder of the girl in Covent Garden—

"Miss? Miss?"

On a sharp inhalation, Beth forced herself to concen-

trate. Mr. Waters was standing by the cart, looking at her in that peculiar way of his.

"I'm sorry, I—" Beth stared at him, having no idea what she meant to say. She shook her head.

After a moment, he rounded the back of the cart, climbed up by her side, and taking up the reins, he clucked at the horse.

Curling her fingers over the edge of the seat, Beth stared straight ahead as they went down the drive, through the massive open gate, and then turned east on the road toward the school.

On instinct, her gaze slid to the windows on the second floor, and she searched for the one she thought was Isobel's. Then she turned her gaze to the road, a pale ribbon unfolding before them.

Mr. Waters seemed little inclined to conversation, and Beth was grateful for that. Grateful, too, for the chance to return to Burndale Academy, to sit alone in her chamber and sort through the roiling turbulence of her thoughts.

Isobel stood in the dark, looking out her window. It was very late, and she had woken from a strange dream feeling restless and . . . something else. She could not seem to find the right name for that feeling, not precisely unhappy, only . . . not precisely happy. Which made no sense to her because ever since she had met Miss Canham—Daddy called her Beth—she had felt far nicer than she could ever recall.

Frowning, she looked to the sky. The moon was high and bright tonight, casting a glow over the countryside, a pretty silver glow. Miss Canham made Isobel's heart feel like that, pretty and glowing. Warm. For the first time in a very long time, she felt warm.

And Miss Canham made her daddy smile. That made her feel warm and glowy, too.

She pressed her nose right up against the glass, blew a breath, and watched a white cloud form on the pane. Moving back, she let it dissipate, then did it again and again, until a movement in the distance caught her eye.

She paused and tipped her head to the side. There was a cart on the road. Her window offered no view of the drive, but between two great stands of trees, she could see a part of the road where it curved toward Burndale Academy, shining pale in the moonlight. And on the road, she could see a cart, carrying . . . two people.

She leaned closer to the window.

Yes, two people. They were too far away to say for certain who they were, but she thought one was a man and one was a woman and the cart plodded along the road at a very slow pace, listing heavily to one side, and then stopping entirely.

The man climbed down, walked around, and disappeared from view, perhaps to squat down on the far side of the cart. There was one horse, and it dropped its head, then lifted it once more. After a moment or two, the man reappeared and stopped by the side of the cart, and he spoke to the woman for a long time, gesturing and talking. She shook her head. Finally, he threw his hands in the air and turned away.

The woman shifted on the bench, and Isobel caught a glimpse of her hair beneath her bonnet, pale and bright. Miss Canham. The woman on the cart was Miss Canham.

Yes, that made sense. Isobel recalled then that Mr. Waters was to fetch Miss Canham back to the school tonight, and Isobel was to return there on the morrow.

So the man was Mr. Waters.

Isobel shivered. For some reason, he always made her uneasy. She thought he did not like little girls very much, for often she would find him staring at them, his eyes unfocused and distant, his expression completely

blank. She hated when he watched them like that, as though he saw them but *didn't* see them.

Something about him always made her feel a little quivery and anxious.

He had walked back a ways now, leaving Miss Canham sitting on the cart. Pausing on the road, Mr. Waters looked back, and Isobel thought he said something. Miss Canham only shook her head, and Mr. Waters began to walk along the road once more, back toward the drive of Wickham Hall.

Miss Canham stayed where she was, her arms wrapped about her waist, the lantern at the side of the coach casting a yellow glow. There was something in her posture—all curled over onto herself with her head bowed—that made Isobel unhappy. Because Miss Canham was unhappy. Isobel was certain of it.

For a long moment, Miss Canham stayed where she was, and then she, too, climbed down, took up the lantern, and began to walk after Mr. Waters.

Isobel was glad for that. She had no liking for Mr. Waters, but she had even less liking for Miss Canham sitting in the broken cart alone on the dark road. It seemed that Miss Canham felt quite the same way, for she quickened her pace and hurried along as Mr. Waters rounded the bend.

Then the light from Miss Canham's lamp went out. Snuffed, just like that, the suddenness of it making Isobel's tummy drop to her toes.

Wrong. This felt *wrong*.

Isobel knew it in her heart, in her soul. Miss Canham disliked the dark. She never went anywhere without a candle. Many a night, Isobel had slunk through the silent hallways of the school, paused outside Miss Canham's door. There was always a rushlight burning. Isobel had seen the faint glow from beneath the door.

Miss Canham would not walk that road in the dark. She had not snuffed that lamp.

But someone had.

Isobel pressed right up against the glass, her breath coming fast and the glass going white where her mouth huffed against it.

Then she saw a curricle outlined by the shine of the moon. A curricle moving at a brisk pace along the bright ribbon of road, rushing away into the night.

Into the darkness.

Chapter Twenty-Five

Stepney, London, March 15, 1818

Henry Pugh swallowed at the sight of the blood. He had known there must be some. Still, he would have preferred that there be none.

The midwife glanced at him, her frown fierce and furious. She had not wanted him here in the birthing room. Had not wanted him in the house. But he had been adamant.

His wife was birthing his babe, and he had no intention of leaving her.

"No pushing, now, Mrs. Pugh. You just breathe like I told you," the midwife said as she leaned close to take a better look.

Melanthe panted, short sharp breaths, her brow furrowed with pain and concentration. Her eyes met his, locked there, and he stepped forward as she reached for him with her scarred hand.

"Almost there, love," he murmured, weaving his fingers through hers. "Almost there."

"Push, Mrs. Pugh! Now!" the midwife cried.

Her face contorting with her efforts, Melanthe pushed, gripping his hand like a vise. He was amazed that she could find such strength. Her belly undulated and rolled, squeezed in the fist of another mighty contraction.

Leaning down, he brushed her sweat-damp hair from her brow. She groaned and pushed, her face red, her shoulders rising from the pallet.

There was a saying in Stepney, that to marry a laundress was as good as a fortune. As he looked at his wife, he thought he had found the truth in that, though for him the fortune was not in coin, but in healing.

"Again! Push again!"

Melanthe cried out, a long, low groan.

"Lovely," the midwife murmured, and Melanthe fell back, a look of wonder washing away the pain that had etched her features only seconds past. Her gaze sought his, and she smiled, a tired and weak smile, but beautiful to him.

Henry saw not her scars. He saw not the place above her ear where her hair had burned away in the fire and never grown back. He saw only the woman he had come to know in small smiles and shared laughter, the woman who had made emotion unfurl in his heart, a little at a time. The woman he loved, the mother of his—

"A son," the midwife said, her voice pitched to carry above the infant's sudden cry. "You have a son, Mr. Pugh."

A son.

Tears stung his eyes and he leaned down to press a kiss to Melanthe's brow. She was laughing and sobbing, his sweet wife. Turning her gaze to his, she offered a watery smile. A special smile.

Their life together was a surprising gift, unanticipated and extraordinary.

Neither had expected to find love in this match. Neither had expected *anything*.

They had married with the sole intent of saving the child. The Trotters' granddaughter. With no relatives to care for her, and the Black Swan worth little after her grandfather's debts were paid, the parish had meant to send the girl to the poorhouse.

No one wanted her, a cursed little girl whose parents had died of plague and whose grandparents had died of foul and bloody murder. The child herself had barely survived. For a time, the doctor had said she would not, for the wound in her side had bled so much, and the infection that followed was so vicious.

But Henry had wanted her. Wanted her though they said he could not have her. That an unmarried man could not raise a little girl.

As if the poorhouse could raise her better.

He was determined not to let her go. He was the one who had found her in the empty linen chest, bloodied and silent, her lips blue. He was the one who had lifted her out, his chest working with uncontained sobs, his arms tight about her as he carried her through the street to the doctor.

Ginnie George was dead, murdered, and he had not saved her. But he had saved this little girl, the Trotters' granddaughter.

And the parish meant to deny him, to rip her from his care and send her to wither and die in a terrible, sad place.

When he had failed to sway the tide with rational argument, he had found another way. With the memory of his beautiful Ginnie bright in his mind, and the heartbreak of her loss a burden he could scarce carry, he had gone to the fire-scarred laundress, Melanthe Smith, asked her to marry him, asked her to be a mother for the child and save her from the poorhouse.

And, bless her, sweet Melanthe had agreed.

"Bring our daughter," she whispered now, cuddling their newborn son to her breast. "Bring our daughter to meet her brother." She glanced at the window. "But first, open the curtains. You know she cannot bear the dark."

"I know, love."

And so, despite the clucking and protests of the midwife, who warned of evil spirits and the dangers of vile humors, Henry opened the curtains, let the sunshine flood in. Then he went to find his daughter, his Elizabeth.

Chapter Twenty-Six

Northallerton, Yorkshire, October 7, 1828

Beth woke in darkness. There was a pounding ache in her head and the sound of breathing, harsh and wet, close behind her.

Confusion surged, and with it, a tide of fear.

She could smell damp earth, feel the coolness of it against her cheek. She was lying on the ground.

Disoriented, she tried to move, to sit up, tried to call out, but her wrists were held tight, one to the other, and her mouth was filled with something that left her tongue dry and dusty.

Her hands were bound together before her. And she was gagged.

She writhed and jerked, testing her bonds, desperate to be free, her fear no longer a tide but a swelling, crashing wave. Awkwardly, she reached her bound hands toward the gag, frantic to tear it from her mouth, but something stopped her. A hand on her arm?

Panting through her nose, she tried to move her feet and found she *could*. Though her hands were tied, her feet were free.

Who—

Where—

Beside her, her captor shifted, moved to stand behind her, his feet shuffling along the ground. He touched her, a strong grip on her upper arms, holding her still, then he dragged her to a sitting position and held her there as she wove and swayed and finally found her balance.

She could barely breathe, the gag and her panic combining in a sickening brew, her heart thudding a desperate rhythm.

But she forced herself to be still. To listen.

Who was he? What did he want?

He squatted behind her, what felt like his bent knee bumping her shoulder. She jerked as he touched her hair. He had unpinned it, or perhaps her pins had come free on their own, and she could feel him stroking the length of her curls where they fell along her shoulder and arm.

Again, he shifted at her back, his hot breath on her neck.

Bile crawled up her throat, bitter and stinging. Beth swallowed, forced herself to repeat the action again and again, willed herself not to vomit.

Through her terror, she forced herself to assess her situation, to hold on to what shreds of calm she could gather. She was gagged. She was bound. And she thought he had tied a cloth over her eyes, for she could see nothing, but she could feel a slight pressure, like a scarf around her head.

"Be still. That's a good girl," he whispered, his lips against her nape.

The sound of his voice made a chill skitter across her skin. She struggled then, though she knew it was useless. Her hands strained against the rope until they were numb from the pain, and she screamed into the gag, though little sound escaped.

"Be a good girl." Another stroke of his hand on her

hair, his tone a low caress. "No tears and tempests, now. No tantrums."

The sound of his voice was familiar. Frightening. A nightmare slithering out from the past.

She trembled, willed her emotions under her control. Terror would mean her death. Her only hope lay in keeping her wits about her, her mind sharp.

The pounding throb of her fear was a knife piercing her, a bludgeon beating her. The power of it swelled and rose, a black, oily torrent that obliterated reason.

Oh, she knew this feeling.

Knew how to *fight* it, to *control* it. She had spent her life learning those lessons.

A slow breath in. A slow breath out. She counted the seconds for each breath, blocking all else. There was only the feel of her lungs filling and deflating. Slowly. Slowly.

"That's a good girl." His voice was far away from her now. She made it far away. Down a long empty tunnel where it could not touch her. She had lived with panic for so long, her fine companion. She could control it. She could do this. She could *do* this.

"Nod for me, Elizabeth." The sound of his voice was familiar. So familiar. If he would only speak in a normal tone, raise his voice above a whisper, she would know him. "*Beth.* Nod so I know that you hear me. So I know you will be a good girl."

She heard him. She nodded.

And all the while she counted the seconds for each breath, felt the swelling tide of dread and horror threatening to tear free. She held it back. Forced it back.

Because to let it free would mean her death.

His fingers moved at the back of her head. The cloth that wrapped her eyes was pulled free and she blinked against the light of the candle.

Keeping her head bowed, she breathed in a careful,

steady pattern, one contrived for composure. One-two-three-four. A slow count in. The same count out.

She glanced about from beneath her lashes, a rapid assessment of her surroundings.

A shack? Wooden walls. Wooden roof. Dirt floor. And in the center a . . . *coffin* . . . buried in the dirt, with the top open.

Do not put me in the box. Do not put me in the box. Oh, please, do not put me in the box.

But in the touch of his hand on her hair, the rapid cadence of his breathing, the way he leaned close and breathed her scent, she read his excitement. And she read the truth.

He meant to put her in the box. Bury her in the box. *Before or after he kills me?*

Isobel flung her door wide and ran down the passage, her bare feet flying. She had no candle to light her way. No lamp. She did not care. Miss Canham was afraid of the dark, but Isobel was not, and there was moonlight enough spilling through the windows at the far end of the hall.

At the top of the staircase she paused only long enough to feel the solid curve of the banister before rushing into her descent. Sliding her hands along the polished wood, she hurried down the stairs, terrified that she would fall.

More terrified that she would be too late.

She had seen her. Miss Bodie-Stuart. From the window at Burndale Academy, she had seen Miss Bodie-Stuart climb into that very same curricle.

And Miss Bodie-Stuart never came back.

Instead, she went into the ground in the churchyard on a cold, gray winter day. All the students from Burndale had attended her burial. They had cried, and the teachers had cried, and Miss Percy, as well. And Isobel had stood to the side, dry-eyed, and never thought about the curricle.

Until now.

Gripped by an awful terror, Isobel thought of Miss Canham, of the churchyard and the cold ground, and she stumbled, her feet sliding off the edge of a stair. She gripped the banister with all her might, panting as she righted herself, tears streaming down her cheeks. Then she rushed on, urgency and fear driving her.

A sob of relief burst free as she reached the gallery, and she ran to the staircase at the far end as fast as she could, her long nightdress swirling about her legs. Finally, she took the last stairs, slipping and sliding and almost falling, her chest heaving, her heart racing.

She flew to the library door, flung it wide.

Found the room empty.

No! Frantic, she spun, ran back into the hall, and froze.

Where would he be? Where would her father be?

Where?

She looked right. Left. Took a step in one direction, then the other. No time. There was no time.

Daddy.

Her throat worked convulsively. Her mouth shaped the word, but no sound came.

Daddy.

Harder, she tried harder, her breath coming so shallow and fast that she felt sick.

Daddy.

"Daddy!" The word was barely a sound, barely a breath, but she had done it. She had *said* it.

Hope burgeoned, and she tried again, and finally the sound did break free, rising through the dark, quiet house, a high, keening cry.

"Daddy! Daddy! Daddy!" Again and again she cried out, the words tumbling together until they were only noise without form. Endless noise.

She screamed, wordless shrieks, even after she heard the echo of running feet, even after she saw the flicker of a lamp moving fast along the gallery, even after she saw him coming down the stairs in great leaps, his expression stark and tense.

Only when he grabbed her and hugged her close did she stop. Not abruptly, but more a slowing of the flood, a quieting of the torrent.

"Daddy," she whispered.

He drew back so he could see her face and she could see his. His cheeks glistened, wet with tears.

Reaching up, she laid her fingers flat on his cheek.

He cried. For her.

She had never seen her father cry.

"Isobel, my beloved. I am here. I am here," he murmured, pulling her close against his chest once more and stroking his big hand along her back.

"Daddy, he took her. He took Miss Canham."

"Yes, Isobel. Mr. Waters took Miss Canham back to Burndale. We knew he would. Miss Percy sent a note." Another gentle stroke of his hand along her back. "But you shall see her on the morrow."

She shook her head, swallowed. "The curricle . . ."

Her father drew back, studied her face, and said, "The footman said that Mr. Waters came to fetch her in the cart."

"No." Her voice failed her, the word fading to a croak. Isobel dug her fingers into her father's arms, forced her lips to shape the sounds, prayed he would understand. "Not the cart. *He* took her in the curricle. He *took* her, Daddy. Like he took Miss Bodie-Stuart."

Beth's gaze darted to the coffin, buried in the earthen floor save for the open top, and she found that she could not look away. The single candle that sat in its holder on a low stool in the corner cast creeping shadows along the walls and floor, and into the open coffin, a black pit that would swallow her.

Her terror knew no confines. It was a swelling, bulging mass that stole her breath, stole her thoughts.

No!

Think of nothing but each breath. Think of this *second,* this *breath, and nothing else.* And as the crushing panic bore down on her, she breathed and counted and listened for the sounds of him behind her, her focus and the force of her will the only things keeping her from dissolving in a sobbing, whimpering heap.

She could feel her captor close at her back, feel his hands on her hair, touching her. The smell of old sweat mingled with the scents of damp earth and hair tonic and tallow from the candle.

"Be a good girl," he crooned. "Be still."

He lifted a curl. Inhaled deeply. Her stomach pitched and rolled.

She held herself as still as she could, though her limbs shook and her teeth chattered against the cloth of the gag, and she ached to fling herself to her feet and run and run and run.

Not yet. Wait for your chance. Do not waste your one chance.

Was there anything she could use as a weapon? Anything at all? A quick glance about. There, in the far corner, a heavy wooden bucket.

"Be still. Be silent." His lips were at her ear, and his voice was low and soft. "And speak only when I bid you."

She nodded again, without prodding. He seemed pleased by that, for he took the gag from her mouth.

"You are not to soil yourself," he said, his tone chilling and void of inflection.

Her gaze shot to the bucket in the corner once more, but she held herself as still and silent as she could.

"Foul refuse makes a haven for vermin." Again, a long slow stroke of her hair. "I cannot abide vermin."

She cringed as he grasped two strands of her hair,

drew them apart, and leaned close. This he did again
and again . . . looking for vermin. Shuddering, she
fought the urge to jerk away, to cry out in horror.

Beth ran her dry tongue over even dryer lips.

"May I—" The words came out as little more than an
indistinguishable rasp. She ran her tongue over her lips
once more, and tried again. "May I speak?"

He made no reply, and so she dared to continue. "M-may
I p-p-please go just beyond the door to . . . um . . . to . . .
s-s-see to my needs? So I do not soil myself and invite . . .
vermin."

She kept her tone as even as she could, though her
whole body trembled now with sick terror that left her
clammy and choked. He would not agree. Of course
he would not agree. But that was not what she wanted of
him, anyway.

Silence greeted her request. Cold sweat trickled down
her back.

Her gaze flicked to the open coffin.

"Please," she croaked, strangled by horror and fear. "I
promise to be a good girl."

She heard only the horrible pounding of her blood
in her ears, a violent throb, and the scrape of his foot as
he stepped away. She held her breath, then exhaled in
a whimpering rush as he shoved her—with his foot?—
along the ground toward the coffin.

He was going to bury her. Bury her alive. In a tight
little box with her shoulders banging the wood on each
side—

Breathe!

One-two-three-four. She counted the beats like the toll
of a bell, slow and even, drawing air in equal measure.

*You are intelligent and courageous, Miss Canham, stronger
than all your terrors combined. You can master this. You have
mastered this.*

Griffin's words sounded in her thoughts and the memory
of the way he had looked at her, admiring, caring. She drew

on that recollection, made *his* confidence her own. There
was no one to save her but . . . *her.*

"Please, sir," she rasped, imbuing her tone with docil-
ity. "I have no wish to soil myself and displease you.
N-n-no wish to provide a nest for vermin."

Silence.

She trembled so hard that she twitched and jerked,
her knees bent up, her bound hands on her thighs, her
head bowed.

Please. Please.

"Use the bucket," he said, not in a whisper, but in a
crisp tone.

She knew him then.

A monster in the guise of a man. Not outstanding.
Not memorable. Thin, sandy hair. Pale eyes.

It was *he* she had spied that morning in Northallerton. Not the gentleman from the coach, but someone
of similar unremarkable coloring and build.

The trustee, Mr. Moorecroft.

He had stood there, in Griffin's library only hours
past, and accused *Griffin* of these heinous crimes. To distract any investigation from himself.

She barely had time to register the shock of her realization when he grabbed her, his fingers biting into her
arm. He jerked her to her feet, spun her to face him.

The candlelight flickered and danced, reflecting off
the length of the blade he held. Long. Sharp. Her gaze
locked on that and her body went cold clear down to
the marrow of her bones.

"I see no vermin," he said, and with careful concentration, he drew forward a lock of her hair and sliced it
neatly away, close to her scalp.

Beth sank her teeth hard into her lower lip to hold
back her cry of horror. He had done this to the others,
the other women, the ones he had killed. But he had
not stopped at a single lock.

He had shorn off their hair at the scalp.

With a hideous grin, he drew a silver watch from his pocket. A large watch, like the one she remembered from when she was very small. Her grandfather had had a watch like that.

Why did she think of that now?

Pressing a button at the top of the pocket watch, he released the lid, flipped it open, and tucked her hair inside. It was pale against a darker gold lock already within. The sight of that, the knowledge that it was the hair of one of the women he had killed, made her weave in place, her fear so great she thought she might die of it.

He had something else in his hand, something small. Reaching out, he touched her bodice, his fingers working there for a moment. Nausea churned in her belly.

"A gift," he said, and ran his palm along her hair. "You gave me a lock of your hair and I give you a trinket in return."

She glanced down. There was a small watch pinned to her bodice.

As she raised her gaze to his, he smiled. "Do you like your gift, Beth?"

Her fear was so strong she thought she would collapse under the weight of it, but she managed a shaky nod.

"Now you may use the bucket," he said, and put his hand to the small of her back to shove her toward it. She stumbled forward.

This was her chance. This was her one chance.

Dare she take it?

The candlelight caught the edge of the knife, bounced off and away, accentuating its length. In her mind's eye, Beth saw Sarah Ashton, saw her body lying in the woods, saw the things he had done to her.

And she knew that it was not a question of daring to take this one chance in the face of his murderous blade. She would be dead if she did not take it, carved like a Christmas goose.

Using her skirt to hide her actions, she bent and

closed her numbed finger not on her hem, but on the bucket handle.

She must not focus on her fear. She must not.

She thought of the pocket watch, and she thought of her grandfather, dead these many years.

"Who was the first?" she whispered, staring at the bucket, knowing that he understood exactly what she asked. Knowing his answer before he said it.

"A girl in a tavern. In Stepney. It was a messy business. Too quick. Not well planned. There were too many people in attendance, too many people for me to go through before I got to her." He sighed. "So that was a muted pleasure. But I got better with practice. Much better." He sounded proud and pleased, bragging of some great accomplishment. "The first? Her name was Ginnie George. Pretty Ginnie, with her bouncing curls."

Beth closed her eyes, tightened her fingers on the bucket handle.

He had killed them. All of them. Her grandmother. Her grandfather. He had butchered them on the floor of the Black Swan Tavern, and gone to the parlor to kill the serving maid.

It had been so long ago, she barely remembered their faces. Or perhaps she could not bear to remember. But the watch, *his* watch, had brought the horror of it flooding back, bright and clear.

He had left her on the floor by her grandmother's body, left her to bleed and die, while he had gone to the parlor to kill Ginnie. But Beth had lived. She had crawled up the stairs to hide in a box, certain he would come, certain he would butcher her as he had butchered them.

She remembered huddling in the linen chest in the dark, the metallic stink of blood filling the close, thick air, and the horror of her grandparents' murders fresh in her thoughts. She remembered her fear. She remembered the pain. One doctor, many years later, had said it was the way she curled in the tight box that saved her life, her position pressing on the wound in her side and slowing her bleeding.

From the corner of her eye, she could see the blade glinting in the candlelight.

He had stolen *everything* from her. Her family. Her childhood. Her sanity. He had left her damaged and afraid.

Always and forever afraid.

Crimson rage surged and swallowed her, monstrous and strong. Stronger than her fear. She closed her fingers around the handle of the bucket and knew her moment had come.

Drawing in the deepest breath she could, she then opened her mouth and let free a violent cry, loud and wild, a testament to her terror and the crashing torrent of her rage.

She swung the heavy bucket up and around, throwing everything she had, everything she *was* into the movement, feeding the momentum, wielding the thing like a club. She swung from the bottom up, so the heavy base of the bucket caught him square on the underside of his chin.

The crack of wood on bone was loud. Louder than her pounding heart. Louder than the harsh grunt that followed her scream.

He made a sound of surprise and pain, and sagged down onto one knee.

Heart slamming against her ribs, she hit him again, this time in the temple, the force of the second blow far weaker than the first.

Tossing aside the bucket, she spun, ran.

The door. The door. She threw herself against it, her bound hands reaching above her head for the rope that would free the latch.

Silent screams ricocheted through her like bats in a cave, and she sealed her lips against freeing the sound, pressed them tight together and bit down until her teeth cut through and she tasted blood.

To free the screams was to free her panic, her terror, to leave her weak in the face of it.

To hold it back, to control it, was her only hope.

Straining up on her toes, she scrabbled at the rope, her heart hammering, her vision tunneled to a narrow black tube. She saw only the rope, high above her.

She could hear stirring behind her. A scraping sound.
Oh, dear God.
The knife. He still had his knife.
He was coming.
One chance. One chance.

She yanked hard on the rope, and the door opened, pushed wide by the thrust of her shoulder. Stumbling, she nearly fell, but with two lurching steps, she righted herself and ran into the night, her bound hands twisted in her skirt, holding it up as high as she could.

Her feet flew toward the dark outline of the trees. Not far. Trees and shadows. Places to hide.

She dared glance back only once. He was there, behind her, a dark shadow with a long, glinting knife.

Chapter Twenty-Seven

Griffin was not subtle in his approach. He came upon Moorecroft's house on the outskirts of Northallerton and rode past, beyond the courtyard and manicured lawns to the orchard that spread in neatly aligned rows.

At the far end of the orchard was a shack. Isolated. Abandoned. Griffin knew of it only because Moorecroft had once allowed the girls from Burndale Academy to come to the orchard to pick apples.

Griffin had been there that day, watching the girls put apples in their baskets, because the trustees were to meet and discuss the school's finances. He recalled Miss Stillwell standing under a tree, engaged in conversation with Moorecroft, the two of them alone and apart from the rest of the group, the moment frozen in his mind like a vivid painting.

The event took on sinister significance now, having taken place the fall that Katherine Stillwell was killed.

Hindsight made all so clear.

With new understanding he recalled the look on Moorecroft's face, intent, a hunter stalking its prey.

He would die before he let Beth become Moorecroft's prey.

Leaning low against the horse's neck, he rode to the

wind, then reined the beast to a halt when he reached
the shack at the end of the property. He could only pray
that his instincts were true, that Moorecroft had indeed
brought Beth here.

He threw himself from his mount, landing on the balls
of his feet, knees bent, senses alert. Reaching down, he
drew his blade from his boot.

The door to the shack was open. Peering around it,
he took in all at a glance. The coffin. The candle. And
the fact that there was no one there.

Agony speared him, the horror of possibilities. Was
she dead? Had he killed her already? Taken her somewhere in the woods?

Too late. I am too late. As he had been too late for Amelia.

Dread sank talons deep into his heart.

He forced himself to stay in the moment, to study the
scene.

There was no blood on the ground. No blood in the
coffin.

She was alive. Beth had to be alive.

He could not lose her. Could not lose the light she
had brought him after so many years of darkness. Could
not lose her warmth.

She had woken his child from her life of silence.

Woken *him* from a frozen death sleep, woken his
heart, woken his spirit.

Beth. His light. His love.

And he had not told her. He needed to tell her, to
touch her, to love her for a lifetime.

She deserved a lifetime, his Beth.

He recalled the look on her face, the tone of her
voice as she had stood by the window last night. *He has
done this before. Will do it again. He likes it more each time.
He likes to kill.*

That eerie knowledge should have alerted him even
then. She knew the monster because she had met him
before, seen him every night in her nightmares. But *this*

nightmare was real, and Griffin meant to end it, meant to save her and make certain that the monster never killed again.

He realized now who she was: the child who had survived all those years ago at the Black Swan Tavern. Beth had escaped this madman then. She would escape him now.

And Griffin would find her.

Spinning, he studied the orchard, the road, the manicured expanse of lawn that spread toward the dark shape of the house. Nothing stirred. Nothing breathed.

He rounded the shack, scanned the woods that encroached on Moorecroft's land, the trees shaded black against the night sky. His gaze was unhurried, careful.

He forced himself to stay calm, to beat back the anger that threatened to burst free of its confines. Such emotion was dangerous now. He needed calm. He needed intellect.

If he was to save her, he must find her.

Where? Where?

There. He saw a hint of movement, slate-black shadow against blacker trees, but it moved, slithered, a snake about to strike.

The bastard is after Beth.

His brilliant, brave Beth. Somehow, she had escaped Moorecroft, escaped the coffin, the shack, and now Moorecroft hunted her in the woods. Worry and anger melded into an icy mélange, and Griffin tapped the rush of emotion, waiting for his moment.

Shifting his grip on his knife, the heft familiar and smooth, he was glad for his years on the streets of Stepney. Glad for the villainy he had learned and done.

Glad that he knew how to kill a man with a single, deep thrust of his blade.

Watching, he waited for a clear view, and then his patience saw its reward. The shadow he had glimpsed a moment past swayed and danced, Moorecroft weaving through the trees. Griffin freed his primitive instincts, let primal emotion and impulse fuel him as, with a dark sense of purpose, he moved forward.

The predator had become his prey.

Beth knew that attempting to outrun Moorecroft was a fool's errand.

Instead, she found a place beyond the orchard, deep in the gloom of the forest. A place to hide. She made herself very small and very quiet, and let the shadows cloak her.

Shivering with cold and fear, she dragged her hands rapidly up and down against the rough bark of the tree. At her feet lay a thick branch she had stumbled over. Fate had smiled upon her, for it was a worthy weapon, one that offered her hope. All she needed to do was fray the rope enough that she could tear her hands free.

Fear was a poison oozing through her veins, making her heart clutch and her throat close. Every sound, even the whisper of the wind through the leaves, made stark terror bite at her.

He was out there. Looking for her. And he might well find her.

Faster, faster, she dragged her hands over the bark, feeling the warmth of her own blood as she tore her skin. The rope was thick. The bark broke away from the trunk in chunks.

Choking back a sob of frustration and despair, she crunched her back teeth together to stop them chattering and gave up on fraying the rope. With her back pressed to the tree, she bent her knees, squatted down, and closed her fists around the thick branch. Her weapon. Her hope.

She was grateful that Moorecroft had tied her hands before her rather than behind.

A sound came from her left, the crack of a twig, and she forced herself to stay still when every nerve screamed at her to leap up, to run. But he would hear her. He would chase her.

He would catch her. Do to her what he had done to the others.

Never.

So she stayed where she was, made herself just another shadow, her back braced against the tree, her feet set flat, her body angled so she could spring to her feet if she must. Before her, she held the branch like a club, her bound hands making it difficult, but not impossible.

Her father had taught her ways to defend herself. Henry Pugh had seen far too much of the dark ways of evil men to trust Beth's safety to a whim of fate.

Footsteps, drawing closer, slow, careful, crushing the dry leaves with a faint crackling noise.

She dared not move.

Another step, closer.

Tightening her grip on the branch, she strained to see in the shifting gloom, faint beams of moonlight filtering through the foliage, dancing about as the leaves swayed in the wind. She remembered another night when this predator had stalked her, not in a forest but in her grandparents' home.

The memories that had haunted her for a lifetime coalesced now into flesh and bone, the monster from her past come for her in truth.

Pressing her back to the tree, she pushed herself to her feet, her thigh muscles screaming at the slow rise, her back scraping the rough bark. She held her weapon ready, her heart pounding a rhythm so wild and frantic it hurt.

And then the shadows moved and he was there before her, perhaps ten feet away—

No . . . *two* shadows, facing each other.

Moorecroft and *Griffin.*

Oh, dear God.

"He has a knife," Beth cried, and neither man turned.

"As do I, my love. As do I." Griffin's voice, calm, smooth. A pause, and then he said, "I am pleased to find you well."

He did not sound pleased. He sounded grim and savage and saturated with rage. Still she did not doubt the sentiment. He was pleased that she was alive. That he had found her. That he had a chance to use his knife.

She ached to run to him, to let him envelop her in the safety and warmth of his embrace. But it was not time yet; there was still Moorecroft to face with his knife and his horrific intent.

My love.

A tumult of emotion raced through her, the words dampening her terror just a bit. She knew he would never say such a thing as a casual endearment. He was a man who said only what he meant. She had learned that much of him by now.

In the pallid light that filtered through the trees, she saw the set line of Griffin's jaw, the ease of his posture, the glitter of his eyes as he followed Moorecroft's every move.

Here was the man she had seen that very first day on the road before the stonebuilt church, the man who made her think of the panther in the cage. Only, the bars were gone, the panther set free. He was lithe and dangerous, and he was here for her. To protect her. *Griffin.*

"Go, Beth. Run now. I have no wish for you to see what will come." He did not look at her, his attention focused wholly on Moorecroft, who said nothing, but shifted a step to the right, and another, with Griffin matching each move.

"No." She would not leave. She would stay and see the end of this, the end of the horror that had begun so many years past.

A part of her believed in him with everything she was. Believed that he would emerge victorious, and that she would have a chance to tell him of the emotion welling in her heart. But a part of her was still the terrified little girl, hiding in a box. The little girl who had never had a chance to tell her parents she loved them one last time before they were taken by the plague. Never had the chance to tell her grandparents of her love before a monster ripped them from her life.

She needed Griffin to know, to carry her love with him, a shield. She dared much, dared all, and whispered, "My love."

He heard. She sensed it in the subtle tension that laced his frame, but he kept his attention firmly fixed on Moorecroft, who was circling, slowly, so slowly. It was a terrible place to share such emotion, to reveal the depths of their hearts, and yet, somehow, with all that had passed before, it was the right place.

Griffin had come for her. She was not alone in the dark.

Trembling, she watched the two male forms blending with the shadows, both crouching and moving as though skilled in this act. She shuddered. Griffin clearly knew of the way of things, but Moorecroft was a madman who liked to kill. Did that offer him a horrific advantage?

Griffin did not tell her again to flee. He had such confidence that his knife would be the one to taste blood, that he would be the victor. Dear heaven, how was she to think of that? What was she to think of herself that it gave her comfort to know he could do this, could stab a man, could kill him if he must? If he *wished*.

How many times had Griffin told her he was a villain?

And here, in the dark wood, with the faint moonlight glinting off two blades, she was *glad* of that, fiercely glad. Whatever villainy he carried was both a gift and a blessing if it meant he would live through this fight.

The sound of harsh breathing carried to her as they shifted in a ghastly dance. She wanted to scream, to sob, but she did neither, terrified to distract Griffin even the slightest bit.

Bodies shifted between the shadows and beams of pale, cool light.

The scuffle of feet. The chuffing of rapid breaths.

A lunge. A retreat. Griffin jerked his torso back and away as Moorecroft slashed at him. Beth lost her breath, her heart pounding so hard she felt sick with it.

Circling. Circling. And every now and again, the moonlight danced off the deadly edge of a blade.

Trembling, Beth sank her teeth into her lower lip and pressed her back hard against the tree trunk.

Now both lunged, a collision of bodies. The two men were shades cast in a macabre tableau, tight up against each other, and Beth could see nothing of their hands.

A sharp snap, the crack of a dry branch underfoot, made her gasp.

She could not say what she expected—an arm upraised, a wicked slash—but there was none of that. Both men kept their hands low and close to their bodies, each movement careful and guarded.

Clutching the branch before her, her bound hands unwieldy, she crept forward. The moon slid behind a cloud and all around her were shades of black.

There was a grunt and a hiss of breath from between clenched teeth, a rapid slash, and one man—which one?—slumped forward on a sharp exhalation, as though he'd been punched hard in the gut.

"Griffin." His name was a plea, a prayer. She no longer crept but lurched toward the two, her makeshift weapon raised, her pulse pounding a mad tattoo.

A dull thud, and she saw the glint of metal on the ground. One of them had dropped his knife.

She felt weak, sick, filled with horror and despair.

"Griffin," she whispered again as, breathing hard, both men fell back a pace and sank to their knees.

Close enough now to see their faces, she cried out

as, with a hissing exhalation, Moorecroft listed to one side, weaving where he knelt, then falling hard to the ground.

Griffin stayed as he was, balancing on his knees, breathing heavily.

For a frozen second Beth hung between hope and horror, the moonlight dappling Griffin's hair, sparking off the blood-stained edge of his blade. She could not see if he was cut, could not be certain.

Crying out, she jerked forward, dropped to the ground by Griffin's side. Was she to lose him now, when she had only just found him? Oh, God, she could not bear it.

On a harsh exhalation, Griffin grabbed the branch she yet held, tossed it aside. He caught her bound wrists, brought his blade up to slice her free, and dragged her against him.

"My brave, brilliant Beth. I see you got yourself free and found a weapon," he said, the catch in his voice undermining the effort he made at a light tone. Then he touched her cheek. "Do not cry, love. Do not cry."

"You could have died." She could barely breathe, barely speak, the lump in her throat was so heavy and thick. She buried her face in his shoulder.

After a moment, he spoke. "I would not die unless I saved you first."

There was a faint thread of humor in his tone.

A strangled sound escaped her, half laugh, half sob. She could not stop them, the silent tears that streaked her cheeks, had no wish to stop them. They were tears of healing. Tears of hope.

He shook his head, drew her closer against him. "Cry, then, my Beth. And I will kiss your tears away. But first, you have a choice to make."

"A choice?" She raised her head from his shoulder.

"Vengenace or justice. You must decide." He drew back a little, enough that she could see the hard glint in his eyes, and he gestured at Moorecroft, who lay on the ground where he had fallen, unmoving. Then Griffin lifted his knife, as though offering a toast. "Vengeance or justice, Beth. The choice is yours."

Three nights later, Beth stood by the window in Griffin's chamber, looking out at the perfectly trimmed expanse of lawn, bathed in moonlight. Each night since the horror of Moorecroft's attack, she had slept in the caring shelter of Griffin's arms. Each night, he kept a candle in the wall sconce burning to chase away the darkness.

And still she dreamed and jolted from sleep to sit panting and wide eyed in the center of his bed as he rubbed gentle circles on her back. The nightmares and fears that had dogged her for so many years were not gone—might never be gone—but with Griffin by her side, she felt better able to brazen them out.

A sound made her turn, and she saw Griffin in the doorway, robed in shadow. The sight called to mind another night when she had stood in the drafty, echoing corridor of Burndale Academy, holding the bloodstained handkerchief in her hand, and the fraught moment when she had been almost certain that she saw Griffin standing in a darkened niche.

"Were you there that night, in the hallway at Burndale?" she asked as she stepped away from the window. "Or did I imagine your presence?"

The shadows and moonlight played across his features, hollowing his cheeks, accenting the line of his jaw.

"I was there." He made a faint grimace. "And I apologize now for frightening you then. 'Twas not my intent, my love."

She shook her head. "I thought I had conjured you from my darkest dreams, or perhaps summoned your image to act as a sentinel."

"I *was* there as a sentinel of sorts. More than once on

my visits to the school to see Isobel, I spied Richard Parsons lurking in the shadows. What was I to think but that he was up to no good? I was of the mind that he would sneak in and steal the teachers blind while they slumbered." He grinned, a flash of white teeth. "So I went hunting."

Crossing to the window, Griffin cast her a glance, then drew the curtains, blocking out the moonlight, closing in the space.

Beth took a slow, calming breath. She was accustomed to this chamber now. It was large and spacious. There were no tight walls here, no choking space.

"Why did you not make yourself known to me? Why did you leave me pondering my own sanity?"

He laughed then, a low, rich sound. "I thought you came out only to fetch a handkerchief that you had dropped in the hall. I had no idea that you espied me. In fact, I hoped you had not. How was I to explain my presence outside your chamber door at such an hour of the night?"

How indeed? Whatever explanation he might have offered, she would not have been in a frame of mind to believe him.

Griffin turned away from the window and crossed to the wall sconce.

He wanted to snuff the light. She knew that. A part of her wanted him to. She wanted to step past what Moorecroft had done to her, to step past the constraints his actions had chained her with for so many years.

But she was afraid.

"Beth?"

"Go on," she whispered.

He hesitated only a moment, then snuffed the candle flame, letting the darkness fall about them, heavy and absolute.

Beth gasped.

"I am here, love," Griffin said. "You can face the darkness. I am here with you."

She was afraid. Afraid of the dark as she had been for as long as she could recall. But there was something else, too, a burgeoning pride and a different sort of excitement that thrummed in her veins.

A soft shush heralded Griffin's movement, his feet shifting on the floor as he came toward her. She remained where she was, frozen in place.

With her sight stolen, she could only hear and touch and smell. Each breath she took filled her with secret knowledge. The subtle, masculine scent of him, spice and musk and man. The feel of his strong fingers working her laces and buttons, drawing pieces of clothing from her body until she was naked in the cool night air. Naked in the dark.

Another breath. In then out. A rise and fall of her breasts, her nipples aching though he had yet to touch her there.

"Beth," he whispered, his lips against her ear. She moaned as he kissed her neck, her shoulder, leaning against his warmth, his strength. A mixed slurry of emotion touched her, anxiety, fear, excitement. Anticipation.

He kissed the side of her breast, her waist, dipping his tongue into her navel, and she wove her fingers through the silky strands of his hair.

Trailing his tongue down her belly, he kissed below her navel, and lower, until she gave a sharp exhalation and an equally sharp tug on his hair.

He held her still, closing his hands about her hips. He kissed her *there*, between her thighs, his tongue sliding between her lips to kiss her as he would kiss her mouth.

"What—" She closed her eyes, laughed, a jittery, staccato burst, and made to pull away, but he tightened his hold, and after a moment, she forgot why she fought him.

What he did was lovely. It was wicked.

She could not breathe, could not think, so shocked, so . . . lustful.

Opening her eyes, she was confronted by impenetrable darkness, and again she felt the surge of mixed emotion, a nervous edge tagging on to her pleasure. Her heart hammered and her limbs trembled. She could see nothing. She could only feel.

"I have no liking for the dark," she said.

"I know. And that is why you sought it. To replace the memories you have with sweeter ones. To prove that the darkness can be welcoming," Griffin said, the sound of his voice soothing. Thrilling. "Trust me, love. I will keep you safe." He made a hushed laugh, the sound incredibly arousing. "Or perhaps I should say, we will keep each other safe."

With his hands still at her hips, he guided her back until she felt something press against the backs of her knees.

Trust me. She did. With her heart. With her life.

"I will catch you, love."

He would. She knew that. And if her nightmares, her memories, came for her, he would stand by her side to chase them away.

As she would stand by his to battle his own dark demons.

"I love you, Beth," he whispered, the words so wonderful, so special, warming her heart, shining like a thousand candles. He kissed her again, there, in her most private place, the thrill of it making her quake. "Let yourself go. Trust me. There can be no love without trust."

"Then I give you my love," she said, the words soft and filled with emotion. "And my trust."

Falling back in the darkness, she gave herself up to him. Trusted him.

Knowing that *together* they were far stronger than either was alone.

* * *

A week later, Beth stood in the churchyard, three small posies of wildflowers held in her hand. She had collected them herself, and tied ribbons about the stems. The chalice-shaped flowers were pretty, with heart-shaped leaves and ivory white petals and distinctive glistening yellow centers.

There was a chill wind today carrying the promise of a storm, and she drew her dark cloak close about her as she glanced to the heavens. The sky was a blanket of dreary gray and the scent of rain flavored the air. Clouds gathered on the horizon, pewter and ash, charcoal limned, ready to burst.

She hoped the rain would hold off just a little longer, at least until after the service.

Looking to the stonebuilt church with its peaked roof and squared tower, she was reminded of her arrival at Burndale. She had expected that the church would be in the hub of activity, the center of the village. She had not expected it to be an isolated place surrounded by rolling hills, and she certainly had not expected to be left, forgotten, at the crossroad.

Bittersweet memory touched her as she recalled her very first sight of Griffin Fairfax, so handsome, so masculine, a little frightening. She had fallen a little in love with him that day.

Turning, she studied the road, looking to each direction for a span of seconds.

Choices. The crossroad offered choices, as life offered choices. One need merely pick a direction to explore.

She tucked a stray curl behind her ear and made her way between the gravestones, stopping first to place one of the three small bouquets at the base of the stone that marked the grave of Katherine Anne Stillwell. Next she moved to the headstone of Helen Bodie-Stuart, and she put flowers there, as well.

The third posy was the largest of the three. She fussed with the ribbon she had used to bind the stems, fixing the bow so it lay neat and flat.

Walking on, she approached the drystone wall. There sat Isobel, holding a small bouquet of her own, her feet kicking back and forth, her dark hair tumbling down her back. Beth had brushed it that morning and fastened a section with a blue ribbon.

As though sensing her regard, Isobel turned to look at her, then clambered off the wall and ran to her side.

"Will they be here soon? Will they come before the rain?" she asked, her brow furrowed with worry.

Beth smiled and smoothed her palm along Isobel's hair.

"Very soon," she replied, and as though to prove her right, the sound of a carriage approaching at a grave and sedate pace drew their attention. It was a closed carriage, gleaming black, sleek and well-sprung, drawn by four matched horses.

Resting her hand on Isobel's shoulder, Beth watched as the conveyance drew to a halt before the gravel path that led to the church doors. The footman opened the carriage door and two people emerged: Miss Percy and a dark-haired man of middle years.

Miss Percy saw Isobel and Beth, and she made her way toward them, her face a little pale as she accepted the bouquet that Beth handed her.

The dark-haired man turned back to face the open carriage door. "I told you it was an affair of the heart, and you scoffed," he said. "I trust you believe me now."

"I shall believe you when the deed is done," came the reply.

Griffin stepped down from the carriage, his gaze slipping directly to Beth.

Though she had seen him less than an hour past, her

heart clutched and her spirits soared to see him now, so dashing in his buff breeches and blue coat. His dark hair fell across his brow, sleek and shiny, and his eyes held hints of mischief and amusement as they met her own.

"Daddy," Isobel cried, and ran to him to be swept up and spun about then set down on her feet once more, slightly rumpled but very happy.

Beth did not even try to hold back her smile as she approached at a more decorous pace.

"Your arrival is timely," she said with a glance at the sky.

"I am always timely," Griffin replied with a grin. He caught her wrist and dragged her close, ignoring her halfhearted murmur of protest, and then he pressed his mouth to hers.

"Christ, I love you so damned much," he muttered, and she could not help but laugh at his aggrieved tone, as though loving her was more than he could bear. Which made him laugh, the sound wonderful and deep and wicked.

"Come along," Griffin said, clapping a hand to his friend's shoulder even as he cast a wink in Beth's direction. "Let us get you wed, Richard."

"Indeed," Richard replied, and sent him a sly glance. "I'd best be showing you the way of it, dear boy, given that your nuptials are soon to follow." He heaved a mighty sigh. "It has always been thus, me showing you the way of things, guiding you on the right path."

Griffin snorted. "I need no guidance. I dally only long enough to allow for the arrival of my bride's family."

The right path. Beth smiled. What a convoluted journey both she and Griffin had taken to reach this place in their lives. Feeling the rightness of her own path, she could only be grateful.

Gwendolyn Percy, soon to be Mrs. Richard Parsons, glanced at the brooding sky.

"Before the deluge, if you please, gentlemen," she

said in her most stern headmistress voice. "I would rather attend my own marriage in dry clothing."

They proceeded into the church, Isobel leading the way, carrying the small bouquet that Beth had fashioned for her.

"I received a letter this morning," Griffin said for Beth's ears alone as they followed the others. "Two bits of news. Moorecroft is to be tried in London."

"Yes," Beth murmured, glad that Griffin had not killed him that night. Vengeance was a tempting brew, and a part of her had wanted that, wanted revenge for the deaths of her family and for all that Moorecroft had stolen from her. A part of her had ached to take Griffin's knife in her own hand and plunge it deep in Moorecroft's breast.

Griffin had looked up at her that night, the moonlight glinting off his blade, and he had offered her the choice. There in the woods, near the blood-soaked shack where Moorecroft had done his foul deeds, Griffin would kill him. For her. So she could have her vengeance.

Or he would truss him up and send him off to London, to face trial.

The decision was hers. Griffin loved her too much to make it for her.

Beth recalled that moment so clearly, the tone of Griffin's voice, the rasp of his breath, the way she felt to know the lengths he would go to keep her safe. She recalled, too, the way he had bidden her make her decision with care, for she would live with it for the rest of her life.

Those words had decided it for her.

She did not want Moorecroft's blood staining Griffin's hands or his conscience. She wanted the monster to face a trial and a hanging. To face justice.

"We expected that the trial would be in London," she said. "And the second bit of news?"

Griffin drew her close against his side.

"The second bit is that your parents have accepted my invitation. Your family will be arriving within the month to witness our marriage and to take up residence in Rose Cottage. I trust that with a good cleaning and a fresh coat of paint it will be acceptable as a domicile."

Beth glanced at him askance. "Given that my parents' entire flat would fit in the parlor of Rose Cottage, I suspect they will find a way to make do."

She paused, waiting until he stopped and looked at her, offering his full attention.

"You know I am grateful for this. For everything. For the offer to give my family a home nearby," she said in a rush. "My mother's most recent letter says that my father is improving a little. He can say some simple words. I am very hopeful that he will show further improvement."

"I have sent word and funds to a doctor in London. A specialist in apoplexy. I asked that he make a visit to your father."

"I am"—she swallowed against the lump that formed in her throat, blinked against the tears that filled her eyes—"I am so grateful."

"No." His lashes swept down, and he picked at bits of imaginary lint on his sleeve. "I do not do this for your gratitude, Beth, but for my own pleasure, and for the debt I owe your parents. Without them, I would not have you in my life. Isobel would not have you. And without you, we would both yet be shades, ghostly beings walking in this world without hope or succor."

"Griffin—"

His lashes came up, revealing dark eyes lit with gold and green, beautiful, intense, so full of emotion it made her breath catch.

"I do not want your gratitude, Beth. I only want one thing from you." His voice was low, a rasp of emotion that wove through her veins and into her heart. "You. I only want you."

"You have me," she laid her palm against his cheek. "My love. I love you. *I love you.*"

"And I you." He leaned close then, until their breath mingled and her heart pounded. Her eyes closed and she waited, waited, for the touch of his lips, the taste of him in her mouth.

He brushed her lips with his, and she could not stifle the sound of disappointment as he drew away.

"Later." He made a low laugh, filled with promise. Taking her hand, he drew her into the church. "Right now, we have a wedding to attend. Later, we can have a private celebration."

"But it is not our wedding," Beth protested.

"No matter." Griffin shrugged and sent her a wicked, sinful grin. "We will enjoy the wedding night."

Discover the Romances of
Hannah Howell